THE DEVIL NEXT DOOR
By
Tim Curran

"Man is a predator with an instinct to kill and a genetic cultural affinity for the weapon."
—Robert Ardrey

"Human aggression is instinctual."
—Konrad Lorenz

Prologue

Somebody had painted the walls with their own feces.

The naked man sat there on the floor, his body a map of bruises and contusions, and smiled at this. His skin was crusty with blood. Some of it was his own and some of it belonged to others. He could tell by the taste. He stared at the walls, licking the salt off his fingertips, trying to make sense of the elaborate graffiti of fingerpainted shit on the wallpaper around him.

Somebody marked this place with their own filth so they could smell it, find it even in the dark.

He wondered what all the childish scrawls might mean, sensing there was important ritualistic symbolism behind them. They seemed familiar. Like maybe once, perhaps as a child, he'd painted a room like this, smeared shit on the walls to marks it as his lair.

What if whoever did this came back?

There was a knife. He looked at it, marveled at the dark stains on it. Sniffing them, he remembered each one.

He put the knife away and went to the window.

The sun was up, all the night things retreated back into their holes. There were wrecked cars in the streets. Several bodies were sprawled on the pavement. One of them didn't have a head. Two others, a man and woman, had been arranged so it looked as if they were copulating. Whoever did that had a sense of humor.

He sat back on the floor, running fingers through his grimy hair.

There was a corpse in the corner and a collection of knives. A fine nest of leaves and sticks and boughs. The scent on them was female and familiar.

He smelled the shit on the walls. It was a fine, earthy smell. The sort of smell that made one comfortable, relaxed, grounded to nature. Not fighting against it, but *part* of it. There was serenity to be had in a lair decorated with feces. He thought about the girl and wondered where she was. If he found her again he would claim her. For it was his right and he had fought for that right.

There was grit on his teeth. A bit of something tasty wedged in his molar. Licking and digging, he worked it free, sucking the juice from whatever it was, and swallowing it. He sat there, hugging himself, humming a low melody under his breath. The stench of his own sweat and pungent body odor made him feel strong. Later, he would piss on the walls, the chairs, so all that came here would know this place was now his.

The ripe stink of a man's bodily excretions was all he really had in this world. His true fingerprint and it was important to spread them around, mark territory and conquests. Others would smell them and know him.

There was something under a rocking chair.

He crawled over there and seized it.

Meat.

He sniffed it and licked it, not knowing where it came from or how it had come to be there. It was salty and gamy smelling.

He put it in his mouth, chewing.

And waited for the girl...

I

Friday the Thirteenth...

Greenlawn, Indiana. The high, hot outer edge of summer. Louis Shears breathed in deep, let that pure green heady aroma fill him to bursting. He could smell freshly cut grass, azaleas in full glowing bloom, hot dogs sizzling on backyard grills...and then something else that stopped him, disturbed him, passed through his mind like an ugly dark cloud: blood. Just a momentary psychic whiff of it, but one so strong he could feel it churning down in his guts. *Blood.* The blood of the town. A blood that was rich and vibrant, almost seductive.

Then it was gone.

He just shook his head as people will do, dismissing it.

And dismissing it mainly because he did not know what was about to happen. That good old Greenlawn, Indiana—like the rest of the world that was old but not nearly so good—was poised at the brink of a pit of absolute yawning blackness.

But back to summer.

Back to clean air and green grass and cars sudsed in driveways and kids on skateboards and the long tanned legs of young ladies pumping away in short shorts. Little pink houses for you and me, smiling children and happy faces, clean fresh-scrubbed places. The American dream. Condensed.

Louis had the afternoon off and the weekend was stretched out before him fat and slothful like a plump tabby sunning itself. He'd landed two new accounts over at CSS, the steel vendor he was a sales rep at. All seemed right with the world. He was looking forward to a lazy Saturday morning of yard work followed by an afternoon nap, maybe brunch with Michelle over at Navarro's on Sunday. And tonight? Well, they were celebrating.

In the backseat of his little Dodge were two nice seasoned porterhouse steaks, a couple baked potatoes, a bottle of Asti Spumante.

After the meal, Louis figured, maybe they'd jump in the hot tub, have a glass of wine or two, and get naked.

These were the things going through Louis' mind in a happy rhythm as he turned the Dodge onto Tessler Avenue, saw a couple walking hand in hand down the sidewalk beneath the spreading oak branches. It was a warm, muggy day as late August always was in those parts and he had his window open, his arm hanging out. He could smell the thick green odor of clotted vegetation on the riverbank. In the powder blue sky he saw a couple gulls winging past, a kite skimming against the fluffy white clouds. It was just the sort of day to be alive and to be happy. The sort of day you wanted to wave and smile at people.

He saw Angie Preen pass on the walk pushing a baby carriage. Her sapphire eyes sparkled in the sunlight, long autumn chestnut hair swept back in a ponytail. It swished from shoulder to shoulder, keeping time with the admirable jiggle of her bosom. She waved. Louis waved. Angie. Single-mother, but proudly so. Independent, strong, reliable. Came from good stock, as they liked to say in Greenlawn at baked bean suppers and church socials when the lives of anyone and everyone were examined like rare old pottery, checked fastidiously for inconsistencies and flaws.

Ah, Angie. Louis had always thought that if he hadn't hooked up with Michelle, then Angie and he might—

Dammit. He remembered the envelope sitting on the seat next to him.

The check for the car insurance. Michelle had given it to him two days before to mail and as was his way, he'd simply forgotten. Forgotten the way he sometimes forgot things.

He spotted a blue iron mailbox up Tessler and pulled to a stop. He got out, whistling under his breath, and dropped the letter in.

Then he glanced down the street.

A primer gray sedan pulled to a stop and two men with baseball bats hopped out. There was a teenage boy standing there, a paperboy, his sack dangling limply over his shoulder by a neon orange strap. The men spoke with him, laughed, and the boy followed suit. A perfectly ordinary exchange, it seemed, but Louis was suddenly disturbed. The sky suddenly seemed not blue but iron gray and there was a chill on the breeze. He could still smell the freshly-cut grass and river bottoms, but now they did not smell of life and growing things, but of rank sun-washed death.

Blood.

He smelled it again.

Louis stood there, something expanding in his chest.

The two men laughed again and swung their bats at the kid.

He went down with a strangled moaning sound. They'd caught him in the belly and the hip. For one split second they stood over him and then they started swinging again. Suddenly, the air was split with the meaty sounds of wood impacting flesh and the kid's wavering screams. The bats kept coming down and Louis plainly heard the splintering of bones.

It all happened in the span of ten seconds.

And like anyone faced with random, extreme violence, Louis' initial reaction was one of disbelief and even skepticism. This was not happening. These two guys— perfectly ordinary-looking guys—were not beating the shit out of a paperboy with Louisville Sluggers. It was a gag, a joke. Surely there was a camera rolling nearby. Some director would shout, "CUT!" and the two guys would help the kid up, all of them laughing about it.

But that did not happen and the screams coming from the kid's mouth were surely not play-acting. The men stood there looking at the kid, the ends of their bats stained red. They were laughing.

They just beat the fuck out of that kid and now they're laughing. Laughing.

It was at this impossible juncture that something shattered inside Louis because he realized that this was the real thing. Then he was running, running as fast as he could towards the kid and the two men. He had no idea what it was he thought he was going to do when faced with two psychos with baseball bats, but something inside compelled him to intervene.

By the time he got near enough to see the kid and the red pool expanding around him, the two men had already hopped into their car. It passed Louis at a casual speed—a primer gray sedan with a wired-up front bumper and a shattered rear window, a UNION YES! sticker on the trunk—and the two men smiled at him and waved, kept on driving like they were just on their way to the store to grab a six-pack and had not just viciously beaten a paperboy with baseball bats.

Louis thought of chasing the car, but instead he memorized the plate number, and went to the kid.

"Oh Christ," he said when he got a good look at him.

The kid was curled up like a dying snake, the femur of his right leg poking through his pants. His left knee was shattered, the leg twisted off at a crazy angle. His right arm was like some lumpy purple contusion and his face was swelling to the point that it was nearly impossible to make out his features. His head looked like some garish, knobby Halloween pumpkin capped by spiky tufts of blonde hair.

"Shit, shit, shit," Louis heard his own voice say.

There was blood everywhere...soaked into the kid's clothes, spreading onto the sidewalk, running from his mouth and ears and eyes. Louis saw a bunch of white things on the walk and realized they were the kid's teeth.

"Don't move," Louis told him, caught between the need to cry and the need to throw up. "I'll...I'll get an ambulance."

But as he turned to run back to the Dodge for his cell, the kid grabbed his ankle with a bloody hand, the pinkie of which was broken and nearly turned right around in its socket. He lifted his head up and vomited out a spray of blood and bile, his entire body jerking, making a sucking, sticky sound as it convulsed in its own pool of blood. Louis just looked down at him, disgusted and afraid and too many other things he was not even aware of. The top of the kid's head was shattered, plates of bone sticking up like shards of glass. You could see his brain in there, lots of blood. A trickle of clear fluid ran down his face.

Intercranial fluid. Jesus, that's intercranial fluid.

"Please...just don't move," he said.

But the kid was moving.

He was holding onto Louis' ankle tightly, very tightly, convulsing and squirming. Louis bent down, had to put his hands on the kid and the warm, fleshy wetness of that made waves of nausea roll through him.

"It's gonna be okay," Louis said, sobbing now, looking wildly around and wondering why no one else was seeing this.

And that's when madness became horror.

The kid let go of his ankle and threw himself at him.

He was so badly broken and injured he should have been capable of little more than moaning, but he suddenly was filled with life, a demented and diabolic life. His fists came up and wrapped around Louis' throat with a grip that was vital and strong. He gagged and spit blood, but he hung on, things inside him snapping and popping. His eyes were black and intense, his mouth hooked in a ragged sneer, toothless and hanging with ribbons of blood.

Louis screamed.

None of this could have happened in the first place and surely not *this*. Mortally wounded kids did not react like this...with rage and ferocity. But that's what was happening. The kid had him by the throat and it was definitely not some weak half-hearted gesture born of brain trauma. This was something else. The hands were strong, immoveable, crushing Louis' windpipe with a strength that was frightening. Louis grabbed those moist hands and tried to pry them loose...first gently, not wanting to further hurt the kid, and then with a manic desperation born of utter terror.

Because the kid's face...it just wasn't right.

He was insane, possessed, something. Those black eyes were flat and relentless; the swollen face bulging with exertion; the mouth contorted into a bloody blow hole, jagged teeth jutting from his gums.

Louis began to see black dots before his eyes as the pressure increased and his air was shut down. What he did next, he did without thought, out of pure instinct. He lashed out blindly, punching the kid in the face with two or three heavy shots that snapped his head back. It was like punching a bag filled with moist bread dough. But it worked. The kid fell away, rolled onto his back, shuddered for a moment or two, then went still. Blood still ran from him and that fluid oozed from his smashed head, but that was the only movement.

He was dead.

A couple bluebottle flies seemed to know this, for they lit on his face. A third settling onto his left eyeball, rubbing its forelegs together.

Panting, dizzy, half out of his mind, Louis pulled himself away from the wreckage of the kid. His white short-sleeved dress shirt was untucked, several buttons gone, the front muddled with brilliant red stains. He put a trembling hand to his throat and felt the slick, greasy blood there from the kid's fingers. The world canted this way, then that. He thought he'd go out cold.

But he didn't.

Sweat ran down his face, a cold sour-smelling sweat, and he was finally aware of the sidewalk beneath him and the birds singing in the trees and the sun in the sky.

That didn't just happen, a voice kept saying in his head. *Dear God, tell me none of that just happened. Tell me I wasn't attacked by a dying kid and that I had to punch him out to get him off me.*

But it *had* happened and the realization settled into him with a weight that almost pressed him to the concrete. He breathed in and out, blinked his eyes, looked around. Same late summer day. Butterflies winging through the grass and flowerbeds. Bees buzzing. Sun hot and yellow in that endless blue sky. Same smell of cut grass and roasting hot dogs, kids laughing and shouting in the distance.

It was the same. It was all the same.

Yet, down deep where the worst intuitions brooded, he knew it was not. Something was wrong. Something had changed. A shadow had fallen over the streets.

A cry twisting in his throat, Louis ran for the Dodge and his cellphone...

2

The police arrived.

Two thick-necked characters in blue uniforms pulled up in a patrol car, parked at the curb, chatted for a moment or two and stepped out. They seemed to be in no hurry. Which was amazing to Louis, because his call to 911 was frantic, bordering on out-and-out hysteria. Still, the cops took their time. They got out, slapped their hats on their pickle jar heads, nodded to each other, and strolled over to the kid's body.

Standing there, incredulous, Louis just thought, *No, no, take your fucking time...*

He didn't know their names at that juncture, but he'd seen them around. There were less than 15,000 people in Greenlawn, so you pretty much saw all the official muscle in town if you stayed around long enough. One of them was fat with a sheen of sweat under his nose; the other was tall and muscular, the tattoo of a shark on his huge forearm. They stared at the kid's body and kept staring. There was no remorse or shock at seeing the brutally disfigured body of a teenage boy. If Louis hadn't known better, he would have associated what was in the cops' eyes as indifference tinged by mild amusement.

One of them bent down to get a better look, waving a few flies off.

"Watch it," his partner said. "Don't step in that blood."

And Louis was, of course, thinking the same thing. It was a crime scene, after all, and he'd seen enough of those shows.

Michelle always made him watch *CSI* with her whether he wanted to or not. So he was thinking that the cop meant, don't step in the blood, because you'll screw up the crime scene.

But the fat one just said, "I don't want you tracking that blood in the cruiser. I just washed the mats."

Louis widened his eyes, but said nothing.

The fat cop looked over at him. "I'm Officer Shaw and this is Officer Kojozian. You the guy that called? Louis Shears?"

"Yeah, I called," Louis told him.

"What happened?"

So Louis began to tell his story and as he told it, he started realizing how terribly ridiculous it sounded. The cops just nodded and it was hard to say whether they believed him or not. Their eyes were just dead and gray like puddles of April rain.

"You get a plate number on that sedan?" Shaw said, scribbling in his little notebook.

"Yeah. ZHB three-oh-one."

"You got a good memory," Kojozian said, like he found the idea laughable.

Louis swallowed. "I work with numbers all day. I remember them."

"You an accountant?"

"No, I'm a—"

"Mathematician?"

"No," Louis said, sighing. "I'm an account rep which has absolutely nothing to do with what I've just told you."

"Just take it easy," Shaw told him.

Sure, sure, take it easy. Great idea. Problem was, Louis did *not* feel like taking it easy. After seeing two guys beat a kid's brains in with baseball bats and then getting himself attacked by the same kid, something which seemed impossible to begin with, taking it easy just wasn't in him. He needed to shout and rant and maybe even crack the coconuts of these dumb cops together so they would see the light shining in their bovine faces. And maybe after that, a good cry and a good drink.

Shaw had his hands on his hips. "Let me get this straight, Mr. Shears. These guys beat this kid near to death and then when you went to help him...he tried to strangle you?"

"Yes," Louis said. "Yes. I know how crazy it sounds, but, Christ, I didn't get all this blood on myself at work. He jumped at me, wrapped his hands around my throat. He was strong...all broken up like this, he was still strong."

Shaw and Kojozian looked at each other.

"Then what happened? He just died?" Kojozian said.

"No, he wouldn't let go of me, he was insane or something. He kept trying to strangle me, so I...I mean I..."

"Yes?"

"I...I guess I hit him."

Kojozian let out a low whistle of disbelief. "Now we're getting to it."

Louis gave him a hard look. "What the hell do you mean by that?"

Kojozian shrugged. "You got blood all over yourself. Your fists are bloody. You just admitted you punched out a dying kid..."

Louis laughed. He had to laugh. This whole exchange was ludicrous. "Oh, I get it. You think I assaulted this kid. Well, yeah, that makes perfect fucking sense, doesn't it? I was bored after work so I beat this kid to death and then I called you guys and made up a story about a gray sedan and two guys with baseball bats. Okay, you got me. Your mind is sharp as a tack, Kojak."

"That's *Kojozian*," he corrected, totally missing the jibe. "And maybe you ought to quit with the mouth...how's that sound, hotshot?"

"Both of you calm down," Shaw said. "We don't think you killed the kid or beat him up, Mr. Shears. It's just that the whole thing is a little wild."

Louis was starting to feel like he'd done something wrong. Like maybe he was in the hot seat here. Was this why people in big cities looked the other way when a crime was committed in plain view? They didn't involve themselves for fear a couple

Keystone Cops like these two might try to implicate them in something they were completely innocent of?

"Sure, it's wild," Louis said. "I'm just telling you what happened. I wish I could tell you something that makes more sense. Trust me, if I was going to make up a story, I think I could do better than this."

Shaw nodded. "Sure, sure. Maybe the kid panicked or something. Maybe he thought you were the guy that did it."

"I wonder why he'd think something like that," Kojozian said.

Louis was burning inside.

He had half a mind to punch Kojozian right in the nose. And maybe he would have if he wouldn't have gotten thrown in jail...right after he got out of the hospital, that was. Because if he took a swing at this ape, he would have gotten his ass not only kicked, but pressed and folded. The funny thing was, he had a pretty good idea that Kojozian wanted him to try something like that. The man was baiting him, intimidating him, pushing him. But Louis would not be baited or pushed, not by an animal like Kojozian.

He made himself breathe very slowly to calm himself. "I'm just telling you what happened, that's all."

"Sure," Shaw said. "Sure."

Kojozian looked at him and Louis felt a chill run up his spine. Those eyes were just as black and intense as the kid's when he'd attacked.

Like the eyes of a mad dog.

"So you're telling us this kid attacked you?" he said. "He don't look like he's in much shape to attack anyone."

"He was."

Kojozian shook his head. He walked over to the corpse. "Let's see...compound fractures, split-open head, massive internal injuries...I'm not seeing it, Mr. Shears. I think you're full of shit. This guy couldn't have done nothing but die." And to prove that, apparently, he kicked the corpse. It made a wet thudding sound. "Nope, he's all busted up inside." He kicked him again. "Hear that, Mr. Shears? Hear that slopping sound like Jello in a Ziplock bag? That's his insides and they're splashing around. People with injuries like that don't do much attacking. What they do is they puke up blood and shit out their intestines, but that's about it."

Louis felt something drop inside of him.

Not only was this offensive and sickening, it was absolutely insane. The kid was dead and this cop was kicking him, saying those awful things. Louis backed away, his head beginning to spin and he wondered if maybe he was in a padded cell somewhere dreaming all this. Because it could not be real. It could not possibly be real.

"What's a matter?" Kojozian said. "You got a weak stomach?"

Louis shook his head. "You can't...you can't treat a dead body like that. You can't kick it."

Kojozian kicked it again. "Why not?"

"Tell him to stop that!" Louis cried.

But Shaw just shrugged. "He's just making a point, Mr. Shears. That's all. Just a point. The kid don't mind."

Kojozian decided he needed to make another point.

He put his foot on top of the kid's chest and pumped his leg up and down. The body shook and rolled with a slow, fluidic motion like it was filled with jelly. The sound of everything sloshing around inside was almost more than Louis could take. More blood pissed out of orifices, a blood that looked almost black.

"Yeah, I'm just making a point, Mr. Shears. I'm teaching you something, that's all," Kojozian explained. He kept his foot up on the corpse's chest, his shiny black shoe and the bottom of his creased pantleg wet with blood. He began pumping his leg up and down again but with much more force, so much that his shoe sank into the kid's chest and came back out again with an appalling sucking sound like somebody working a plunger in a clogged toilet.

Louis took another step back, then went down on his knees, vomiting into the grass. It came and went quickly enough. But when he again looked at the two cops, the fever was still on him. Because Kojozian still had his foot up on the corpse's chest and Shaw still looked unconcerned.

"Please," Louis breathed. "Please stop that."

Kojozian shrugged and pulled his foot free. "Weak stomach," he said.

Shaw was looking at his shoe and pants. "Lookit the mess you made. You're not getting in my cruiser like that. Wipe your shoe off on the grass."

Louis could feel a scream building in his throat...

3

If viewed from above, Greenlawn would have looked roughly like a postage stamp with the Green River intersecting it. The north side of town was the oldest and the houses there could bear witness to this to any with an architectural eye. The closer you got to Main, the better they were kept up. But the farther you went, the shabbier they became until ultimately they blended into a strip dotted with neighborhoods of ramshackle company houses and old railroad hotels, industrial concerns and saloons and sooty apartment buildings. All of which ended at the very doorstep of the train yards. South of Main things were much more prosperous and here flanking nice antique blocks of tall, narrow Victorians and frame houses thrown up before the Second World War were neighborhoods of post-war ranch-style houses of brick and stucco. And at the southern edge, modulars and pre-builts that had blossomed in the last twenty years, taking over fields and ball diamonds and any available open space. The west side of town was marked by a looming assortment of warehouses, mills, and machine shops, most of which were closed and rotting. The Green River passed through town, running through old neighborhoods and new, coursing beneath Main Street and continuing north up through the train yards before leaving town entirely and making for the wheat fields, farmlands, and scrub forest beyond.

All in all, Greenlawn was an ordinary town in the Midwest, no different from any number of towns to the east or west or south. The same families had lived there for generations and what new blood came in, generally settled in and toughed it out or moved away. The schools were good, the streets clean, the crime rate low. There were fireworks in the park on the Fourth of July and parades for Christmas and Veteran's Day. There was a county fair in August and a circus passed through in May. There was a winter carnival and another come September. The summers were hot and humid, the winters long and white and frigid. It was a great place to raise a family, a great place for fishing and hunting and outdoor recreation. There had been a bad fire in 1915 that started in the shanty village at the western edge and swept through the northern half before it was contained. Old timers still spoke of it. There had been a few murders, though no more than you could count on one hand and nothing in recent memory.

Greenlawn was just an ordinary small town that could be found anywhere.

This, then, was the scene on Black Friday...

4

Maddie Sinclair slid the knife out of her husband's throat.

Cocking her head like a dog listening for its master's approach, she studied the blood-streaked blade of the carving knife. She sniffed it. Then she tasted it. She made a bestial groaning noise in her throat.

She stiffened.

A sound.

She waited, gripping the knife, ready to fight, to pounce, to kill. Whatever it took to protect what was hers and hers alone. Footsteps. Slow, stealthy. Maddie's lips pulled back in a snarl. She tensed. Sniffed the air. Waited. She could smell the musk of the others that were coming. It was an odor she recognized. The odor of female.

She brought the knife up.

Squatted in a killing stance, ready to leap.

Two girls came into the living room. Something in her chest jumped at the sight of them. There was recognition. A warmth that was quickly replaced by something cold, plotting, and atavistic. Maddie recognized them as her brood, her young, her daughters, but there was no emotion at this: the two bitches were not to be trusted. Not yet.

Hissing at them, Maddie sniffed the air they brought with them.

She smelled urine. Blood.

It was a satisfying odor, one that calmed her somewhat. They smelled of the hunt. Not like others out there, not soapy and repugnant. She waited to see if the bitches would challenge her kill, try to take it. But they did nothing but stare. They did not run. There was no fear on them. Just hesitation. They were both naked. They had taken needles and poked their breasts, stomachs, chests, and arms with them, creating a bleeding series of welts that ran in decorative, concentric patterns. The elaborate scarification was symbolic, tribal, and resembled the intricate cicatrisation of certain African bush clans.

Maddie liked it.

If these two bitches were to hunt as part of her band, she would decorate her flesh likewise.

The bitches moved in closer, intrigued.

Maddie allowed this, watching them. Like her, they were pale, streaked with grime and gore, leaves and sticks braided into their matted hair.

She hissed at them.

They did not make any threatening moves.

Maddie motioned them in with the knife. They squatted by the carcass with her. They laid fingertips upon the kill, touching, feeling, instinctively probing muscle mass and fat deposit, knowing which would be spitted first.

Maddie swallowed. "Down..." she said, her voice dry and scraping, the words difficult to pronounce. "Take the kill down...below..."

The bitches did not argue.

Each gripping an ankle, grunting and gasping, their young scarred bodies rippling with muscle, they dragged their father's corpse away across the carpeting. Maddie watched them. She was pleased. Her kill was made and her clan established. It was good.

Moaning some long-forgotten tribal melody deep in her throat, she retreated into the corner and defecated there on the plush sea-green nap. When she was done, she sniffed what she had produced.

She heard the bitches dragging the carcass below to the cellar.

Its head thumped on each step.

Sniffing the air for intruders and poachers, ever aware of danger, Maddie followed the scent trail of the carcass to the cellar door and below. When she got down in the cool, damp darkness, she schooled the bitches.

Together, they dressed out the carcass...

5

The scream started out small in his guts and now it was rolling upward, gaining mass and volume along the way. And Louis was going to set it free and mainly because he didn't really think he had a choice. Maybe he would have, too, but another Greenlawn police car rolled up behind the other one. The guy that got out was thin and tall, white hair poking around the edges of his cap. His mouth was hooked in a crooked scowl.

"What gives here?" he said.

Louis finally felt some sanity coming back. He knew this guy. His name was Warren and he was a sergeant or something, an old hand on the force. Louis knew that he handled the safety programs at the schools and was always in the newspaper involved in some civic or charitable organization. Warren also sang in the church choir over at St. Stephen's and had a hell of a set of pipes on him. He was okay. Old school all the way, he'd sort this clusterfuck right out.

"Well, it's a real mess, Sarge," Shaw said.

"Let's have it," Warren said, pulling a cigarette from behind his ear and showing it some flame.

So Shaw told him all about it and the whole time Warren's eyes shifted from the stiff to Louis and it didn't look like he cared for the looks of either. When Shaw finished, Warren just nodded.

"They treating you okay, Mr. Shears?" he said.

And Louis launched right into it. The re-telling of this tale sounded no better than the other one, but the evidence was all over Kojozian's shoe and pantleg.

"He's got a weak stomach," Kojozian said. "He got sick in the grass over it all."

Warren grinned. "No shit? Well, take it easy, Mr. Shears. Dead is dead. You can tap dance on this kid or drop your knickers and take a dump in his mouth. It's all the same to him."

Louis stared up at him, pale and wide-eyed. "You're all crazy," he said.

"Boy, he does have a weak stomach, all right," Warren said, exhaling smoke through his nostrils. "No offense, Mr. Shears, but you wouldn't make much of a cop. Lots of bodies, always lots of bodies."

"We had a guy last week," Shaw said, "over on West Rider Street. Mail piling up and all that. Neighbors call us and we go over there. We had to go in through a side window and that stink when we opened it up...holy Jesus! We found the stiff on the shitter. Old guy had a heart attack while he was delivering the mail. Must have been about a thousand flies on him. Another thousand on the windows and flying around. They were buzzing so loud, you couldn't hear yourself think."

"That's nothing," Warren said. "When I was first on the Department, we got a call to go out to the airport. Middle of summer, some guy's sleeping in his car with the windows all rolled up. A real hot bastard it was, too. Some kids were riding their bikes around, saw the guy laying in there, said he had rice all over him. *Rice*. Ha, what a mess! The smell would have put you right down to your knees, swear to God. He'd been in there almost a week, came apart like boiled chicken when we tried to pull him out. Most of him stuck to the seat..."

Louis got to his feet and then he was running, running dead out for the Dodge. His brain was filled with a screaming black noise and he was certain that he had lost his mind. Nothing else could possibly explain it.

"Hey, where you going?" Kojozian called out.

"Let him go," Shaw said. "We don't need him. What we need here are a couple shovels to scrape this kid off the sidewalk with..."

And then Louis was in his Dodge. He could feel the seat beneath him and his hands gripping the steering wheel. He held on tight before the entire world went flying away beneath him. Because it was coming, he knew it was coming.

He squealed around in a U-turn and saw Warren wave to him in the rearview. As he screeched away down Tessler Avenue, barely missing a parked car, his face was slicked with sweat and his entire body was shaking. He needed badly to pull over and be sick, but he didn't dare. He just did not dare. He had to make Rush Street and home. And the most insane, impossible thing of all was that the cops did not come after him.

They did not come after him...

6

At Greenlawn High, things began to happen.

Macy Merchant, a junior and honor roll student, sat down in her fifth hour Mass Media class and tried to shut out the teenage soap opera that played around her as it did on a daily basis. Macy was not a popular girl. She was smart and ambitious and serious, qualities which certainly did not endear her to the more socially elite of Greenlawn High.

Not that any of this really bothered Macy.

At least, not that she was willing to admit openly. Some kids were funny and some kids were jocks, some were drop-dead gorgeous and some were burgeoning criminals, and some, like her, were just smart. A thin, flaxen-haired girl, she knew her one true attribute was her brain. And she was adult enough to know that in the real world, this is ultimately what counted. Sometimes she wished she had looks like Shannon Kittery or Chelsea Paris or some of the other senior vixens, had guys worshipping at her feet. But not too often. For she knew that looks faded, as they said, and that both Shannon and Chelsea would probably end up living in trailers with three screaming brats each and the obligatory alcoholic, abusive husband who once upon a time had rushed for a hundred yards in the big game, but now only rushed to the refrigerator or to the TV set to watch the WCW or *Girls Gone Wild* on DVD.

Unlike so many of the others that ran the maze of high school looking for their slice of cheese, Macy had ambitions. School and study came easy to her, so early in her freshman year she decided to go to law school upon graduation and commenced to arrange her classes accordingly. Yes, a good law school. Then maybe criminal law followed by district attorney and even judge. After that, a leap into politics and who could say where it would all end?

Yes, Macy had high ambitions, lofty aspirations, but no one save the school counselor knew this. None of her classmates would have suspected that brainy, quiet little Macy was aiming at positions of great power.

And the reason for that was Macy herself.

She was, sadly, shy and introverted and much-ignored. Much as she fantasized about being a great wolf of the courtroom, the fact was that she found it nearly impossible to give even a three-minute oral report before the class or to even speak up unless directly called on. These things, she well knew, were something she would need to work on.

On her way into Mass Media, she steered her way through the mulling bodies in the hallway and slipped into her seat. No one noticed her outside and nobody noticed her inside. She was simply a fixture in the minds of the other students, much like a chair or a desk. She sat up in front, arranging her materials, trying to shut out all the gossip and bitching that was going on around her. Sometimes it all seemed so terribly juvenile she could barely stomach it.

"—and if he doesn't call tonight, that's it—"

"—thinks she's got me wrapped, dude, but she's in for a surprise—"

"—so they blamed me, can you believe it? It's just a little dent—"

"—that top cost me fifty bucks, so the dumb bitch puts it in the dryer—"

"—he told us to hand it in tomorrow, like I have the time—"

"—if that's what he thinks of me, he can kiss my ass—"

And on and on and on.

Macy could hear Shannon Kittery and her pop squad discussing something almost breathlessly and she figured it probably had something to do with hair color or shoes or something else equally as revelatory.

"All right, all right, pipe down!" Mr. Benz said as he waltzed into class, chewing a big wad of bubble gum as usual. "Everybody in their seats or I'll get my whip out."

He opened his briefcase and snapped his gum. Everyone took their seats and the commotion died to a low murmur.

"You're not supposed to chew gum unless you have enough to share," Shannon Kittery giggled. A few stifled laughs broke out, mainly from her group.

Benz strode over to her, grinning. "All I've got is this piece," he said, pulling the blob of wet gum from his mouth and sticking it about an inch from the end of her nose. "But you're welcome to it. Go ahead."

Shannon made a disgusted sound and shut up.

"Anybody else want it? No? Heck with ya." He shoved it back in his mouth and went up to the board. He ran his fingers across the bald pate atop his head and said, "My hair look okay?"

Everyone laughed.

"Good. My hair is my life." He sorted through some papers on his desk. "Today, I want all of you to break up into twos with your assigned study buddy and get to work on your reports. Yeah, yeah, I know it's only the third day of school, but those reports are still due next Friday. Any questions?"

A few hands shot up.

"Good. Get to work."

Benz sat down at his desk and read a newspaper, ignoring everyone.

Macy felt a slow painful groan well up inside her for this was the moment she dreaded most of all. For some ungodly reason, Benz had teamed her up with Chelsea Paris, one of

Shannon's ratpack. Chelsea was a varsity cheerleader and after Shannon herself, the reigning queen of the hive. Chelsea had no use for Macy and that undying love went both ways. Chelsea came over, looking like she was approaching a septic tank, and sat down at the desk nearest Macy. She crossed her arms over her impressive bosom, rolled her eyes and proceeded to look very bored.

"I don't like this any more than you do," Macy told her, surprised that she had even said it.

"Oh, spare me, you little nit," Chelsea said, examining her lustrous auburn hair for split ends. "Spacey Macy. I'm so sure."

"I was just saying—"

Chelsea held a hand up, palm towards her study buddy. "Yeah, yeah. Whatev."

"Knock it off," Macy said, something hot bubbling inside her. "Bitch."

Chelsea looked like she'd been slapped. *"What did you say?"*

Macy just licked her lips.

She couldn't believe she'd just said *that*.

Not that it was uncalled for, really, but she wasn't like that, she never spoke up...but suddenly it just felt *right*. For years now she'd wanted to tell Chelsea and Shannon and the rest of the bimbo bunch exactly what she thought of them. And now, she had. It was amazing and more than a little shocking for both girls.

Macy sat there, staring at Chelsea, and it was crazy, but it was almost like there was a voice in her head, telling her what to do, egging her on. But not a thought voice, but an *actual* voice, one that was deep and confident. *Haven't you taken enough shit?* it seemed to be saying to her. *Haven't you given these insufferable, vacuous, superficial little bitches every chance? You've been pushed and pushed and pushed and each time you've been kind, each time you turned the other cheek, they rewarded you with treachery. It's high time you gave a little back, don't you think?*

Macy smiled. "Bitch," she said. "Rotten slutty fucking cheerleader bitch."

Chelsea looked like she was going to cry. "You, you can't talk to me like that, you little—"

"I'll talk to a little cunt like you any way I want."

Both girls stood up now, facing each other.

Everyone was waiting, anticipating bloodshed.

Chelsea was taller, athletic, but inside she was weak and frightened like the rest of her ratpack. Terrified of rejection, of the curse of unpopularity. Afraid to be told the truth and particularly by a socially inferior nit like Macy Merchant. And Macy? For the first time in her life, there was no fear, no indecision. She stood there, smiling, her eyes the flat gray of tombstone marble. She wanted to hurt Chelsea, she wanted to draw blood and make the little cheerleading whore beg for mercy.

The animal in her was hungry.

"Cunt," she said.

"Ah, girls..." Benz said.

Chelsea's eyes narrowed to slits and she slapped Macy across the face.

There were muted cheers from the ratpack.

Macy grabbed Chelsea by the throat, yanking her right over the desk and bouncing her face over its top not once, but twice. Chelsea made a strangled sound, eyes bulging, blood running from her nose. And before anyone could intervene or hope to, Macy yanked Chelsea's head up by a handful of hair, grabbed a sharpened No. 2 pencil off the desk, and buried it in her left cheek. A few gasps rose up as Chelsea stumbled back, a look of horror on her face, the freshly sharpened No. 2 Ticonderoga jutting from her cheek, a wet trail of blood running down her jaw. Whatever sort of shock had gripped her, it now faded, and she opened her mouth to scream. Opened it wide enough that Macy could see that the tip of the pencil had impaled her tongue, gone right through it in fact.

"Yahhhggg," Chelsea gagged, blood gushing from her mouth now and right down the front of her pink Old Navy tee. "Gaaahhhlllggg..."

It was not a pleasant sound.

Macy could smell the blood.

It made her mouth water...

7

And, at the moment Macy Merchant lost control, upstairs in Mr. Cummings 5th hour BioLab, Billy Swanson waited.

Waited.

Because even the best plans were really a matter of timing and stealth. The new Billy knew this even if the old one was too goddamn stupid to realize such basic laws. So he waited until Cummings paired them up for their lab assignment. He waited until Cummings asked for a volunteer to pass out the dead frogs for dissection.

"I'll do it," Billy offered, grinning pleasantly.

Cummings looked surprised, but shrugged. "Go to it," he said.

Tommy Sidel laughed as he passed by. "Think you can handle it, dip shit?"

Billy kept smiling. "I can handle anything, douchebag. Didn't you know that?" He leaned in closer. "You still going out with Shannon Kittery, Tommy? Lucky boy. I think I'm going to fuck that bitch in the mouth."

Tommy tensed. "You're fucking dead," he said.

"We're *all* dead, Tommy. Take my word for it."

Tommy looked like he was ready to piss nails and Billy knew that after school, old Tommy star-running-back-scumbucket-pencil-dick was going to be thinking payback and it would be the worst decision his little pea brain had ever come up with. But then, everyone knew that Tommy Stick-Up-His-Ass-Sidel had all the cunning of a box of petrified camel dung and all the charm of an open sore. Yeah, he'd come looking for payback and Billy would give him a little treat he'd never forget. And when he was done cutting on him, he'd do something to that uppity prick's corpse that would make his own mother puke.

They were all assholes.

They all deserved to die.

For like Macy Merchant, something inside him had suddenly changed. Whoever and whatever Billy Swanson had been all those years was gone. The worming caterpillar named Billy had crawled into its cocoon and emerged as a pissed-off butterfly with a brand new attitude, one that looked down in disgust at the mess the old Billy had made out of his life.

There came a time, the new Billy assured him, when enough was enough. When you stopped chewing other peoples' shit and asking for seconds.

And that time was now.

Because the old passive shit-eating Billy days were all over. History.

He'd been picked on, put down, and shit upon...but no more. That was for the weak. And Billy was no longer weak.

The supply room in which the frogs were stored was in a large, bulky stainless steel refrigerator reached by a door at the back of the classroom. The storeroom had another adjoining door which led to the chemistry classroom. It was closed, the room on the other side empty. The storeroom was where the chemicals and lab glassware and utensils were stored.

It was also where Cummings and a few other science teachers stored their lunch bags and coats.

Billy saw Cummings' red Thermos.

He smiled.

There was a yellow metal cabinet on the other wall which read DANGER HAZARDOUS CHEMICALS! in brilliant red letters. As always, the key was in the lock. Calmly, purposefully, Billy opened it and removed the jug of sulfuric acid. He slipped on the elbow-length protective rubber gloves and did what had to be done. Afterwards, he got the frogs out. They were in heavy plastic bags. He passed one out to each lab team and placed them unceremoniously on the wax-lined dissection trays.

It was simple.

All things truly wonderful usually were.

Then he took his seat. His lab partner was Lisa Korn, another much put upon student who always looked a bit ragged. She was jittery and prone to fits of crying and sudden fainting spells. She had all the earmarks of a future neurotic, a condition that was in many ways fostered and encouraged by the incompetence and blind eyes of the public school system. Billy always felt sorry for her, because he knew what her life was like. The abuse the other students handed out to her which the faculty simply preferred to ignore. By the nastier students and uppity bastards like Tommy Sidel and his posse, Lisa was known simply as Lovely Lisa Korn-Hole.

She looked nervous as always, afraid maybe that she had done something wrong or would say something wrong if she dared open her mouth.

"Don't worry, Lisa," Billy told her. "It's all about to change."

She just looked at him and he smiled.

He could smell the sex between her legs. It made him giddy.

"Let's do it," he said.

Taking the scalpel, he slit open the frog's belly like it was something he'd done a thousand times. While Lisa turned an amusing shade of green, he pinned back the frog's skin with tiny dissection needles and got to work.

And waited for the shit to hit the fan.

He did not wait long.

Mr. Cummings went into the supply room and came out with his Thermos, pouring himself a cup of coffee. He made it all the way to his desk before he took his first gulp. Like he always contended, he was nothing without his caffeine and today was the day when he would finally get his fill. He raised the cup to his lips, scanning the lab teams with disinterest, and swallowed a big gulp.

No one was really paying any attention to him at that moment.

No one but Billy Swanson.

Cummings drew the cup away from his lips with dawning horror. What was at first a scowl of distaste soon became a twisted rictus of agony. The coffee cup slid from his trembling fingers and shattered at his feet.

And then everyone was suddenly paying attention.

Cummings was staggering around and shuddering, clawing at his throat as gouts of steam wafted from his mouth like cigarette smoke. No one said a word in that split second of realization that something was *very* wrong with him. His glasses flew off, his eyes bulging, his face the color of Wisconsin cherries. Rivers of sweat coursed down his brow.

"What's he doing?" Tommy Sidel said.

Cummings fell back against his desk, overturning a stack of graded test papers. His fingers were hooked into claws, thrashing and tearing at himself and everything in sight. "Ggggghhhhlll," he gagged, blood running from his mouth in dark ribbons.

"Mr. Cummings?" Tommy Sidel said, the first one on his feet. "Mr. Cummings! Are you all...right..."

Cummings collapsed to the floor, his fingers tearing open his shirt, cutting deep red welts in his corded throat. A high, inhuman wailing came from him. He thrashed around, thumping his fists and moaning just moments before he began to vomit out great clots of steaming, bloody tissue.

"Mr. Cummings," Tommy said, at first trying to get a hold of him, but now backing away in disgust as gore sprayed in the air. "Mr. Cummings! *Goddammit, somebody get an ambulance, a fucking doctor! He's dying or something...*"

And he was.

His mouth opened in a terrible continuous scream, his teeth snapping and gnashing, tearing his lips to shreds. His face was a contorted red fright mask, his tongue dangling from his lips until his teeth literally bit it in half. All the students were gathered now in a tight circle to watch his agony. He was like some nightmare cartoon run in fast motion. An evil caricature of someone possessed by a demon, hopping and flopping and moving with epileptic speed and at such impossible angles that they could hear his tendons popping and bones dislocating.

Nobody rushed out for help.

Not a one.

Something was happening to them, something they did not understand or really even question. It passed from one to the other like cold germs and when it was done, the students of 5th hour Biolab were not who they had been a few moments before. They were altered, changed. They looked down at Mr. Cummings and there was not a single twinge of remorse or sympathy in them. What they felt was rage, a stupid and insane rage that consumed them. And one that needed to be voided on something, someone.

Billy stood behind them with Lisa Korn at his side. "Watch, Lisa," he said. "Now you're going to see what they really are down deep."

Lisa just stood there, speechless, her eyes unblinking, her mouth pulled into a straight colorless line.

Billy was smiling, smelling the raw stink of atavism coming from the crowd.

It was delicious.

For maybe twenty or thirty seconds, the students ringed around Cummings did not move. They stood in mock surprise at what had happened, at the dying thing at their feet. Then they began to move. Slowly, inexorably, like some machine cycling up, they started to move as one. Cummings was barely moving, but that didn't stop them. You could see what was coming in their eyes, in the grim set of their mouths.

There was a sudden flurry of voices that combined into a steady, flat droning:

"—gave me a C on that report—"

"—wouldn't have gotten kicked off the team if it wasn't for you—"

"—coulda let me slide, you rotten fuck—"

"—just had to tell my old man you saw me smoking—"

"—always making fun of me—"

"—flunked me—"

"—narced on me for changing grades—"

It all kept rolling, the petty hatreds and accusations and suspicions until it became a sort of mindless chant, building inside each and everyone of them to a pulsing, deadly crescendo and the very air was roiling with heat and malevolence.

And it was then that the first true incident of mass insanity in Greenlawn struck. The students went after Mr. Cummings, kicking and scratching and punching and biting him. They went after him like animals with sheer bloodlust and brutality. Something inside them needed voiding and that something needed a common enemy and in their dying teacher, they found it. They crowded in, beating him to a pulp, trying to twist his limbs off and stomping his guts to sauce. They did not even slow down until their fingers were red, their mouths drooling, their clothes spattered with blood.

And the only thing that really slapped them out of it was a voice that cried: *"What in the name of hell is going on here?"*

The voice belonged to Howard Sullivan, the head custodian. Known as "Sully" to faculty and students alike, he was much loved and had been at Greenlawn High since the days of the Kennedy administration, was only a year shy of retirement, in fact. Anger was a rare commodity for Sully; he liked the kids, year after year, he honestly liked the kids. Liked their fads and music and devil-may-care attitudes. He said they made him feel young and custodian at the high school was the only job he could land where he never really had to grow up.

But today, Sully was mad.

He was shocked and sickened and beyond words. He waded right into the mass of students, pulling them away from Mr. Cummings, actually shoving them out of his path.

When he got a good look at Cummings' corpse, he looked at the circle of students around him. He saw their vacant eyes, their grinning mouths, all that blood on them...smeared, splashed, dripping. Tears rolled from his eyes. "Kids...Jesus Christ, what...what the hell are you doing here? What have you done? *What the fuck have you done?*"

The students pressed in closer.

Sully looked from face to face, saw what was coming, tried to get away, but it was just too late.

They fell on him.

Like lions falling on a gazelle.

And behind them, Billy Swanson grinned...

8

Louis Shears made it home and as he walked through the door, he swore to God he would never leave it again.

The world had gone mad and he was content to leave it to its own devices. He shut the door behind him, locked it. And then on second thought, he threw the deadbolt. He walked into the living room and then the kitchen, feeling like some wind-up toy soldier going first in this direction and then that. He sat in his recliner, got up, sat on the couch, then he got up again. Went to the cupboard above the refrigerator and pulled out a bottle of Chivas Regal. He poured himself two fingers in a water glass, swallowed it down, then poured himself another.

You better get a grip already, he told himself, and that sounded good in theory, but in practice...well, it was something else again.

He sat back in the recliner.

Pulling from his drink and peering out the picture window, the world seemed all right. Cars passed on the street and leaves fluttered gently in the trees. He could hear the sound of a lawn mower and some kid going up the sidewalk on a skateboard.

These things were the normal sights and sounds of an August afternoon.

But what about what happened on Tessler Avenue? Where did any of that fit in? How did he qualify what he had seen this day? Two guys beating a kid near to death with baseball bats and then the kid attacking him and those whacked-out cops showing up? Where did that fit in the annals of a late summer's day? Where did you find the box that would hold such things or a label to slap on it?

"You don't," Louis said. "You don't even try. You just sit here and get drunk. Get shitfaced and forget about it."

Very nice, very nice, indeed.

But hardly practical.

He thought about the steaks and the wine out in the back of the Dodge. The meat needed to be gotten into the fridge before it started to turn. Those porterhouses were nearly two inches thick, custom cut, and had cost him nearly fifteen bucks a throw.

He just couldn't leave them out there.

But that's exactly what he was planning on doing.

The cell phone in his shirt pocket jingled and he jumped, nearly spilling his drink. He put it to his ear, almost expecting one of those crazy cops to be on the other end. But it wasn't them. It was Michelle.

"The weekend stretches out before you," she said. "I hope I didn't interrupt your nap."

Louis started laughing. *No, honey, I wasn't taking a nap. I was sitting in my recliner sucking down whiskey. You ought to see me. Buttons popped off my shirt, bloodstains all over it, my throat bruised from some mortally wounded kid who decided to have one last hurrah and strangle me.*

"What's the matter, Louis?" Michelle said. Even half way across town over at Farm Bureau Insurance, she could sense it on him. That something was most definitely wrong.

"Where should I start?"

"Oh no...you didn't get the accounts, did you?"

"Oh no, I got them. That part of my day was fine. It's just that this town is going crazy. I'm just wondering if you can buy straightjackets in bulk, because I'm thinking we're going to need a lot of them."

Michelle said, "Oh, you heard then?"

"Heard what?"

"About the bank."

Louis felt a heaviness in his chest. What now? "Tell me," he said.

"I only know what they're saying," she said. "I guess an hour ago some old lady came into the bank across the street, you know, First Federal, and wanted to close her account. The teller told her she needed a slip to do that and the old lady just went ballistic. Get this, she whipped out a knife, a big knife, from her purse and stabbed the teller. Stabbed her like five or six times. At least, that's what they're saying. We heard the sirens. It was awful."

"Shit."

"It gets worse. The old lady supposedly walked right out with her bloody knife, sat on the bench outside, and then...well, she just slit her wrists. *Slit* them, Louis, and then folded them in her lap and calmly bled to death."

"Who was it?"

"I don't know. But they said she was smiling. Just sitting there, bleeding to death...and smiling."

Louis swallowed. "The teller survive?"

Michelle said she didn't know. "She lost a lot of blood, I guess. Louis, it was Kathy Ramsland."

"Kathy?" Louis said. "Oh, Jesus, Vic's kid sister?"

"Yeah, I guess."

Calling Kathy a "kid" was maybe overdoing it in that she was nearly thirty. But, hell, Louis had grown up next to her, hung out tight with brother Vic right through high school.

Sitting there, the booze bubbling and acidic in his belly, he was picturing Kathy as a kid. Pushing her around on her bike when she was learning to ride without the training wheels. Making her up as Bride of Frankenstein for Halloween. The awful stories Vic and he used to tell her to scare the shit out of her. The time her hamster died and she buried it in the backyard in a metal Band-Aid box and then he and Vic digging it up a week later to see what it smelled like.

Not Kathy, Christ, not Kathy.

"Louis?" Michelle said. "I don't know what's going on but something happened over at the high school."

Louis swallowed. "Like what? A shooting?" he said, making the quick assumption as most did after Columbine.

"I don't know. But I guess there's like ten cop cars out there...the townies, sheriff, state police. Whatever it is, it must be pretty bad. That's what Carol said. She just drove by there."

The heaviness wasn't just in his belly, it was laying over him, crushing him down in the recliner. He was now starting to wonder and as he wondered, he worried. Maybe you could write off one or two weird things happening, but when they occurred in bunches then you started thinking things. You started seeing the sort of connections that canceled out coincidence. The sort of connections that made paranoia leap into the back of your mind.

"What the hell is going on?" he said out loud, though he'd honestly meant only to think it.

"I don't know," Michelle said. "But it's weird, isn't it?"

"It gets weirder," he said and then he started telling his own tale. The assault. The dying boy. The crazy cops. And as he told that story, realizing yet again that it sounded positively absurd in the telling, he began to turn it all over in his mind. What he'd seen. The stabbing at the bank. Whatever was going down at the high school. Sure, it could have been a series of grim coincidences, but he couldn't seem to wrap his mind around that. For deep down, he was almost scared. Scared that something was happening to Greenlawn.

Something on a huge scale.

In the distance, he could hear sirens. Lots of them. And he wondered what else was going on out there, what other awful things were occurring behind locked doors in all those neighborhoods piled up end to end.

But he stopped himself right there.

It was not healthy thinking. Just because some very odd things were happening did not mean for one moment the town was going insane. That was just paranoia doing his thinking for him. He wasn't about to go down that road. You started thinking crazy bullshit like that, next thing you knew you were afraid to leave the house. Louis had had an aunt like that. She became a shut-in, terrified of everything outside her own door. He wasn't about to become like that.

Yet, the feeling that something was wrong, really wrong, persisted. Like a bad taste, he just couldn't seem to wash it out of his mouth.

"Louis? Louis? Are you there?"

"I'm here," he told his wife.

"Are you telling me that cop was really kicking that boy's body? Stomping on it?"

"Yeah, that's what I'm telling you."

"That's scary. That's really scary."

"Sure," he said. "And goddamn Greenlawn, of all places."

"You better report this," Michelle said. "Call down to the police station right now or go down there, tell them what those nuts were doing. Good God. It's horrible." She was breathing very fast on the other end. "Louis? Are you all right?"

"Yeah, I'm okay."

"No, you're not."

"Well, I'm okay as I can be." He paused, studying the whiskey in his glass. "I wish you could come home. I know it sounds stupid, but I'd just feel better if you could."

"I'll get there soon as I can. I have to finish up some things here first, though. I'll be about an hour, maybe an hour and a half."

That wasn't good enough, but he didn't tell her so. Every minute she was away from him made that hollow in his guts open wider. But how could he honestly explain any of it to her? How could he make her understand, make her feel what he was feeling himself?

"Okay," he said. "Get home as soon as you can."

"Louis...are you sure you're all right? You don't sound good."

"I'm okay."

"You're positive?"

"Yes."

"All right. I'll be home soon as I can."

"Okay. I'll be—" He paused.

"What? What is it?"

Louis wasn't sure himself. He heard the creaking of the steps out on the porch. It didn't mean anything really. Could have been the kid delivering the paper or the mailman. Yet, with what he'd been through and what Michelle had told him, he was expecting something bad.

"There's...there's someone on the porch," he said in almost a whisper.

"Louis...you're scaring me, okay? Just stop this now."

"Hurry home, baby. Please just hurry home."
Hurry...

9

Louis broke the connection, slid the phone back in his pocket.

Setting his drink aside, he started wondering what he had for a weapon in case he needed one. He wasn't a hunter or a hobby shooter, so he didn't have any guns. His trout rod and reel didn't count for anything. There were knives in the kitchen, of course. He went to the closet by the front door and dug out a driver from his golf bag. Then the step out there creaked again. He pulled the sheer aside from the oval window set in the door.

Just the mailman.

Old Lem Karnigan.

Louis sighed. What the hell was wrong with him? Why was he inflating this all into something bigger than it was, some crazy conspiracy?

Lem saw him out of the corner of his eye and waved absently.

Louis pulled the door open.

Lem was pushing seventy, but hadn't retired and there was no talk of him doing so. They'd probably have to force him out. Lem's wife had died two years ago this past winter and his kids were all moved away. He probably didn't have anything but the job. And that was sad when you thought about it.

He was standing on the bottom step sorting letters and fliers. The mailbag strapped over his shoulder looked impossibly bulky and heavy. Almost too much for a skinny old guy like him.

"One of these days, Louis," he said without looking up, "I'm getting out. I'm going down to Florida with the rest of the old coots. I ran into Ronny Riggs last week, just up from Miami Beach. You know what he said? He said there's beaches down there where the girls don't wear no tops. How do you like that? he says. So I say, Ronny, I like that just fine." Chuckling to himself, Lem looked up and his laughter stopped. He saw Louis' disheveled appearance, the crusted bloodstains on his shirt.

"Jesus. H Christ, Louis! What the hell happened? You get in a fight?"

Louis shook his head. "Some kid got in an accident...I had to help. It was a real mess."

Lem just stood down at the bottom of the steps, staring at him.

And as Louis watched, it was almost as if a shadow passed over his face. Lem shuddered, his mouth pulled into a scowl. It looked as if something, something necessary had just drained out of him. And that quick.

Then he did the most amazing thing: he sniffed the air.

Sniffed it like he could smell the blood all over Louis. Like an animal.

"You okay, Lem?"

"So you helped that kid, did you?" Lem said. "Well, that was kind of you."

Louis just swallowed. Gooseflesh had broken out on his arms. *Look at his eyes. Look at his goddamn eyes.* What Louis saw made him wish that he'd brought the golf club with him. Because Lem's eyes were flat and black and shiny like those of a rattlesnake right before it strikes. Just like the kid's eyes...nothing in them.

"You okay, Lem?" he said again.

Lem squinted, his lips pulled back from his teeth. "No...no I ain't all right, Louis Shears. I ain't all right at all. I was thinking...I was thinking about last Christmas...you never left me a tip like you used to do. Yeah, yeah, I know it's my job to deliver your fucking mail, but a tip tells me you appreciate the job I do. That I bust my ass six days a week in good weather and bad, bringing you you're fucking mail."

Louis made ready to spring back inside. "Well, Lem, I'm sorry about that. Last Christmas was a bad time for us. Michelle's mom got sick and all. Everything was crazy."

Lem ran his tongue along the fronts of his teeth. "Sure, Louis, sure. Guys like you, they always got an answer for everything, don't they? Well, don't you worry, Mr. Louis Shears, I know my job. I do my job. Ain't nobody that has to tell me how to do my job, least of all you. Here's your goddamn mail." He crunched it up in his fist, letters and magazines and fliers, threw at Louis. "There you go, you sonofabitch."

And then he ambled away, glancing over his shoulder from time to time at Louis like he hated the sight of him. He moved up the sidewalk, talking to himself. The real frightening thing was that he was moving with a rolling, loping gait like that of an ape.

And worse: he was digging in his mailbag and tossing letters in the air.

Tossing them in bunches.

Then he stopped at a row of rose bushes at the Merchant's house next door, unzipped himself and took a piss. Right there in plain view.

Louis just stood there.

There was something in the water, something in the air. He didn't know what, but they were all starting to lose it. What in the hell was happening? He'd seen it come over Lem, that emptying of all he was or ever had been, leaving something behind that was primal and uncivilized, raging.

He wondered if it was the blood on his shirt.

Lem had been all right until he'd seen the blood. Didn't they say that the sight and smell of blood could create a sort of aggressive response in animals? In dogs? Was that true for people, too? No, that was ridiculous. There had been a sudden inexplicable aggression in Lem, but it had been more than that. He was like the kid or the cops. Suddenly, somehow, things like ethics and self-control had suddenly vanished, leaving a predatory anger in its void.

Louis shut the door.

Then he locked it.

He peered out the window.

At the Merchant's house next door, Lem left mail scattered on the lawn. Two houses down at the Loveman's, he dug into his bag, scratching around in there like an animal rooting in soil for grubs. Then he put a hand to his face and shook. He tossed the bag aside and just wandered away up the walk like he was sunstruck.

It was happening and Louis knew it.

Something horrifying and unknown was taking the town one by one...

10

An easy three blocks away from where Louis Shears was being introduced to the new postal system in Greenlawn, Tessler Avenue crossed Ash Street and right there, right at the bottom of the grassy hill where all the houses were whitewashed and the flowerbeds bloomed lushly with black-eyed susan and rose-pink spider lily, there was a store called Cal's One-Stop. It was named after Bobby Calhoun, who had run it since just after World War II until his death six months ago. Cal's was the sort of place to grab a six-pack or a gallon of milk or a pack of smokes, but not much else since everything was vastly overpriced.

When Angie Preen set out for Cal's, tucking little Danny in the buggy, she did so not because she needed beer or milk or cigarettes or even paper plates or a bottle of ketchup. She had other reasons. None of which were altruistic.

She was going there to turn the screw, as she liked to call it.

And said screw just happened to be firmly lodged in Brandi Welch's back.

And I'll twist it in that little witch, God yes, I'll make her squirm.

"We're going to the store, Danny," she announced. "We need some things."

"We always need things, don't we, Mommy?" said little Danny and for one uneasy moment there, Angie was almost certain that there was a deep salty rut of sarcasm behind his words. But that was silly. He was barely two-years old.

Paranoia, that's what.

Besides, it was that time of the month and her flow was heavy. She was moody, quick to anger, ready to scratch out eyes for the least infraction. Some women, she knew, did not get crazy like she did when they were menstruating. Lucky them.

She looked down at Danny, struck, as always, at how much he looked like his father and how little he looked like her. He had his father's smooth flawless Mediterranean skin and moody, chocolate-dark Sicilian eyes. As such, he was beautiful. Just like his father. Pleasing to behold. One could only hope that he was *nothing* like his father in every other way.

"I want a candy bar," Danny said.

"Okay. We'll get you a Mounds or a Three Musketeers or something."

Danny seemed satisfied with that, then he furrowed his brow, said, "I want a gun."

"Stop that!" Angie chided him, a bead of sweat popping at her temple.

"I want a gun so I can shoot people dead!"

Angie stopped the buggy right there, right on Tessler where the streets are handsomely lined with oak and yellow poplar. "Stop it, Danny. Don't you let me hear you talk like that again. Only bad men shoot people. And bad men get thrown in cages for the rest of their lives. You don't want that, do you?"

A tear in the corner of his eye, he shook his head.

God, she wondered if he was already becoming his father.

Jimmy Torrio. Angie had met him in Terra Haute. A week later she was sleeping with him and the transition between stranger and lover had been exceptionally smooth. But Jimmy Torrio was nothing if not smooth. He gave her Danny, who was beautiful and precious, but that's the only thing he had given her.

Then why did you keep spreading your legs for him?

Ah, the question of the day, the year, the century. Why? She had a good job, she was from a good family, at least by Greenlawn standards. Jimmy was an asshole, he was selfish, he was corrupt. He had a criminal record that he had not revealed until she was in too deep to care. He was really good at nothing beyond drinking and gambling and mooching money. He was not even really very good in bed. Yet, Angie had stayed. At least until she'd found out that she was only one of many. Then she ran straight back to Greenlawn, a bun baking in the old oven, no money, and absolutely no self-respect.

Two years later, she was still obsessed by him. Maybe it was smoldering hate now, but they always said that hate was merely the flipside of love.

"Can I have two candy bars?" Danny asked.

"Of course you can," Angie told him. Why not?

It was a beautiful day and Angie was thinking about Louis Shears who had just driven by, how he always smiled at her, how his eyes flashed like coins in a streambed and behind that look, just behind it, a touch of heat and a touch of interest. Louis was nice. Louis was funny. But he was also married to Michelle who was a very nice lady. So Angie would admire from afar. As always.

Across the street, she saw Dick Starling walk by. He was a very nice man. Everyone loved him. His daughter, Brittany, was on the archery team. Angie had won three state championships in archery when she was in high school and Dick Starling had been instrumental in getting her to take the job of archery coach. Angie hadn't wanted to at first...but she finally submitted. Putting an arrow in a target was not only a great distraction from the stresses of life, it was sheer joy when you imagined that the target was in fact Jimmy Torrio. Bullseye every time, heh, heh.

She waved to Dick Starling...he did not wave back. He was gripping his head in his hands and staggering up the sidewalk like he had a good hangover going. Angie decided it was none of her business.

Cal's was just up the block now.

Angie grinned.

Other than archery, tormenting Brandi was her only true joy in life.

Maybe I should use that bitch for target practice.

Danny's birthday tomorrow. Maybe Jimmy was already in town. Sometimes he did that. He'd show up in Greenlawn, look up some of his old cronies and throw together a card game, indulge in a little whoring with cheap sluts like Little Miss Saucy

Tits Brandi Welch. *Asshole.* He'd probably screwed the little witch last night. Maybe this morning. You could never tell, oh God in high Heaven, you could just never tell.

Angie pushed her buggy through the door of Cal's.

There were maybe six or seven people in there, buying bread, examining the beer in the cooler, chit-chatting as people in Greenlawn will do.

Angie swept the store with acidic eyes.

Ha, there she was. Right behind the counter: Little Miss Saucy Tits. Look at them everyone, admire them, see how plump they are. Women, wouldn't you just love to have a set like these and, men, wouldn't you just love to squeeze them or bury your face in the sweet valley between, yummy-yummy?

At the sight of her, a slight headache bloomed in the back of Angie's skull: it was sharp, insistent. It made her squeeze her eyes shut. And for the briefest of moments, it cast a dark shadow over her thoughts. A shadow that she instantly recognized with some fundamental half-submerged awareness that was ancient and misty. It crawled up from within her, breaking the sleep of reason.

Then it was gone.

Brandi looked up from her Soduku magazine, pencil pausing, saw Angie and tensed, God how she tensed.

Angie smiled at her, a lethal meat-eating smile.

Poor Little Miss Saucy Tits. Look how nervous she is. See how her breasts, so jutting and firm, have deflated somewhat. See how her liquid black eyes shift about nervously like those of a rat wary of the cat. She trembles. Her lips so full and pink and juicy are now pulled into a pale gray line of despair.

Poor little thing, Angie thought. *It's nothing truly personal, you know, but you shouldn't have been fucking my ex. He comes to town maybe once a year and you fuck him and I know it and you know it and I'll never let you forget it.*

Angie lifted Danny from the buggy. "Go find yourself a candy bar," she said, then turned her full hating attention on Brandi Welch who was already withering away like a flower before October's first frost.

"I'd like a lottery ticket," Angie said.

Brandi swallowed. "Um...which kind?"

"What kinds do you have?"

Hee, hee. Make her go through the whole list from Megamillions to the state drawings to instant scratch-offs like Pot-o'-Gold and Million-Gazillion and E-Z Street. It took her about five minutes to go through them all and tell Angie how much they cost and how much you could win, all the unnecessary details. And when she was finished, a fine dew of sweat on her brow, Angie said, "No, I've changed my mind."

What Angie badly wanted to do was to read the little whoring witch right out in front of everyone. What a scene it would be with little Danny at her side! Just tell Little Miss Saucy Tits what she thought of her in plain terms. Refer to her openly as that part of the female anatomy that you generally reserved for the worst, evil little shrews, the old Cee-U-Next-Tuesday. Which was a word that Angie would not allow herself to say out loud or in mixed company because, dammit, she was from a good family and she was better than that...wasn't she?

"I want some cigarettes."

"Cigarettes?"

Angie flashed her the dead smile of a window dummy. "Yes, cigarettes."

"I guess...I mean, I didn't know you smoked."

"Lots of things you don't know, isn't there?" Angie told her. "But trust me, Brandi, in time you'll get to know all about me."

Brandi swallowed. She recognized the implied threat and the tension was so thick on her you could have sliced it like cake. "What kind? What kind of cigarettes?"

"What kind do you have?"

Brandi sighed. "Listen, do we have to go through this every time?"

"Through what?"

"You know damn well what I'm talking about."

"I only know that you're being very rude to a customer."

Danny, damn him, came running up and tossed two Almond Joys on the counter, breaking up the fun which had all the earmarks of being exceptional.

"Is there anything else?" Brandi asked her, a thin smile on her lips.

Angie, pissed-off, cheated, and trembling with barely-concealed rage, dug through her purse, clawed through it really, found her wallet...and it was at that precise moment that the little headache blooming in her skull like a corpse-orchid suddenly flowered and its petals filled her head and its fragrance consumed all that she was.

With moonstruck eyes, she looked from the purse to Brandi, recognizing neither or their place in the scheme of things. She made a guttural grunting sort of sound deep in her throat. Her fingers continued to dig in the purse, finding a wallet, a cosmetic bag, a cellphone, a box of crayons for Danny...things she no longer recognized or understood.

Then they found something else.

A box-cutter with a curving steel blade like that of a scimitar.

Angie had no memory of throwing it in there when she'd sliced open boxes for the recycling. She only knew that it felt good in her hand. It conformed to her palm and begged to be put to use.

"Um...are you all right?" Brandi asked, caught somewhere between confusion and fear.

Angie looked up at her, drool running from her mouth. Her eyes were fixed, staring, almost reptilian. She brought out the box cutter and slashed Brandi across the throat. Brandi stumbled back, shocked, stunned, overwhelmed. Blood bubbled from her torn voice box and she tried madly to stem it with her fingers. It squirted between them like a flow of rich red wine, catching Angie in the face.

The hot spray of blood was not unpleasant.

It was pleasing.

Angie came right over the counter. She slashed Brandi's outstretched fingers to ribbons, she took the tip of her nose off, she opened one breast, and then she ripped the box-cutter across

Brandi's lovely dark liquid eyes, the hooked blade catching in the left pupil and yanking the bloody, glistening orb out by a section of optic nerve.

People fled the store.

But more disturbing, others did *not*.

When Angie came around the counter from the hacked, bleeding thing on the floor, two men and one woman stood there, smiling at her, staring at her with dark troglodyte eyes. Eyes that understood. One of the men, middle-aged and balding, stepped up behind her and slid his hands up her shirt, gripping her breasts roughly.

Angie liked it.

Her blue eyes were like crystal drowning pools, lips pulled away from teeth. The front of her pink tee was soaked with blood, crazy whorls of it had splashed over her face. She enjoyed the smell of it. It excited her, stirred primal memories of the hunt. She licked it off her lips.

The others following, she went back behind the counter. She dipped her fingers into Brandi's gored throat, swished them around in the wound, then, her fingers dripping with blood, she went over to the wall. She knocked a display of Hostess cakes out of the way, kicked aside a cardboard standee of Dale Earnhardt hawking Budweiser...and proceeded to draw on the wall in blood. Elaborate looping symbols, complex intersecting linear marks, bloody handprints and stick figures, repeating them again and again.

Using Brandi Welch's corpse as their palette, the others joined her, covering the walls in ritualistic hieroglyphics that looked oddly like the cave paintings of Paleolithic man.

They instinctively knew what she was drawing and they followed suit until the wall was crowded with primitive art.

When Angie walked out of the store, the others followed in her rich, savage blood-wake. It was her scent now and it drew them to her.

And behind in the store, forgotten but unconcerned, Danny reached into the meat case and found a moist, well-marbled slab of sirloin. It dripped with blood. He brought it to his mouth.

Humming, he began to suck the juice from it...

II

After Louis was long gone, Officers Warren and Shaw and Kojozian stood around staring at the dead boy on the sidewalk, each happily reminiscing about other stiffs they'd been called in on. How they looked, how they smelled, what happened when they tried to bag them up. Warren was an old hand, just like Louis thought, and he seemed to have the best stories by far. But the other two kept trying to outdo him like a couple guys reliving their high school glories on the gridiron.

Kojozian, who'd only been a cop five years by that point, kept trying to come up with something that would impress Warren. "I tell you about that nut over on Birch Street a couple years back? Some old guy, retired railroad man, he took to the bottle and took to it hard."

Warren nodded, as if he'd heard it too many times. "The sauce gets 'em every time. Take my word for it. I could tell you some stories, boy. The old Sweet Lucy, they get a taste for it, look out, brother."

"Sure," Kojozian said, "sure. This guy's got it so bad that his wife decides he's going cold turkey so she up and locks him in the coal bin down in the basement. Keeps him there like a week. You believe that shit? He's in there, living in the straw, shitting and pissing himself. She slides food under the door for him, but no booze. She wouldn't have called us, but she broke the key off in the lock. Well, let me tell you, we broke the door down and the smell that came out...oh boy, not nice. The old man was out of his tree with the D.T.s. He'd torn up his nose, clawed it right to hamburger because he thought there were bugs crawling in and out of it. We took him out and it was no easy bit, he bled all over my uniform shirt, just screaming about the bugs living inside him."

Warren just kept nodding, watching the flies gathering on the kid's corpse. Right then, they were investigating the crater at the top of the head. Warren finished his cigarette and flicked it at them. It scattered them, but the butt lodged right there in the sticky goo coming out of the skull.

It sizzled and went out.

Kojozian said, "Hot out today."

He yanked his tie off and threw it. Then he unbuttoned his uniform shirt, took it off, and pulled off his T-shirt beneath. He threw it in the grass. He put his uniform shirt back on, but did not button it back up. The sun felt good on his bare chest.

Shaw mopped sweat from his face, just shaking his head. "Sure, goddamn booze. You remember old Father Brown over at St. Luke? Oh, now that was long before your time, Kojozian. Father Brown was a hell of a guy, let me tell you. That old sonofabitch ran the church, St. Luke's school, the whole nine yards. Christ, he'd been over there since the forties."

"Forties?" Warren said. "Try the thirties."

"Yeah, well, Father Brown he had quite an operation going over there. Everyone loved him right to death. The church picnic in the summer, the fall carnival, the Halloween spookhouse, the Christmas programs...hell, what a guy. Every old lady in town worshipped that man."

"He used to have supper at our house twice a month when I was a kid," Warren said.

"Sure. He was like that. But what very few in this town knew was that he had an awful thirst. Once a week, usually Thursdays, old Father Brown would just get pissed three sheets to the wind. His housekeeper would always call down to the station and we'd go off looking for him. One time, there he is on Main, leaning up against a parking meter, pissing on the sidewalk." Shaw was grinning now and couldn't help himself. "Well, we get out of the squad car and he sees us right away, tells us to go get fucked and when we're done with that to go fuck our mothers. That's the truth, Kojozian. He was one mean sonofabitch when he got a bellyful."

"He was," Warren said. "Christ, was he ever."

Shaw went on. "Well, me and my partner, Bill Goode...you remember Goody, Sarge? Yeah, well we had a hell of a time with him. Brown had been a boxer in the old days and he still thought he was. He was swinging at us and we were dodging and ducking, but finally we got him under control. Neither of us thought about his johnson that was hanging in the wind. He pissed all over Goody, saved a few squirts for me. What a goddamn mess that was."

Kojozian tried to think of another one, but drew a blank. He worked his shoe under the dead kid's arm and made it bounce up and down, made the palm of his hand slap the concrete in a jumpy rhythm. Slap, slap, slap-slap-slap.

"Boy, I'd hate to get piss all over me."

"Well," Warren said. "That's nothing. If all you get in this job is some piss on you, you're doing all right. We picked up this character on a parole violation out at his house down by the train yards...one of those old houses down there, you know? Well, we came right in and the guy says, I gotta take a shit. Just let me take a shit. But we weren't buying it. We cuffed him and threw him in the back of the squad car. We're pulling out of the driveway and he shits his pants. Damn, I don't think he shit in two weeks. He filled his drawers and it overflowed right down the leg of his pants. Christ, the smell. We took him down to the jail and hosed him off. I spent the afternoon cleaning shit out of the back of the squad car. Every time it got warm in there, even a month later, you couldn't smell nothing but that guy's shit."

"Oh yeah?" Shaw said. "I can live with the shit. That's nothing. It's the vomit I can't stand. I pulled over a guy for drunk driving when I was working midnights. I pulled him out of the car and he vomited right on me. It was summer and I had my collar open and he puked right down the front of my shirt. For the next two hours, my belly is coated with this guy's puke."

Warren just laughed. "Puke is just puke. I ever tell you about the train that plastered that bum the first year I was on the Department? Holy O. Christ. It hit him and he got tossed underneath, cut into about fifty pieces. Middle of goddamn winter and we're poking around in the snow, bagging up pieces of him. There I was, just green with it, carrying around an arm in one hand and a foot in the other. Another rookie found a hand

and he stuffed it in my pocket because we didn't have anywhere else to put it. We had those old leather coats with deep pockets then. It fit just fine. Well, it was a busy night and I forgot about the hand in there. We got off shift and we went and got loaded. I come home and I hit the hay. You shoulda seen the look on my old lady's face when she looked through my pockets!"

They had a good laugh over that one.

Cars kept coming by, slowing down to get a look and Kojozian waved them along. This was police business here. When they got a look at him, they sped away.

"Well," Warren finally said. "This isn't getting this stiff off the public sidewalk."

"We need a shovel," Shaw said.

Kojozian was wondering where they'd get a shovel when he saw a guy down the block trimming his hedges outside a trim little ranch house. They all saw it same time he did.

Warren in the lead, they went on down there...

12

"Excuse me, sir," Warren said, taking his hat off. "We're on police business here. What's your name?"

The guy stood there in blue jeans and a tank top, clippers in hand. He was very neat and immaculate as was the lawn behind him, just as green as emeralds. He was staring at Kojozian. His shirt open, chest glistening with sweat.

"What are you looking at?" Kojozian asked him. "You never seen a cop before?"

"No...no...it's just that...um..."

"I asked you your name," Warren said.

"Um...Ray Donnel. What's going on here...what's this about?"

Kojozian chuckled. "He wants to know what this is about."

"Sure, he does," Shaw said. "He's just being a concerned citizen, that's all."

But Warren shook his head. "Sorry, Mr. Donnel. This is police business and we're not at liberty to discuss the particulars. We need a shovel, maybe those clippers, too."

Donnel looked from one to the other. The blood had drained from his face. "I have tools in the shed."

"He says they're in the shed," Kojozian said.

"Sure, where else would they be?" Shaw said.

He led them back behind the house and they all commented on his yard, how nice it was, how green the grass was, the nice edging job he'd done on his walk. They were all really impressed and they told him so. Inside the shed there were racks of gardening tools, spotless and shining. Shovels arranged by size. Donnel was definitely a guy who believed everything in its place and a place for everything.

Warren grabbed a shovel, admired the clean blade on it. "Nice," he said. "Real nice. We'll try not to dirty it up too much."

"That's okay," Donnell said, fumbling over his words. "I'm...I'm just a neat freak, I guess."

"Nothing wrong with that," Shaw said, mopping more sweat from his face.

"As long as I get 'em back, I'm not worried."

Warren handed the shovel to Kojozian. "You'll get it back. I'll see to it. We're cops and you can trust us. We're not thieves, you know."

"Oh, I didn't mean that."

"You believe this guy, Kojozian?" Shaw said. "He thinks you're a thief. Thinks you won't bring his shovel back. How do you like that?"

The big man bristled. "I don't like it at all."

Donnel looked at them like maybe it was a joke, but they were deadpan to a man. They saw nothing funny about a guy like him who thought cops were thieves. In fact, in their book, there was nothing worse than a guy like him that didn't trust cops. What was the world coming to?

Donnel just shook his head, smelling something on these three he did not care for. Something savage, something desperate.

"Listen, officers, I didn't mean anything. I didn't mean anything at all."

The three of them were circled around him now like they didn't want him getting away and Donnel was starting to sense that. Their faces were hard, their eyes shining like basalt. They licked their lips with the pink worms of their tongues. Shaw's belly growled.

"Maybe he wants the shovel back right now," Warren said. "You better give it to him."

Kojozian shrugged and swung it with everything he had at Donnel's head. There was a clanging and Donnel dropped to their feet, a gash opened from his left ear to his right eyebrow, blood pooling out. Kojozian kicked him with a gore-encrusted shoe, but Donnel did not move. He just bled some more.

"What a guy," Shaw said. "You just can't reason with some of 'em, you know that, boys?"

They knew, all right.

They gathered up three shovels, a rake, and a wheelbarrow which would make carting the stiff around a lot easier. Shaw and Kojozian stepped out into the sunlight.

"Hey," Warren said. "You're not gonna just leave him there, are you?"

"Why not?" they said.

Warren shook his head. "This guy likes things neat. We should at least respect that. Give me a hand with him."

Kojozian lifted the body up to where a hook was sticking out of the wall. While he held Donnel, Shaw and Warren pushed the body onto the hook. It entered just beneath the back of his skull with a moist, grating sound. He hung there just fine.

"That's better," Warren said. "Donnel would have appreciated that."

"I hope I look so neat when I'm dead," Shaw said.

Kojozian studied the blood all over his hands. He was fascinated by it in a way that blood had never fascinated him before. He kept sniffing his fingers. Finally, a loose and almost comical smile on his face, he rubbed blood all over his right index finger and painted his face with it. A huge red X that went from jawline to temple, the apex being dead center of his nose.

The other two did not seem to notice.

They all just stood there for a few minutes, approving of what they had done. Donnel was hanging from the wall, blood running down his face and out of his left eye. They listened to it drip to the floor for a time, then they went to take care of the kid...

13

Macy Merchant walked home from school that day in something of a daze. She did not understand what had happened. She only knew that it left her feeling very scared. Very disturbed. She thought it over and kept thinking it over and all she came up with was a blank. An absolute blank.

It just did not make sense.

Sure, she couldn't stand Chelsea Paris or Shannon Kittery or any of the rest of their uppity, elitist pack. But she'd never mouthed off to them before. She'd never dared. And she certainly had never attacked one of them. Macy couldn't remember ever being in a fight. Chelsea and Shannon had been mean to her long as she could remember, but even when they shoved her in the halls in junior high or knocked her books out of her hands, she'd never fought back.

You did more than fight back, Macy, a stern voice in her head informed her. *You attacked. You attacked Chelsea. You stabbed her in the cheek with a frigging pencil.*

Oh, God. Oh, dear God.

Thing was, she could remember doing it just fine.

She could remember the absolute hatred and loathing she'd suddenly felt for Chelsea. It had been like a poison working its way through her, until...until she had just lost control. All of it boiled in her and she'd started calling Chelsea names.

Then she'd grabbed her.

Pounded her head off the desk.

Then stabbed her with the pencil.

And the blood...God, the smell of it. It had made her hungry. It had made her mouth water. And worse, far, far worse, it had made her *horny*.

Just the memory of that sickened her.

Mr. Benz had dragged her down to the office and Chelsea was taken to the school nurse. She remembered Mr. Shore, the principal, reading her the riot act, asking her again and again why she, a straight A honor roll student with a spotless record, would do something so vicious and cruel. Chelsea was being taken to the hospital. She would need stitches. And as Shore went on and on, Macy just sat there, that black poison still seething in her guts. She kept smiling even though Shore told her to wipe that goddamn smirk off her face. But she hadn't been able to. It was like someone was smiling for her, thinking awful things and doing worse things, and she had only been along for the ride.

While Shore raged, she had stared at his belly. It was so full and round beneath his starched white shirt. What a mess it would be, she thought, if someone opened it with a knife.

Then...whatever had taken hold of her, just faded.

Macy started crying.

And not your average boo-hoo crocodile tears, but the real thing. Whatever that awful compulsion had been, when it released her, it was like she had been torn open inside, cut right to the bone, and then the blood had flowed and kept flowing. This blood was clear and ran from her eyes, but in her mind it was just as red and just as hot as it spilled down her cheeks. Even Shore had melted when he saw it happen.

Macy...sweet, gentle, kind...was back and maybe he saw this.

That other *thing* was gone. Shore had tried to console her, tried a great many things, in fact, short of telling her it was okay, it was nothing to get upset about. But, truth be told, Macy was in such a state of tearful despondency by then, it had even crossed his mind to say *that*. Then the school secretary, Mrs. Bleer, had come in and did what many men seemed so incompetent at and incapable of: she soothed Macy. She talked her down, hugged her, let her know that while, yes, it was bad attacking another student, that they would work it out.

Had it been someone other than Macy Merchant, the treatment would not have been so sympathetic or understanding. But Mrs. Bleer knew Macy just as Mr. Shore did and Macy was a good kid. Smart, well-adjusted, dutiful...she was not some wildcat that routinely assaulted other girls.

Both of them kept asking her the same thing again and again: *Why?* Why had she gone after Chelsea like that? What had Chelsea said? What had she done? Because neither of them were ignorant of Chelsea Paris and the sort of girl she was. And the way they were seeing it was that Chelsea must have really, really done something bad this time around to get a reaction like that out of Macy Merchant, of all people.

Yes, they wanted to know why.

And as Macy walked down Colidge Street, making for 7th Avenue and Rush Street, she wanted to know why, too.

She saw Kathleen Soames standing on her porch. She waved.

She kept walking, aware only of the thoughts that filled her head and this was enough. Clutching her books to her chest, her head slumped down, she stared at the sidewalk. The cracks in it. The anthills blossoming every few feet.

The thing that absolutely terrified her about it all is that she had felt no control, as if someone or *something* else had simply taken over. She wondered if that's how crazy people felt when they opened up with a gun in a supermarket or took an axe after somebody, like they were not really to blame, that it had been someone or something else, some terrible urge that had taken control of them completely, one they were powerless to stop.

Is that how it was?

Was she now in that category?

God, there'd never been anything like this, no indication that she was crazy. She had bad thoughts like anyone else, but she'd never hurt a fly before in her life. Right then, despite the fear and sadness, she did not feel essentially different than she had two weeks before or two years before. And that was the scary thing...would it happen again? Just out of the blue would she attack someone? And have no control over it when it happened?

What a mess, what a terrible mess.

Maybe she had a chemical imbalance like schizophrenia or one of those things they'd learned about in Personal Psych last year. Multiple personalities. Good Macy and bad Macy. If that was true, then there would be medications and therapy. Regardless, her life would never be the same again. At school, she would be tagged as a psycho by some and be a hero to all the others who'd always wanted to put Chelsea Paris in her place but had never dared. Yeah, that was some kind of fame. The sort of fame she could live without.

Mom would not be happy with any of it.

Macy's dad had died when she was five from a heart attack and, although she could not remember *exactly* what her mom was like before that, she had a pretty good idea that her mom was not a drunk. That she was capable of holding onto a job for more than two or three months at a crack. And that she had not been sleeping with anyone she happened to run into at the bar.

At least, she hoped so.

But the truth was that sometimes it was really hard to say *who* was doing the parenting. There was only the two of them now and mom was usually pretty hung over which dumped just about everything in Macy's lap. She generally did the cooking and washing and house cleaning. She was the one that balanced the checkbook when there was actually any money in it. If it needed doing, it fell on Macy. She knew what the gossip in the neighborhood was, the common assumption that mom was a drunken whore and that Macy, with no true parental supervision, would soon enough follow in her tracks. The apple didn't fall far from the tree, as they said.

But they were all wrong.

Macy did not smoke or drink or do drugs and at sixteen, she was still a virgin unlike Chelsea Paris, Shannon Kittery, and the rest of the pop squad. Maybe as far as the virginity thing went, there had been precious few opportunities because she was not a natural vixen with all the necessary equipment in place by the eighth grade. Still, even had she been like Chelsea or Shannon she did not think she would have hit the mattress as fast as they had. It was the same with drinking and drugs, all the other assorted temptations that commonly led teenagers astray.

Macy did not indulge because she chose not to.

Maybe she had self-control and maybe she had self-respect and maybe she was more emotionally mature than her peers. Regardless, she set a high standard for herself and sometimes she wondered if it was because of her mother *and* her father. Her mother because Macy was honestly embarrassed at what mom was and had no desire to be like her. And dad because he had died young and Macy had never gotten a chance to really know him, but she felt that she owed it to his memory to conduct herself in a way that would have made him proud.

Macy, of course, never admitted this to anyone, let alone mom.

Because mom didn't like to talk about dad. Whenever his name was mentioned she dropped into one of her funks and the only person who could get her out of it was Jim Beam. Macy sometimes thought that mom wanted her to run wild, would have been much happier if her only daughter fell from grace, stopped being such a "goody-two-shoes" as she often called her.

And how was that for parenting?

Mom would get a kick out of this, though. Macy attacking another girl and getting suspended—dear God, *suspended*—pending an investigation. Macy had a funny feeling she would laugh when she heard, say something stupid like, *well, well, you're just like the rest of us after all, aren't you?*

And that was the thing, wasn't it?

Macy did not want to be like the rest.

She worked hard, studied hard, set high standards for herself to follow and now that had all come crashing down. She'd assaulted Chelsea Paris. Of all the impossible, unexplainable things.

She'd never live this down.

Half way down 7th, Macy suddenly looked up.

Looked up and couldn't believe what she was seeing...

14

The Hack twins, Mike and Matt, were standing on the sidewalk, lording over a pile of rocks, and casually tossing them at a minivan parked at the curb. Macy just stood there, watching as the boys threw them one after the other. The windows were spider webbed from the impacts, the doors and quarter panels scratched and dinged in.

Macy couldn't believe it.

She'd babysat the two of them off and on for the past three years. They were monsters at heart, but they were not wantonly destructive like this.

"Mikey!" she called out. "Matt! What do you think you're doing?"

They looked over at her, smiled in recognition, and began throwing rocks again. The impacts were loud enough so that everyone in the neighborhood must have been hearing them, but nobody was paying any attention. Mr. Chalmers was even sitting out on his porch in plain view, just reading his paper.

"We're throwing rocks," Mike said with typical ten-year old honesty.

Macy rushed over to them. "Stop it! What the heck is wrong with you two? Can't you see you're wrecking that minivan? Your mom will go nuts! God, what's wrong with you two?"

Mike scratched his sandy-blonde hair. "Mom said we could."

"Yeah," Matt agreed, "that's what she said."

Macy just shook her head. "Oh, I'll just bet she did."

"It's none of your business," Mike said. "You better go."

"Mikey..."

Matt stared at her and his eyes were funny. "Get out of here! You don't belong here!"

As Matt said that, Mike was behind her, too close for Macy's liking. And what he was doing...this is what made her jump away and give Mike a shove that planted him squarely on his ass.

He'd been sniffing her.

Like a dog.

Sniffing her ass.

Mike got up, looked like he was fighting against something. "Maybe...maybe you better just go, Macy. Things are different now. Things can happen."

"That's it," Macy said, reaching out and snaring Matt by the wrist. "You're coming inside right now, the both of you."

But Matt yanked his wrist free.

Macy took a step back when she got a real good look at what was in his eyes. Neither of them had ever been openly defiant like this, but now they were not just defiant but almost savage. Their freckled faces were damp with sweat, hair plastered to their foreheads. And those eyes...so intense and hating, almost reflective like black glass.

Macy suddenly felt a shift of power around her.

The boys were not afraid of her. Not in the least. In fact, they were looking at her with no fear whatsoever and something even deeper and more caustic like absolute hate. They looked like animals, like they wanted to take her down with teeth and claws, gut her right there on the sidewalk.

"You guys...you better go in," she said.

Mike grinned at her. "Fuck you," he said.

"*What?*"

Macy stepped forward to grab him, even though the idea of touching the boy was suddenly repulsive to her. She stepped forward and Matt kicked her in the shin. Mike punched her in the arm. And then they both took hold of her and she had to fight with everything she had to throw them off. Her books went one way and she went the other. She made it maybe ten feet when the first rock struck her in the back. Then another glanced off her brow, slicing her open.

"Stop it!" she cried. "That hurt! You better stop it right now!"

But they weren't going to stop and she knew it.

They had gone crazy, the both of them. Something in them had just snapped and she could not only see it in their eyes, she could *smell* it wafting off of them in a hot, pungent odor. Trying to reason with them now was like trying to reason with wild dogs that were intent on taking you down. Another rock hit her in the stomach, another in the crook of her arm and hard enough so that it went numb right down to the wrist.

Macy ran.

The boys followed, flinging stones at her with everything they had. Rocks glanced off her back, whistled over her head. She outdistanced them quickly, vaulting over the hedges and running right up to Mr. Chalmers' porch. The boys hopped the hedges and then skidded to a halt when they saw him.

"What the hell's going on here?" Mr. Chalmers said. "Why're you boys chasing this girl? That you, Macy?"

"Yes," she panted. "They've gone nuts! They're pegging me with rocks!"

"They are, eh?" Mr. Chalmers tucked his reading glasses in his shirt pocket and set his paper aside. "What the hell's got into you boys?"

"We were throwing rocks at her," Mike said.

"Yeah, we were going to kill her," Matt added.

Macy felt all the spit in her mouth suddenly evaporate.

There were no words to adequately describe what went through her head at that moment. Fear and shock and horror, too many other things. It all left her feeling weak and hopeless.

Mr. Chalmers stood there, hands on hips, appraising the situation. Though he was in his sixties, he was still a large, well-muscled man with broad shoulders and a thick chest, the result of his twenty years in the Army as a paratrooper with both the 82nd and 101st Airborne Divisions. He still had the requisite thick neck and bristly crewcut, though now gone white.

"Mr. Chalmers," she said. "There's something happening here. I don't know what. But some kids at school went crazy like this and attacked a teacher and the janitor. They killed them."

But Mr. Chalmers was not interested in that. "You boys want to kill this girl, don't do it in my yard, you hear? This is my territory! *My* territory! I marked it with my scent and you better not cross my scent, you understand?"

Macy was shaking her head from side to side.

Mr. Chalmers, too.

It was in his eyes like it was in the eyes of the Hack twins: that seething, primal emptiness. That blankness that was without bottom.

"How'd you mark your territory?" Mike asked. "We want to mark ours, too!"

Mr. Chalmers laughed. "Like this, boys. Just like this."

And as Macy watched, he unzipped his pants and pulled his penis out. Still smiling, he proceeded to urinate on the steps, washing them down so all would know the boundaries of his territory.

When he was done, the boys sniffed it, recognizing his smell and remembering it.

Macy let out a scream.

"Get her, boys!" Mr. Chalmers said. "Run her down! Whichever one takes her down first gets her!"

Macy took off running, the twins in hot pursuit.

She darted down the sidewalk and then cut between two houses, ducked behind a garage. The twins came running, looking around, and then jogged away down the alley. Macy hid there, panting and sweating, something broken loose now in the back of her mind.

She saw the twins in the distance.

They had stripped off all their clothes now.

They were pissing on trees like dogs.

Macy tried to catch her breath, tried to hold her world together before it flew apart.

It was some kind of mass insanity, she decided, that's what it was. That's what had made those kids go crazy in Biolab and attack Mr. Cummings and Sully and that was what had made her go after Chelsea Paris. It was like some kind of insanity bug.

And now it had the Hack twins and Mr. Chalmers.

I have to get out of here, Macy found herself thinking. *They could be everywhere. The whole town could be crazy...*

And that was a possibility, she supposed.

She calmed herself the best she could and crossed the alley, slipped through a couple yards and thankfully saw no one. She didn't know what was going on. But what she kept thinking was that if she had snapped out of it, maybe the others would, too. What amount of damage would be done by then she could not know and did not want to guess at—

"Hey, Macy," a voice said. "How's my favorite girl?"

Macy turned, flooded with fear, and then for maybe two or three seconds she relaxed. She breathed. Why, it was only Mr. Kenning who lived up the block. Mr. Kenning was a Boy Scout troop leader, he announced football games for the Greenlawn High Wildcats, and he sold cars for a living. A nice man who loved sports and kids and his Irish Setter, Libby. He always had a few kind words for Macy.

Except...this was not *that* Mr. Kenning.

This Mr. Kenning was standing in the back yard, completely naked and covered with blood. Neither of which seemed to bother him in the least. He was smiling, hacking on something with a knife. Blood ran down his forearm and dripped from his elbow.

"Come here, Macy. I have a secret I want to share with you."

Macy just stood there, the instinctual need to flee very overpowering. She stepped around the hedges, knowing she shouldn't, but needing to see just how bad this situation was.

"Come here, Macy. I won't bite you."

I have a secret I want to share with you.

But Macy could see his secret quite plainly: there was a carcass hanging from the limb of Mr. Kenning's apple tree and he was in the process of dressing it out. It was skinned, fleshy, bleeding. There was no doubt what it was. Even if she hadn't seen the ragged pelt of lustrous orange fur at his feet, she would've recognized the dog. It was hung by the throat.

Mr. Kenning stabbed his knife into the torso, slitting it upwards. Libby's viscera spilled out in a coiled, bloody mass. Mr. Kenning studied his dripping red fist that held the dripping red knife. He sniffed it, then licked the back of it.

"Oh no," Macy said, the world beginning to spin around her. "*Oh no...oh no...oh no...*"

Her whole body was shaking, tears rolling down her face, nausea rolling in her belly with the hot, rank stink of slaughtered dog.

Mr. Kenning kept smiling. That grin was depraved and obscene, filled with a raw unflinching appetite. He would rape her if he could, Macy knew, then he would feed on her.

"Come here, Macy," he said, his blood-spattered penis standing erect. "I'll share my kill with you...if you share what you have with me."

Macy screamed and ran and, thankfully, he did not follow. He called out to her to bring her mother over, the whole time hacking and chopping at the dog. Macy threw up in the Maub's hedges, cut through the Sinclair's side yard, then ran across the street to her own porch.

She stopped right there, catching her breath, trying to make sense of it all. Everything looked so positively *normal* that what she had just gone through seemed ridiculous. She heard a siren in the distance, but that didn't really mean much. Not by itself.

Behind her, there was movement, feet coming through the grass.

She whirled around, eyes wide and mouth open, ready for just about anything. She saw Mr. Shears standing there. He lived next door. But this was not the Mr. Shears she knew. His eyes were glassy, his hair wild. His shirt was torn and hanging open, bloodstains all over it.

In his hands was a golf club and he looked ready to use it.

"Please," Macy said. "Oh, please, just stay away from me..."

But Mr. Shears kept coming...

15

Mr. Chalmers wasn't real happy with them for losing the girl. In fact, when they got back and told him that Macy Merchant had slipped away, he came right off the porch. He tossed his newspaper and came right at them. His eyes were filled with a simmering blackness. They were shiny like those of a mad dog.

"Simple goddamn job I give you two," he said, pulling his belt out of its loops and snapping it in his fists, "and you fuck it up."

Mike and Matt Hack stood there, knowing they were going to be punished, but not even thinking of running off. They had this coming and they knew it. So they stood there when the belt came at them, lashing them in the faces, the pain sharp and cutting. They cried out and fell to their knees, curling up in balls as the belt laid open their backs in hurting welts.

"You *feel* that, you little shits? That's *pain* and nothing teaches, nothing instructs quite like *pain*," Mr. Chalmers told them, studying the belt in his hands. He was grinning now, satisfied, his eyes mocking and filled with venom. "You two gotta quit acting like fucking little boys. This is war. This is survival. When I send you out to get something, you don't come back without it. Those other neighborhoods, they're gonna try and take what we got, so we got to hit them first. We gotta take what they got. Their women, their food, their weapons. Do you see? Do you see? DO YOU FUCKING SEE, BOYS?"

Both boys were naked, their faces caked with dirt and sweat. But their eyes were wide and bright and somehow primal. Mr. Chalmers had hurt them and they seemed to like it. The pain had unlocked something in them and it was something they wanted more of.

In the distance there was a sudden chorus of howling. It rose up high and shrieking and then faded away. It was hard to say whether it was from animals or people. At the sound of it, Mr. Chalmers nodded his head as if he understood the need to howl all too well.

"Don't make me school you again," Mr. Chalmers said. "Now go out there and bring back a woman. Don't come back empty handed. Bring me some gee-gee, some nice young gee-gee and don't come back without it. Go!"

Mike and Matt raced away, less human than they'd been even an hour before. They ran through yards and down alleys, crawled through vacant lots where the grass was yellow and crisp and dusty. This was the high, hot end of green summer and they smelled it, tasted it, knew it like they had never known it before. They rubbed their sweaty naked bodies with dirt, with crackling brown leaves, with chaff and loam until they smelled of summer, of rich earth and low wild things.

They were supposed to get some gee-gee, some nice young gee-gee for Mr. Chalmers, which was pussy and they understood the need and want of fine pussy, but fuck Mr. Chalmers because they were young and free and lost in the heady bouquet of absolute atavism.

So many houses.

So many places to raid.

And behind so many of those doors, the owners had already tasted the new primeval blood of Greenlawn which was the blood of the world now. They were drunk with it as Mike and Matt were drunk with it. Many were already gathering their weapons and stockpiling their food, herding their women and children together, living out their sweet, secret animal joys, just waiting for the night when they would run wild, killing and raping and plundering and tasting the hot blood of their prey upon their slavering tongues.

Many were like that.

And those that weren't, were quickly becoming the minority. But even in that dim, shocked, confused minority, there were stirrings of ancient drives, the need to run on all fours and fill their senses with the savage delight of simple regression.

The first place Mike and Matt stopped was a trim white ranch house with pink shutters. The yard was immaculate. The flowerbeds bursting with color. They rolled in the grass like dogs, then dove into the flowerbeds and smashed all those vibrant blooms beneath them. They grabbed up bunches of zinnias and marigolds, sweet pea and snapdragon, rubbing the crushed flowers and fragrant petals against their bodies. There was a goldfish pond out back. They caught every fish and smashed them with rocks. Then they went inside the house.

They knew whose house it was.

It belonged to Mrs. Cannon, a retired schoolteacher. If you trespassed on her lawn she would call the police. If you kicked your ball into her yard by accident she would seize it and never give it back. That's the sort of person she was. A woman who spent her life teaching children, but secretly despised them and their youth. If the parents on the block thought she was a miserable old bitch, the children were sure she was a broom-riding witch.

When Mike and Matt came through the door, Mrs. Cannon, a widow of seventeen years, dearly wished that her husband was still alive because even though she had dealt with some real bad boys in her time, she knew that she had finally met the very worst.

Mike and Matt Hack.

Naked and dirty, leaves and sticks in their hair, their bodies scratched and bruised and plastered with bits of flowers, they were about the most horrible things she had ever seen.

"Hello, Mrs. Cannon," said Mike.

"Hello, Mrs. Cannon," said Matt. "We were supposed to get some young gee-gee but we came to see you first."

Mrs. Cannon, well past eighty, was thin and weak and did not move so good anymore. But her ire was up and she directed it with vehemence: "Get out of my house! You filthy little monsters! Get out of my house!"

And bare seconds after she had said this, she knew it was the wrong thing to do. Because you didn't try and intimidate rabid dogs. And that's what these two were. She could see it in their eyes: that blank, glaring animal hatred. They had parted company with civilization. Just the sight of those eyes and what was behind them made her bladder let go. She shook. She trembled. But tried not to move because didn't they say that if you did not move, made no aggressive posturing, that a mad dog would not attack?

But it was too late because they smelled the fear on her.

Matt leaped forward and Mrs. Cannon swatted him in the face, but that just enraged him, made him let go with a coarse growling sound that filled her with more terror than she'd ever known in her life. He grabbed her by the wrist and threw her to the floor and with such force her left arm snapped upon impact. She was old, her bones fragile and reedy. She cried out and he stomped down on her side with his foot. Three ribs gave like dry twigs.

Mrs. Cannon screamed, cried, sobbed, just beyond herself with agony.

She looked up at Matt Hack and knew that what she was dealing with here was not a boy, it was something else. Something evil and cunning and inhuman. There was no boy left inside that dirty husk, all of the culture and learning and civilization that had been hammered into his head for the past ten years had been stripped away, peeled back, revealing this primordial monster.

While she squirmed on the floor, Mike rushed in and helped his brother. They stripped Mrs. Cannon, revealing the shriveled used-up body she hid even from herself. Skin and bones, not much more. Mike took up her unbroken arm, studied it, sniffing his way up the forearm and, deciding that the flabby bicep was by far the meatiest part, bit down on it with everything he had while Mrs. Cannon screamed and flopped and he drew blood. He did not particularly care for the taste of old lady flesh, so he promptly spat it back in her face.

She didn't last long after that.

The boys jumped up and down on her, shattering her bones until shards of white erupted through her skin. When they were done, Mrs. Cannon was not moving anymore. She was just a bloody, loose-limbed heap and they soon lost interest in her.

They ravaged the house.

They emptied closets and dressers, shredding clothes and bedding with steak knives from the kitchen. They broke mirrors and emptied cupboards, pulverizing dishes and crockery on the floor. They urinated on the sofa and chairs and on the corpse of Mrs. Cannon. Mike took a shit in her bed. Matt did the same on the living room carpet. Like an animal, he was amazed and excited by the raw stench of his own feces. He played with it. He sniffed it. He held it in his hands. He threw it at his brother. Then he knocked the pictures off the walls and wrote his name again and again in brown looping whorls of excrement.

And by that point, his name meant very little to him.

But he enjoyed how it looked on the walls...

16

Louis Shears stood there with the golf club in hand, looking at Macy Merchant. She was standing by the porch steps of her house, battered and terrified, her forehead gashed open. She was wearing baggy cargo shorts and an oversized T-shirt that she practically swam in. Both were streaked with dirt.

"Macy," he said. "Macy...it's okay, it's me, Louis."

But Macy was not buying his line. She looked around, wondering maybe if she could get away from him before that golf club came down. "Please," she said. "Just go away..."

Louis lowered the golf club. She seemed all right. After his experience with the beaten kid, those cops, and then Lem Karnigan...well, he was a little on edge. He'd been standing there by the door, peering outside, waiting for he did not know what, that awful paranoia brewing inside him. When he saw Macy come running across the street, he knew he had to go to her. She was either crazy or just scared. And he had to prove to himself which it was for his own state of mind.

Thing was, she was looking at him as if maybe *he* was the crazy one.

"Macy, it's okay, really it is. I'm not nuts."

She sighed, but didn't look convinced. She just kept staring.

Then Louis remembered the blood on him, how he must look. "I had a run in with a...with a crazy man," he explained. "I haven't changed my shirt yet."

She sighed again and lowered herself to the steps. She buried her face in her hands and wept.

"Macy...what happened? Did somebody do something to you?"

Macy looked up at him, her face streaked with tears. Her shirt was torn, her arms and face bruised, crusted blood smeared on her forehead. She nodded, sniffed. "The Hack twins...I babysit them. They were throwing rocks at a car. I told them to stop and they pelted me..."

She told him it all, including what Mr. Chalmers had said. How they were not to kill her in his territory. Louis could just about imagine what was going through her mind. The unreality and disbelief of her own experience. He'd felt that way telling his story to the cops and then to Michelle on the phone.

When she was done, he just shook his head. He knew Mr. Chalmers and you couldn't hope to meet a nicer guy. The image of him whipping out his business and showing the kids how to piss to mark your territory was not only ridiculous and disturbing, it was actually kind of funny in a mad sort of way. Had anyone told him this yesterday or even this morning, he supposed he would have laughed.

But he wasn't laughing now.

And certainly not when Macy told him about Mr. Kenning and Libby.

Shit.

"There's been weird things happening all over town, honey. I don't know what's going on."

"At the school, too. A bunch of kids went nuts and killed a teacher. At least, that's what I heard."

It's building, Louis thought. Whatever's happening, is building now. It's not even slowing down.

He wanted to get out of town with Michelle...but he'd had the TV on before and this crazy shit was happening everywhere. Did he dare tell Macy that the whole country was unraveling? No, he couldn't freak out, not in front of the girl. She did not need that. He was an adult and he had to act like one. Give her some reassurance that the whole world had not just been shoved into the pit. That's what he had to do.

"What's going on?" she asked him. "It wasn't like this this morning."

"No, it doesn't make sense. But a lot of people in this town have just went off the deep end."

"I've been hearing sirens all the way home from school."

"Yeah, I think we'll be hearing them for awhile. Until this stops."

Macy just nodded, staring down at her feet.

Louis wanted to say something to her that would make it better, make her not worry or be afraid. He figured that's what adults were supposed to do with kids, but the problem was he couldn't think of anything. He had been looking for something that would make himself feel better, too, but he hadn't been able to find it. Maybe if he had been a parent, he could have. Maybe he'd be well-practiced in the art of clever, consoling bullshit. But he had no kids. Michelle couldn't have any and he'd just accepted that, as she had. And as a result, he was simply no good at this.

Macy looked up at him. "What if this doesn't stop?"

"Well, it has to."

"Why?"

Well, there was a good one. The simple logic of it floored him. "Because...because it has to, that's why. I mean, the entire town hasn't gone crazy, just some people. I'm not nuts, though I probably look it, and you aren't either. I don't imagine everyone at school was or you wouldn't be here. Am I right?"

She nodded. "I guess. But what about everywhere else?"

"Let's just worry about Greenlawn for now."

Louis went and sat beside her.

He liked Macy. Everyone in the neighborhood liked Macy. Maybe part of it was Jillian, her mother, white trash if he'd ever seen white trash, but mostly it was just because Macy was, well, likeable. She wasn't a stuck-up, eye-rolling, empty-headed, self-absorbed princess like a lot of girls her age. She was a good kid. She was smart and sincere, mature and very funny when you caught her off guard or she relaxed around you.

Louis just looked at her, smiling.

If he had a girl of his own, he'd want her to be Macy. She was small and thin, blatantly sexual around the mouth and eyes, almost hungry-looking. Although her curves were definitely making themselves known, she had not really blossomed completely yet, but judging from Jillian who pretty much had everything in the right place, when that happened Macy would be fighting off the boys with a sharp stick. Her eyes were huge and liquid brown, shimmering. They lit up her face. Why the boys weren't after her now, Louis did not know. Maybe you had to be older to appreciate a calm, understated beauty like Macy had or to revel in her almost sensual schoolgirl charm...things she probably didn't even know she possessed.

He found that he was staring at her and she was watching him do so, a slight blush blooming in her cheeks.

Oh Christ, he thought, *did she know what I was thinking?*

She turned away and he wondered what had gotten him on that train of thought.

Louis and Michelle had only lived on upper Rush Street for the past four years, but they knew all the local gossip. Macy's father had died when she was very young and Jillian had just crashed and burned, becoming a drunk that played it pretty free and easy with men of any age, if you could believe all that was said. One thing that was true, though, was that Jillian had never recovered from her husband's death and had retreated to her eighteenth year where she still was, an adult woman with a child who acted like a wild college girl out sowing her oats for the first time. It was too bad. Macy probably needed her mom to *be* a mom, but that just wasn't going to happen. Around the neighborhood they said that Macy had raised herself. That she took care of the house and just about everything else, including her mother.

Louis did not doubt that part of it.

Every summer, Michelle and he threw a neighborhood bash. There was beer and pop, hamburgers and hot dogs. Just a social event where all the neighbors and their kids could spend some time together, get to know each other better. And Jillian always came, of course. Sometimes she just got drunk and sometimes she got really loaded and fell flat on her face. Sometimes she picked fights with the other women, but mostly she just pursued their husbands in ways that were practically indescribable. That first summer when Louis and Michelle had spread the word, Dick Starling, a heavy equipment operator that worked for Indiana Central Railroad and lived across the street, had taken Louis aside and over a few beers, laid it all out for him.

"This is a pretty good neighborhood, but we got a few odd ducks here," Starling said. "I think everyone will show for your party. Old man Onsala won't. He's a crazy old Finnlander. You can always tell the Finnlanders by the pile of firewood in their front yards. They like to hang gutted deer in the front yard come season. Onsala don't like anyone, barely speaks anything but Finnish. Les Maub and his wife'll come, but not if you invite the Soderbergs. Bonnie Maub and Leslie Soderberg have been fighting about something since 1963 and they still won't talk to each other. They won't show. On the other hand, Jillian Merchant *will* show and that's not necessarily a good thing. But if there's booze, she'll be there. Oh yes, Lou, count on that. She's not bad looking, you know? Long legs and nice set of jugs on her. You'll get a look at her and you'll be thinking what every man in this neighborhood has already thought: that you wouldn't mind getting into that shit, having a little fun. But you won't, buddy, you won't dare because she's nuts."

That was Louis' first introduction to Jillian Merchant.

The party that year came and Jillian came with it. She was actually quite attractive, like Dick Starling said, but her eyes were wild and hungry-looking. The more liquor she poured into herself, the hungrier those eyes became until she was scoping out the men at the party like a dog sizing up red meat, wondering which cut to take a bite out of first. She was wearing a black leather miniskirt which put her long, slender legs on fine display right up to the thigh. She completed the look with a tight tube top that barely contained her cleavage. She kept drinking and making the rounds and anytime she found a lone man, she hopped right on his lap and gave him a free bump and grind, whether his wife was present or not. Louis had managed to keep his distance as she moved around, flirting and running up to the men like a horny feline. But, finally, she cornered him. Right there by the keg of beer she was all over him, asking him to give her a private tour of his bedroom.

Louis couldn't believe it.

With Michelle there, too.

Jillian was just out of control and liked it that way, apparently. Later, playing cards with the boys at the picnic table, Jillian had zeroed in on him again. She kept hanging around and sticking her tits in his face while the other guys chuckled about it. Louis kept her away from him, but he did not realize the level of her determination until she went right up to Michelle and asked, "You mind if I give your husband a lap dance?"

Michelle claimed later she thought it was a joke, even though she should have known better by that point. "Um...no...yes...no, I don't care," Michelle had said.

The stage was set. Jillian jumped right on Louis' lap, facing him yet, her tits pressed into his chest and her crotch right up against his own, her miniskirt practically pushed up to her hips. She went right at it, moving her ass and legs with almost professional zeal, grinding into him and making him first turn red, then start to sweat. He could feel the heat of what was between her legs just fine. He put a stop to it then and there, figuring he better before something embarrassing popped up in his pants. He pulled Jillian off of him, but she came right back, wrapping her arms around him and one of her long legs, trapping him, encircling him. Finally, all the boys laughing at him, he picked Jillian up to carry her back to her own seat and that was a mistake. For as he threw her over his shoulder, drunk himself, he saw the looks on everyone's faces. What happened was, with Jillian over his shoulder, everyone saw that she had no underwear on. Her skirt had really hiked up to her hips and there was her fine, round ass on display along with her business.

The women were either laughing or angry; the men laughing, too, or just staring with delight at all Jillian had to offer which was considerable. Most of them had not seen such an offering since their high school days...at least not in such wonderful proportions. Dick Starling, being the smartass he was, snapped a shot of that embarrassing moment with his digital camera: Louis standing there looking surprised, Jillian over his shoulder, one tit popped out of her tube top, legs kicking, ass and privates on full display. He liked to bring that picture out and show it to Louis whenever he came over.

And, of course, Michelle never let him live it down.

But that was, essentially, Louis' first taste of Macy's mother and each summer since she put on a similar show at the backyard parties. The sad thing was that Jillian carried on like that right in front of her daughter, had absolutely no qualms about it. Louis was not a parent, but even he knew there were things you did in front of children and those you did not.

Macy sat there with him beside her for five or ten minutes before she spoke again. "But it's all funny, isn't it? Funny/scary? I mean, I can see a couple people losing it on the same day...but like this? Aren't the odds against dozens of people going whacko on the same day, the same afternoon? Or thousands across the country?"

"Yeah, I guess they would be."

"Insanity—if that's what this is, Mr. Shears—isn't catchy. It's not a disease, a germ, a microbe, whatever. It does not pass from person to person."

Well, he couldn't argue with any of that.

It made him think of all those end-of-the-world movies he'd caught on the late show. There was always, ultimately, something to blame. An atomic bomb or a mutant germ or chemical warfare...something that made people change into monsters or crazies. There was always something. He could rule out radiation, he supposed, but the jury was still out on the biological or chemical agents. But if it was something like that, something in the soil or water or air, why hadn't he been infected? That dying kid surely had it, whatever it was, and Louis had been in pretty goddamn close proximity with him.

Shouldn't he have been contaminated?

But what if it's nothing that simple, nothing that quantifiable, Louis. Not a germ or a chemical. Then that would make it even worse, wouldn't it? The idea that what's happening here and everywhere will keep happening until the streets are filled with bodies until there's no bodies left?

Yeah, that was somehow worse.

That there was a force or influence that could change people into savage, brutal things. Yeah, that was terrifying. There would be no safeguard against it. Whatever it was, it was absolutely fucking dangerous. Equally as lethal, as far as the human race was concerned, as thermonuclear weapons or an unstoppable plague. Hadn't Einstein said something to the effect that if the Third World War were fought with atomic bombs, that the Fourth would be fought with bow and arrow? Yes, civilization would be utterly destroyed. From the rocket age to the stone age in five minutes, as they said. And wasn't this like that? Something that could take men and women, strip their civilization away, turn them into primal, violent monsters just as bad?

Louis stopped himself there.

No point getting carried away. Not yet. This all might blow over or maybe it already had and there would be nothing left but a lot of questions when it was over. He didn't believe it was done with. Maybe he couldn't believe it. All he knew for sure was that whatever was out there doing this, it was terribly dangerous. But for now all he could think of was getting Michelle home and getting Macy safe. That's what counted.

"Macy," he finally said. "I don't know what this is about. But it's not the end of the world."

"What if it's the end of Greenlawn?"

"Then we find another town."

"What if they're all like this?"

"Then we build a new one that isn't."

Louis was liking his new pragmatic self. He had never been that way before this moment. He had had very little trouble in his life, a minimum of adversity, so like most people, he fell apart when things got rough. But that was no way to be. This would be sorted out and it would be sorted out by people like him one step at a time.

"Is your mom home?"

Macy just shrugged. "They called her from the school, but there was no answer. She's probably sleeping one off."

"Why did the school call?" he asked, realizing it was probably none of his damn business.

Macy was studying her tennis shoes again. "Um...well, I suppose I should tell you. You'll hear about it sooner or later anyway."

She told him briefly about the Chelsea Paris incident. He nodded as she spoke, but did not seem judgmental.

"And you think that whatever's getting to these people got to you, too?"

Macy just shrugged. "It had to have, Mr. Shears. God, I wouldn't do something like that. I don't even swat flies. I catch them and let them go outside. I don't like hurting anything or anyone. It's...it's just not me."

Louis didn't think it was either. But it brought up an interesting idea and that was that maybe it would just go away. This madness. Maybe it was temporary. That gave him some hope, at any rate.

He patted Macy on the wrist. "Let's go see if your mom's around."

As they stood up, a pickup truck passed on the street. It slowed as it came by, a couple tough looking teenage hoods in it. They stared at Louis and Macy and he stared right back. Gave 'em everything right back in like doses. That wasn't the way he was, either. He did not indulge in stupid staring contests with other men or play the my-dick-is-bigger-than-yours game. That was strictly for idiots with a total lack of self-esteem and self-worth. Yet, he did it right then. Those kids looked tough, looked mean—Louis was pretty certain they were infected—just out cruising for prey. What bothered him most was how they looked at Macy, like they were sizing her up for their stable.

That pissed Louis off, so he gave them the hard look.

They kept going.

He wondered if the look he gave them was like what Mr. Chalmers had been doing: marking his territory. Maybe they sensed that he was willing to fight for what they thought belonged to him, so they went off in search of easier pickings. They said dogs could smell fear on you and maybe these *people* could, too. Like the old adage went, if you don't want to be a victim, then don't act like one.

"Come on," Macy said.

They went up to the door and paused there, Macy reaching out and taking hold of his hand. He clenched it, liking the feel of another sane person nearby.

"What if she's...what if she's crazy, too?" Macy said.

"Then we'll deal with it," Louis told her.

He went to the door and threw it open. The house was silent inside. No TV or radio going, not so much as a toilet running. Just that immense dead silence that in its own way told him that there was no one there, no one alive at any rate.

"Let's go," Louis said, pulling her across the threshold with him.

And soon as he crossed and stood inside on the worn shag carpeting, something inside him plummeted very low and he waited for whatever was coming. Because it *was* coming and it was going to be bad. Real bad...

17

There had been a foul wind blowing through Greenlawn all day and it was only a matter of time before it reached the door of Kathleen Soames, settled there in a ghastly miasma of rot. She had been expecting it.

She had felt it inside herself more than once that afternoon, something boiling, something simmering, something making her think things and want to do others.

Alien things, awful things.

Things she was not capable of.

But it had been there, scratching away in her brain, a darkness and a dankness and an awfulness. A shadow that had fallen over the town was trying to fill her head with shades and unthinkable impulses. Sometimes she was sure it was her imagination and at other times she was sure it was not. For sometimes it was as palpable as cold hands ringing her throat or moldy breath in her face, a hot voice whispering in her ear.

She had told Steve about it twice now, but Steve was not interested.

Steve said it was her nerves. That she was just tired. She needed a good rest. Her nerves and the muggy heat of late August were brewing up a storm in her mind. She'd been working too hard again, trying to keep house and do her gardening and taking care of the kids and waiting hand and foot on Mother Soames upstairs. Christ, that crazy old woman was enough in herself to wear you to the bone. What she needed was a drink and nap. He'd take care of supper. When Ryan got home from his paper route, the two of them would make a nice supper while she slept.

And it was nice, really nice of Steve to offer.

During the whole of that long, listless, and somewhat upsetting day, it was the first thing that had made her smile. Maybe Steve was right. She'd been nervous all day...stomach upset, rolling in waves more often than not; hands shaking; face sweating. She kept screwing up the most simple tasks. Dropping things, knocking things off shelves. She'd tripped on the stairs twice that afternoon when she went up to look in on Mother Soames. She'd cut her fingers with a knife making the old lady's lunch and bumped her head on the same cupboard door three times. Nothing was right. The town, the neighborhood, the house, and, yes, even Kathleen herself. Off kilter. Askew. Something.

Like a door, she was either open too wide or not wide enough.

And when she tried to sort it out, to make sense of it, all she got was confused. She'd tried to settle in with her soaps that afternoon while Ryan was still in school and Mother Soames was napping, but she couldn't seem to concentrate. Couldn't sit still. The TV was too loud or too soft and the pictures were too bright, too hard on her eyes. She looked, but none of it made sense. The storylines were as incomprehensible as hieroglyphics.

It was a hot day, but not so hot that even in the cool of the living room she should have sweated, felt dizzy, felt the need to vomit, been on her knees before the toilet some four times in one hour. Not that anything came of it: just wracking dry heaves that left her breathless and frightened, her head spinning and her temples pounding, her throat tight as braided rope and feeling as if it was coated in a fine, scratchy fuzz.

Kathleen had even taken Steve's advice and stretched out in bed.

But all she did was toss and turn. There was no position that was comfortable. Her pillow felt warm and damp like some breathing, dormant thing that was waiting to wake. And the one time she'd almost drifted off, she thought she'd heard a voice from inside that pillow say, *"Now, Kathleen. Do it now."* She'd come out of that sitting up, not remembering doing so. Sitting up with her knees drawn to her breasts, her arms wrapped around her legs, sweat dripping from her brow, making her eyes sting.

No, she would not sleep.

Despite Steve's protests she went right back to it, organizing cupboards already fastidiously organized; cleaning out drawers; wiping down shelves; sweeping and dusting and mopping because she dared not sit still, afraid that voice would speak to her again or she'd start thinking bad things. She had to keep busy, she had to keep moving, she had to beat it out of herself, wrench it from her mind and the only way to do that was with hard work. Thing was, she had become some mindless automaton, just repeating the same tasks over and over again until Steve had demanded to know what the hell was going on.

He'd come back from the garage that day complaining about the heat and the three rings jobs he'd had to perform and goddamn automatic transmissions and vacuum lines and his boss who was just pissing him off, pissing him off so much, he admitted, that he'd almost picked up a torque wrench and knocked his brains out.

Steve was calm and easy by nature, but not this day.

He was wired and irritable and he drank his beer and tried to watch CNN and all the time, Kathleen couldn't stop cleaning. She vacuumed right past him, picked lint from under the couch cushions and straightened pictures and washed walls and emptied plastic fruit from the same bowl five times and polished the bowl, chased every speck of dust from every vinyl grape leaf and plum stem. Steve drank and smoked his cigarettes and every time he flicked his ash in the ashtray, she was right there, emptying it and wiping it clean. Finally as she reached over to do it again, he grabbed her arm like he wanted to break it.

"Listen to me, Kathy," he said, sweat beaded on his upper lip. "If you don't sit down and fucking relax, I'm going to tie you to a goddamn chair. You're getting under my skin, you hear me? Knock it off."

"I...can't seem to stop," she admitted. "I feel so wound up. Like I'm one of those toys with a key you turn, you know? Just wound tight."

Steve pulled off his cigarette. "Okay, sure. Now I'm pulling the key out and throwing it away. So stop it, all right? I'm not up to this. You don't stop and God help me, but I'll...I'll...just stop it. Please, just stop it."

"I'll go check on Mom."

"Piss on her," Steve said. "Goddamn parasite sucking the life out of us, that's what she is."

"Steve...Steve, she's your mother."

But he didn't seem to care.

All he cared about was CNN and the bad news everywhere: murders and beatings, fires and mob violence. Crazy things. Awful things. But he could not stop watching it all; he was transfixed.

There were things going on in his head, Kathleen knew, just as there were things going on in hers. He could pretend as she pretended, but they were there. Things that did not belong and had no reason for being, malefic shadows reaching out and enveloping, making them into people they were not, demanding that they be everything but what they were.

After that little exchange, Kathleen tried working outside, but, dear God, that sun was hot. It burned the skin from her muscles and bleached her eyes white and evaporated the blood from her veins. And she sweated, God, how she sweated, but not the good sweat of hard work but an acidic-smelling poison that was gray and pungent like the run-off from a sewer. That sun...that burning sun.

She prayed for darkness.

Finally, her head aching and her teeth chattering, she went inside and splashed water in her face, but that stink was still on her. She took a shower, trying to get that smell off with body wash and Camay and Steve's Irish Spring, but the more she scrubbed and deodorized, the more that stink came off her in hot, rancid waves.

God, what was that smell?

She stood under the cool spray, gagging on the stench that reminded her of hospital waste and the juice dripping from infected abscesses. Her skin was rubbed pink, rubbed red, just raw and hurting and she kept thinking that it was inside her, that whatever it was, she had to cut it out, she had to slice it free like a tumor before it spread.

And then there she was, standing in the shower with her razor, slicing the blade down her arms and over her wrists and the blood ran and flowed and the smell of it...Christ, the black and putrescent smell of what was inside her.

With a cry, she tossed aside the razor and stepped out of the shower, seeing herself in the mirror, naked and wet and smeared with blood. But her mind was beyond shock by that point. She had to get back to work. She had to get outside and get some fresh air before her head flew apart.

So she did that.

And on her way to the stairs, she paused by the door to Mother Soames room, standing there and listening to the old woman breathe and thinking what it would be like to stop that breathing. For she hated the sound of it. Some nights she lay awake listening to it, that ragged and wheezing respiration. It came through the walls and got in her head and she waited,

waited for the breathing to stop in the dead of night as they said it often did with old people. Yes, she waited, tensing, *wanting* it to stop. She hated herself for it, but deep down she wanted that old bitch to die in her sleep. That breathing, that perpetual hollow breathing, it was like...yes, it was like that story she'd read in school by Poe where that heart would not stop beating even after the old man was dead.

Kathleen actually reached for the tarnished brass doorknob of Mother Soames' room...but she stopped herself. Made herself stop, even though that same whispering voice said, *"Do it, Kathleen. Do it now."*

She yanked her hand away, eyes filled with tears, knowing that if she opened that door there would be no going back. For when that door was opened, something, whatever was whispering to her, it would take her, it would possess her and she would like it, she would surrender herself completely to the sweet violation of that other. She would smell the hot, sour perspiration of the old woman, the urine-smell, the age-smell, the medicine-smell, and it would sicken her. Then she would hear that rasping breathing and she would really have no choice but to squeeze the life out of that old, repellent slug.

Squeeze until the breathing stopped and those blanched eyes rolled shut and the foul juice ran from her mouth.

Placing hands to her ears, Kathleen ran downstairs, unaware that she was naked or why such a thing would matter. She grabbed up rugs as she went, two and three and four, wrestling them out the door and standing on the porch, naked and bleeding and mad, beating dust out of them that had already been beaten out five or six times.

She stopped and sniffed herself.

She smelled like Camay and body wash. The fresh, clean scent of it made nausea roll in her belly. That was the problem. Chemicals. All those chemicals and preservatives, dyes and fragrances and artificial things they put in everything these days. It was all making her rot from the inside out.

She wanted that other smell back, the dark poison smell of what was inside her.

There was a garbage bag on the porch. Steve hadn't brought it out to the cans yet.

She could smell the trash in it boiling, stewing.

It made her mouth water.

That's what you need, Kathy. You need rotten and foul things, dirty things.

Yes, that was it. Going down on her hands and knees, she tore open the bag and scattered trash everywhere. Panting, drooling, sweating profusely...she grabbed up egg shells and banana peels, tuna tins and used tampons, stinking hamburger cartons with raw, graying meat still clinging to them, anything that stank or had gone over, and began rubbing it all over her skin. She scented herself between the legs with banana peels, loving the greasy sensation. She rubbed old meat and smelling juice over her breasts until her nipples stood erect. She greased her hair with fish oil and rubbed tampons under her arms and down her legs.

She was so excited by it all, feeling so free and so vital, that she slid a filthy finger into herself and brought herself to orgasm right there on the porch. Her body blazed with heat and her fingers vented it, let it all come flowing out.

Some kid was watching her.

Some teenage boy from down the street, watching her with his mouth hanging open. Kathleen knew he was there. She liked him watching. She wanted him to sense her heat, to recognize her scent by sniffing all her parts. She gasped and cried out and then it was over.

The silly boy looked terrified.

On her hands and knees, Kathy pulled her lips back from her teeth and hissed at him.

He ran.

Little worthless shit! He should have taken the bait! He should have come up on the porch and rutted with her! Then she would have had him! Then she would have sank her teeth in his throat and tasted what came splashing out, filling herself.

Kathy leaped down into the yard and crawled through the flowerbeds, tearing out azaleas and mums in handfuls. She ripped out hollyhocks and zinnias, decapitated bluebells and buttercups with her teeth. She flattened them all, rolling through the sweet, gagging, flowery wreckage she had created.

But it wasn't enough.

She yanked flowers out by their roots until she reached the cool, moist black soil beneath and then she rubbed it on herself, digging through it, swimming in it, loving the earthy dank smell of dirt.

A worm had been disturbed and she snatched it up, threw it in her mouth and chewed it to a pulp.

She was feeling better than she had felt in weeks now.

If only that damn sun would go down.

Because when it did, when it did...the night would be like no night this miserable, stagnant, shit-grubbing town had ever seen before.

And Kathy knew it.

"What the hell are you doing?"

It was Steve. Silly man, he'd missed her show on the porch, but now he saw her...dirty and bloody and stinking. He looked afraid. He looked confused. Kathleen ran up the porch steps on all fours and dove through the screen door. Steve fell over and she jumped on him, rubbed herself all over him as he fought against her...hitting her, scratching her, bringing delicious waves of pain. But then she had his head and she banged it off the floor until he went limp beneath her.

Panting and sexually aroused, Kathleen took his hand in her mouth, licking it and swooning with the taste of man-sweat. She bit down as hard as she could on his fingers until the flesh crushed and the bones snapped beneath. She worried and chewed until she got some good meat free to eat.

Then dragged him into the kitchen.

She used the carving knife.

She slit his throat, slashed open the carotid until hot, dark blood splashed over her breasts. She cut his clothes off, chewed at his throat and belly, leaving bloody punctures all the way down until she found what she was looking for between his legs.

God, how good it tasted in her mouth.

How delightful it felt smashing to a pulp between her teeth.

Sometime later, Kathleen took his blood and painted the walls in loops and whorls and scraggly hex signs she remembered from a book long ago. When she was done the kitchen was hers. It smelled of raw meat and blood. This was her place, her warren and she had to keep others out.

Squatting by the kitchen door, she pissed to mark her territory...

18

When the door to her office opened, Michelle Shears almost came right out of her skin. She didn't know what she was expecting, but it was only Carol, her boss. Usually she knocked, but today she burst right in. Stood there with a glassy look in her eyes.

"Have you heard?" she said.

Michelle felt butterflies winging in her belly. "What now?"

"It's all over the radio."

"I...no. I've just been trying to finish up some things. I want to get out of here."

Carol just stared with those dead eyes. "It's everywhere now."

"What is?"

"What's happening in this town. It's happening everywhere. There's rioting in LA. People are setting fires in Chicago. There's been some kind of mass suicide in New York. Things are going crazy."

Michelle tried to swallow but couldn't.

Mass insanity...all over the country? Right away, like everyone else, she started looking for reasons, connections. She started thinking about terrorists letting loose some bioweapon, some kind of germ. She saw a show once where they said that if such a germ were let loose in a major airport, commuters would spread it from one end of the country to the other in a matter of hours.

Was that it?

No, it didn't make sense. She could see it hitting Chicago and New York and LA, all the major arteries of the airlines. But Greenlawn? Unless someone just happen to have been infected on a flight and come back here, spread it around real fast...no, it didn't make sense.

"What the hell's going on, Carol?"

"I don't know. But it's all over the place. They said on the news some guy in Fort Wayne murdered a family with an axe. They were his next door neighbors for godsake."

Michelle felt something beginning to fragment inside her.

She'd been entertaining some fantasy all afternoon of getting home and getting out of town with Louis until the madness blew over. But if it was everywhere...where could you run *to?*

"The governor of Texas has declared a state of emergency, Michelle. It's all over CNN. People are killing each other. Like animals."

"Good God."

Carol just stood there a moment, hugging herself. Then she looked over at Michelle with dark, simmering eyes. "Animals," she said. "Animals. I wonder what that's like..."

She left the room.

Michelle looked out her window.

She saw the sunny streets of Greenlawn. Everything looked perfectly fine. In the distance, there was the whine of an ambulance. *All over the country. Good God. All over the country.* But she knew she couldn't worry about that. Not now. She had to worry about this place.

About Greenlawn.

Suddenly, she could see nothing else, know nothing else. Tunnel vision. One place. Her town. Her territory. Everything else faded as something important and vital inside her went with a warm, wet snapping noise. There was purity then. There was joy. She could smell her own skin and taste the salt on her lips and feel the heat between her legs.

She rummaged through her desk drawers.

Found something she could use.

A letter opener with a six-inch blade...

19

Dick Starling stood watch over his wife's corpse.

This was the love of his life, his happiness, his heart, his everything. That's why he had to kill Megan because she just hadn't understood. When it had come over him as it was now coming over everyone, she had fought against it. And even though he could no longer really remember what he had been like before, he knew that this was better and Megan was an alien entity, a disease germ in the midst of a healthy body. So he had taken his axe and split her head open.

That had been several hours ago and now he had her strung up in the kitchen by the feet, had dressed her out as he dressed out his deer in November. He'd taken her head off and gutted her, placing her organs and entrails in neat piles in the sink on the drain board.

There was blood all over the floor.

There was blood all over him.

He sat in a sticky, drying pool of it, the blood-stench up his nose and down his throat, permeating every pore and every cell and the joyous, pleasing smell of it made him swoon, made him hard, connected him to the simple rhythms of life in a way he had never known before. He sat there, studying the blade of his axe. It was stained with blood. There were clots of hair and bits of tissue stuck to it.

Cocking his head, he listened.

For intruders.

They had already tried to take his kill once. A woman and two ratty-looking girls with kitchen knives. Some near-submerged, misty portion of his brain told him that they were once Maddie Sinclair and her two daughters, Kylie and Elissa. But that meant nothing to him. They were scavengers, predators. He had chased them off. He had wanted the woman. He wanted to fuck her on the bloody floor, maybe the girls, too. But they had run off.

He wondered where his own daughters were.

He studied the walls of the kitchen. They were splattered with blood and decorated with bloody handprints. When Dick had been dressing Megan out, he had been amazed at his bloody hands so he pressed them against the walls and made prints. He liked the way it looked so he kept dipping his hands into his wife's torso and painting the walls with red handprints. Those who came here would know this was his lair. That he would defend it.

He heard voices in the distance.

Crawling across the floor with his axe, he pulled himself up by the sink. The smell of organ-meats and intestines made his mouth water, his belly growl. He peered out the window. He saw a man out there, across the street. A man and a girl. It took him a moment, but then he remembered that the man was Louis Shears and the girl was Macy Merchant.

Dick wondered if Louis would give him the girl.

Maybe he would trade her for meat.

Dick slid down to the floor and studied his handprints on the wall and contemplated his wonderful new world. He would need to go out soon. Go out and hunt. But first there were other considerations.

He needed to eat.

Breaking apart several kitchen chairs, he built a fire on the kitchen floor.

Soon, the smell of roasting meat filled the room...

20

Louis stood there with Macy by his side, listening to the empty house.

They called out a few times and listened to their voices echo and die out. Louis had been in a lot of houses and it was funny how something as subtle and abstract as an echo could tell you things. Maybe it had something to do with sound waves and maybe it had something to do with some buried sixth sense we all carry within us. Regardless, he could tell that the Merchant house was empty...though that wasn't exactly the word that was bouncing around in his head at that moment: *unoccupied.* As in, *Louis, this house isn't so much empty as unoccupied, if you can dig the subtle nuances of that.*

He stood there, swallowing down a sour taste in his mouth. "Maybe she stepped out or something," he suggested and wondered why he did not believe that anymore than Macy seemed to.

"No," she said. "She's always home now. She has a job, Mr. Shears, but she doesn't go on until eight tonight."

Louis was almost afraid to ask what that job was. The way Macy said it, not going *on* until eight, made it sound like Jillian had found a job stripping on stage. Thing was, his mind drew a blank when he tried to make small talk, so he just asked. "Oh yeah? Where's your mom working these days?"

"She's a cocktail waitress over at the Hair of the Dog," Macy told him. "Do you know the Hair of the Dog, Mr. Shears?"

The way she said it, Louis just bet that she knew all about the Hair, as it was called locally. The Hair of the Dog was a sleezy bump-and-grind joint out on the highway that catered mostly to truckers and bikers and tough working class types from the mills and factories. Nice place. Louis had only been in there once with a couple guys for a bachelor party and they'd left pretty quick. They were worried the women there might kick their asses, let alone the men. As he recalled, the waitresses were all topless.

"Sure, nice place," he lied.

Macy grunted. "You're either a bad liar or you don't get out much, Mr. Shears," she told him. "No offense, but there's nothing nice about a place like that."

"I'm sorry, Macy."

She shrugged. "Why? I gave up trying to babysit my mom years ago."

There were things Louis could have said, but it was absolutely none of his business so he kept his mouth shut. Poor Macy. Such a good, sweet kid. She deserved better than Jillian. That was for sure.

They made a quick search of the main floor and Jillian was nowhere to be found. There were a couple overflowing ashtrays and empty beer cans on the kitchen counter, a sink filled with dirty dishes, the remains of a frozen pizza on the table with a couple flies mating on it, but that was about it. In the living room there was a basket of washing that had spilled over onto the floor, scattered magazines and newspapers with rings on them like they'd been used for coasters.

But no Jillian.

"This place is a dump, isn't it?" Macy said, obviously embarrassed.

"No...I wouldn't say that."

"It is, too, Mr. Shears. Quit being nice about things. It's not necessary. I know what everyone thinks about us. It's no big deal. My mom is a lazy, drunken slob and a...a...well, I know what people say."

"Who cares what they say?" Louis told her. "It's nobody's goddamn business but your own."

"Thanks, Mr. Shears," Macy said. "That was nice."

"Quit calling me Mr. Shears. You make me feel like I should be walking with a cane. Call me Louis or I'll start calling you Miss Merchant."

Macy reddened. "Oh God, not that! Mr. Hamm at school calls me Little Miss Merchant all the time. It's embarrassing, you know?"

Louis just smiled. "Hamm is *still* there?"

"Yes, and just as weird as ever."

Mr. Hamm...dear God. Mr. Hamm had been there when Louis was in high school and he'd graduated twenty years before. Mr. Hamm was this large, very obese man who stood around in the hallways drumming his fingers on his impressive belly. Back then, Mr. Hamm had been partial to medieval forms of punishment if you acted up in his class. He'd make you stretch out your arms and balance a stack of textbooks in each hand until you thought you were going to drop or stand on one foot with your nose touching the blackboard. It was never anything violent like a ruler across your knuckles—that was Mr. Hengish—but it was just as painful after you did it for fifteen or twenty minutes.

Macy went and checked out the downstairs bedroom and bathroom while Louis took a turn through the dining room. Nothing, nothing.

"You know," Macy said when she came back, "I feel really stupid. You don't have to stay here, you can go home. I can handle this. I'll just lock myself in."

But Louis shook his head. "No, let's stay together."

"I was hoping you'd say that...Louis." Macy looked around. "I have to clean this place up. What a dump. Well, I suppose we should look in the basement in case she fell down or something."

Louis got a funny feeling when she said that. For reasons he did not understand properly and never would, he said, "I'll check the basement. You go check upstairs. If she's anywhere, she's probably up there. I don't think Jillian would like me just bursting into her bedroom."

"Oh no, she'd *hate* that," Macy said with all due sarcasm.

He watched her pad up the stairs and he went down the hallway to the cellar door. He opened it and started down the steps. He was worried about more than Jillian; Michelle should have been home by now. He'd looked out the upstairs windows twice and her car was not in the driveway. He pulled his cellphone out and dialed next door. No answer. Nothing but the answering machine kicking in. He called Michelle's cell, but there was no answer there either. He wasn't liking any of that a bit.

"Jillian?" he called out. "Are you around?"

He hadn't been down the Merchant's basement since the summer before. The pilot light had gone out on Jillian's water heater and she had been waiting for him to get home from work, sitting out on the porch. He got it lit, all right, Jillian hanging over him the whole time, her tits bursting out of a halter top. He barely got out of there with his virtue intact. Jillian had cornered him at the dryer, on the stairs. He thought she was going to have her way with him on the washer. When he got home, of course,

Michelle was waiting for him. He told her Jillian's pilot light had gone out and Michelle had said, *Oh, I'll just bet. Did you get it lit for her, dear? Get everything burning high and hot again? You're such a good little neighbor.*

She had hounded him for weeks about that.

Louis went into the utility room where the washer and dryer, furnace and hot water heater were. No Jillian. There was a junk room and a furnished bar room, but she wasn't there either. He called out for her a few times and just stood there, feeling...well, he wasn't sure *what* he was feeling. Only that he did not like it. He did not like it at all. He was feeling what he'd felt when he'd first walked into the house, that something bad was building around him. Standing there, his guts twisting up, he felt like a kid standing in a deserted house on a dare. Waiting for the boogeys to come sliding out of the walls. It was like that. He did not know what to expect, but it was there, all around him, gathering strength and thickening in the air like poison.

"Jillian?" he said, his voice sounding very dry and very old.

There was one last room to check, a spare bedroom at the back.

It was where he had to go and exactly where he did *not* want to go. But he had to. Just go in there and get it done, get back upstairs to Macy, because honestly, he just did not like the idea of leaving the girl alone. Not with how things were. He walked over past the bar and to the doorway leading to the bedroom. There was no door, just a set of old plastic hippie beads hanging down. The kind of thing Greg Brady had in his bedroom...or had it been Davy Jones on *The Monkees?* Louis brushed them aside, smiling, remembering similar beads his sister had strung in her room. Ah, the seventies.

As soon as he got in there, he stopped smiling. It did not seem to be a conscious effort on his part.

"Jillian?" he said.

The bedroom was long and narrow and ran the length of the back of the basement. It wasn't a bedroom really, but more of storeroom where everything went that didn't seem to have a place anywhere else. There were cardboard boxes stacked right up to the bare rafters overhead, stray pieces of furniture, racks of clothes with aisles in-between. It was dim in there, no window to the outside. Louis felt blindly along the walls until he found a switch. A single bank of fluorescent lights buzzed on overhead. Only one tube worked, the other dirty and flickering. It cast an uneven, surreal illumination, shadows jumping all around him.

Louis walked down the aisles of clothes that were hung from rods connected to the beams overhead. Lots of the clothes were Jillian's and Macy's, old coats and snowsuits and you name it, but much of it was men's suits and jackets, a couple dusty overcoats. This must have been Macy's father's stuff. Jillian had never thrown any of it out, just relegated it to this rummage sale, this morgue of cast-offs.

Everything smelled moldy down there, like mothballs and rotting linen.

Louis moved down the rows of coats and dresses, brushing them with his fingers as he passed. He wasn't even sure by that point why he was even bothering.

"Well, I suppose you're not here, Jillian," he said.

He pushed on to the end, stepping over cartons of Macy's baby clothes, boxes of old toys, a stool, his hands parting clothes as he went. Denim and corduroy and twill...and then his fingers touched something cool and rubbery at the same moment that his eyes caught sight of a hulking shape that did not belong. Yes, right there, tucked between a couple coats.

Louis let out a cry and stumbled back, falling right over a carton of toys.

Jillian was here, after all.

She was hanging there amongst the coats. She was naked, her flesh pale, her head cocked to the side from the noose encircling her throat. Her face was livid like a bruise, her eyes open, and her tongue dangling out thickly.

"Oh no," Louis heard himself. "Oh, Jillian...not this..."

She'd tied clothesline rope around her throat—and very tightly by the looks of it—and tied off the rope around a roughhewn rafter above. Then she'd jumped off the stool and hanged herself, tucked neatly amongst the other hanging things.

Louis just stared up at her with a horror that was shocking and depthless, his eyes wide, his tongue stuck to the roof of his mouth. He wondered what it had been like, what had gone through her head. He was picturing her almost casually undressing, her mind filled with blackness. Maybe folding her clothes very carefully. Coming down here and tying off that rope, fastening it around her throat, maybe whistling the whole time.

Dear God.

But he would never know what she had done exactly or what she had thought and he was glad for this.

Jillian just hung there, swaying slightly from side to side, turning in a slow and lazy semicircle. What struck Louis the most was not her puffy and purple-blue face, but the fact that she was naked. Even in death, she was somehow sensual and well-proportioned like maybe wasn't dead at all.

Louis did not look away from her.

For some reason, he did not dare.

The idea of taking his eyes off that hanging corpse was unthinkable. His belly rolling with nausea, his hand feeling oddly cold where he'd brushed hers, he backed away, finally finding his feet and dashing out of there.

"Louis?" Macy called.

Good God, he'd forgotten about her.

Louis stood in the barroom, looking from the dangling hippie beads that were still moving to the steps leading upstairs. He could hear Macy coming down them. He started to sweat, to panic. *Okay, buddy boy, are you going to let Macy see her mother like this or are you going to move?* There was no real choice in the matter. He went over to the stairs and stopped her before she got down there and got any fool ideas about looking around herself.

"She's not down here," he said, a little louder than he'd intended.

"Okay," Macy said. "Okay."

Taking her hand, he led her up the stairs and didn't relax any until the cellar door was shut, hiding its sins in its dark belly. He stood there a moment, just breathing. Macy was staring at him. She looked concerned.

"Louis...you're not...*losing* it, are you?"

He almost burst out laughing. "No, no, no."

"You had me worried," she said. "You sure you're all right? You look a little green or something."

Sure, he was green. Who wouldn't have been? His stomach kept trying to crawl up the back of his throat like it wanted out, wanted to jump out his mouth and pirouette on the floor. He touched his face and it was cool, clammy, moist with sweat.

"Tell me what's wrong," Macy said. "Please."

Louis thought quick because he had to. "Um...it's just closed-in spaces. I get kind of claustrophobic sometimes. It's nothing."

"Oh, that's too bad. You were in the back bedroom, weren't you? It's creepy in there."

It's even worse now.

"Well," he said, "Jillian's gone. We'll just have to wait for her. Maybe we should go to my house. Michelle should be home soon. Then we can figure out what we're going to do."

"Okay."

Macy was easy with it and Louis had to wonder why.

Was it just the paranoia about what was going on in Greenlawn or was it something more? Was she feeling the badness in her own house just as he was? Good God, his mind was all mixed-up and he did not know what to do. Sometimes he stressed so easily. This time, it was understandable. He needed Michelle home. She would know what to do. She always knew what to do. What scared him most was the idea that she would *never* be coming home. That she was dead somewhere, perhaps swinging from a rafter like Jillian.

But that was just paranoia.

They crossed through the Merchant's sideyard and climbed up onto Louis' porch. Michelle's car was still not in the driveway. Maybe that meant nothing, but he was beginning to think otherwise.

"When will she be home?" Macy asked.

But Louis could only shake his head. "I wish to God I knew..."

21

The smell of raw meat was overwhelming.

Mike Hack knew that he and his brother were supposed to find some nice young gee-gee, but the meat...oh God...such a wonderful odor. He had smelled it down the alley and traced it here. To this yard. Nothing had ever smelled this good before. He would have the meat. He must have the meat.

But wait.

Careful.

Remember what Mr. Chalmers said.

This is war.

This is survival.

Those other neighborhoods, they're gonna try and take what we got, so we got to hit them first. We gotta take what they got. Their women, their food, their weapons.

Yes, caution was advisable. Next to him, sweating and grinding his teeth and breathing hard, Matt could barely contain himself. He wanted the meat, too. Mike put a hand on him, stayed him from diving over the hedges and taking what was offered.

Mike held a finger to his lips.

He saw—

A plate of raw meat slabs sitting on the picnic table. Raw, ready for grilling. He could smell the juice, the fat, the blood pooling on the plate.

The meat was unattended, except for a few flies. No one was around. On all fours, down low, smelling the earth and feeling he was part of it now like a worm tunneling through mulch, he crept forward into the yard. Matt was behind him. Still grinding his teeth. Still breathing hard.

Mike sniffed the air.

He scented the raw meat.

But something else, too, something that made him alert for danger: the scent trail of others. People were near. Hunters like him, perhaps. He could smell their passage in the yard as a wolf can smell a game trail: a gamey, vile musk.

It excited him.

Still on his hands and knees, fighting the very simple need to roll in the grass and scent himself, Mike crept forward. Past a kid's pool. Around a swingset and a row of decorative peony trees. The meat was close now. Just a matter of reaching out for it.

Careful.

With Matt at his back, he sidled up to a little potting shed, lost himself in the cool fragrance of cedars. But the fragrance was not so strong that he did not scent the others and know they were near. Very near. He could smell their sweat, their heat, almost hear the thudding of their hearts and the rush of blood in their veins.

Where were they?

Matt made a moaning sound in his throat and jumped out of the shadowy protection of the cedars. He ran to the picnic table and grabbed a raw meat cutlet, shoving it in his mouth. He chewed and slurped, pink juice running down his chin. He made a squealing sound in his throat that was nearly orgasmic.

But then—

A woman and two naked girls came rushing out of the potting shed where they'd been waiting all along. Mad things with wild hair and grime-streaked faces. Their eyes were huge and staring, lips pulled back from teeth.

And Mike, his brain reeling and misfiring, recognized them.

Or who they had once been.

Kylie...Elissa...those girls are Kylie and Elissa Sinclair. And that's their mom...Maddie, Maddie Sinclair.

This passed through his mind like a dying echo, but had no true substance and quickly faded.

Matt turned and kicked out at the woman, driving her back. But as he did so, one of the girls took a long-tined meat fork and stabbed him in the side. He let out a yelp of pain and turned to fight and the other girl slashed him across the throat with a knife.

No!

Mike jumped in, diving on the woman, trying to thumb out her eyes and get his teeth to her throat, but she threw him off. Threw him down. Kicked him and kicked him again until he rolled away, panting and stunned and breathless. She left him there and joined the two girls in goring Matt, taking him down, hunters to prey, slashing and cutting and stabbing him until he was a coiled up thing on the ground, raw and red-stained.

Mike crawled off towards the hedges.

One of the girls came after him.

He tripped her up and punched her twice in the face, feeling her lips mash against the teeth below. She went down but not before laying his face open with her nails in four red stripes.

Mike ran off.

He looked back once, knowing his brother was beyond help.

The woman and the girls were poking Matt with their forks and jabbing him with their knives. He was making a hoarse bleating sound, but he was all used up. He barely moved. The woman and the girls were spattered with blood. It stood out in bright, vibrant contrast to their pale faces.

As Mike ran off, he saw the woman hike up her sundress and piss on his brother, scenting him with territorial pheromones.

Marking her kill...

22

For the longest time, there were only the sounds of shovels scraping concrete, of things popping and snapping and dripping. The kid was stuck to the concrete and it took some work for them to shovel him free. It was back-breaking labor, all right, messy, dirty, stinking work. But under Warren's direction, they finally got the kid's body into the wheelbarrow and by then they were sweating and filthy and not in the best of moods. Then they stood there in sweat-stained and gore-streaked uniforms, not saying anything, just looking at the stain on the sidewalk and the red sprawl of arms and legs spilling over the sides of the wheelbarrow.

"That's it," Warren said, studying his pink-stained hands. "That's it."

"Now what?" Shaw said to him, his fat face beaded with sweat.

Kojozian smeared blood over his chest.

A crowd had gathered to watch—men, women and even children—and they pressed in close as they dared, not really amused or horrified or suffused with any other emotion you would readily expect. Others had came, sure, but they got out of there right away when they saw what was going on and maybe when they saw how that crowd looked, what was in their eyes and, more importantly, what *wasn't*. Their eyes were dead, distant moons that looked and watched, but did not seem to see. Some of the men pulled off cigarettes and a few of the women held babies. Many were naked. Many had painted arcane symbols on their chests. They admired the X on Kojozian's face. One old lady had brought her knitting. A little boy had a sucker in his mouth that he slurped on.

"Our uniforms are a mess," Shaw said. "They smell."

Warren scratched his head, wondering why that mattered. They were cops. They had to keep the uniforms on, especially the shiny badges. People would know them by these things. Symbols of office, of authority.

Kojozian said, "What do we do with this kid? We just gonna wheel him around all day?"

"Why don't you dig a hole," one of the crowd said.

"Sure," said another. "A hole is where something like that belongs."

"Plant flowers on top so it looks nice," said the old lady with the knitting.

But Warren explained to them that this was police business, official business, and you just couldn't go burying a dead kid anywhere you wanted. There were rules and regulations to be followed. Rituals. Yes, *rituals* that must be observed. They just didn't understand.

"I say we find out where he lives and bring him over there," Kojozian suggested.

Warren shrugged. "Yeah, that might be the thing to do. Whoever he belongs to will like that, don't you think?"

Kojozian grinned. "It's the least we can do."

The kid who was working the sucker stepped forward. "That's Ryan Soames. He delivers our paper. I know where he lives. It's just a block over."

"Okay, kid," Warren said, "lead the way."

Kojozian pushed the wheelbarrow down the sidewalk, the kid out in front, marching like he was in a parade. Behind them, the crowd plodded along. They were all excited to get to the kid's house. This was really gonna be something...

23

After Ray Hansel and Paul Mackabee of the State Police CSI left Greenlawn High School and Principal Benjamin Shore and the crime scene in general, they drove through the town, trying to get a feel for it. And what amazed them most was that they couldn't.

The town felt...what?

Hansel wasn't sure exactly, but almost blank, empty, deserted. The way a ghost town would feel: unoccupied. That you were the only thing in it. And that didn't make much sense because he saw people out in the streets walking, washing their cars, shopping, women pushing baby strollers and men leaning on the backs of pickup trucks, chatting, as men will do. There was life, there were people, but why could he not *feel* them? Although it made absolutely no sense on the surface, Greenlawn was like a town peopled by mannequins, dummies. Things that looked like people, pretended to be people, but were not people.

You be careful with that, Hansel told himself, *you be real careful. There's something wrong here and you know it. If all goes to hell as you are suspecting it will, there's going to be need of a few clear, clean heads that can do some thinking.*

"Don't know about you, Ray," Mackabee said, "but I'm getting a chill right up my spine."

"Me, too."

They listened silently to the squawk coming over the radio and it did not allay their fears much. There were a couple of old houses burning on Water Street on the north side. A couple kids had drowned in the Green. Lots of domestic disturbances. A couple of assaults. A child had gone missing after school. And there had been no less than three reported suicides within the hour. All this in Greenlawn. Whatever this was, it was building, gaining momentum.

Maybe if it had just been here and not the rest of the country they might have felt a little relieved. But it was everywhere and that scared the shit out of both men.

Hansel thought: *Nowhere to run. No matter how bad it gets here, there's nowhere to run. Nowhere to hide. No safe harbor. One town will be just as insane as the next.*

Jesus.

He drove downtown and pulled up before the police station, a tall and narrow slab of pale brick. He stood there on the sidewalk, sensing things that he did not like.

An old man walked past and his eyes were filled with murder.

A woman walked by holding a little girl's hand and there was something almost synthetic about the expressions on their faces.

"I'm gonna go grab a cup of coffee across the street," Mackabee said.

Hansel nodded. "Keep your eyes open. Watch yourself. I'm gonna go see Bobby. See what he has to say."

Sighing, Hansel went directly upstairs to Bobby Moreland's office. Moreland was the chief of the city police. He was a fat, funny man who seemed to know just about everyone in town on sight. Some said he would advance soon into politics.

Hansel found him sitting behind his desk, sipping coffee. He was still large, but there was no humor in those eyes and certainly no laughter wanting to come out of that dour mouth.

"Ray" he said.

Hansel sat down. "What's going on?"

Moreland was staring at the screen of his laptop. "Things are going mad over in England. There's a group of hundreds that are currently laying waste to central London...they're murdering, raping, pillaging. Unbelievable. They're practicing a scorched earth policy, Ray. Burning and destroying everything. They're even killing the animals in the stockyards. Slaughtering them. Have you ever heard of such a thing?"

Hansel shrugged, considered it. "Sure. It's going on in Washington and New York right now. The army is fighting a house-to-house guerilla war in the Bronx and Brooklyn. Baltimore is burning. So is St. Louis. Cleveland is a war zone. Dallas and New Orleans are so bad that they sent in the Marines. Except, from what I'm hearing, discipline has broken down and scattered bands of Marines are raiding at will. And did I mention that the governor of California ordered an airstrike on East LA?" Hansel just shook his head. "Civilization is crashing, Bobby. But to be honest, I don't really give a shit about those other places. I'm mostly concerned with this state, this county, and Greenlawn in particular at the moment."

"Well, we have a little bit of everything, as you well know." Moreland picked up his Styrofoam coffee cup, realized it was empty and set it back down. "I can't keep a handle on it all. Between my boys, yours, and the county boys, we got our hands full. I keep hoping this is going to die down...but it's not dying down, Ray. Can you tell me why that is?"

But Hansel just shook his head. "I don't know. Something has this town, this country, this whole goddamn world, and it's squeezing the guts out of it."

Moreland looked defeated. "My wife...she's a little soft on religion and all...she thinks...she thinks it's the Devil. Devil come down to Earth. Armageddon, the Rapture, all that happy horseshit."

Hansel did not laugh as he might have a week ago. "Well, Bobby, if it *was* the Devil, then at least we'd have an enemy to fight. Something to go after. But this...shit, there's no rhyme nor reason. It's coming down everywhere and there's no fucking reason for it."

"Yeah."

"Wanna hear something funny?"

"Sure, I could use a laugh."

"Oh, you won't laugh, trust me." Hansel got up and went to the window, peered through the Venetian blinds to the streets below. "I see people out there, going about their business, but I don't *feel* 'em. Does that make sense? They're there, but it's like they're not there at all."

Moreland just nodded. "Town feels empty, don't it? Things going on, more things than we can ever handle and a lot more we won't know about for days and days, yet it's quiet out there. You know? Just quiet."

"People you see don't smile, Bobby. They don't even talk. They just walk around like they're lost, like they're trying to find their bearings."

"Maybe they are."

Hansel thought so, too. All of them out there were feeling it. Some had been affected by it, many in very devastating ways. But the majority were just confused, trying to make sense. Trying to understand why reality had been unplugged and they were about to fall headlong down a steep incline. One without a bottom.

"I got units that aren't reporting in," Moreland said. "That scares me the worse. But what can I do? Call the governor and say that this town needs psychiatric help? How would that sound?"

"Like you were cracking up," Hansel told him.

"I am."

"No, not yet you aren't."

Moreland studied his hands for a long time and when he spoke, he did not look up and meet the other man's eyes. "You want to hear a confession, Ray? One that won't sound so good at all."

"Sure."

"I'm scared," Moreland admitted. "I'm scared like I've never been scared in my life. I'm scared for the world. But more than that, I'm scared for Greenlawn."

But Hansel understood. For he was scared himself. He licked his dry lips, said, "Sad thing is, by the time this is over, Bobby, I'm afraid there won't be anything left of civilization. Now how's that for drama? People going crazy, people acting like animals. Six months from now we might be living the way our ancestors did. A world lit only by fire..."

24

When they got over to his house, Louis went upstairs and cleaned up, got a new shirt on. Then he came back down and took a belt of whiskey. It didn't do him much good, but he figured he was better with it than without.

Michelle still wasn't home.

She was not answering her cell and Louis was starting to worry. Mainly because when they'd been outside, he could smell smoke like maybe there was a house burning somewhere. Smell smoke and hear more sirens and all that told him that whatever was going on was far from finished. It was still rolling. Maybe gaining momentum.

He picked up his cell and called Farm Bureau Insurance.

The phone rang and rang over there, but nobody picked it up. It was after hours now. Well past closing time. Michelle was not there and neither was anyone else. That meant she was either on her way home or...

Well, he wasn't going there.

Not yet.

"I wish I knew where my mom was," Macy said, sitting there on the couch, tense and expectant.

Louis just swallowed. "She's...she's probably out shopping or visiting someone."

"I guess."

Louis could not look at her.

He walked over to the window by the door and watched the streets, wishing as he'd never wished before to see Michelle's little Datsun come swinging down the block. But he was disappointed. Not only was Michelle not coming but no one else was either. It was Friday night. People should have been coming and going.

And what is that saying to you, Louis? What exactly do you think that means?

Honestly, he thought it was time for a good panic attack, but that would hardly solve anything. And he had to consider Macy. She was scared and he knew it. Maybe she was sixteen years old, but that was still a kid. He could not go to pieces on her. She needed him and for the first time in his life, Louis had a newfound sense of respect for parents. Because parenting was an awesome responsibility when you actually thought about it. He was worried sick about Michelle, but she was an adult and whatever was happening out there, she was better equipped to handle it than Macy was.

"Listen," he said. "Do you have any relatives in town? Somewhere your mom might have gone?"

Macy shook her head. "Not really. They all live other places. There's Aunt Eileen, but she's way down in Greencastle. She sends a Christmas card every year, but her and mom don't get along."

Surprise, surprise. "Anybody else?"

"Um...well, there's Uncle Clyde. He lives here. On the other side of town, but him and mom never talk. I haven't even seen him in two or three years."

Louis figured that this Uncle Clyde was family anyway. That was something. Worse came to worse, he could farm Macy off on him. But that was later.

"I got an idea," Louis said. "Let's take a ride."

"A ride?" She brightened a bit.

"Sure. Beats sitting around here staring at each other. Let's see if we can find Michelle and we'll keep an eye out for your mom, too." He shrugged. "Michelle will probably pull in the driveway five minutes after we leave, but at least we'll be doing something besides twiddling our thumbs."

"Yeah," Macy said. "Okay. I just thought of something, though. Mrs. Brackenbury down the street. Sometimes mom goes over there."

Mrs. Brackenbury was an old lady who lived alone with about twenty cats. She had to be pushing eighty. Her husband had been dead for years. Just her and the cats. Louis had heard about Jillian going over there, not to visit, but to borrow money from the old lady. It was rumored she had quite a pile.

Louis tossed Macy his cell. "Why don't you give the old gal a ring? I'll go write Michelle a note."

Macy pulled back her hair and tightened her pony tail ring, then started punching up Mrs. Brackenbury's number.

Louis walked into the kitchen, glad to be away from her for a moment.

God, she was a sweet kid, but he felt so responsible for her. He didn't like that. And mainly because he did not know if he was up to it. Up to watching over anyone in a crisis. He quickly scratched a note to Michelle and hung it on the fridge.

They'd take a drive and at least they'd be able to see what was going on. Something had to be done and quick. He had to tell someone about Jillian's body over there and then he was going to have to break it to Macy.

But first things first.

He jogged down into the basement and grabbed his tackle box. He took a Schrade lockblade knife out. The blade was six-inches long and razor sharp. He stuck the knife in his pocket. Maybe there would be no trouble out there at all, but you just never knew. If things continued like they had been, Greenlawn was going to be like the deep dark woods come nightfall and you just never knew when the wolves might show when you were on your way to grandmother's house...

25

Across the street, Dick Starling covered himself in mud.

After roasting his wife's corpse in the kitchen and feeding on it, he went out into the backyard, feeling the sun on him. It warmed him. He stripped off his filthy clothes which were crusty with bloodstains and danced around, arms upraised, soaking in that sun and feeling its wonder.

The sprinkler was going.

Down on his haunches, tensed, ready to spring, he watched it shooting gouts of water into the air. He was fascinated by it. He honestly had no cognitive recall of setting out the sprinkler that morning to water the flowerbeds. In fact, by that point, he really did not know what a sprinkler was. There was some gray area in his brain associated with it, but he shook it away.

He crept over there on all fours.

The water splashed against him. He liked it. He seized the sprinkler head and brought it to his mouth. As the water pulsed into his face, he licked and gulped at the flow until he was sated. Then he tossed it aside. Blades of grass were stuck to his belly and legs. He liked the way they smelled. He went over to the flowerbeds. The bright colors of the blooms were nice. He snatched an azalea, chewed it, spat out it back out, disgusted by the sweet taste. Then he tore all the flowers up and cast them about.

He did not want flowers.

He wanted mud.

With the sun beating on it, the dark earth of the flowerbeds was warm and mucky. He scooped up handfuls, sniffing each one, and smeared it all over his chest and legs and arms and genitalia. Especially his genitalia. It was warm, thick, and comforting like primordial ooze. He greased his wet hair back with it and painted black bands across his face.

He felt safer then; camouflaged, stealthy.

He grabbed up his bloody axe where he'd left it by the back door. It felt good in his hands. A hunter needed a weapon and this one had already been blooded. On his hands and knees, he crept around the side of the house. He was full now, his belly stuffed with meat. His needs were quite simple: food, shelter, weapons. But there was another desire as well: *sex.* Since his daughters had not returned, he knew he had to go hunt a woman.

Peering from the hedges that flanked the front of his house, he watched the home of Louis Shears across the way...

26

Kathleen Soames was not surprised when she saw the crowd.

She had felt them coming for some time as she dismembered her husband on the kitchen floor and decorated the walls with his blood. She had *willed* them to her. She wanted them to come and marvel over what was hers. She wanted them to try and take it so she could fight them, roll in the dirt with them.

But when she saw them, she knew they had not come to raid.

They had come for other reasons.

So she looked at them and they looked at her, each recognizing one another for what they now were, grateful that they had found each other at long last.

The crowd.

Dear God, yes, the crowd.

Men, women, and children tagging behind three cops in filthy untucked uniforms. The big one in front was bare-chested and painted for battle. He was pushing a wheelbarrow and in it was what Kathleen expected to see. Something broken and bloody and tangled. Something that made her heart split open momentarily, made her remember things, remember a swollen belly and a kicking, a chubby pink thing pressed to her breast, a growing and hungry thing, blue-eyed and wheat-haired. A smiling face and a boy's laughter and a world drowning in love and joy. But it vanished so quickly maybe it never existed at all. The heat of the memory became a frost that settled deep into her, a killing frost that withered roots and closed blossoms and then there was just a winter deadness inside her that no spring thaw would ever melt again.

The crowd.

They came up to the porch and stayed there, watching her, smelling her scent and recognizing it as their own. She had marked the porch with her urine and now they smelled it. They would not cross her scent unless she allowed it. Not unless they wanted to fight.

They pushed in, compressed into a single mass, a single breathing machine, something with eyes that did not see and hearts that barely beat and minds that were flat and metallic and cutting. They waited at the edge of the porch.

The white-haired cop who had no hat on looked up at her and said, "Ma'am, I'm Sergeant Warren. This is Officers Shaw and Kojozian. We brought this back to you because we knew you'd want it."

Kathleen just stared.

She could feel her breasts rising and falling, the blood drying on her arms, taste the sweat on her lips. Smell the darkness oozing from her, content that they, the crowd, smelled as she did now. A stink of things dead and things horribly alive, things pulsing with a morbid vitality. She stared at Warren and at the thing in the wheelbarrow. Her mind was a hollow oblong that filled with blackness drop by drop.

Wary as any animal with others intruding so close to its warren, she hopped down the steps to inspect the offering they had brought. She examined the tangled corpse in the wheelbarrow. She sniffed it carefully. Bending her head down, she licked the skin of a stiffened arm.

"Yes," she heard herself say. "Yes. It's mine."

"We bring this to you," Warren said, indicating the corpse of her son. "Have you something for us?"

"Yes. Inside. Upstairs." She was breathing hard. "Would you like to see my husband?"

"Yes."

Then they filed past her and she heard them in there, heard them laughing, heard them snarling and fighting over things. She would share. Of course she would share. She'd always been a good neighbor. The crowd filled the house with motion and voices, claws and teeth and intent. Kathleen watched them file from the living room. She touched the dirt and blood ground into her skin, fingered the filth in her hair. The crowd was in awe of her. They stood in silence, faces like yellow wax and dead moons, mouths painted red and fingers still redder.

"Well," Warren said, wiping blood from his cheek "What do you offer?"

Kathleen grinned and her teeth locked tightly together. They felt long and sharp and ready. "Upstairs," she told them. "Upstairs is the one you want."

The crowd moved up the stairs, leaving a blood-smell and a meat-smell in their wake. They smelled as she did, only more so. Just dirty and rank and repulsive. A bouquet of death lilies and graveyard roses and mortuary orchids pressed into cold, waxen fingers. A good smell, a fine smell, a real and true smell.

As they filed up the stairs, Kathleen grinned.

The sun outside was so hot, so very hot, burning and blinding. She wanted sunset and shadows and steaming darkness, the feel of cooling pavement under her hands and feet, night-smells and night-tastes. The pure and atavistic joy of running wild and free and hungry with the pack.

Upstairs there was the pathetic, broken scream of an old woman.

Kathleen grinned.

Hurry sundown.

Hurry...

27

Well, that's how it ends. That's how it all crashes down around you.

This is what Benny Shore, Principal of Greenlawn High School, was thinking as he left school that day, just amazed at all of it. Yes, beside himself with the horror of it, surely, but more than that, just amazed. Like they said, what a difference a day could make. He'd come to work that morning, chipper and happy, whistling some silly tune...and now he was leaving, depressed and hopeless, wanting to slit his wrists.

Yes, one day could make all the difference in the world.

There was little to do now but wait and see what came next.

The school board were beside themselves, the city and state and county cops just scratching their heads. Shore's phone had been pretty much ringing off the hook ever since it all happened and then, for the last hour or so...it had been oddly quiet. He was expecting to be besieged by parents once their workday had ground to a halt, but it had been quiet.

The calm before the storm?

Or a sign of something worse?

The sign of a world going into the shitter, that's what. It's breaking out everywhere now...random violence, bloodshed, savagery. And, for once, old boy, you don't need to turn on CNN to see it: because it's HERE. It's in the STREETS...

Shore hopped into his Jeep and buried his head in his hands.

He sat there like that for maybe ten minutes and then just stared out into the deserted parking lot. There were a few police vehicles there, but that was about it. He was thinking about what Ray Hansel had been telling him as the State Police CSI unit combed through the wreckage, about the violence not only at the school but in the town as well. So much of it in one day that it made even the most skeptical onlooker more than a bit nervous. Was there an underlying cause to it all as Hansel had suggested? Was there a pattern very much evident, but one they could not see because it did not fit the usual parameters? And probably the worst and most unthinkable thing of all, was it possible, as Hansel had hinted at, that this was only the beginning of something much larger?

Would this infection of violence gut the world?

Shore shook his head.

Too much, too much. His head was beginning to hurt from it all. There had been a nasty headache threatening all day and now it was coming, landing hard in his head with reinforcements.

He dug a bottle of Ibuprofen from the glove compartment and chewed a few tablets up, washed it all down with a swig of coffee from this morning that had been sitting in the Jeep all day. It was awful tasting, but he did not notice. He fumbled a cigarette into his mouth, lit it, and blew smoke out through his nostrils.

He felt so...helpless.

So utterly helpless.

He'd been principal at Greenlawn High for nearly eleven years, before that assistant principal and guidance counselor. This school was *his* school and he did not like the idea that he could do absolutely nothing. That this was all in the hands of others, most of them with no true personal interest in the school, the kids, their combined impact on the community at large. He felt like he was giving up without a fight.

He unrolled his window the rest of the way and stared up at the school.

Two stories of red brick that had been standing since 1903, right on the spot where the old schoolhouse—tall and narrow, whitewashed clapboard with a rising belfry—had been until it burned to the ground in the winter of '01. He thought of all the classes that had passed through those high, arched doors, the class pictures that had been taken out in the grassy courtyard. All the football games and track meets that had been held in the athletic field behind. He could almost hear the cheering and laughter, the boom of drums and thunder of the high school band. Yes, he could smell autumn in the air, leaves and bonfires and apples.

That's what it was all about, he suddenly knew.

Tradition.

It was all about *tradition*.

And those goddamn kids in Biolab had taken that all away.

Not just from Shore himself, but from the whole goddamn town and the generations that had yet to set foot in the school. Those kids had tarnished that and it would never be the same again. For the next hundred years, maybe, if the school stood that long and the world was still turning, kids would be telling stories of that terrible day. Horror stories. That was the ultimate legacy of this day, this Friday the 13th, grist for horror stories.

Shore felt the headache building in his skull. *Fucking kids,* he thought. *What the hell were they thinking? What the hell came over them? How dare they do something like this, turn my school into a goddamn sideshow!*

The headache amplified and Shore actually cried out, pressing his hands to his temples. The cigarette fell from his lips and landed on the seat between his legs, burning a hole there, but he neither noticed nor cared. The pain passed and he swore under his breath. He was actually hoping that none of those little shitting monsters from 5th hour Biolab was ever found. He hoped they did the right thing and threw themselves into the deepest, darkest hole they could find and pulled the dirt in after them. Hell, yes. Let the evil of this day die with them and then nobody would point their fingers at Greenlawn High, they'd just speculate and speculate and finally accept the fact that those kids were all fucked-up on drugs.

Shore smiled at the idea.

He started the Jeep and threw it in reverse, then drive, coasting it slowly through the parking lot. He lit another cigarette and brushed the burning one on the seat to the floor. He pulled around behind the building, taking the circle drive, so he could take a good long look at *his* school.

He liked to see it.

It made him feel good inside, important maybe.

Necessary.

This was his territory.

His.

As he came around the corner, passing through the faculty lot, he decided he had better not see any of those damn dirtbags smoking cigarettes or necking in the trees behind the lot. If he did...well, if he did, he was going to come down on them like never before. He'd bust their heads open. He'd bust their goddamn heads right open.

But he saw no one.

At least until he came around the back of the school and then he saw a kid standing there, right in the middle of the road. Some dumb kid staring at the oncoming Jeep like he had no idea what a moving vehicle was. Shore grimaced and hit the horn a couple times. The sound made his head throb.

Dumb kid...what the hell was he doing?

Then Shore got a good look at him.

No, just not any kid. That was Billy Swanson. Goddamn *Billy Swanson* from 5th hour Biolab.

"Billy," Shore said under his breath. "Well, well, well."

He knew Billy fairly well.

A little nothing shit, an outsider dwelling in a world of fantasy. He didn't try out for sports, volunteer for any of the clubs. He did absolutely nothing and like any kid that did not fit in, he took the standard ration of shit. Shore had disciplined kids like Tommy Sidel—another 5th hour Biolab monster—for picking on Billy, for shoving him in the halls or punching him in gym class or tripping him up outside. Yeah, yeah, yeah. It had fallen on Shore as it always fucking fell on Shore. But right then? Had he been able to go back, he would have picked on that little shitting mama's boy himself. Knocked his ass to the floor and kicked his fucking *Star Trek* paperbacks away, wiped his ass with them.

Kind of shit was that for a growing boy to be reading anyhow?

Feeling it rising in him, the anger, the rage, the frustration, Shore slammed on the brakes about ten feet from Billy. He hopped out. "Billy! Get your ass over here, I want to talk with you! You hear me?"

Billy just looked at him, his eyes dead and flat and somehow defiant.

Shore did not like how the kid looked at him, because not only was there defiance there, but an absolute lack of fear. Shore did not like that in the least. Billy should have been cowering, hanging his head, but he was not. He was glaring. Shore glared right back at him, his lips peeling back from his teeth. It occurred to him that they were facing off like two dogs disputing territory, which had the right to piss on a given tree. But he dismissed that, for suddenly things like metaphors made no sense to him.

"Billy..." he said.

The kid just smiled.

Smiled and spit at his feet, made sure Shore watched him do it, too. Why, the defiant little shit. He had no idea what he was stepping in this time. Benny Shore did not take crap from losers like Billy Swanson. He stepped on them. He crushed them. And Billy was about to find out all about that.

But Billy had no interest.

He turned and walked off at a very leisurely pace, again indicating no fear.

Shore reddened, fumed. *"Billeeeee..."*

He thought he heard the kid laugh, was almost sure of it.

Billy was now moving off at a casual jog, the sort of jog that said, you couldn't catch me anyway, you stupid fuck.

So that was the game he wanted to play? All right, all right.

Shore jumped behind the wheel of the Jeep and threw it in drive.

He squealed out and rocketed right at Billy Swanson. Although he was not aware of it, something had finally and ultimately burst in his head like a sore, filling his mind with pus and diseased drainage. All he knew is that Billy Swanson had really stepped in it this time. Really and truly. He accelerated, gripping the wheel and the very act felt so good, so liberating, so very right. The Jeep came speeding up behind Billy at almost forty miles an hour and the stupid kid just didn't have the sense to get out of the way. He tried to dart to the left at the last possible moment, but no dice. Shore struck him and the impact tossed him up onto the hood. He rolled off and tumbled into the parking lot.

Shore squealed to a stop and spun the Jeep around.

Billy got up.

He was young and the impact had hurt him, but he was hardly down for the count. He glared at Shore with wild eyes and then limped off like a wounded animal. But Shore wasn't having that. He gunned the Jeep and swung the wheel when Billy hobbled up over the curb. He almost got away, but then the Jeep hit him again and Shore cackled. Billy was thrown face down and the Jeep rolled right over him.

In the rearview, Shore saw him back there, broken and bleeding. But still no fear. Billy was scowling and snapping his teeth. Shore threw the Jeep in reverse and rolled over him again. This time he clearly heard the sound of bones snapping. It was a good sound, one that Shore had wanted desperately to hear.

But it wasn't enough.

So he drove over Billy again.

And again.

And again...

28

Ray Hansel was just leaving Bob Moreland's office at the Greenlawn Police Station when he saw the woman coming up the stairs. Under ordinary circumstances, he probably wouldn't have paid much attention. It was a police station, after all, and people tended to come and go at such places. Particularly today where there was a constant stream of visitors...some were out of their heads and went straight to lock up; most were just normal, or nearly, normal and scared and worried. They came in to report assaults and arson and even a few murders, but mostly it was just to report missing family and friends or neighbors that were just acting a bit off.

But the woman Hansel saw was not one of them.

He shut the door to Moreland's office—where they had just decided that it might be a good idea to call together an emergency meeting of the city council because what they were looking at was civil unrest—and he saw her step into the corridor. What drew his attention to her was the fact that she was wearing only a bathrobe, a ratty old terricloth thing that was dirty and dusty with strings of cobwebs stuck to the collar and sleeves like maybe she'd been hiding out in an attic. Her face was pale, terribly pale, her hair teased into a great rat's nest. And her eyes were like black holes burned into her face.

"Ma'am?" Hansel said, his hand instinctively going for the butt of the bluesteel Beretta 9mm in his holster. It did this automatically without any help from him. "Can I help you?"

She took two steps forward, moving with an odd mechanical cadence, not seeming to see or hear Hansel. Her attention was focused on Moreland's door with such intensity that it was almost scary.

Hansel stepped in her path. "Ma'am?" he said.

She turned and looked at him and snarled like she'd been scalded.

Her hand came out of the deep pocket of her gown and there was a seven-inch carving knife in it. Without hesitation, she slashed at Hansel, going right for his throat. He ducked away and grabbed her arm before she had a chance to repeat the maneuver. She screamed and fought, but he got her off balance and tripped her up. She dropped the knife and immediately went after him.

"*Need some help out here!*" he called out as she scratched and kicked at him.

Two cops came running from an office down the corridor and took hold of her, pulling her off Hansel and throwing her to the floor. She landed with a thud, rolling over, and coming up on all fours like a dog ready to bite. Her bathrobe was wide open, her pasty white breasts on display. Her teeth were clenched, a rope of saliva hanging off her chin, black and leering eyes darting from man to man.

"Okay, lady," Hansel said. "Just take it easy, we're not going to hurt you."

She made a hissing sound, blowing air through her teeth. Her face was contorted, deranged, and there was no getting around the fact that she needed to be put in restraints. There was something blatantly vicious about her and Hansel was certain she would have sunk her teeth in his throat given the chance.

One of the cops took out his Mace and she charged him.

He never even got his finger on the button.

He was a big boy, outweighing her by an easy hundred pounds, yet she struck him with such force that all he had time to do was cry out as she slammed into him, knocking him flat. His partner grabbed her around the throat with an armlock and she came alive in a loose, writhing mass, head whipping from side to side, spit spraying from her mouth. She jumped up in his grip, kicking back with both feet and catching him in the shins, her splintered nails laying his arm open. He released her with a gasp and she seized his arm and sank her teeth right into it. He screamed a high and whining sound and Hansel saw the blood well from where her mouth was attached to his arm.

Then she turned on Hansel himself.

Her teeth snapping, her chin smeared red, she came right at him and he brought down his gun, butt-first, catching her right between the eyes. The impact knocked her back and she spun around in a crazy circle, hissing and shrieking, and then just collapsed, out cold.

"Holy shit," Hansel said.

The cop with the bitten arm let his partner drag him down to the first aid station, leaving Hansel alone with the unconscious woman. She was breathing hard, her bathrobe hooked up around her waist, legs splayed in opposite directions. Catching his breath, Hansel pulled out his handcuffs and kneeled beside her. One eye was open and staring, a metallic gleam to it; the other was closed. He took hold of her left arm and the flesh was hot and greasy feeling. He snapped a cuff on it and as he was about to put the other on, Moreland appeared.

"Oh, my Christ," he said.

Hansel lifted her and snapped the other cuff on her, breathing easier when it was done with. He couldn't stand the feel of her beneath his hands, her flesh feverish and moist, almost reptilian in its slipperiness. He looked down at the one eye and it reminded him of the eye of a jungle snake, flat and predatory.

"She was heading right for your office, Bob," he said. "She had a knife."

Moreland just stared dumbly.

"You better get that council together, Bob," he breathed. "We need people in here. The mayor can give the governor a jingle, I'm thinking. We need bodies in here. National Guard and maybe the CDC out of Atlanta. This goes on, we'll have a fucking revolution by tonight. You hearing me, Bob? We need martial law here."

That's what came pouring out of Ray Hansel's mouth, even though he knew none of the above was remotely practical. Knee-jerk, that's what it was. Whole state was going crazy, governor wouldn't give a high hot shit about goddamn Greenlawn.

But Moreland was oblivious to anything he was saying. He kept staring at the woman sprawled on the floor. Hansel did not like what was in his eyes.

"Bob...Bob, do you know her?" he asked.

Moreland slowly nodded his head. "Yes...yes, I do. It's my wife..."

Hansel swallowed.

And then downstairs, the screaming started...

29

When Susan Donnel pulled into the driveway of her house on Tessler Avenue, she was in a state of high panic. A Darvocet at lunch was followed by two Bacardi and Cokes. The world was unraveling. So much was happening in so many different places that she refused to even listen to the radio anymore.

Doom.

Gloom.

Horror.

And this time it wasn't just in Afghanistan or the Left Bank. It was here. It was everywhere. Even Greenlawn, her oasis, had lost its collective mind. As she drove through town, she saw devastation. Burning houses. Trash in the streets. Dogs running in packs. People running wild and naked in the streets.

And when she pulled in the driveway, hoping Ray was home and wondering why he wasn't answering his cell, she had to sit behind the wheel for five minutes. It took that long to pry her fingers off it. They were white-knuckled claws. Her stomach was upset. Her head was aching. She was shaking, every muscle drawn taut.

She stepped out into the driveway.

Into the absolute silence of Tessler Avenue. Not so much as a passing car. A kid on a bike. The hum of a lawnmower. Nothing. Oh, Jesus, that silence was worse than just about anything. Holding back a cry, she ran into the house.

"Ray!" she called. *"Ray!"*

Dammit, it was his day off. His car was at the curb. He had to be here, he just had to be. The house was neat. There were the remains of a sandwich on the table. Ray's lunch. She dashed from room to room in a frantic, sweaty panic. They would get out of town. They would pack up what they needed and get up to the cabin on Indian Creek, wait for this...*madness* to blow over. For God help her, it had to, it just had to.

He wasn't in the house.

Dammit!

She ran outside, looked in the backyard, saw the door to the garage was open. Of course. Of course. The garage. His private haven. Probably practicing his OCD, arranging his gardening tools or numbering his screws.

"Ray! Ray! Goddammit, Ray, why aren't you—"

A dank clamminess spread over flesh, her head spun, cold sweat ran down her face in rivers. She went down to her knees, a scream breaking loose in her throat. *"No, no, no, no, no, Jesus God, no..."*

Ray was hanging on the wall.

He was hanging by a hook there amongst the shovels, rakes, and hoes. Her husband. Her lover. Her rock. *Hanging there.* His eyes were wide and staring, the crown of his head ruptured, cleaved open in a grisly, jagged rent. Fingers of scarlet blood had run down his face, accentuating his chalk-white pallor.

Screaming, crying, her mind gone to sauce, Susan crawled out of the garage on all fours. She found her feet, staggered a bit, went down in the grass, vomiting. A voice in her head kept saying that such things as this could not be. They'd gotten up together this morning. Ray had made her breakfast. They'd laughed together. They'd showered together. He kissed her goodbye at the door and now...and now...

Susan ran.

Marge, she thought, Marge.

She ran next door, diving right over Ray's carefully sculpted hedges and landing face-first in a flowerbed. She scrambled through the yard. The Shermer's. Marge Shermer was practically like a mother to her. Her husband, Bill, was cranky, but he would know what to do. He was a crusty old war vet that always seemed to know what to do. Susan saw his pick-up truck in the driveway. The windshield was shattered.

Oh, no.

She went to the door, didn't bother knocking. Inside, there was wreckage. Paintings had been yanked off the walls. The TV set was tipped over. Potted plants scattered from one end of the living room to the other. She trampled across black potting soil, not daring to call out. Something inside her, long dormant, was aware now. It sensed danger. No sense alerting anyone or any*thing* to her location.

She slipped into the kitchen, flattened herself up against the refrigerator.

The same, dear God, it was the same. Cupboards had been emptied, the contents of drawers scattered over the floor: knives, spoons, forks. Canisters of flour and sugar had been spilled about. There were bloody handprints on the countertops. The walls looked like they'd been gouged with knives.

There was a stink of raw urine in the air.

Somebody had gone insane in here and then pissed with glee.

Susan went down to the floor, grabbed a knife.

Tears ran from her eyes, drool filled her mouth. There was a wild tic at the corner of one eye. Shadows jumped in her brain. She was hearing a creaking sound. It was coming from the backyard. Tensing, Susan crept over the floor, leaving footprints in the flour. She eased herself up the counter so she could peer through the kitchen window out into the yard.

Careful, don't give yourself away.

She saw the bushes back there, the potting shed. She craned her neck. There was the clothesline. A gentle breeze made sheets flap. But that creaking. That continual creaking. It reminded her of—

She craned her neck. Her body was prickly with sweat, her blouse stuck to her back. She saw...she saw Marge. Marge was hanging from the oak tree back there. Susan saw it, wanted to scream, to cry out, to do many things, but by that point something had shut down in her.

So she just looked.

Marge, poor old arthritic Marge, was strung up from that oak like a lynched desperado in an old western. She was naked, her body bloated and purple and broken. Her face was a swollen contusion. She was only recognizable by her fine silver, moon-spun hair. It looked like she had been beaten to death. With bats. With boards. With hammers. It was hard to know. Her limbs were shattered, bent at unnatural angles.

Susan didn't bother looking for Bill.

Not running now, but moving with a quick, stealthy burst of speed like a hunted animal, she went to the Lychek's next door. They were a bunch of Bible-thumping Jehovah's Witnesses who were always leaving pamphlets and leaflets in everyone's mailboxes: SIGNS OF THE SECOND COMING or JESUS IS HERE NOW ON EARTH or YOU CAN BE GOD'S FRIEND! Nobody liked the Lychek's. They didn't believe in things like Christmas or Halloween. Pagan holidays, they said. The neighborhood kids always pranked them on October 31st. Oh, the awful things they did.

But Susan didn't care what they believed or what they didn't believe. For she could not be sure at that moment, as the world lost solidity and focus for her, just exactly what she believed in herself anymore.

She didn't bother knocking.

She stepped right in, brandishing her knife, waiting for attack that never came. She could smell blood, shit, piss, worse things. The living room was trashed. Bound volumes of *The Watchtower, Awake!*, and *Our Kingdom Ministry* had been yanked from bookshelves, pages torn out in a wild rage. They lay everywhere like fallen autumn leaves along with dozens of pamphlets preaching against progressive ideas like evolution and the separation of church and state. Then someone had defecated all over them. And by the amount of shit heaped and smeared on those pages, probably quite a few people. Susan immediately had a lunatic scenario in her head where a bunch of crazies came in here, tore up the books, and then, dropping their drawers, squatted down and happily shit together.

It was ridiculous.

But she feared it wasn't far from the truth.

Apparently they'd been using the pages as toilet paper, too, which was probably the most constructive use any of it had ever been put to, she decided.

Thump, thump, thump.

Susan went down in a crouch. The knife trembled in her hand. That thumping. What was this now? It was coming from a doorway at the far side of the room, possibly a dining room. She thought of running. Her animal sense demanded it. But being that she was still more or less a reasoning being, she was curious.

Tensed, ready for battle, she stepped across the room, very aware that she was stepping through human shit. The smell was overpowering, sickening. She noticed that there were bare human footprints in the waste, that filthy tracks led away into the room she was now creeping up on.

She got to the doorway.

Thump, thump, thump.

Louder now. She could hear a man grunting, a woman gasping. The sound of flesh slapping against flesh. No, no, it couldn't be *that*. Not here. Not with shit spread all over the place. No human beings could be that vulgar, that crude, that low and bestial. But the sounds were getting louder and louder. There was

121

no mistaking them. Despite herself, Susan felt a stirring inside her.

She chanced a look.

A man and woman were screwing on the floor. The man was entirely naked, his body covered with scratches and dried bloodstains. The woman wore only a short skirt and this was pushed up around her hips. Another woman, older, was crouched by them, rocking back and forth in mimic of their motions, gnawing on an apple.

And beyond them...in fact, only a few feet away...the remains of the Nychek's, Jack and Wendy. Her legs were missing. He'd been split open like a suckling pig, his abdomen wide open, entrails bulging out, heaped on the floor in a fleshy, coiling mass. Blood had spread out from the remains in a sticky red pool. The couple were fucking in it, streaked with blood and shit, just happily going away at it.

Susan just stared, appalled and sickened.

In the back of her mind there was a memory. Some show on TV. Something about man's modern world, his cities and technology, being like a cage that he had locked himself up in. The captivity repressed his natural instinctive desires, his animal impulses. In the cage, man no longer had to fear predators or hunt for food or defend his territory. Like a monkey in a zoo, he had no other instinctive outlet but sex. That's why people were so obsessed by sex. Simply because all the other impulses nature had installed were repressed. All that remained was *sex, sex, sex*—

There were low voices in the kitchen, the sound of bottles or jars smashed on the floor.

Susan made to back away...and then something hit her from behind. Right between the shoulder blades with an explosion of impact and agony. She was tossed into the room, slipping on the blood and landing atop the lovers. The man paid her no notice; he was intent on what he was doing. The woman hissed at her. She struck out with a backhanded fist, catching Susan in the mouth and sending her sprawling. This time she landed in the viscera on the floor. She cried, slipping and sliding on it, feeling it under her shoes like greasy snakes.

The old woman spit phlegm at her.

Susan crawled away, whimpering and shaking.

And there, right before her, standing high and almost proud, was a nude woman with a baseball bat in her hands. Her breasts and belly and face were painted with snaking transverse bands of blood. Her hair was wild, caked with filth. Her blue eyes were wide and bright, filled with a glacial coolness. They stared down with a catatonic glaze that was shiny and wet and utterly inhuman. More like the hungry stare of a wolf.

Now you got it, hon. Wolves. As in were-wolves. You know, shapeshifters, Lon Chaney and all that horseshit. Werewolves. That's what these things are. Not people. Not really. Not anymore. Maybe they're not sprouting hair and fangs like movie werewolves, but please be assured, my dear, these are fucking werewolves and you are now in their lair.

And all of that was disturbing, *hell yes*, but what seemed even worse was that this crazy woman had a leather sling of arrows on her back and a shiny onyx bow over one shoulder like she was some demented Amazonian.

"Please," Susan said, holding out her hands for mercy, trying to catch her breath, trying to find her center which was so lopsided, inverted, and upside down by this point she could have slid right off it like a fried egg in a grease-slicked pan. *Over, Under, Sideways, Down,* as The Yardbirds had once said. She swallowed, feeling the dryness of her throat. Her heart pounded, blood rushed at her temples. "Please...I didn't mean to barge in, I was looking for someone, but they're not here so I'll just be on my—"

"*Hhhhsssssssttt!*" the woman said by way of reply, forcing hissing air through clenched teeth.

Susan shook her head, not understanding such gibberish. At least on the surface...but down below where the wild things were, where they ran crusted with blood and gamey with their own rancid animal stink, she understood all too well. She was being told in a very rudimentary way to shut her fucking mouth. For the werewolf woman did not want to hear shit like that. She was not accustomed to her prey blabbing on and on; she liked her meat to know its place, to sit on the plate and exude a tasty pink juice, to be tender and filling, to satisfy both tongue and gut...but that was it.

"What's...what's your name?" Susan said, trying a different tact even though her animal instinct told her she was literally fucked here like the virgin on prom night in the old joke.

The woman cocked her head, her face scrubbed of emotion like that of a mannequin. There was excrement all over her feet. Her pale thighs and calves were bright with fingers of blood that seemed to have run from between her legs as if she were menstruating. And judging from the hot, meaty smell wafting off her, Susan knew she was.

"Please," Susan said again.

The woman grinned. Her teeth were stained red. "I'm Angie," she said. Then she said it again: "I'm Annnngeeeee," the way a little kid would say it, enjoying the way it filled her throat and rolled off her tongue. And this more than anything told Susan Donnel all she needed to know about the brain behind those eyes: simple, childlike, the cunning and savage appetites of a beast coupled with the rudimentary reasoning of a child.

Susan opened her mouth to speak and as she did so, Angie swung the baseball bat with a smooth muscular grace. It hit Susan in the mouth and she in turn hit the floor, her teeth scattering like dice. She was barely conscious, just gagging on her own blood. She was barely aware of the two men that stepped into the room and ripped her clothes off beneath the full approving glare of Angie Preen.

Susan came awake to the sharp stab of penetration between her legs, a heavy man that stank of sweat and shit pumping away on her. The horror of this floored her: the invasion, the brutality, the violation of the act. She let out a wild, whooping scream as those hips pistoned and the man's greasy, hot flesh pressed into her own. His breath blew in her face and stank like meat green with rot, like blood and vomit and boiling fevers. His face was a mask of dried blood, just that grinning mouth and gnashing yellow teeth, the stupid bovine staring eyes, unblinking.

The woman named Angie looked on with amusement. She licked her lips. Her free hand went down to her crotch. Gasping, she slid a finger into herself as Susan was raped.

Oh God, oh God, oh God, please please please no no no—

Then there was a keening cry and another man, a heavy, bulky man, kicked her attacker off and then mounted her himself. Then the first man pulled him free and the two of them were fighting, rolling through the shit-stained papers in the living room, kicking and biting, snarling and scratching.

Angie squatted down by Susan, she grabbed her by the hair and brought her contorted, tearful face to her own. As Susan trembled, Angie sniffed her like a dog. Her throat. Her breasts. Her hair. Then she threw her down.

"When you're done," Angie told the fighting men in a low grating voice that was practically a growl, "bring the cunt along. We'll need her..."

30

When they got outside, Macy said, "Well, Mrs. Brackenbury said she hasn't seen mom. It was worth a shot, I guess."

"Did she say anything odd to you?"

Macy shook her head. "No...well, I mean, she's always a little flaky, isn't she? Her and those cats? I told her to be careful, to lock her door, but she wouldn't listen. I don't even think she knew what I was talking about. She's in her own little world or something."

Louis had to smile. "Well, she's getting on in years, you know," he said, trying to be diplomatic.

"Tell me about it. She calls me 'Nancy' half the time."

Louis suppressed a giggle and led Macy over to his Dodge. There was still a smear of blood on the handle from when he'd jumped in there after his encounter with those wigged-out cops. But the driver's side rear door was open. He hadn't left it open. He was sure of it. Without alerting Macy to his concern, he casually closed it, but not before noticing that his bag with the steaks in it was gone. Just...gone. *Somebody came and stole raw steaks, Louis. What do you think about that?* He was not very surprised. He looked down the street. Nobody was around. Not a soul. Was that good or bad? The smell of smoke was heavier in the air now and he wondered what was burning out there. A house or was it maybe a block of them?

"Hey, Louis!" a voice called.

He paused at the car, craned his head back, wondering what it could be now. It was just Earl Gould from next door. Earl was okay. A retired anthropology professor from Indiana U with far too much time on his hands these days, he just liked to talk. Sometimes Louis could barely get out of the yard without a lengthy chat over Earl's meticulously trimmed hedges.

"I better talk to him," Louis said. He checked his pockets. "Do me a favor, Macy, will you? Run inside and grab my wallet. It's up in my room on the dresser. I won't be a minute."

Macy strolled away and Louis went over to the hedges. Earl was there with a pair of trimmers and Louis approached him very cautiously. It didn't look like he was crazy, but then it hadn't looked like the mailman was either...not at first. Louis wasn't really too concerned about driving without his wallet, but he thought it might be a good idea to get Macy out of there in case Earl snapped.

"How's things?" Earl said.

Louis shrugged. "I don't know, to be honest. Pretty weird things going on today."

Earl nodded, peering up at Louis over the rims of his glasses. "That's what I'm hearing. Goddamn country is flipping its wig."

"Whole world, Earl."

"You know what I say, Louis? Screw the world. Let's worry about this place."

"Yeah. I guess."

"Small towns can be very funny places, Louis. On the surface they're boring and ordinary and even serene, but deep down you can never truly say what might be boiling, you know?"

"Sure."

"Just one day, things happen. Not just one thing, but many. A chain of circumstances that seem to have no common root. At least, not one that you can see. Take Greenlawn for example. No, just humor me. From what I've been hearing we suddenly find ourselves faced with what seems to be a wave of random violence. It's disturbing, isn't it? Certainly, but it'll play itself out given time...won't it?"

"I hope so, Earl."

"Violence. It's the core of the human beast. It's what we are and where we came from and what we descend into with the slightest provocation. It's true, Louis. We carry within us the animal aggression of our simian and proto-human ancestors. Every beating, every rape, every witch hunt and mass murder is evidence of that. Even a child threatening another with a stick or a gangbanger with a switchblade in an alley is an expression of animal legacy in its purest form. The armed predator. Everything we do—from our urge to find and maintain territory, or real estate, to pecking orders and hostility to those outside our social grouping, the competition for females or males, race hatred and fear of strangers—all of it based on ancient animal patterns, like it or not."

Louis licked his lips. They were very dry. "But it'll stop. It has to."

"And if it doesn't?"

Louis absently looked at his watch. "I don't know."

"This town is a perfect microcosm for the world. People don't see it as such, of course. Because they're too close, too involved, that's why." Earl worked his clippers, taking out a stray twig. "You need a bird's eye view of this town to understand what ails it. The people who live here can no more examine their lives objectively than you or I can study the tops of our heads."

Louis just stood there, not in the mood for it.

Earl Gould was a nice old guy and he was very smart, but he had the sometimes annoying tendency to over-analyze and over-intellectualize things. Louis figured it was the fact that he no longer had a classroom to occupy or students to lecture. So he grabbed anybody that happened by—a neighbor, the meter-reader, the guy from the gas company—and discoursed at length on anything from politics to world economy to small town culture to that patch of weeds growing under the elm in the front yard. Louis would have liked to tell him what he'd seen and experienced, but that would mean sacrificing another hour or two that he just did not have. Because Earl would have to minutely examine each shred of evidence and then play devil's advocate for a time before finally rendering his hypothesis.

He was a smart guy, sure, but now was not the time for such things.

"Look at it this way, Louis. There is reason and cause if we can only open our minds to see them. And the people of Greenlawn cannot see beyond the ends of their noses, God bless 'em, each and every one." Earl leaned closer over the hedges. "I think, though, if they were able to, what they would find would scare them. Because small communities like this are often quite scary to an outsider, eh? Isolated, inbred, insular, paranoid even. Tribal. Oh yes, very tribal. Places like this always have one or two episodes of explosive violence in their pasts. Mostly you don't hear about them because small towns know how to keep their secrets and to lock their closets most securely so that the skeletons do not get out where they can be seen by shocked eyes."

"Yeah, you're probably right, Earl."

"Oh, I am. You can bank on that. I'm not a native. We only retired here because my wife spent her childhood in this very town. But that gives me an advantage, doesn't it? No rose-colored glasses or troublesome blinders on this old man's eyes, eh? I can see the mechanics of this town, where decay has set in and where new growth may yet bloom. The very anatomy of Greenlawn is mine to view." He chuckled at the idea, but there was a sharpness to his laughter, a darkness welling just behind his eyes. "I think, deep down, Louis, that the good citizens of our fair city of Greenlawn are not surprised at any of this. I think they've been expecting it. In the primal blackness of their souls, I think they've been waiting for something like this, something terrible to happen for a long time. And now the cork has been popped from the bottle and all that fermented juice is leaking out, spoiling everything and everyone it touches. I think, Louis, some will welcome this, what today has brought and tonight might still bring. They'll see it as an inevitability, won't they? All those tensions and frustrations building all these years, needing to vent themselves. Oh yes, Louis, they've been running hot and rancid like bad blood for too long now. Something that's needed purging, a sore that's needed lancing. Yes, my friend, things have been approaching critical mass for some time and I've been watching it happen. Critical mass has been reached and now comes savage fruition. All it took was a catalyst and do you know what that catalyst was?"

"It isn't just this town, Earl. It's the whole damn world."

Earl smiled at that as if he was amused by it. "Of course it is, Louis. The whole world. One race trapped in this disquieting moment in time when the shadows of antiquity are crowding in upon them." Earl nodded. "Do you want to know *why* this is happening, son? Why the human race is descending into savagery? Why our psychological evolution is being thrown clear back to the Paleolithic? Well, I tell you, I'll tell you. But first ask yourself this: Why do locusts swarm? Why do lemmings purge themselves? Why, indeed? When their populations reach critical mass, some biological imperative is activated in order to cull said populations. Hence, locusts swarm, lemmings purge. Locusts take to the skies in a swarm, descending on fields and stripping them, going into an eating frenzy. And they do this to cull their populations, for inevitably only a fraction of the population will *survive* the swarming. And lemmings? They do not consciously purge themselves as some think. They overpopulate, that unknown imperative switches on, and they migrate en masse. Again, only a fraction *survive* the migration. Most starve. Again, population culled."

Louis just stared at him, pretty certain now that Earl was mad, too. They had all gone mad, each in their own way. And this was certainly Earl's way. "That's very interesting, Earl."

"Isn't it?" Earl stabbed a finger at him. "But what does this have to do with human populations? I think you've already made the connection. Our population has reached dangerous, critical proportions. We are destroying the environment to accommodate this massive population explosion. Nature has thrown every conceivable stumbling block at us to slow it down...disease, famine, natural disaster. But we've beaten them off one by one. And now? Yes, *the ace in the hole*. That same biological imperative that exists in locusts, lemmings, even rats. We are, essentially, swarming. We are purging ourselves. We are cleansing the stock, so to speak. There was a very intelligent man name of Hutson. Roger Hutson. Hutson was an ethnologist from Oxford, over in jolly old England. He wrote a marvelous book called *Swarm Mechanics* many years ago where he warned of just such a species-threatening event. He claimed that in each of us, as in the aforementioned animals, there was a rogue recessive gene that would become activated if our population reached hazardous levels. That it would bring about unprecedented savagery, that we would literally exterminate ourselves until our population stabilized. And it has come to pass, has it not? This gene is activated, Louis. God help us, but it is. All of them out there...animals, they are regressing to animals, throwing off the yoke of intelligence and civilization, returning to the jungle and survival of the fittest..."

Earl went on and on, unable to stop himself. He cited studies with rats. How when they were overcrowded as humans were now in their towns and cities they began participating in degenerate, self-destructive behavior just like people. Murder, incest, homosexuality, cannibalism. Anything to weaken the overburdened population, to burn it out at its roots. To poison it out, cull the weak, preserve the identity and genetic purity of the breeding pool.

"The human garden will now be weeded," he said.

"But, Earl—"

"Oh, how arrogant we were!" Earl raged. "To think we were the masters of this planet! To think we could rape the environment and subvert natural law! And all the time, it was not nuclear war or some deadly pathogen waiting to undo us, but *ourselves! We are the instruments of our own destruction! Inside each and every one of us there is a loaded gun and radical population explosion has pulled the trigger! God help us, Louis, but we will exterminate ourselves! Beasts of the jungle! Killing, slaughtering, raping, pillaging! An unconscious genetic urge will unmake all we have made, gut civilization, and harvest the race like cattle as we are overwhelmed by primitive urges and race memory run wild!"*

"Listen, Earl," Louis said. "I need to get going, I have to—"

"WHO'RE YOU TALKING TO OUT THERE, EARL?"

It was Maureen, Earl's wife. She was hard of hearing and shouted everything. Even if you were in the same room with her. But Louis was glad for the intrusion.

Earl shook his head. "I'm talking to Louis! Louis Shears from next door!"

"WHO?" Maureen shouted through the kitchen window.

"Louis! Louis from next door!"

"LOUIS? IS MICHELLE OUT THERE?" she cried. "I SAID, IS MICHELLE OUT THERE?"

"No, she's not!" Earl looked apologetically at Louis and shrugged his shoulders.

"WHAT?"

"I said she's not out here!"

"WELL, WHAT ARE THE TWO OF YOU DOING?"

"We're not doing anything! We're just talking!"

"WELL, IF YOU WON'T ANSWER, I BETTER COME AND SEE MYSELF!"

Earl sighed. "Christ, but she's getting bad, Louis. Real bad. All day long she asks me what I'm doing. I'm taking out the trash and she wants to know what I'm doing. I'm cutting the grass and she wants to know what I'm doing. What the hell does she think I'm doing? You take out the trash because it's full and you cut the grass because it's getting long just like you take down the Christmas tree or throw the Halloween pumpkins in the can, because it's time! Because it's time!"

The screen door creaked open and out came Maureen with her cane, looking suspicious as she always did that something was going on and she had not been informed about it.

Louis looked over his shoulder, wondering what was taking Macy so damn long.

"WHAT IS GOING ON OUT HERE? THAT'S WHAT I'D LIKE TO KNOW!"

"See?" Earl said. "It's like this all day. How would you like to deal with what I deal with?"

Louis sighed. They were a nice old couple, but now was not the time for this shit. But he knew he wasn't leaving. Not yet. Not until Maureen came over and got her two cents in. She always had to know what was going on even when nothing was.

"LOUIS! DID YOU HEAR ALL THEM DAMN SIRENS?" Maureen shouted. She was a little woman with a bent back, bad knees, and glasses that made her eyes look about the size of golf balls. She looked frail and she probably was, but her lungs were working fine, despite the two packs she smoked every day. "I SAID...DID YOU HEAR THOSE DAMN SIRENS?"

Louis felt a headache building at his temples. "Yeah, I heard 'em."

"WHAT?"

"He said he heard 'em for chrissake!" Earl interpreted.

Maureen nodded and pulled a Benson & Hedges 120 from her pack and lit it. But her eyes were bad and it took some doing. She held the lighter with both hands and as she brought the flame to it, she kept backing away from it as if she was afraid she was going to light her nose on fire. It took some doing, but soon the old chimney was stoked and clouds of smoke were blowing from it.

"WHOLE TOWN'S GOING TO HELL, LOUIS! FROM ROOT TO ROSEBUD, JUST A MADHOUSE! A MADHOUSE, I SAID!"

"She said it's a madhouse, Louis."

But Louis had heard just fine and wondered as always why Earl felt the need to repeat a woman who was on the same decibel level as a Metallica concert. Already his ears were ringing.

"WHERE'S MICHELLE?" Maureen wanted to know.

Louis swallowed, wondering the same thing. "She's at work," he said, refusing to shout. He just wasn't up to it. "I have to go pick her up."

"WHAT?"

Earl tossed his hedge clippers aside. "He said she's at work! He has to go pick her up!"

"WHY IN THE HELL ARE YOU WHISPERING, EARL?" she wanted to know. "WHEN I ASK A QUESTION HAVE THE DECENCY TO ANSWER IT!"

"I did answer it!"

"NOT THAT I COULD HEAR!"

"Well you can't hear a damn thing anyway!"

Louis stepped back from the hedges, trying to get a look at his house. Macy had been gone too long. He was starting to get a funny feeling about that. What if she'd decided to dart over to her house to write Jillian a letter...and then gone downstairs?

"WHERE DID LOUIS GO?" Maureen asked.

"He's right here!"

"HE DIDN'T EVEN SAY GOODBYE! HOW DO YOU LIKE THAT?" Maureen just shook her head, staring right at Louis but not seeing him. A few feet out of the direct line of sight and she lost you. She pulled off her cigarette. "WELL, IT'S A WONDER MICHELLE PUTS UP WITH HIM! HOW LONG HAVE THEY BEEN MARRIED AND STILL NO CHILDREN! DON'T TELL ME THERE'S NOT SOMETHING FUNNY ABOUT THAT, EARL!"

Louis reddened, but was not surprised. You could pretty much hear Maureen up and down the block when the windows were open in the summer as she routinely gossiped about the neighbors.

"Jesus Christ!" Earl said to her. "Louis is right here! Are you blind?"

"WHAT?"

"I said, Louis is right here!"

Maureen pulled off her cigarette and squinted. "OH! WELL HE CAN'T HEAR ME WAY OVER THERE!"

"I need to get going, Earl. I have some things to take care of."

"Okay, Louis. Sorry about Maureen." He tapped a finger to his head. "She means well, but her eyes are shot, her hearing's no good, and she's getting soft upstairs."

"Don't worry about it," Louis told him.

"Think about what I said, Louis."

"IS LOUIS LEAVING?"

"Yes!"

"WHERE'S HE GOING?"

"He's got errands to run, goddammit!"

"EARL GOULD, YOU QUIT THAT DAMN WHISPERING AND SPEAK UP LIKE A MAN! YOU KNOW I CAN'T HEAR SO GOOD!"

"Shut up!"

"WHAT?"

Louis saw it coming just as he'd seen it coming when Earl started talking about the inevitability of the town going insane, of rogue gene expression sacking civilization as we knew it. The darkness was there. Hiding in the cracks and crevices of his mind and now it was bleeding out like shadows when the sun went down.

He turned to his wife. "I told you to shut the fuck up!"

"WHAT DID YOU SAY? QUIT WHISPERING LIKE A LITTLE GIRL FOR GODSAKE!"

And that was it.

Earl was talking about critical mass and catalysts and all the rest, well here it was for him. Critical mass had been reached and things were about to explode out of control. Race memory descended. He was a fine, gentle old man, but that all changed in an instant. He took two steps right over to Maureen and hit her in the face with everything he had. She went right down, blood splashing from her mouth right up to the bridge of her nose. Her dentures were hanging out like a set of wind-up chattery teeth.

It happened that quick.

Louis actually looked across the street toward the Maub's house, the Soderbergs, to see if anyone had seen what he'd just seen.

But there was no one around.

"Earl!" he said. *"Jesus Christ, what do you think you're doing?"*

But Earl did not hear him or care what he said.

He walked right over to his wife and gave her a good kick in the side and she howled with pain, gagging and gasping and spitting drool and blood into the grass.

Louis was about to intervene, but he heard Macy calling out to him. "Louis! Louis! *Mr. Shears!"*

Louis suddenly forgot about what he had just witnessed. He turned on his heel and ran to the house. He could hear Macy crying out and whatever was going on, it was bad. Real bad. He jogged up the steps and went right through the front door and it wasn't hard to follow her voice.

She was in the kitchen, but she wasn't alone.

She was behind the kitchen table and facing her was Dick Starling from across the street. But not the Dick Starling Louis knew. Not the same Dick Starling that had taken a picture of him with Jillian Merchant over his shoulder, that same funny and wisecracking man that had helped Louis lay the slab for his garage out back or threw Sunday afternoon backyard barbecues during football season.

No, this was not *that* Dick Starling.

This Dick Starling was covered in mud and dirt, hair wild and matted, completely naked, his penis standing erect. And his eyes...God, cold and dark like undersea caves. A rank stench of blood, death, and moist black earth blew off him. And he had a bloody axe in his hands.

"Hey, Louis," he said in a clotted, dirty voice. "I'm gonna get me that little cunt and when I'm done, you can have what's left. It's only fair that I have some, don't you think?"

Dick Starling was a monster...

31

Inside Benny Shore's head, there was a mirror maze like the kind you could find at a carnival. You looked into this one and you were a compressed little dwarf, into that one and you were a tall skeleton man. You looked here, there were ten of you, over there and there were fifty Benny Shores. Sometimes they were the principal of Greenlawn High School and sometimes they were little boys with frightened faces lost in the expressionistic tangle of their own jagged thoughts.

Careful, careful, Benny, those thoughts will kill you.

See how they glisten?

See how the lights catch their razored edge?

Yes, yes, easy now, because those thoughts will slit you right open, spill all your goodies out in coils of red, slopping things.

After he ran over Billy Swanson, Shore drove home taking a most leisurely route to his house over on Tessler Avenue near the river. He was in absolutely no hurry. When that headache had finally found him, delivered him from the here and the now into some distant and possibly primeval place deep in the core of his being, it had done things to him. It had changed his needs and wants and ambitions.

What had mattered before was now rendered meaningless.

Everything was different.

In his own way, perhaps he was still a scurrying insect, but the nature of the colony had certainly changed. It was like a shade had been drawn and the light was finally, thankfully shining in.

For some time, Benny Shore felt in touch with the world at large, with the community, with nature itself. None of that silly nonsense of budgets and meetings and planning boards...what the hell was that about anyway? No, what he felt was deeper, bigger, more fluid. Like some psychic channel to his fellow man had been opened and he was tuning in. With what they were and had always been and what they all soon would be. It was marvelous. So marvelous, in fact, that Shore was almost offended by the vehicle he drove. He wanted nothing better than to strip his clothes off and run mad through the streets.

At least, that's how it was for a time.

Then, suddenly as it had come upon him, it began to desert him.

What had been warm and inviting and peaceful became cold and awful, a December wind blowing through his skull and turning everything inside him into white ice. And that voice, that terrible goddamned voice began to say things, things that reminded Shore of who and what he was and that was not a good thing. *Benny...Benny, just what have you done?* it kept saying. *What in God's name has happened to you? What do you think you are doing here? You just ran over a kid at the school, goddamn Billy Swanson...you ran him over and kept running him over...that's murder, you crazy sonofabitch! Don't you realize what you've just done? You've committed MURDER!*

And, God in heaven, why didn't that voice just leave him alone?

Why didn't it go away? Because that voice was cruel, inflexible authority and Shore did not want to be part of that world of board meetings and budgets and committees. He wanted to run free with his nose to the ground. He wanted to lift his leg and piss on trees. He wanted to find a female and mount her. He wanted to hunt prey and bring it down with his hands. He wanted to feel the meat beneath his teeth and the blood on his tongue.

He wanted, *needed,* these things.

Alive and vital and free, stripped of boring authority and meaningless purpose.

But the voice reasserted itself and it began to speak to him like he spoke to kids at school, kids that cut class and smoked in the bathrooms and got into fights. It kept at him and at him, cutting and sharp. *Murder, murder, murder.* And that's when the mirror maze opened in his head, showing him as he now was—shaking and sweating and shocked, streaks of white in his hair—and as he had been—demented and giggling and kill-happy—and as he would soon be—a mad thing hunting through fields and woods.

No, please, no, no, no...

Yes, the mirror maze was open and it didn't even cost a dime for admittance and Shore was lost in its corridors, seeing himself, reflections of who and what he was and who he would never be again. Yes, Benny, Benny, Benny. And not just himself, but high windy gallows and cold graveyards and rising tombstones with open, waiting graves. It was all there in the mirrors, all the insidious things that had been set loose inside him, they were all showing themselves. Dirty, monstrous, crawling things.

And they all looked like him.

Distorted, narrow and blown-up and slinking, jumping and dancing. But *him*.

Oh, dear God.

He tried to squeeze his eyes shut so he would not see those faces, those Benny Shores sticking out their tongues at him, laughing and drooling and jibbering. Would not see himself running over a boy named Billy Swanson and giggling madly at the very idea.

Yes, slowly, painfully, it all began to fade.

Even the mirrors were dissipating like morning mist. The last things he saw in their smoky, polished surfaces were all those deranged Benny Shores running away from him, hating who he was becoming again, hating his authority and his look and his smell and his touch that was sterile as fresh bandages. Yes, Benny, Benny, Benny, childhood Benny and teenage Benny and adult Benny and Principal Benny running and running with a flurry of night-echoing footsteps. And then it was all gone, not even a reflection of the heat and perfection of that other simpler, baser world he had known and loved even as it now repelled him.

Now there was just...Benny Shore, the principal of Greenlawn High School. Just Mr. Shore and his stern voice and disapproving glare. *No running in the halls! Where's your hall pass? Don't throw food in the cafeteria! What's wrong with you kids? What are you, animals? Savages? Do you think this school is somewhere to run free and wild? Is that it?*

A block away from his house, Shore stopped the Jeep and jerked at the reflection of himself. That silly, sweating, trembling middle aged man who was broken, shattered, reduced to pieces like Humpty fucking Dumpty. He had to think, he had to reason.

Yes, he had to get home.

To Phyllis and little Stevie and Melody. Yes, he had to get to them and gather them up, get them out of town before the madness got them, too, and they did something truly horrible. He would not let his family be sullied like that. He could not and would not allow it.

Drive, you idiot.

He made Tessler and saw people standing on the street, looking either lost or mad and maybe they were both. Some woman was laughing uncontrollably on the sidewalk. Just beside herself. And as Shore passed he saw why. There was a little hill that led down through the grass to the river. And in the water, maybe ten feet out, was a baby stroller bobbing...something small and pink bobbing next to it. She had pushed it down the hill, laughing maniacally as it bumped its way to the river and went into the drink.

Shore sped up.

They were all crazy just as he had been. Down the block from his own house a girl was getting raped by a couple men, right there on the lawn of a house. And like the crazy mother, she was not only laughing, but crying out with mad ecstasy. Yes, this was the world, the new and not so shiny world of Greenlawn.

Shore pulled into his driveway and ran up to the porch.

He could smell supper cooking as he entered the door...spices and herbs. Phyllis was preparing the evening meal, humming as she always did. He could hear her chopping things and dicing things on the cutting board. Water was boiling and steam made the air in the house heavier than it already was. Shore mopped perspiration from his face.

"Phyllis!" he called out. *"Phyllis!"*

She kept humming and he darted into the kitchen. There were carrots and celery and potatoes chopped on the table. Two big pots of water boiling on the stove. The oven preheating. Jesus, the heat in there was unbearable, just stagnant and consuming like midday in a tropical jungle. The windows above the sink were steamed white. Water was dripping.

"Phyllis!" he called again.

"What is it, Benny?" her voice said, coming from the doorway that led into the pantry.

"We have to leave! We have to get out of town!" he said, pulling off his coat and loosening his tie. "C'mon, something's happening out there! We have to get out of here right now! Get the kids and your Aunt Una! We have to go right now!"

"Oh, don't be ridiculous, dear," Phyllis said. "You're overreacting. We'll have supper and talk about it."

"Goddammit, we're leaving! We're leaving right now!"

Before he could make the pantry door, Phyllis came walking out, completely naked, her body moist with a sheen of sweat. Her eyes glittered like jewels, shining and glimmering, an odd almost reddish tint to them.

And her head was shaven completely bald.

"What in the hell are you doing?" Shore said, even though something in his belly already knew the answer to that one.

"I'm making supper," she said, her eyes wide and staring.

He kept shaking his head. "But your hair...Phyllis, listen to me, we're leaving—"

"Oh, no we're not," she said and came right at him, was on him well before he could do anything about it. "We're staying, Benny, we're all staying, staying, staying..."

And as she spoke, the gleaming butcher knife kept coming down, finding Shore's throat, his eyes, his chest, his belly, until he fell at her feet and still the knife came and kept coming until the hairless, insane thing that had been his wife was spattered with drops of blood...

32

Mike Hack had the girl roped-up and he dragged her down the alley, kicking her when she wouldn't move. He had caught her digging through an overturned garbage can and jumped on her, beating her senseless. Like him, she was naked. A scavenger. Once she was unconscious, he dragged her into the Sinclair's backyard. Then he cut some clothesline from their clothes poles and tied her up.

Bring me some gee-gee, some nice young gee-gee and don't come back without it.

That's what Mr. Chalmers had said.

He would be pleased with what Mike brought him.

"Move piggy!" Mike told the girl, yanking her along. "Move, piggy, piggy, piggy!"

The girl snarled at him. She was naked, streaked with dirt, her hair hanging over her face, stinking like the garbage she had been feeding on. Mike did not know who she was. He had never seen her before. He figured she was from some other neighborhood, come raiding, stealing what was theirs.

Those other neighborhoods, they're gonna try and take what we got, so we got to hit them first. We gotta take what they got. Their women, their food, their weapons.

Oh yes, Mr. Chalmers was going to be pleased that Mike captured one of them. And a young one, too. Female. When she was out cold, Mike had fondled her pert, upturned breasts and the wetness between her legs. It was the smell of this more than anything that had intrigued him.

But he was hungry.

God, how hungry he was.

He had been thinking of meat ever since Matt and he had tried to steal the meat in that yard and were ambushed. Now Matt was dead. The others had gotten him. Mike felt no remorse over this. His simple reptile brain had inserted its practical impulses: feed, fight, flee, find shelter.

The girl hissed at him and Mike kicked her, being careful never to get in too close so she could use her nails or teeth on him.

Up until five or six hours before, her name had been Leslie Towers. She was an honor roll student, a member of the Key Club and president of the freshman student body. That was five or six hours before. Now who and what she was was really anyone's guess.

Mike kicked her again and paused.

He was smelling meat again. Savory, juicy meat. But not raw. Cooked. A pleasant, mouth-watering odor of smoked meat. *Delicious.* He forgot about Mr. Chalmers momentarily and followed the meat smell. He dragged the girl along down the alley until he reached the Kenning's yard.

Oh, the meat.

A carcass of dog was spitted over a low fire, the air redolent with the fine, juicy smells of its dripping shanks. Mr. Kenning was squatting there, slowly turning it over the flames with absolute patience and absolute rapture. His primitive mind was fascinated by the cooking meat, the flickering flames.

Mike knew he had to have some of that meat.

One way or another.

But the girl snarled again and Mr. Kenning turned. He had a knife in one hand. He rose from the fire, his body greasy with yellow dog fat he had smeared over it and slicked his hair back with.

"Are you hungry, boy?" he said.

Mike nodded.

"I have a nice dog here. It's very tasty. I will share it with you if you will share what you have with me."

Mike's simple brain tried to reason it out, but reasoning was getting harder and harder. Mr. Chalmers would be angry if he didn't bring the female to him. But Mike did not care. He wanted the meat. And he could have it without a fight, just by sharing. Simple animal desire quickly overcame reasoning.

"What do you bring me?" Mr. Kenning asked. "What do you offer?"

"This," Mike said, yanking on the clothesline that snared the girl's wrists and dumping her into the grass.

Mr. Kenning appraised her. "Lay it at my feet."

Mike dragged the girl over to him and Mr. Kenning kicked her until she stopped thrashing. He sniffed her length, licked her throat, slid a finger into her. He nodded. The offering was pleasing to him.

Using his knife, he cut a greasy slab of meat from the dog and handed it to Mike. It was hot, sizzling, but Mike tore at it with his teeth, filling himself with its salty richness.

Together, wordless, they ate.

When they were done, Mr. Kenning raped the girl. Then he showed Mike how to do the same...

33

"Listen to me, Dick," Louis said to the mud-covered man with the axe, the man who had once been Dick Starling. "Just listen to me, Dick. We've been friends for years, you and I. Just please put down that axe, all right?"

"Friends?" Dick said, as if he were trying to make sense of that word.

"Yes, Dick. We're friends. I trust you and you trust me."

Dick cocked his head like a confused animal and grunted. A low guttural sound that was completely unnerving. Filthy with mud and blood, dry leaves and sticks clinging to him, he looked like some primeval savage.

"Dick? Do you understand?"

Dick Starling just stood there, darkness filling his eyes and looking like it wanted to spill out like tears. His mouth was hooked in a contorted grin and he was breathing very fast, his chest rising and falling. He looked from Macy to Louis, couldn't seem to make up his mind what he wanted to do.

But he was thinking.

You could almost hear the primitive machinery of his mind whirring. And Louis was pretty much thinking that it was a very simple mind that Dick Starling now possessed. Gone were all the things that had made Dick, *Dick*. Whatever powered that brain, it cared not about the NFL or swimsuit calendars or basketball pools or sports betting. It had lost interest in the '66 Camaro kept under the tarp in the garage, the one the old Dick babied, buffed and polished and tuned, taking it out only for vintage car shows. Things like that meant nothing to the new and improved Dick Starling. He didn't even give a shit about his wife or his two daughters.

All of that had been replaced by much simpler imperatives...to hunt, to kill, to fuck, to eat. Maybe Earl Gould was right.

All of them out there...animals, they are regressing to animals, throwing off the yoke of intelligence and civilization, returning to the jungle and survival of the fittest...

"Dick," Louis said, his voice very calm even though his heart was trying to pound a hole through his chest. "Dick...listen to me. It's important that you hear what I say."

But Dick didn't seem to think that was important at all.

What was important here, friends and neighbors, was getting this fine piece of teenage snatch and raping it, then maybe slitting its throat, letting that hot blood pour into your mouth because that was the world's oldest orgasm, the smell and taste and *feel* of the blood. Only tightass Louis Shears didn't seem to know that because...well, because, he was still hung up on outdated, trifling things like morals and ethics and civilization.

"Louis," Dick finally said and it looked like it took some real effort just to be coherent. He shook his head, licked his lips. "Louis, goddammit, don't go fucking up things. I'm taking that bitch and you can either join in or I'll go right through you. How's that sound, old pal?"

Louis was scared.

Hell, yes. Like watching your best friend change into a werewolf right in front of you. Because, honestly, the change was that complete, that total. Dick was a slavering, shaggy monster, hungry for conquest and meat. Everything that civilization, his parents, and environment had taught him were acceptable behavior had been thrown right out the window. What was left, what was in control of him, was something much older, something atavistic and basic, something from the dawn of the race.

"Dick, you're not touching the girl. I can't let you. I think inside you know that. Just try and think, Dick. Try and be rational, okay? You were always a good man and I think some of that goodness is still in you."

"Fuck you, Louis."

Louis stood his ground. "Don't do it, Dick."

Don't be threatening, Louis warned himself. *He's just an animal. If you get territorial on him, he'll have to fight you. He won't have a choice. You push him into a corner, he'll come out clawing.*

Which was pretty good advice, but Louis figured Dick was locked hard in an aggression mode and he was going to attack either way. The thing was, though, you couldn't let him see fear and at the same time, you couldn't appear too threatening. Dick had to be treated like a mad dog, nothing more.

"Where's Nancy, Dick? Where's your wife? Where are the girls?" Louis said, hoping this would be like a slap across the face.

"Nancy...Nancy's dead. I killed her, Louis. She didn't understand how it is. She fought against it. She didn't see how...*pure* things are now. So I took this axe and I fixed that bitch."

"Louis..." Macy said.

But he couldn't risk taking his eyes off Dick for even a second. He was not a fighting man. He was not a violent sort. But down deep he was a man as any other and if it came down to it, he would fight to protect what was his. He would not sacrifice Macy to Dick Starling. He could not and would not let that happen.

"Get out of my way, Louis."

"Can't do that, Dick. You know I can't." He just shook his head. "C'mon, Dick. Think, try and think—"

"I don't wanna think! I hate thinking!"

"—please, Dick, just try. Something's happening in this town. Some kind of sickness has gotten people and it's got you, too. It's making you do bad things."

"Yeah, you're right, Louis," he said, "and I've never, ever felt so alive before."

Enough conversation and they both knew it.

Louis would have had an easier time convincing an ironing board it was a doorstop than changing Dick Starling's mind. Louis steeled himself and Dick attacked. He made another coarse grunting sound in his throat and swung the axe with everything he had, two-handed. Louis ducked past it and the blade struck the refrigerator with a clanging sound, denting the front right in and leaving a six-inch gash. Macy screamed and Louis shouted and Dick snarled, bringing the axe back around. The blade missed Louis' chest by a scant two or three inches. But the backward swing through Dick off balance and Louis went right at him, grabbing the axe handle in both hands and fighting with everything he had for it. Under ordinary circumstances, it might have been a dead heat. Louis was taller than Dick, but Dick outweighed him by thirty pounds.

But there was nothing ordinary about this situation: Dick Starling was an animal filled with animal fury.

Louis threw everything he had into it, trying to throw Dick off balance, but Dick wasn't having it. When he couldn't wrench the axe free from Louis' grip, he kicked and stomped and then put all his maniacal strength into it. And, dear God, what they said about crazy people being strong was true. Louis held onto the handle and Dick still swung it, swung it *and* Louis through the air, slamming him down on top of the table. Dick was just mad. His eyes were wide and shining, drool foaming from his lips, a stink of blood and bad meat coming off of him in rank waves.

"*I'll kill you, Louis!*" he muttered with almost a growling sound. "*I'll fucking kill you, kill you, kill you...*"

Louis hung on, giving Dick a few good kicks to the legs that did nothing but infuriate him. He kept lifting Louis up and slamming him back down again and again and Louis knew, just knew, there was no goddamn way he was winning this one. Dick would tire him out, kill him, and then...and then...

And that's when Macy stepped up behind Dick and struck him with an empty wine bottle. The impact was heavy. It made a hollow, thudding sound and it stopped Dick. He looked more confused than anything. Then Macy swung it with everything she had and it smashed right over his head in a spray of green glass.

He folded up instantly.

Dazed and disoriented, he tried to crawl across the floor at Macy, groaning and spitting. Louis jumped off the table and kicked him in the side of the head with everything he had. Dick went out cold.

"Thanks, honey," Louis panted, trying to catch his breath.

"He isn't dead, is he?" she asked.

Then Dick moaned. Nope, not dead at all.

"We better do something with him," she said.

Louis smiled at her. Little Macy was no cringing wallflower, not when she got her ire up. There were plenty of teenage girls who would have screamed and ran, but not this girl. If you had to be trapped in a nightmare like this, then Macy was the girl to be trapped with.

Louis reached down and grabbed Dick's ankles. "Open the door," he said.

Macy opened the back door and Louis dragged him from the kitchen, grunting and puffing. It was no easy bit. Maybe it looked easy on TV, but in reality dragging a full-grown man around was hard, sweaty work. And Dick was nothing but dead weight.

Louis got him to the steps and let him roll down. He heard Dick's head bang off the steps, but he didn't feel a single twinge of guilt over it. With Macy's help, he dragged him through the grass to the garage. It was no easy trick getting him through the door, but they did it.

"He's going to thank us for this later," Louis panted.

He took duct tape and taped Dick's wrists together behind his back, using a lot of it. Even a madman couldn't tear his way out. Then he took a length of chain and passed it around Dick's taped wrists and wound it around a support beam that went from floor to rafters above. He slapped a Masterlock on the chain and that was that.

Macy stared down at Dick. "You heard what he said, Louis. About his wife. About Nancy."

"I heard."

Louis hoped it wasn't true, but he figured it was.

Nancy, for godsake.

She was one of the nicest people you could hope to meet. When Michelle and he had moved into the neighborhood, she had been the first one at the door. She brought over a wicker basket with a bottle of wine and a loaf of bread in it. That's the kind of person she was.

Outside, Louis tried Michelle's number on her cell. Nothing.

"Maybe she's still at work."

Louis shrugged. "She should have been home an hour ago even if she worked late."

But he dialed up Farm Bureau anyway. It couldn't hurt. It was answered on the fourth ring and Louis brightened a bit. "Hello? Carol? Carol, is that you?"

Carol was Michelle's boss. "Who's this?"

"Louis. Louis Shears."

"What do you want?"

Louis was not feeling so bright now. He could hear it in Carol's voice: the madness. It didn't have her all the way yet, but she was close. Just teetering on the brink of darkness.

"Is Michelle still there?"

"No, she's not here. I'm here."

"Carol, when did she leave?"

"Who cares? What do you want her for, anyway?" There was a smacking sound on the other end that might have been Carol licking her lips. "I'm here, Louis. Why don't you come down. I'll wait for you."

Louis hung up. "C'mon, Macy, let's get out of here."

They ran to the car, but Louis already had the feeling that he was simply too late...

34

"I don't want to go crazy again," Macy said as they pulled away from the house. "I don't want to feel like that again."

Louis licked his lips, wondering if he should ask what he needed to ask. "Was it...was it very bad?"

Macy just stared straight ahead, but didn't seem to be so much looking out as looking *in*. She nodded her head slightly. "It was horrible. It was kind of blurry before, but now I'm remembering more. I mean, I knew what I did, I could recall it all right, but I couldn't make sense of it."

"But now you can?"

She nodded. "Yes, I can. I never liked Chelsea...that's the girl I attacked...I didn't like her then and I don't like her now. She's just a preppy, stuck-up bitch. I know I shouldn't say that, but that's all she ever was. She treated me like dirt. Always had. I never did anything to her, I never smarted off to her...nothing. But she always hated me, always had it in for me. She's just one of those people, right? Oh, look at me, look at how wonderful I am. I'm popular and special so that gives me the right to turn my nose up at everyone and be a snotty, uppity witch. So, yeah, I guess I hated her. I think most kids do, except for the idiots in her little posse and all the boys that drool over her."

"And you think the way you felt about her, that had something to do with it?"

Macy wrapped her arms around herself. "Yeah, I think so. Something in me always hated her, you know?"

Louis nodded. "I know, believe me, I know. Kids like Chelsea are nothing new, Macy. They've always been around, always treating other kids like shit. There were plenty of them when I was in school, too. Most of 'em need a good kick in the ass or a good slap across the face, but they never get it. The social elite. Most of 'em have money and think they're better than everyone else. That kind of nonsense starts at home and if the parents don't jump all over it when they see it, it only gets worse and worse and then what you have is a monster on your hands."

No, Louis did not have kids of his own, but plenty of his friends did and he saw it first hand. Spoiled, demanding, snotty brats that became impossible teenagers. Parents usually spoiled kids out of love, but that was the wrong kind of love. They weren't doing them any favors by letting them think they were better than anyone else and that the whole world simply existed for their convenience. Louis didn't know Chelsea Paris—thank God—but he'd known plenty of others like her. Kids so wrapped up in themselves and their own fleeting teenage food chain, spoiled and bossy and whiny, that when graduation came and they were thrust out into the real world, they were totally unprepared for it.

You were the most popular kid in school, eh? Prom queen? Cheerleader? Varsity quarterback? You knew all the right people and moved in all the right circles?

So what?

Once you stepped out of high school, the world at large did not care. It did not exist to assuage your ego or worship you or hand you things on basis of who you knew and who you blew. All that snotty, selfish, uppity behavior came back to bite you in the ass.

Show me a snobby little teen princess, Louis thought, and I'll show you a girl in for real trouble, in for a very rude awakening.

"Well, that's Chelsea, all right," Macy said. "A monster from hell. Her and Shannon Kittery and all the rest."

"Kittery, eh? Her mom must be Rosemary Kittery. I went to school with her. She married Ron Kittery. Back then she was just Rosemary Summers. Great to look at, but with all the personality of a rattlesnake. Cheerleader, prom queen, the works. A petite little blonde with a big set of...ah, well the boys liked her. Ron Kittery was a stoner in school. Just a total waste. Rosemary wouldn't even acknowledge his existence. Then she got out of high school and found herself in the real world. Ron's mom and dad had money, Rosemary's old man—Shannon's grandpa—was broke. He was president of First Federal, but they lived way beyond their means and he started embezzling. He was caught, of course. They hushed it up, but this is a small town and everyone knew. So what was little miss prom queen to do? She pursued Ron until he finally married her. And now she's turned out a carbon copy of herself in Shannon, I see."

Macy allowed herself to laugh. "Petite, blonde rattlesnake with big boobs? Yup, that's Shannon the magnificent."

They shared a chuckle over that and Louis was surprised, and not for the first time, how parents often managed to duplicate themselves, good or bad, in their children. It was actually kind of scary, when you came right down to it.

Macy was silent for awhile, then she said, "That's what it was about, Louis. That's what it was really about. I know that now. I'd hated Chelsea for years. And something inside me decided enough was enough. It rose up inside me, only I couldn't stop it. We all have crazy thoughts, but we don't act on 'em, do we?"

Louis nodded. "So you think that this...whatever this craziness is...it just plays on something already inside you? Lifts inhibitions? Maybe frees the beast within?"

"Yes!" Macy said, sitting up and startling Louis. "That's it! I always maybe wanted to punch her in the face or something, but I didn't. I kept those thoughts in the back of my head where they belonged. But this...whatever it was...it brought them to the front and instead of being able to say, no, you can't do that, I was like, well, *why not?* Why not give that little witch what she's been begging for?"

It made sense, this thing freeing all the darkness and black thoughts of the people of Greenlawn. Inhibitions neutralized, social constraints eroded, morals and ethics ground to ash...nothing left to stand in the way of your darkest, most repressed and dangerous fantasies. And when you yanked away things like civilization and morality...what was left? Just the malign shadowy side of the human animal, the barbarity and bloodlust and savagery which was our inheritance: animals...hunting and killing and raping, smashing anything or anyone that got in our way.

It was sobering, very sobering.

But the same dilemma remained: what was the vector, the mechanism which had infected those people? And why had it gotten to Macy and then released her?

Maybe Earl Gould wasn't far from the truth. Maybe he was, in fact, absolutely correct.

God help us, Louis, but we will exterminate ourselves! Beasts of the jungle! Killing, slaughtering, raping, pillaging! An unconscious genetic urge will unmake all we have made, gut civilization, and harvest the race like cattle as we are overwhelmed by primitive urges and race memory run wild!

Louis found that he was sweating.

He was terrified.

Was this how it ended? In a primal fall? A new Dark Ages of savagery that threw the human clock back 20,000 years if not fifty or a hundred?

Louis did not dare repeat any of Earl's theories to Macy. It was enough that he knew. More than enough. *Earl.* Good God, Earl. After the run in with Dick Starling, Earl and Maureen had not been out in the yard when Macy and Louis got out there to the car. And honestly, Louis just didn't have the heart to go looking for them.

Macy was just staring at her hands now as they drove. "The thing was, Louis, I...I didn't feel in control, you know? Maybe those thoughts were in my mind like they're in anyone, but it wasn't like I made a...*conscious* decision to set them loose. It was like being in a car and somebody else was at the wheel."

Louis swallowed. "Did you feel like you were being...I don't know...compelled somehow or controlled, something like that?"

She shrugged. "I guess. I knew what I was doing was wrong, but I couldn't stop myself. It was like something else was in charge. I know that sounds stupid, the Devil made me do it or something, but that's how it felt. And when it went away, I just burst out crying. I was scared, really scared. It felt like I was possessed or something, being taken over. It's dumb, but that's how it felt."

Louis sighed. "It's not dumb, Macy. But it is disturbing."

And it was that, all right. *It felt like I was possessed or something, being taken over.* That was merely Macy's subjective impression, of course, but if Earl was right, *if* he was right, then this possession was not some fantasy like diabolic influence or even mind control exactly, but something inherent in the human condition. Something ancient and absolutely evil.

"I guess I don't care what happens as long as I don't go nuts again," Macy said.

"Maybe you're immune now," Louis said.

"What about you?"

"I don't know. I don't know why it hasn't gotten to me. But maybe if it hasn't, it hasn't gotten to a lot of others, too."

Maybe. He just hoped he *was* immune. For wasn't it possible that if this was a genetic impulse of sorts, an ancient imprinting, that it might have been bred out of certain segments of the race or that it might malfunction in certain individuals?

He hoped so.

For the idea of becoming some primal beast was frightening. The idea that he might get "infected," might become something like Dick Starling.

Because if that happened...what might he do to Macy?

Louis shook it from his head, trying to tell himself that Earl Gould was nothing but a crazy old crackpot whose brain was soft from too much research, too many crazy old books.

But he didn't believe it for a minute...

35

When Rosemary Kittery, the mother of Shannon Kittery—Macy's old pal— tried to lock up K & G Apparel on Main that evening just after eight, three men came in and they had other ideas. She was hanging the CLOSED sign on the door and they burst right through it, nearly knocking her on her ass.

So much for subtlety.

Right away, Rosemary knew she'd made a godawful mistake by not just closing the doors at four or even five. Things were happening in town. Maybe you could, like Rosemary, tell yourself different, but the proof was in the pudding. The pudding in this case being two cops in dirty, ragged uniforms. Then a third whose uniform was unbuttoned, his bare chest and face painted up with what looked like blood. Like warpaint as if he was some fanatical Kiowa warrior preparing to die in battle.

Rosemary swallowed, doing her best not to scream outright.

"Evening," said the older of the three. He had white hair and a crooked mouth, a perfectly lopsided mouth truth be told. "Sorry to barge in on you, Miss..."

"Kittery, Rosemary Kittery," she said in a weak voice, not knowing what else she *could* say. But she knew she had to keep calm. Show no fear. These three were crazy, but she had to act like they were not. "Is...is there a problem?"

"She wants to know if there's a problem," the painted warrior said, a tall muscular fellow with blank eyes. "Don't that beat all."

The other cop, short and fat with a porcine face, just shook his head. "You see it all in this job."

The white-haired cop ignored them. "I'm Sergeant Warren," he said. "These two are Shaw and Kojozian. Don't pay 'em any mind. Last thing you want to do with a couple sick bastards like this is pay them the slightest attention. You do...well, look out."

"Yeah, look out," Shaw said.

Kojozian chuckled. "The Sarge is right, ma'am, you get me going and I'm a real barrel of fucking monkeys. I lose control, I like to start putting my hands on people, you know? Sometimes I touch 'em in all the wrong places. I'm funny like that."

"For chrissake," Shaw said, "you're gonna scare her. She don't need to know about that. Don't you pay him no mind, ma'am."

Rosemary, a slight blonde woman pushing forty who still maintained her varsity cheerleader figure, blinked her big blue eyes a few times. "I won't," she said.

Dear Christ, look at their eyes.

Just look at their eyes.

Something was missing there and something else had taken its place.

"Both of you shut up," Warren said. "We're here on business. If anybody's gonna paw up this broad it'll be me." He smiled at her. "No offense, ma'am."

Okay, this was not good.

Rosemary had seen this one before, this Warren. Maybe in the paper or around town. He'd been a cop forever. At first she hadn't recognized him. It was as if he'd undergone some subtle change...maybe his face was too long or too wide, his eyes too sunken. It was there, something was. Looking at him and the other two, she knew she had to play this cool, play it natural. Because there was no getting around the condition of their uniforms or the fact that they were stained with blood. A lot of blood. What she thought were freckles on Warren's face were not freckles at all.

She smiled thinly, wanting very much to scream. "Well, you said you were here on business. How can I help you?"

"She wants to know how she can help us," Kojozian said.

"Maybe you ought to show her," Shaw said.

Warren sighed and lit a cigarette. "Why don't the both of you pipe down? Thing is, ma'am, our uniforms are looking pretty bad. And we're cops, you know? We have to keep the peace and Greenlawn don't want its peace-keepers parading around in rags like this. We were eyeing up those trenchcoats in the window, the khaki ones. They look pretty smart."

Rosemary just stood there, their eyes on her. They did not blink. They did not do anything other than burn holes right through her. "Well," she finally said. "Why don't you try them on?"

"Yeah, that's what we were thinking," Warren said.

Shaw and Kojozian knocked displays out of the way getting to the trenchcoats in the window and all Rosemary did was keep smiling. It seemed that her smile was painted on. She didn't think she could have pulled her mouth out of it even if she wanted to.

The cops put on the trenchcoats right over their ragged uniforms. Warren's fit him all right, but the other two were big men and they couldn't begin to get them on. Kojozian tried damn hard, splitting open a few seams in the process.

"Look what you did!" Warren said.

"Oh, it's no problem," Rosemary said. "You need bigger sizes is all. I have a couple more in the back room. I'll get them. Try on some hats while you wait."

They bought it, seemed to be buying it.

"Do what the lady says," Shaw told the other two. "Goddamn monkeys."

She went into the back room at a leisurely pace, humming under her breath, taking the time to straighten a display of shoes as she went. She was good, she knew she was good. She'd been in the high school drama club and it certainly showed. In the back room, she moved around some boxes so it sounded like she was doing something. She could hear them muttering to themselves, admiring Warren's trenchcoat. It was hot and muggy out there and they wanted trenchcoats. *God.*

Breathing hard, Rosemary slipped out to the loading dock. She could still hear them. They were arguing. While they were thus engaged, she slipped out the rear door, closing it quietly behind her. Oh, it was going to work, she was really going to escape and she knew it.

The heat of the day hit her as soon as she stepped out into the alley.

She jogged around the side of the loading dock and they were waiting for her.

Not the cops.

No, the children.

Maybe not children exactly, but *teenagers.*

Fifteen or twenty of them and they all looked like the cops...bloody, faces streaked with grime. She recognized more than a few of them from school, from parties Shannon had had. Holly Summer and Janet Weiss, Kalen Archambeau and Brittany Starling. Sure, the gang was all here. Tommy Sidel, Shannon's boyfriend, was even there. All the girls from school.

And Tommy. That was not only strange, but disturbing. But what was even worse was that they were all naked.

Completely naked.

Rosemary opened her mouth to say something, but she knew it was probably pointless. Their eyes were simply dead, their faces pale, their mouths grinning.

She tried to move past them and they tightened their circle, staring and staring. And those faces, dear God, just bleached of anything remotely human. A few of them were drooling and more than a few had dried blood smeared around their mouths as if they'd been chewing on raw meat.

"Please," Rosemary said. "I need to get past."

But they stood their ground.

Behind them was a huge pile of rubble. It was the remains of Hobson's Shoes that had burned down the winter before and finally been demolished. The kids all had chunks of red brick in both hands. Good size pieces, broken and jagged.

"Tommy," Rosemary said. "Let me go, okay? We'll go home and see Shannon, all right?"

But he just shook his head. "No, you won The Lottery."

"Yes, The Lottery," another said.

And soon they were all chanting it with dead voices: "*The Lottery, The Lottery, The Lottery, The Lottery...*"

The Lottery? *The Lottery?* It didn't make any sense, but then again, maybe it made all the sense in the world. They sure as hell weren't talking about the state lottery drawing, Winfall or Megamillions, no this particular lottery was of a much darker variety and she damn well knew it. Because right then as they ringed her in and she saw the stark madness in their eyes and what they were holding in their hands, she knew. She *knew.* Because they were all around Shannon's age and Shannon had been reading a story for school called "The Lottery." Rosemary knew the story. She'd read it in school herself. And in that story, the person that won the lottery was—

"No!" she said to them. "You can't do this! You can't do what you're thinking!"

"Yes, we can," Tommy said.

"Please!" she cried, holding out her hands in supplication. "That's just a story! It's not real! You can't do this! You can't do something like this!"

Now they were grinning and raising the shards of brick in their hands. Behind her was a wall and before her, only the kids themselves. If she wanted out, she would have to go right through them. But it was too late, because it began. Rosemary ducked under the first few shards, but others struck her legs and chest. She cried out in pain and two more shards struck her head, putting her right down to her knees.

And then all the children came forward.

They threw more chunks of brick and with everything they had. Rosemary's scalp was cut open, her flaxen hair going red with a blossom of blood. Another hit her nose hard enough to break it. Another knocked three teeth out of her mouth and still another peeled the flesh away from her cheekbone. And they kept coming, stones and rocks and missiles, knocking her senseless. Before she fell, a cruelly aimed hunk of brick caught her right in the left eye, smashing it to pulp right in the socket.

And through bloody vision she saw her daughter there amongst them.

Shannon stood there, grinning.

"WHAT IS THE LAW?" she said. "WHAT IS THE LAW?"

With a wet and tormented moaning coming from her lips, Rosemary pitched straight over and then the kids circled around her, pummeling her from above with more shards of brick until she stopped moving, until her legs kicked with weak spasms and blood ran from her shattered skull and punched-in face.

Laughing, the kids kept at it for some time...

36

Night was coming fast now and Mr. Chalmers, content now for perhaps the first time in his life with who and what he was, smelled it on the breeze. Dogs howled in the distance and he listened, judging from the sounds just how far away they were and if they presented any danger to his clan.

He was watching his hunters by the fire.

In what had once been his backyard, they were hard at work applying what he had taught them. Using the limbs of straight saplings, they were fashioning spears. After the limbs were peeled, the ends were split so the blade of a knife could be inserted and lashed into place. Now they were fire-hardening the points as he had also showed them. Chalmers himself had learned this technique in survival school while he was in the Army. And though much of his former life was now misty, indistinct, or absolutely incomprehensible, he remembered this.

Somewhere, a few streets away probably, there rose a chorus of blood-curdling screams. They came and went, rising and falling with a rhythmic cadence. These were not the screams of agony or fear, but of *joy*. The night was coming and the clans were getting excited for the barbarity and promise that only darkness could bring.

Chalmers had once been married. Many, many years ago. His wife had passed on and he had never remarried, remained childless to this day. But he had always wanted children, felt the paternal pangs for a brood of his own. And then, as he entered his sixth decade, the pangs for grandchildren.

Now he was satisfied.

Now he had children.

They were his hunters: a ragged, disparate group with naked, oiled skin, dirty faces and grubby bodies painted up with earthen browns, electric blues, and blood reds. As he watched them by the fire, he saw that they had threaded and knotted beads, feathers, and tiny bones into their hair. With their naked, lithe bodies and the ritual painting, it made them look fierce.

There were a dozen of them. The youngest was six and the oldest was twelve.

Their parents had abandoned them—heeding the call of the wild that had been activated within them to run free—and Mr. Chalmers had brought them together into a cohesive whole. And tonight, he would lead them against the other clans.

Mr. Chalmers still wore his favorite khaki pants, though very dirty now, and boots, but he had torn off his shirt and took to wearing his dead wife's fox coat that had been stored in mothballs in the spare bedroom. He had cut off the sleeves so that all could see the many tattoos sleeving his arms from his days in the Army. Although for many years he had kept them covered, grim reminders of his days in the Vietnam War when he led reconnaissance patrols and hunter/killer teams deep into enemy territory, he now revealed them. They were badges of honor, symbols of military blood rites, of combat and life-taking.

The children, his clan, respected him and knew he was their leader.

Those that dared question that, he had beaten. And one particularly arrogant fifteen-year old boy, he had murdered, slitting his throat using the same knife he had carried during the war: a K-Bar fighting knife with a ten-inch carbon steel blade. He now wore the boy's ears on a necklace around his throat along with his scalp.

The screams rose up again.

The clan jumped around the fire, imitating the sounds, bristling with excitement for the hunt that would begin soon, the raiding against other neighborhoods.

His blood running hot and sweet, Chalmers felt more like a man than he had since his days laying ambushes along the Ho Chi Minh Trail many years before. He had a plastic tube of eyeliner in his hands. Breaking it open with his K-Bar, he covered his fingertips in the black make-up. Carefully, just as he had in the war, he painted black tiger-striped bands across his face, darkening his chest and arms.

Tonight, after so long, he was returning to the jungle...

37

As they got closer to downtown, they stopped talking. Maybe the conversation hadn't been much to begin with, but as they started getting a good look at the town and what was going on, it was like they had been gagged, rags shoved into their mouths and taped in place.

"It's the whole town," Macy said, not trying to hide the emotion that welled up in her now. It filled her, sank her down to new depths of despair. "It's the whole town, Louis! The whole town has gone crazy!"

"Just take it easy," he said, finding it extremely hard to take it easy himself.

But it was everywhere and it wasn't just a matter of feeling something was wrong now, for you could see it: cars were smashed and left out in the middle of the street, houses were burning, garbage cans were overturned, windows smashed, naked corpses sprawled in yards. Like a tornado of destruction had passed through.

Something had snapped here.

Something had given way.

The whole damn town needed to be buckled down in a straight jacket. Louis watched it all and he was just beyond words to sum it up in his own mind. You'd pass through blocks of wreckage and madness, then, two or three streets over, things seemed perfectly ordinary. People were washing their cars and walking their dogs and cutting their grass. But he had a pretty good idea that those people were not sane either. There was no way they had not heard of what was going down around them, yet they went about their boring little chores like all was well with the world. The only thing that gave Louis hope were the neighborhoods where there were no people at all, nothing to suggest there was anyone around but a few curtains parted to see who was driving by.

"Why isn't something being done?" Macy wanted to know. "They can't...they can't just let this happen. Where are the police?"

Louis was wondering the same thing himself. They should have been out in force, but he had yet to see a single patrol car. Though, in the distance, he *was* hearing sirens. Lots of sirens. He couldn't be sure if they were police vehicles or ambulances or fire trucks, but there were a lot of them.

He'd only seen a small portion of the town now, but he suspected it was going on everywhere. If that was the case, there would be way more happening than the locals could handle. Even with the state and county boys chipping in, it would be way too much. They would need the National Guard or something. Maybe they were already on their way and maybe not. Because, realistically, whatever was turning people into maniacs and animals, it wouldn't just be afflicting the civilians. Cops, too, would be mad as hatters.

Seeing it, unable to understand any of it, left him feeling confused and reeling. A chill went up his spine. It was just too much. A few crazy people was scary...but an entire town?

A country?

A *world*?

This is nothing, Louis, a voice coldly informed him. This is absolutely nothing. You just wait until tonight. It'll be dark soon and then you'll see some shit. Oh yes, you certainly will.

But he had no intention on being around by then.

Macy had had an episode herself, but it had been temporary. Was he hoping for too much in thinking that maybe it would only be temporary with the others, too? Was that even possible now? He didn't and couldn't know. But, the fact remained that he had not gone crazy. He had no wild urges or black thoughts. Absolutely nothing.

Not yet.

But if Earl Gould's theories were true—and Louis was beginning to think they were—then it was only a matter of time.

Regardless, if he was still normal, there had to be others. Maybe those quiet neighborhoods were full of normal people. People that had decided to lock their doors and wait things out. But what happened when the crazies were the majority? What happened tonight when they took the town and started kicking in doors and diving through windows, slaughtering the last of the rational ones?

Louis felt more afraid than he'd ever been in his life.

He wanted to drive out of town before such a thing became impossible, but he couldn't abandon Macy and he sure as hell could not just leave Michelle. And just where could he drive *to*? Another town filled with savages?

His hands were white-knuckled on the steering wheel, his teeth chattering. He had to do something, say something. Macy was just beside herself.

"Listen to me, Macy," he finally said, trying to sound cool and collected and probably failing miserably. "I need to get down town, I need to find Michelle. When we do, we're going to find that uncle of yours. What's his name?"

"Clyde," she said. "Clyde Chenier."

"Okay, we'll track him down."

"And if he's nuts?"

"We'll deal with that then."

But she was not reassured in the least. She was a tough kid. Louis fully realized that now, if he hadn't before. She was tough as nails. She was shaking in her seat, wanting to come apart, wanting to cry and scream and whimper, but she wasn't. And she wasn't because she was literally holding herself together.

"Macy," he said to her, touching her hand. "I'm going to get you out of this, okay?"

She nodded.

"I don't know what this is about, but we'll figure it out."

She turned and looked at him. "But it's not just here, Louis. It's everywhere."

He turned on the radio. Very few stations were even on the air and those that were, were not broadcasting live. Just taped stuff.

The local station was WDND, Cozy 102. It was the butt of endless jokes by the locals. But it was the only one broadcasting out of Greenlawn. Macy punched up the AM band and found 102 quickly enough. Louis didn't have it programmed in. An old school thrasher of the Black Sabbath/Deep Purple ilk, he just couldn't handle that tirade of elevator music. Give him some Zeppelin or Nazareth, but go easy on Bobby Vinton and The Kingston Trio.

"Here it is," Macy said, turning up the volume.

For a moment or two, there was only a building static that made them both tense up. Then the announcer came on, the same morbid-voiced guy who did the Daily Obituary Report at noon every day. He droned on in his usual monotone: "*Well, that was 'April in Paris' by Count Basie and his Orchestra. And before that, we had 'See Saw' by the Moonglows. Boy, I remember that one like it was yesterday. Yes, it's another lovely day in downtown Greenlawn. The sun is shining and the birds are singing and allll is right with world. Now don't go away, we got more mellow sounds for a mellow evening...Bobby Darin and the immortal Patsy Cline singing, 'Crazy.'*

"*You gotta love that. Craaazeeee. It really fits, don't it? I don't even know if anyone's listening by this point. In case any of you are, there's been no news out of continental Europe for six hours now. Same for Australia. In the Middle East, Tehran is burning. CNN reports that London is completely blacked-out. Satellite images confirm that the only light in London town is from burning buildings. God help us. And here at home...here at home, New York has fallen. There's a firestorm sweeping through LA. Chicago is a warzone. Don't know about anything else...internet is down now. Lost my AP feed an hour ago. I'm going to sign off now. Nothing left to say. Cozy 102 won't be broadcasting tomorrow. There won't be anyone left by then who even knows what a radio is. And, really, there won't be a tomorrow, will there? Only darkness. Bonfires and stone knives by this time next week, animals hunting in the streets...most of them of the two-legged variety. Now comes the time of the primal fall...*

"*Behold, darkness will cover the earth...and night cover the nations of man...*

"*May God help us...*"

Louis reached out and killed the radio.

Maybe the dead immensity of what was happening to the world did not hit him until that very moment. He heard Macy make a moaning sound next to him, but she was light years away. The realization of it all was like a storm of dust and debris and spinning shit inside his head. A sweat that was neither cold nor hot broke out on his face and his teeth locked together so hard that his molars ached. Everything canted this way, then that, and he knew he was going to pass out. Prickly heat swam up his belly to his chest.

*That kid and those cops and the mailman and Macy's mother
hanging in the cellar and Dick Starling had only been appetizers. Just
the beginning.*

Louis was going to black out. God help him, but he was
going to black out. He swung the wheel and hit the brakes,
popping the curb. Then slowly, the world stopped spinning and
he was just sitting there behind the wheel with Macy.

She looked at him and her eyes misted with tears.

"I'm okay," he said. "I'm okay."

But he wasn't. A person with a tumor chewing a hole in
their belly could say they were okay, too, but it didn't make it so.
Something had settled into this world and you didn't need eyes
to see it, you could *feel* whatever it was. It had settled into every
stick of wood and every brick, every roofing tile and every leaf of
every tree. It had consumed and polluted. And what it had done
to the flesh and blood things of that town was hideous beyond
imagining.

Louis sat there, hearing old Mr. Morbid on the radio,
again and again: *And, really, there won't be a tomorrow, will there?
Only darkness. Bonfires and stone knives by this time next week,
animals hunting in the streets...most of them of the two-legged variety.
Now comes the time of the primal fall...Behold, darkness will cover the
earth...and night cover the nations of man...*

Oh God in heaven, what was happening here and what
would happen tonight when the shadows were thick as sin in the
mind of an evil man and the moon rose high over the rooftops?

As he thought these things, he could see only Michelle.

Michelle with her big dark eyes that always seemed to
look not just at him, but into him, and that sweep of chestnut
hair that fell to her shoulders. He could see her when they'd met
years ago and he could see her now, the way her dark beauty
always made his knees weak and his heart seize up. He did not
even know if she was still alive, some mindless kill-happy animal
stalking the streets. He needed her, needed her like never before,
because he knew very well then and there that she was his
strength. It sounded corny and cliché, but it was true. He wasn't
much without her. He fed off her strength and confidence, that

unflappable sense she had to always do the right thing, the practical thing. He needed her hand to hold, he needed her voice to hear, and not just because he loved her, but because he was almost certain that everything he had done and would now do were the wrong things.

Macy wiped her eyes. "You heard what he said. You heard what he said, Louis. It's everywhere. There's nowhere to run."

"Yeah, I heard it all right. I heard it just fine."

"I'm scared," she admitted to him. "I mean, I'm really scared."

"So am I..."

38

In the Shore household on Tessler Avenue, Aunt Una woke from her nap and felt the crushing loneliness of her eighty plus years well up and fall back over her, crushing her flat with its permanence. Its weight was a physical thing like a graveyard slab pressing her flat, holding her down and letting her feel the ages eating her away, withering her to dust.

Oh God, oh God...

She opened her eyes and realized that, *yes*, she was alone and had been alone for many, many years. Sure, there was her niece Phyllis and her husband Benny, the kids...but that seemed precious scant consolation. Because her life, her *own* life, had been empty and wanting for years and it was only now, in that thin confused veneer of waking, that she realized the truth of her empty, cast-aside life. She went through the motions and put on a smile and urged a laugh now and again from her bosom, but it was all false.

Synthetic.

What she had now was a yellowed photograph in a scrapbook, something cocooned in dirty silk. Her life was not real, just an insect carapace on a sidewalk, dry and flaking, waiting for a boot to crush it or a good wind to blow it into a gutter.

The reality of it was gone and had been for very long now.

Charles had passed some sixteen years ago and her own children, Barbara and Lucy, were far away and rarely did they call and Una could not blame them. Why call a mummy at a museum? Why remind it of its slow dissolution in a glass case greasy with the fingerprints of the living things that watched it decay?

No, all of it was gone and she'd been pretending for far too long.

She sat up in bed, the minty odors of liniment and camphor rising up around her. She began to shake and gasp, clinging to the damp sheets beneath her. *Oh dear Christ, what have I been doing? Why did I allow this to happen? Oh, you silly, deluded, crazy old hag! Forcing yourself into their lives, making Phyllis take you in when you had nowhere else to go! You're nothing but a great sucking parasite that bleeds them of their life and vitality...don't you see that? Oh, you should be out at the town cemetery, right next to Charles, going to earth and feeding the worms and making the grass sprout green under those big, wind-creaky elms! That's what, that's what!*

At least you'd be accomplishing something!

Una, tears streaming down her face, age threading through her like cracks in the foundation of an ancient house, made herself stand. She did not know why she thought these things, but it was amazing she had never thought them before. The truth was a mirror that did not lie. Not about age or circumstance or exactly what you had become or *let* yourself become.

She stepped over to the window and saw Greenlawn laid out before her...the rooftops and spreading trees, flagpoles and church spires. Yes, all of it built and compacted into this space. It was designed for living things, not mummified old broomstick-limbed hags like her. She caught a reflection of herself in the glass and it was like a ghost hovering over the town itself. She could feel the creeping dryness of age, the dampness of the grave knitting her bones. And the horror of what she was and would never be again.

She stumbled over to the doorway.

She could smell things cooking downstairs, hear Phyllis humming and the kids chattering and laughing. Real, rich, living sounds. Those were not *her* sounds. Her sounds were rain on concrete vaults and autumn leaves blown over crypt doors, spiders spinning silent webs in night-black tombs, dead flowers and black soil and nitrous boxes held tight in the rotting belly of the good earth.

Una moved down the hallway to the stairs, standing there, feeling a silence within her that would never be disturbed by noise again. It was all she had, that coveting and enclosing silence, windy and longing and hollow. The sound of graveyards and empty places, listening churchyards.

Down the steps, then, one, two, three, four...

She could smell supper.

She'd always had a good appetite, but now that was gone. Skeletons were never hungry and scarecrows needed no bread. She could feel the aches and pains and stiffness of a life that had long since ceased to be productive.

She made it downstairs and suddenly, the children were quiet and Phyllis stopped humming. They were holding their breath, waiting, playing games on an old woman who had no more sunshine in her heart for games.

Una moved through the living room towards the kitchen. The smells there were meaty and thick and spicy.

Still, no sounds.

No sounds at all.

She came into the kitchen, saw them sitting in the dining room beyond.

Phyllis. Stevie. Melody.

They were naked of all things.

And bald.

They had shaven their heads. All of them were grinning, their chins shiny with grease. A strand of meat hung from Melody's mouth and she sucked it in. On the table was what they were eating, what Phyllis had been cooking. What she had chopped and sliced, stewed and boiled and baked and the smell of it was sickening. And the sight of it...*no, no, no, you old woman, you've lost your mind, you can't be seeing this! You can't be looking at this!*

"Sit down, Auntie," Phyllis said.

"And eat," said Melody.

"It's yummy," said little Stevie, jabbing something pale on his plate with a fork.

Una shook her head from side to side as a scream loosed itself from her throat. What was left of Benny Shore was spread over the table. The provider of this household who was even now *providing*. His limbs had been roasted and his viscera stewed, his blood was a soup and his entrails stuffed with jelly. And there on the platter, surrounded by browned potatoes and carrots, garnished with dill, was his head, glazed like a ham, his screaming mouth stuffed with an apple.

"Sit...down," Phyllis said, drool running from her mouth, her eyes glistening stones, staring with a fixed madness.

Una, screaming and mad, sat down.

Then the children were there, pressing themselves in, stuffing fat and pale meat into her mouth, pushing it down her throat with their greasy hands, filling her with the flesh and blood of their father while Phyllis held her. They emptied tureens and platters and serving dishes, dumping them all over Una, ladling soup over her head and shoving undercooked meat into her mouth until she could not breathe, not swallow, not do anything but fall from her seat, retching and retching, as they stood above her, grinning.

Then they fell on her with knives and teeth...

39

The boy's meat was sweet and rich.

The thing that had once been known as Maddie Sinclair slept off her repast of boy, bloated, gassy, and satisfied. She snored. Her limbs trembled. Naked and crusted with dried blood, fat, and marrow, she lay in a corner of the cellar where she had scooped an earthen nest out of the dirt floor, filling it with dry leaves. A section of the boy's entrails, half-gnawed, encircled her like garland. She lay there with her arms around her eldest daughter, Kylie, who nestled to her mother's pendulant breasts as she had done as an infant. They slept on, bathed in their rising stench, happy as any animals fattened from the kill.

The air was smoky, ripe with an odor of meat, blood, and urine.

Maddie's limbs shuddered as a dream ran through her simple mind. A primordial dream of the chase, the hunt, bringing down shaggy beasts with spears and arrows, bathing in the blood of immense carcasses.

She chattered her teeth, winced as gas rumbled from her backside, and went back to sleep.

The cellar was dim, moist, and smelled of black earth. Rather like a cave. It was this more than anything that had drawn Maddie here. Guided by untold ages of racial memory and primate instinct, she selected her lair as her ancestors had. The gutted remains of her husband were scattered across the floor along with some of his picked bones and drying flesh, garbage from several plastic bags. A wiry, muscular man, he had not been good eating. That's why the trap was laid that snared Matt Hack.

He had been most delicious.

A pit had been dug in the center of the floor and a low fire burned, smoke rising and filling the cellar with a dirty haze. The limbs of the boy, carefully dressed-out and salted, were hanging from the cobwebby beams above on ropes fashioned from his tendons and gut. Over the fire, suspended by a tripod, was the boy's stomach. It had been stuffed with organ meats and fat, sewn-up and now slowly smoked. His torso was dumped in the corner along with his head which had been broken open, brains scooped out.

Maddie's youngest daughter, Elissa, was still awake.

She squatted by the boy's head, running fingers along the inside of his skull, getting the last bits of buttery-soft gray matter that had been missed. Staring at what smoked over the fire with vacant eyes, she sucked her fingers clean. Like her sister, she was naked, streaked with grime and filth from head to toe, her flesh intricately cicatrized in patterns of welts and rising scars. Maddie was now similarly decorated. Elissa belched, ran dirty fingers through her fat-greased hair, dug a hole with her fingers and, squatting, shit into it. When she was done, she wiped her ass with a handful of leaves, then crouched down to sniff what she had produced. Satisfied, she buried it, flinging dirt over it like a cat.

Hopping on all fours, she crossed the room, intrigued by the smell of garbage on the floor. A heap of rotting vegetable matter stopped her. She sniffed it, chewed some, decided it was good. She rubbed herself with decomposing lettuce, pulpy tomatoes, bits of onion.

Then she went over to the nest.

Circling it three times, she wedged herself in next to her sister who reflexively encircled her with her arms. Then together the brood slept, dam and offspring, a knot of foul things, trembling with atavistic dreams, waiting for the night and the good hunting it would bring beneath the eye of the sacred moon...

40

Louis knew that the smart thing to do was to turn the car around and head right out of town. He was guessing there were only about a thousand voices in his head screaming for him to do this very thing...voices of instinct, survival, and self-continuation. But these voices knew nothing of love and devotion and duty. These were vague concepts to the voices, bigger and civilized things and they could not have cared less. All they cared about was living, was continuance, about saving the bacon of one Louis Shears who was preparing to jump right into the frying pan, fat side down.

So Louis ignored them.

He pulled over a little hill and entered Main Street from its far eastern edge, seeing all the familiar sights and familiar places that should have been calming, but now filled him with a mounting anxiety. He took it all in, trying to swallow and finding that he simply could not.

"We'll...we'll go over to Michelle's work, see if she's around. Then we'll go over to the police station," he told Macy and he thought it sounded pretty good, pretty reasonable considering the situation.

Macy was tense next to him. "Okay," she said.

Unlike many towns where the main drag was perfectly linear or seemed that way, Main Street in Greenlawn was a winding, serpentine affair and you could never reach a point where you could see more than a block ahead or behind you. They passed blank storefronts and little cafes, gas stations and bowling alleys, hardware stores and banks. It all looked perfectly fine. All except for one thing.

"Where is everyone?" Macy said. "There should be people around on a Friday night."

"Just take it easy, honey."

"C'mon, Mr. She—Louis. Look around, there's nothing. There's not even somebody walking a frigging dog," she said, alarm bells chiming just beneath her words. "It looks like a ghost town and it feels like one, too. Where are they?"

Louis tried to swallow.

She had a very good point, of course. They had seen life in other parts of town—along with a great deal of wreckage—but here it was simply dead. His window was unrolled and he no longer heard sirens or anything else, just the sound of the Dodge's engine, its wheels rolling on the pavement, a slight breeze in the trees overhead. But not a damn thing else. It was like in the last five or ten minutes, somebody had thrown a switch, shut everything off.

"They must be inside," he said.

"Why? Why would they be doing that?"

"I don't know."

"This is freaking me out."

It was an almost comical statement considering things, but he did not laugh. Main Street was a graveyard for all intents and purposes. Not a thing moved or stirred. There wasn't even a bird singing or a cat sunning itself on the sidewalk. Just a great, empty nothing. Yet, deep inside, Louis was certain that those houses and buildings were *not* empty, that there were people in them or things like people, things with eyes that watched the Dodge slowly roll past, waiting until it stopped, waiting until the man and girl got out and then, and then they would—

"There's the Farm Bureau building," Macy said.

Louis saw it, his heart thudding in his chest now.

It was on the corner, set back a bit with a parking lot out front. The building was red brick, kind of looked like one of those old school houses you'd see in the country sometimes. Even had a little belfry on top, but no bell. Louis remembered that it had been the post office when he was a kid, before they moved it to the end of Main. There were a couple cars parked in the lot, but none of them were Michelle's. Still, he had to look.

He pulled the Dodge to a stop and just sat there, getting a feel for Main as it, he thought, got a feel for him, too. He could smell flowers and grass, the heat boiling from the blacktop. He was feeling those eyes again, watching. There were people nearby and he knew it. They were hiding behind locked doors, in closets and cellars, peering from behind curtains and Venetian blinds. Just watching. Like a group of people waiting to yell, "SURPRISE!" when birthday boy walked in.

Louis figured that's not what they would say to him, though. It would be something unpleasant and dire...right before they slit his throat ear to ear.

"Well?" Macy said.

He stepped out and breathed in Main Street, felt it in his face. It was hot and still with a dark, sweet smell that he could not recognize, but knew did not belong. He listened for someone, anyone, even the sound of a car, but there was nothing but a flag flapping on the pole above Farm Bureau and wind chimes coming from an antique store down the way.

Oh, they're here, all right, Louis. All of them. They're playing the oldest game in the book. Maybe you remember it: hide-and-seek. They know where you are and if you get close enough, they'll jump out and tag you. Maybe with their hands, but probably with their teeth.

He came around the side of the car, noticing with some unease that the shadows were starting to grow long. It would be dark soon. The wind was hissing through the treetops and along the roofs with the sound of someone exhaling. He walked across the parking lot, the fear building in him, unsettling him. It was growing, getting big and unmanageable. He had no reason to be afraid, yet he pulled the lockblade knife out of his pocket and knew that he would use it if he had to.

He found himself looking around Main Street like he was seeing it for the first time. The tight rows of buildings, the alleyways cut between, all the little cul-de-sacs and stairways and shadowy recesses, the overhanging roofs...all the places someone might conceivably be hiding. He was looking at these things the way a soldier might as he edged into enemy territory.

"Louis," Macy said and her voice was heavy, breathless. "Look."

She was at his side, but as he had been scoping out the threat factor, she was only looking at the Farm Bureau building ahead of them. She was pointing at the whitewashed doorway with its gleaming brass knob. There was something on the door. A smear of something dark which he knew instinctively was blood. There was more of it on the doorknob. A few flies were investigating it. Swallowing, Louis unsnapped his lockblade and reached out for the door.

It was unlocked and whispered in without so much as a creak.

He stepped inside, into the chill air conditioning which made goosebumps break out along his arms. Quiet. It was dead quiet in there, but he felt that it was not unoccupied. Somebody had been here. Somebody who had left a vague trace of something dark, something evil.

The receptionist's desk was empty, as was the first office. Both were neat, undisturbed. There was more blood smeared along the walls and several handprints of varying sizes that must have belonged to several different people. Whatever had happened, it had been a group effort.

"I think we should leave," Macy said.

"In a minute."

The next office was Michelle's and as he rounded the doorway, he thought his heart would explode in his chest it was beating so hard. Because he was expecting to see her in there, slit open and covered in flies.

But this room was empty, too.

Her papers were neatly organized, a few potted plants on the desk, pictures from their wedding and others from Cancun last year that made him want to weep openly. File cabinet, computer, coat rack, impressionist painting on the wall...but nothing to indicate violence or anything out of the ordinary.

But something had happened here.

And as he got out into the corridor, Macy so close behind him that she bumped into him every time he so much as paused, he was certain of it. Even without the bloody handprints on the walls, he could smell the badness here. This place was infected like a sore and you could smell the evil oozing from the walls in a stark miasma.

"Louis..."

"Just another minute," he said.

Macy was right, of course. What they needed to do was get out of here before whoever or *what*ever that made those grisly prints returned. But he couldn't bring himself to leave. Something was pulling him forward down that corridor and demanding that he look at what was waiting there. Because there was an aura of menace here and he had to know what it was coming from, had to understand it and look it in the eye. At the end of the corridor there was another door, blood streaked all over it.

Louis could feel Macy tense up behind him.

He took hold of the door and threw it in. This was the office of Dave Winkowski, an adjuster. Louis stepped in there and the smell of blood was so strong he wanted to retch.

"Oh God," Macy said, turning away.

A woman's naked body was sprawled over the desk, drying blood splashed all over it. Louis knew who it was. It was Carol, the same woman he'd spoken to on the phone and not that long ago.

Her throat had been slit, blood splattered around everywhere. But worse, her skirt was pulled up around her waist and it looked like somebody had used a knife on her, flaying open her vulva and carving up her thighs with grisly abandon. It was not a crude hacking, but something almost surgical that had taken time.

Macy had only seen the body. Thank God she had not looked too close.

Louis grabbed her by the arm and pulled her down the corridor. "Let's go."

They left quite a bit faster than they'd come in. Out in the parking lot, the sun felt nice. The coolness of the insurance building left them and for a few minutes they just stood in the parking lot, at a loss for words.

"We better go," Macy said.

"Yes."

"I mean, somebody did *that*, Louis. Somebody who was insane. I don't want to be here when they show."

Louis followed her back to the car and just sat behind the wheel, not knowing what to do or what to say for the longest time. Most people went through their lives without having to find a corpse. But today, he had found two. Carol's butchered body and Jillian, of course. As he sat there he found the words leaping into his mouth, the words he knew he would have to say to Macy sooner or later: *sorry, kid, but your mother's dead. She's hanging in your basement. Tough luck.* And they almost came out, but he swallowed them back down in the nick of time.

"What?" Macy said, picking up on it. "Were you going to say something?"

But he just shook his head. "No, nothing."

"What now?"

He shook his head again. He pulled out his cellphone and called home in case Michelle was there. He let it ring until the machine kicked in. Then he broke the connection and tried again. Nothing. She wasn't home. She wasn't at work. Where in the hell was she?

"Who are you calling?" Macy asked.

"The police. This is fucking ridiculous."

He dialed the station house and then dialed it again because he thought he'd punched in the wrong number. But there was no answer. That was not a good sign at all.

"Nothing?"

"No."

"Try 911."

Breathing deeply, Louis did. The number rang. There was a clicking on the other end. He could hear someone breathing over the line and it made gooseflesh swarm over his forearms.

"Is somebody there?" he said.

"Hey, looks like I got a live one," a man's voice said.

"Who is this?" Louis demanded.

"Who do you want it to be?"

Louis swallowed. His throat was dry as ash. "Listen to me. I'm calling from Greenlawn. We have an emergency here. We need help, okay."

"Where are you?"

Louis almost told him, then he thought better of it.

"Where are you?" the voice wanted to know. "You tell me...I'll send somebody to get you."

Louis broke the connection. He was pale and sweating.

"There, too," Macy said, fighting back a sob. "There's no way out of this."

"We're going to the police station," he said, trying to sound confident.

But even then he knew he was making an awful mistake...

41

The Huntress waited behind the dusty glass of a second hand store.

She watched the man and the girl get into the car.

There was something about the man she remembered, as if perhaps they'd been joined at one time. The more she watched him, the more she was certain of it. Just the sight of him made her blood run hot, made her heart beat in a delicious new rhythm. She licked her lips. She clutched the hunting knife in her hand very tightly.

The Huntress could no longer remember who she was.

She could no longer remember *why* she was.

It seemed that the way she'd been living these many hours was the way things had always been. Flooded with the primal memory and instinctive recall that had swallowed all that she was or ever had been with a simple plunge into the ancient black waters of prehistory, she was content. Content with the hunt, content with the kill. What more was there?

The car moved slowly up the street.

Hiding in the store, the others of her clan waited breathlessly. They wanted to hunt. They wanted to bring down prey with claws, teeth, and gleaming blades. She could smell the raw animal stink of them and it excited her. She led them because she was cunning. They were brutal, bloodthirsty, but almost idiotic in their simplicity. They understood only savagery, the law of the beast, kill or be killed, and they raided in such a fashion: with berserk, screaming mania. She, however, understood tactics, ambush, stealth. They were in awe of her.

One of them made a grunting, slobbering sound.

"Wait," she told them. *"Not just yet."*

She was tall and raven-haired, lean with rippling muscle, her eyes just as dark as the animal inheritance that misted her brain. Intrigued by the man, she trembled. Everything inside her—from heart to liver to lights—was pulsing, thrumming, anxious.

The Huntress had a vague recollection of the girl.

But that was unimportant.

She would have the man to satisfy her curiosity about him. And the girl? She would be killed or enslaved to amuse the sexual appetites of the clan...

42

Ray Hansel was alive.

He staggered down Main to where his patrol car was parked. The streets were silent now, deathly silent. There were bodies strewn about, the carcasses of dogs. Blood and entrails everywhere, a reeking fly-specked stew in the streets and spread over the walks. He was dazed and hurting and half out of his mind. As he walked—staggered, really—the sinking sun still hot on his neck, he tried to put it all together and make sense of something that was utterly senseless. He remembered the insane woman coming in, making for Bob Moreland's office, how they overpowered her. Moreland said it was his wife and then, and then...

And then you heard the screaming, he reminded himself. *The awful torturous screaming and you rushed downstairs right behind Moreland and every other cop that was up there. Remember? Remember how it looked? Men, women, children, and...dogs. Dozens and dozens of people and twice that many dogs.*

He seized up right there on the walk, a dead man at his feet, sprawled over the concrete. He had died in battle with a Doberman. The Doberman's jaws were locked on his throat, the knife in his hand still buried in the animal's guts. They were both tangled in the dog's viscera; it was knotted over them in fleshy ropes. Mangled and gutted, a surreal sculpture of human and canine locked in a fearsome and appalling death. Like two wax figures that had melted into one another. They both looked like they'd been dipped in red ink.

Choking on his own bile, Hansel moved past them, past the carnage spread everywhere.

All that blood, all those mutilated bodies.

He wanted to vomit, but there was absolutely nothing left in his stomach. His uniform was in rags. He was cut and bitten and scratched and generally banged-up. There was blood all over him, human blood and dog blood mixed in with his own.

He saw his patrol car and shuffled his way over, only stopping when he was a few feet away.

He looked around, his eyes glazed and his face scratched to the bone.

Are they all dead? Is the entire town dead now?

Logic told him it could not be, yet he'd never felt so terribly alone and terrible vulnerable. He wondered vaguely where his partner was. Where the hell was Paul Mackabee? Dead? Was he dead, too?

Standing there, he was wondering why the dogs had attacked.

Because when they'd first flooded into the police station with that mob of wild-eyed people, they had attacked *together*, dogs and people. In *unison*. All shrieking and howling and foaming at the mouth. It had been a slaughter, an absolute slaughter. The cops overwhelmed and buried alive beneath people and dogs.

Those weren't people, Ray, he told himself. You saw them...many of them were naked like animals, painted up like jungle savages, their hair wild and matted, their faces set, eyes shining with a moist blackness, just staring and staring. There was nothing human about that mob. Savages. Just savages out to rend and kill, bite and slash.

Same as the dogs that ran at their sides.

Yes, that's how it had been. He remembered pulling his gun as Moreland and the others in front of him had gone down under claws and teeth and fingers and paws. He kept shooting until he'd emptied the clip. He'd brained two women with the butt of his pistol and then ran back upstairs, the pack howling at his heels. He'd been bitten and scratched and nearly taken down by a pair of bird dogs, but he'd escaped.

Barely.

What he remembered most, what he would always see, was not just the blood and bodies, the dogs and crazies dismembering people and biting into throats and tearing open bellies, not just that or the violent, repellent stink or the mist of red that settled over the squad room...no, what he would always remember was that people, human beings, had been running on all fours with the dogs, biting like them, tearing like them, bringing down their prey in packs just like them. And the scariest part was that he honestly couldn't tell after a few moments which were the dogs and which were the people.

He saw only slaughtering, muscled, slashing red forms.

Dear God, dear God.

Hansel climbed into the cruiser and got on the emergency channel. He didn't bother with call numbers or police codes. He simply said, "This...this is Trooper Hansel! Do you hear me?

Trooper fucking Hansel! I'm in Greenlawn! I need back-up, I need troops! We've got bodies everywhere, civil unrest...move it, move it, move it!"

There was nothing but static for a moment or two, then: "Greenlawn! Come in, Greenlawn!"

Hansel brought the mic to his mouth, his hand shaking violently. "This is Greenlawn...do you hear me? This is Greenlawn!"

More static. Then a voice: "How's the hunting over there?"

The mic fell from Hansel' fingers.

They've all gone fucking mad. God help us, but they've all gone mad...

Then he did something that he had not done for six years since his wife passed: he pressed his hands to his face and he sobbed. He could not stop sobbing, his entire body trembling, the tears rolling hot down his cheeks. It all ran through his head, all the awfulness that he'd seen this day culminating with the slaughter at the police station. It all came pouring out of him and he could not stop, could not do anything but shake and sob until there was nothing left.

He was only alive because he'd gotten upstairs, gotten into a closet and stayed there. That's when the dogs must have turned on the people or vise versa. He remembered them scratching at the door, the dogs *and* the people, and then the screaming and shouting and growling and snapping. They had hunted side by side until there was no more game, then they'd hunted each another.

They turned on one another.

The fighting and savagery had gone on for some time and then things had grown quiet incrementally. When he finally dared go down there—about fifteen minutes ago—there had been nothing but death. The squad room was a carpet of bodies, human and dog, and parts thereof, a red sea of filth. There were dozens of corpses locked in death throes with the dogs, dog teeth in human throats and human teeth in dog throats. He had not paused to examine any of it. He made his way outside and threw up on the steps of the police station.

And now here he was, crying like a baby.

Well, this wouldn't do, this wouldn't do at all.

He had to get a grip, he had to get a set on him and start acting like a cop. Goddamn Greenlawn was a fucking warzone and somebody had to start setting things right and that somebody just happened to be Ray goddamn Hansel. Just because you got kicked in the nuts didn't mean you had to fold up and have a good cry, squat to piss the rest of your life.

No, sir, that wouldn't do at all.

Some kind of ugly door had been thrown open on this world, all the dark and crawly things creeping out and having themselves a real old fashioned slash-and-burn hoo-ha, and it was going to take some serious ass-kicking professionals to slam that door shut.

Hansel knew that he had to get ready.

But...shit...it was spreading everywhere. He couldn't fight alone, it just wasn't possible. What in the hell could this possibly be about?

He started up the car and pulled away down Main, taking the first corner he saw and making for the south side. He'd grab the county road outside town and make for the highway, find people, normal people, start marshalling the fucking troops like Patton hitting the Rhine with the Third Army. Kick ass and take names, holy Jesus K. Christ.

As he drove down Providence Street, one of the main thoroughfares that ran from one end of town to the other, he saw wrecked cars, bodies in the streets, burned houses and abandoned city vehicles. He even saw a firetruck, doors hanging open, hoses unrolled and attached to a nearby fire hydrant, but not a soul around to work them.

This will be the biggest, ugliest clusterfuck this world has ever seen. Years from now, they'll still be trying to figure this out.

If there's anybody left to do the figuring, that is.

If the madness isn't permanent.

If I live to see it.

If this whole goddamn country isn't a slaughterhouse by then.
If...
If...
If...

If civilization could survive this fever, the whole goddamn country, the whole goddamn world, would be like ripe meat and the media were the buzzards that would pick it clean. The stain of this day and what was yet to come would never wash off for a hundred years.

He kept driving and then he slowed...slowed right down because something was not right. In his head...something was just not right. It felt like a swarm of black flies had been loosed in there, buzzing and crowding and filling his skull. He hit the brakes and skidded to a halt. He couldn't seem to remember what he was doing or even who he was for a moment or two. It was like there was some devastating influence taking his mind, some invasion that was stripping away who and what he was.

He sat behind the wheel, his mouth hanging open and his eyes glazed.

He caught a glimpse of himself in the rearview mirror and what he saw looking back at him made him want to scream. A stranger. A perverse caricature of himself...something lunatic and twisted.

It's happening, a very tiny voice in his head informed him. *It's happening to you right now, Ray. This is what it feels like when the cellar door of your mind swings open and all the black, shuddery, forgotten things come loping out...*

And that was what he thought.

But he did not think it or even understand the train of thought for long, because suddenly he was *gone.* There was something else and someone else and there was no more rational thought as such.

He threw the cruiser in park very calmly.

He took the shotgun from the rack and stepped out into the sunlight. He could feel its warmth, the dying day and its final gasp of hot breath.

From deep inside, a voice was shouting at him, but he did not listen.

He gasped. He drooled. He shook and sweated and his heart raced. A wetness spread at his crotch. There was a shotgun in his hands and he brought the barrel up to his mouth, fingers on the trigger.

Goddammit, Ray, don't let this happen. Fight, fight.

He would not do that, he *could* not do that. Putting a gun in his mouth was against everything he was. Yes, fight, he must fight. So he strained his muscles, but they were soft and pliable like putty. He had no more control over them than he did his bladder. He fought, but it was hopeless. His hands brought the gun up and the barrel rose, leveling out and dropping until it was in his face. His mouth opened to receive it. A long, strangled moan came from somewhere deep inside him.

The barrel of that twelve-gauge pump slid into his mouth, cool and metallic and tasting of machine oil.

He was powerless, weak, empty. He was nothing. He did not exist. He was just doing what he'd always wanted to do, always needed to do on some subconscious level. He'd known other cops that had eaten the gun and he wondered if this is what it had been like for them in their final moments before they sprayed their brains over the ceiling. Did they feel like this? Overcome, crushed down, broken, violated?

Maybe, maybe, maybe.

It was his own will making him do this, yet it felt like someone else was in charge of him. Making him do things that were against everything he stood for.

His fingers started putting pressure on the trigger.

Then he just lost all strength. Whatever it was, faded and fell apart.

The gun slid out of his mouth and Hansel was overwhelmed with dry heaves. He fell, the riotgun clattering to the pavement. On his hands and knees, wringing wet now with sweat and piss, the smell of blood and dead animals thick on him, he began to sob.

Then a voice, "Hell you doing, Ray?"

He looked up. Paul Mackabee was standing there. His uniform blouse was torn, buttons missing. There was blood all over his hands, streaked across his face. His eyes were filled with shadows. And, worse, he had the bloody pelt of a dog slung over one shoulder.

"Paul...Jesus, Paul...*the whole fucking town...*"

Mackabee kneeled down by him. He stank like oily carcasses. "Sure, whole town, Ray. Whole fucking world. Quit fighting it. Just...relax...and let it happen..."

Hansel thought he was crazy, no better than the rest. But he was tired, drained dry from what he'd seen. There was no fight left. He closed his eyes and let the darkness well up inside him until it spilled out of his eyes in ribbons of night. When he opened them, Huckabee was still squatting there.

Hansel grinned at him. The bloody pelt over his shoulder exuded a rank odor. It smelled delicious...

43

Swinging his nightstick by its thong, Warren moved up the streets flanked by Shaw and Kojozian. He stepped over the naked corpse of a woman and past a couple of dogs feeding out of an overturned garbage can. Across the way, a car had crashed into a fire hydrant and water was flooding the streets. Kojozian went down on his hands and knees and lapped water from the gutter.

"What are you? Some kind of goddamn animal?" Warren said to him, pointing his nightstick at the big man.

Shaw folded his arms and shook his head. "You hear that, Kojozian? He wants to know if you're some kind of animal."

Warren thumped Shaw on the back of the head with his stick. "What are you? An echo? He heard what I said. You heard what I said, didn't you?"

Kojozian nodded, his face glistening wet, his streaked warpaint running some. "I heard you. I was just getting a drink is all."

"Well, don't be lapping like a dog," Warren warned him. "Remember, you're a cop. You're wearing the uniform. You want to drink from a puddle, cup your hands; don't lap."

"I was thirsty."

"Sure, he was just thirsty," Shaw said.

Warren stopped. "You see these hash marks here?" he said, pointing to his sergeant's stripes on his filthy uniform shirt. "These are experience. These say I'm in charge. And when I say a cop doesn't lap water like a dog you better believe I know my business."

They walked on, oblivious to the destruction and mayhem around them.

Yes sir, this was Warren's town. He was a cop and he kept the peace. When you wore the uniform for a living, people expected things from you. Warren was unconcerned that his uniform was untucked, stained with blood and dirt, he only cared that his badge was shiny and his hat was on. Regulations. If a man didn't live by the regulations, he lived by nothing.

He walked on.

The sun was sinking towards the horizon. It had been a fine day, Warren thought. A productive day. He looked up into the sky, noticing that a great many birds were circling above the town now...gulls, crows, ravens. A buzzard was perched atop a mailbox across the street. A flap of something was hanging from its beak.

They came upon the fleshy white corpse of an obese man out in the flooded street. A few more inches and he'd float away. A terrier with a blood-red snout was gnawing on his arm, a thin woman in a skirt and nothing else was chewing on his throat. Both seemed unconcerned that they were being watched.

Warren tipped his hat to her. "Evening, ma'am."

She hissed at him.

Just ahead they paused. There was the sound of screaming. Warren looked at the other two. "Sounds like somebody's having a party. We better break it up."

They jogged to the end of the street, came around a corner and saw something which stopped them dead. Warren tapped his stick against his leg. Shaw patted his round belly and pulled the survival knife out of his Sam Browne belt. Kojozian, bare-chested, painted and wild-looking, bunched his blood-stained hands into fists and raised his haunches. A State Police cruiser was pulled up at the curb across the street. Two uniformed officers that Warren thought looked kind of familiar were kneeling on the concrete. They had knives in their hands. Carefully, grunting and exerting themselves, they were peeling the scalps from two corpses, sawing away happily.

"Of all the things," Warren said. "Cops, Poaching in our territory."

A fuzzy half-memory swept through the archaic ruins of his mind. Those men. He felt he knew those men. *He could see them...around a fire, yes. Cooking trout in a pan. Drinking beer. A fishing trip. Yes, Warren had been on a fishing trip with these men. Ray Hansel and Paul Mackabee. Trooper Hansel. Trooper Mackabee. They were old friends of Warren's. Both old hands on the state force. Warren knew them well. Drank with them. Fished with them. Jesus, Ray and Paul—*

Then it was gone. He didn't know who they were and cared even less. Poachers. Goddamn poachers.

He sighed. "Sonsofbitches," he said.

"You seeing this, Kojozian?" Shaw said. "You seeing what I'm seeing?"

The big man shook his head. "I'm seeing it, but I'm not believing it. I think somebody ought to go over there and remind those monkeys that this is *our* beat."

"Well, why don't you?" Warren said.

"You think I should?"

"I insist."

"Yeah, I insist, too," Shaw said. "Of all the things."

Kojozian slid a length of chain from his belt. It gleamed in the dying light...except where it was stained with something dark. He walked right across the street, huge, long-limbed, almost ape-like in his stride. One of the state troopers looked up. He had a leather sash with human scalps sewed to it tied around his throat. When he saw Kojozian coming, he rose up, brandishing his bloody knife.

His eyes luminous with ferocity, he charged.

"This guy's not real bright," Warren said.

"No, he's not bright at all," Shaw agreed.

The trooper darted in, slashing at Kojozian as the big man swung the chain over his head. The trooper slashed, he jabbed, he tried to get in to draw blood. Kojozian stood there, oblivious to it all. He baited the trooper in. Thinking he had an easy kill, the trooper jumped in for a killing blow and Kojozian brought down the chain with all his muscle and weight behind it. The chain made a sharp whooshing sound and then made contact with the trooper's head. His scalp was peeled from forehead to ear and he went down to one knee, shrieking. Kojozian brought it down again and split the crown of his head open.

The trooper shook and shuddered on the ground, but he was done.

Kojozian stood over him, bringing the chain down again and again until it was dyed red and tangled with hair and meat.

Meanwhile the other guy came after him.

"Hey, you better watch it," Shaw called out.

But Kojozian was too intent on beating the other trooper into about two-hundred pounds of raw, red meat.

The trooper slashed with his knife and caught Kojozian across the ribs. He slashed his face, his arms, almost got his throat but Kojozian snapped the chain to his temple and down he went. Standing there, bleeding and dazed, Warren decided it was time to help him. He and Shaw went over there.

"You could've stepped in," Kojozian said.

"I thought you could handle them," Shaw said. "I guess I was wrong."

Kojozian grimaced. "I don't care for your tone."

"Easy," Warren told him.

"Fuck that," Kojozian said and punched Shaw right in the mouth. When he tried to get up, he punched him again.

Warren stepped between them with his stick. Good thing, too, because Shaw looked pretty mad. "Listen," Warren said. "You guys wear the badge. Act like cops. Use your knives."

They both pulled their blades and circled one another. Kojozian kept wiping blood from his eyes and Shaw tried to stay on his blind side. Kojozian jabbed and Shaw brought his knife around in a quick arc, laying his arm open. Kojozian let out a cry like an enraged bear and, trying to keep the blood from his eyes, slashed out wildly back and forth. Shaw sidestepped him, ducked down low, and jabbed him in the ribs.

"Nice," Warren said, lighting a cigarette.

Kojozian was fighting sloppy now, just whirling around with his blade, slashing out blindly as he wiped blood from his eyes. Shaw played him, let him get in close, and then darted away. Kojozian leaped at him. Shaw jumped away, let the bigger man's forward momentum carry him. Then as blood yet again filled Kojozian's eyes, Shaw slipped behind him and buried his blade between his shoulders. Once. Then twice. Kojozian fell to one knee, crying out, and slashed Shaw on the elbow and Shaw stabbed him in the chest.

Kojozian dropped his knife...lumbering, trying to find his feet, but weak now from the pain and the blood which poured from him.

"Let me see that knife," Warren said.

He took it from Shaw, went up behind Kojozian and slit his throat.

The big man went down, coughing out ribbons of blood, squirming in a red sea of his own making.

"Come on," Warren said. "We have police work to do."

They left Kojozian dying on the sidewalk...

44

Macy did not scream.

When they saw what had happened in the police station, she did not open her mouth and let the scream out that was no doubt building in her. Nothing so Hollywood or dramatic. She did not even bite down on her fist like some damsel in distress in an old movie. In fact, she did nothing. She stood there by Louis' side, absorbing the atrocity before them. It was as if some insane war between dog and man had broken out and they were viewing the aftermath. But maybe it was even more than that. Like some great rending machine had sucked in dogs and men, filling the police station itself with meat and bloody mucilage that had overflowed those walls and spilled out onto the sidewalk.

Louis stood there with her, just sickened and shocked and appalled. A mutilated body or two at the scene of an accident was bad enough. You were offended, but at least you could wrap your brain around it. Two cars met, two cars were smashed, what was driving them was turned to pulp. But what about something like this? How did you view slaughter like this and what did viewing it do to you? The squad room of the police station was a horror, just the bodies of men and the carcasses of dogs all tangled together, split and rent and disemboweled. The floor a river of clotted waste like something that might be shoveled from a slaughter house pit.

Macy opened her mouth and said something perfectly unintelligible, but Louis understood. He understood just fine. Something in her, something good and necessary and human, had been laid bare and she was bleeding inside from a dozen cutting wounds. He took her by the hand and led her from that terrible place, the raw hot smell of death just nauseating.

It was just getting worse. Hour by hour.

And in his mind, he could not stop hearing Earl Gould's voice: *All of them out there...animals, they are regressing to animals, throwing off the yoke of intelligence and civilization, returning to the jungle and survival of the fittest...*

God.

That explained the savage regression of human beings here and around the world...but what of these dogs? Dogs could be very savage, of course, their instinctive behavior was only kept at bay through breeding and discipline imposed by their owners...but what about *these* dogs? From what he was seeing, they had regressed, too, becoming less like domesticated dogs and more like wolves, savage blood-hungry wolves.

Did they have the gene, too? The dogs? Or was it not quite that simple? The regression of humans was more than just psychological, he was thinking. Maybe they didn't sprout fangs or become hairy proto-humans like in the old movies, but the activation of that gene...well, it had to trigger biochemical changes in the human animal. And if the chemistry was different, more basic and animalistic, then obviously bodily secretions would be altered, too. Perhaps it was some chemical signature the dogs smelled, some odor that caused an aggressive response in them.

Louis supposed he'd never really know.

Outside, they stepped over bodies and dogs and that was when Louis went down on one knee and threw up. Oh, it had been coming for some time and when it arrived, it hit him hard like a good kick to the belly. Cold sweat popped out on his forehead and the world spun on its axis and down he went, his knee hitting the concrete hard and his hands slapping hard enough to make them sting. What was in his stomach came out in a warm, almost satisfying gush as if he were voiding toxins or bad meat out of his system. He had no idea what he'd last eaten, but there it was, splashing onto the sidewalk.

Finally, the gagging stopped and blood finally made it back up into his head. "Macy," he said. "Macy..."

She stood there, unmoved by what he had just done and what she was seeing all around her. Her eyes were wide and teary. They blinked. Her chest rose and fell as she breathed. Her hands were knotted into fists at her side. Her mouth hung open. But other than that, she was just gone. She'd seen too much, absorbed too much, and something in her had simply said, screw this, and shut down.

Louis reached out and grasped her left ankle. "Macy? Honey, are you all right?"

But she did not answer.

She was in shock or something, he figured.

He pulled himself up and put his hands on her shoulders. "Macy?" he said in a very soothing voice. "Listen to me now. I

191

know this is bad, but you can't let it get to you. You have to fight against it."

But she was done fighting.

Louis took her hand in his own and it was chilly, moist and limp. She walked with him for maybe ten feet, then she moaned and folded right up. She fell against him and he caught her, which was a good thing because she might have split her head open on the sidewalk otherwise. She fell into him, loose and flaccid and he immediately gathered her up in his arms. She was a small girl, but he was amazed at how terribly light she was. He got her over to the grass, away from the splayed death all around them and gently set her down. She was breathing and her pulse was strong. Just shock. Just nerves. Just your average fainting spell and who more deserved one?

"It's gonna be okay," he told her. "It's all gonna be okay."

Although he did not like the idea of being out in the open and defenseless on Main Street, he knew there were things that had to be done. Things maybe he should have done hours before.

He pulled out his cellphone and dialed 911.

It rang and rang...but there was no answer.

No answer.

That meant emergency services were down and why the hell wouldn't they be? He scooped Macy up and carried her over to the Dodge, wondering how it all looked from above. The bodies and the dogs and some crazy guy carrying a teenage girl in his arms. Jesus, like something off a paperback book cover or a movie poster. All that was lacking was some burning buildings behind him and some rolling plumes of smoke, maybe a couple smashed cars.

Leaning Macy against him, he opened the Dodge, then slid her into the seat. Her face was covered in a dew of sweat. Her eyelids flickered a few times, but she did not wake. He secured her with the seatbelt and shut the door...

45

The shadows were long.
It was almost time.

The Huntress was still waiting in the second hand store which was now growing wonderfully dark as the sun fell behind the trees leaving a smear of blood on the horizon. True nightfall would be in fifteen minutes.

The clan was growing impatient.

She made a grunting sound and they quieted.

Out in the street, the girl was in the car. The man was standing beside it, looking confused, looking troubled. The Huntress could smell his indecision, his weakness, blowing through the screen of the window. He was ripe for the taking. If they rushed out now, he might fight, but it would be half-hearted, without conviction.

She waited, sniffing the air.

She smelled green, growing things, the musky urine scent of the pack. She was catching a curious after odor of the girl in the car, too. The scent of her body wash, her sweat, the perfumed stink of her hair, and the ripeness between her legs that made the Huntress feel hungry.

The males of the clan smelled it, too.

Being who and what they were, they only wanted to follow it to its source. To take the offering of the girl, to break her and fill her with their seed. But the Huntress would not allow it and they knew so. They only wanted to run wild and free; she was teaching them discipline.

As the night air began to push steadily in, pure and sweet with night-blossoms, the Huntress felt her nipples harden. There was electricity in her blood, an expectant rhythm to her heart.

She watched the man.

In a few moments now...

46

Okay, Hero, what now? Louis asked himself. *What you gonna do now? You gonna hang around this fucking graveyard in vain hope that the cavalry will ride in or are you gonna make like a sheep and get the flock out of here?*

Standing there by the car, he was uncertain. Inside, a voice was telling him to run, to get out of town already, but it was not that simple and he knew it. Where were they? Where was everyone? Were they all dead? He could almost believe it, standing there on that deserted street, the shadows growing long, night coming, filling itself with a darkness that would soon fall over the town like a shroud. He could imagine them all, in their houses and garages and cars, just everywhere, all dead from something that was as inexplicable as the regression itself.

He looked around, seeing the bodies and the devastated police station. The buildings and storefronts of Main were just empty and dead like the entire population had been evacuated and somebody forgot to tell him about it. Everything was still, motionless and eerie. Like ground zero at an A-bomb test or a city in one of those post-apocalyptic movies.

Louis stood there, feeling the town around him, and was certain it was not empty. He could almost feel others out there as he had before. Hiding behind those storefronts, maybe waiting for dark like a bunch of ghouls. The idea of that made his flesh crawl.

Yes, he could drive out of town and leave this mess for someone else. But there was still Michelle. There was still his wife and he could not just abandon her. Maybe she was dead, but until he saw her corpse he couldn't bring himself to believe that.

What then?

And then he knew. The most basic mechanism of survival was defense and all he had was the lockblade knife in his pocket. He needed something better. A gun. There were guns in the police station, but that would mean wading through those bodies, looting around through them and pulling a bloody gun from an equally bloody holster. The idea of that was repellent, but he didn't really have a choice.

And then he saw, down the middle of the block, a State Police cruiser parked out front of Dick's Sporting Goods. Cop cars always had shotguns in those racks. He would just borrow one, that's all. He looked at Macy sleeping in the car. She'd be safe for a few minutes.

Louis turned and jogged down the sidewalk to the State Police cruiser. The windows were open, but there was no shotgun in a rack. In fact, there was no rack, just a lot of electronic stuff and a radar gun. So much for that. He turned to leave and then he caught something out of the corner of his eye. Something that made him freeze-up. Through the glass windows of Shelly's Café, he could see forms.

People.

There were people in there.

People sitting in booths. They were not moving, just sitting. Louis felt sweat run down his spine. He made ready to bolt. Surely those people had seen him. Surely they would come after him...but they didn't. He glanced quickly down the block at his car. It looked very far away. Swallowing, he went up to the café, being very careful. Those people sitting in there still paid him no mind. He went up to the door, peered through the plate glass. Yes, there were people in booths and people at the counter. Some at tables. Maybe a dozen at most. All unmoving, just sitting and sitting.

This is where you leave well enough alone, Louis.

Sure, he knew that. He knew that very well. So, ignoring that voice of reason and common sense, he pushed through the door and stepped inside. He could smell the coffee, the burgers, the deep-fat fryers. Hunger actually wormed in his belly for a split second, but it did not last. Because there was another smell: a stench of blood and shit, a death smell that made his belly curl in on itself.

The people were not moving.

Many had fallen over in their booths or right off their stools. Trembling, fighting back a scream, Louis moved amongst them, knowing he had to. They were mannequins and wax figures, sideshow dummies and straw-stuffed effigies. At least that's what his mind was telling him. But the truth was much darker. They were not wax or wood or thermoformed plastic, they were flesh and blood and every last one was dead.

Their throats had been slit.

Yes, the fat man and his obese wife in the booth; the two grimy men in coveralls sitting behind them; the pretty woman in shorts and her cute red-headed daughter; the two guys and the state cop at the counter. All of them had their throats slit. There were a few other bodies on the floor, people that had fallen from their seats. Blood was pooled on the green tiles. It had coagulated on the counter. Run in rivers down the back of the brown plastic seats of the booths themselves where the fat man and his wife's heads hung back. All those throats were laid open as was that of a waitress on the floor behind the counter and a fry cook slumped in the corner by a stainless steel cooler.

Jesus.

It was bad. Just morbid and loathsome and frightening. But what was even worse was that it looked like they had slit their *own* throats. Using steak knives and carving knives from the café's own wares, they had slit their own throats and testament to that was the fact that most of them still gripped the knives in their bloody, stiff fists. Other knives had fallen to the floor. Even the little girl had opened her own throat...if the paring knife in her chubby, dead little fist was any indication.

It hit Louis like it had at the police station, the shock which was huge and physically heavy, overwhelming. He almost went down, but gripped the edge of the counter and clenched his teeth until it passed.

No, they hadn't needed dogs or mad killers here, they'd done the work themselves just as Jillian had. Louis found himself wondering how it had gone down, how it had worked. Had it hit them all at once? The urge to destroy themselves? Was it some kind of unspoken, unconscious decision to avoid regression, to die while they were still human? The same thing, perhaps, that had gotten inside of Jillian?

He stared at the carnage and was almost certain of it.

He could almost see it in his mind, all these people in the café, in their own little world, separated from the raw stench of primeval degeneration that blew through the streets in a hot, rank animal smell. Whatever was human in them rising to the surface like a swimmer desperate for one last gulp of clean air before sinking into the primal waters of race memory. It must have clicked in all their heads at roughly the same time: a complete rejection of that infectious, ancient evil rising from within. The need to preserve something human while they still *were* human and not slavering beasts running naked, killing and fucking in the streets.

There really was no other explanation for it.

The waitress must have passed out the knives and then, in unison, they'd slit their throats. Some had made a clean, almost professional job of it, while others had been very messy, sawing through their throats not once, but two and three times, their necks hacked and gouged and carved. But they'd done it. They'd all done it.

Louis thought: *Get out of here. The rest of it is bad enough, but this is infinitely worse and you goddamn well know it.*

But he didn't leave.

He couldn't bring himself to.

There were horrors and then there were *horrors* and some of them simply demanded examination, regardless of how sickened and terrified you were. Maybe the human mind needed reasons, needed explanations. Maybe it could not look on this without demanding to know: *why?* Maybe the human mind could not just turn away from something so senseless and gruesome without understanding the design of it. Louis leaned against the counter, his head thick with the stink of blood, hearing flies buzz and the clock tick up on the wall. It scared him. This whole thing scared him. And the very worst thing was that all those corpses were *grinning*. Their faces were pale, their throats and chests dyed red, and they were all grinning, just grinning the most hideous smiles imaginable.

And their eyes were wide open...

47

When Macy opened her eyes, her first sensory experience was not the plate of spiderwebbed glass that lay over her lap from the shattered window. It was the stink. The stink of those that had ringed in the car in the fading light. *Monsters.* That's what she thought. Monsters. These were monsters...ogres, trolls, bogarts from a fairy tale that had slipped out of the dark and secret wood to feast on children by moonlight. She seemed to recall something like them from a storybook as a child, but maybe, just maybe, the memory was much older: atavistic recall. For the tales of ogres and trolls and child-eating witches were just ancient memories of primal horrors re-channeled into harmless fable. The truth behind them was dark indeed.

They just stood there, looking at her.

Men, women, children. A couple kids she knew from school.

They were yellow-skinned, dirty, half-naked, faces painted up like skulls, hair greased or tied-up with sticks and tiny bones like those of rodents.

A man standing in front of the car had a huge butcher knife in his hands that was almost as long as his forearm. He motioned with it. He made a low barking sound.

Then filthy, scabby hands were reaching into the car, taking hold of her and she just didn't seem to have the strength to fight. Oh, she reflexively kicked and hit at them, but they yanked her through the window and bounced her head off the roof to take the fight out of her. She cried out, but it was a choked, pathetic sound.

They threw her to the ground.

She looked up at their deathmask faces carved with shadow. Their eyes were empty, shiny, vulpine. She opened her mouth to say something and they rained kicks down on her until she rolled into a heap, barely conscious. When her mouth did open to scream, something was stuffed in it: a foul-tasting, salty scrap. A piece of a shirt soaked with *their* sweat.

Louis, Louis, Louis...please help me...

Help me...

But he was nowhere to be seen. And as Macy fell trembling behind some black wall of terror in her mind, she felt hands grip her ankles, dragging her through the street...

48

Warren was standing there in the fading light with a cigarette in his mouth, ruminating on his life as a cop upholding the law, when the arrow punched into Shaw. Caught him right in the throat with a solid *thunk!* and punched out the other side, the arrow tip shining bright red, a hunk of meat caught on it. Shaw's eyes glazed like a pot fired in a kiln and he pitched straight over.

Warren just stood there, watching him squirming on the ground. Shaw looked positively ridiculous with an arrow through his throat. Sighing, Warren ground out his cigarette and pulled his knife. "Guess we'll be having company soon," he told the writhing, bleeding man.

He was right.

In the fading light, he could not see much out there. Cars at the curb. Alleys. Trees. Houses. Hedges. Nets of shadow overlaying them all and making for a fine killing ground with himself as the prey. He started backing away from Shaw's body. He turned this way. Then that. Yes, they were all around him. Goddamn. He could smell the urine and musk they were scented with, the wild animal stink of them.

A shadow moved behind a car.

The sound of padding bare feet from behind him.

He turned, ready to fight, heard a curious whooshing sound and another arrow caught him right in the belly. It didn't go all the way through. The impact put him on his ass, knocked the wind from him. His knife clattered to the concrete. Then the pain came: sharp, cutting waves of it as what seemed oceans of blood welled from the entrance wound of the arrow. Sweating, straining, his heart pounding in his chest, Warren let out a strangled cry and pulled the arrow from his belly. Blood gushed from the hole. He felt dizzy, confused.

The bloody arrow in his hand had a triple-barbed, four-bladed tip on it, a broad head used for bear hunting. It fell from his fingers. He tried crawl down the sidewalk, but he just didn't have anything left to crawl *with*.

Clutching his bleeding belly, he opened his eyes.

They had ringed him in: the hunters.

There were a dozen of them with clubs and broom handles sharpened to lethal points. They were all dirty and streaked with blood and paint. A high-breasted, blue-eyed young woman with a bow in her hands stepped forward. She made a hissing sound and another woman stepped up. She was older than the first, but well-muscled, sleek, her face painted with red and green bands as was her naked body. Things like beads and sticks and tiny bones were braided in her hair. She had a slat of bone thrust through her nose and had peeled her lips away with a razor so her teeth and gums were on display. She carried an axe in one hand and a sharpened broomstick in the other with a human head, that of a teenage boy, impaled on the tip.

Warren blinked at her through his pain. He recognized her. They'd brought the body of the boy to her in the wheelbarrow. She had given the crowd an offering of the old woman upstairs.

She did not recognize him; her eyes were glassy, translucent.

She chattered her teeth and trembled with rage, her eyes simmering black with a vast, stupid hatred.

Warren did not look for mercy and he did not get any. The others waded in with clubs and began beating him until his bones were heard to snap, until his ribs were staved in, and his lower jaw was shattered. Knobs of bloody bone thrusting through his ripped uniform pants, he inched on the ground like a slug, moaning and groaning.

The woman with the bow came over. A hot stench of blood and decay wafted from her. She was menstruating. Blood all over her legs. It dripped from her. While the others held him, she crouched over him and rubbed her moist red vulva over his face, marking him with a crude cross of menstrual blood.

"Now," she said.

Marked for the reaping.

The other woman handed over her broomstick with the head on it. She gripped her long-handled axe with both hands. With a manic, shrieking cry of delight, she swung the axe and decapitated Warren quite cleanly. His broken body lurched, shook. The eyes in his head blinked a few times and then glazed over with a stark finality.

One of the hunters took his head and impaled it on a broomstick.

He raised it up to the darkening sky and let go with a screeching blood-maddened war cry...

49

Louis kept expecting the dead people in the café to move.

He kept expecting them to wink at him or to call him by name, perhaps take hold of him with their cold, sticky red fists and show him exactly what had gone through their minds when they pressed that serrated steel to their throats, demand that he do the same.

For it was better than the alternative and he knew it.

There was a rustle of cloth and he spun around, his eyes wide and his mouth hooked in a terrible grimace. One of the men at the counter slid from his seat and fell to the floor. The little girl at the table fell forward, striking the plate before her face-first. The fat lady trembled and rolled out of the booth, coming down hard, her bloody knife clattering across the floor and stopping at Louis' feet.

For one split second, he did nothing. His mind was filled with a roaring, whooshing sound and he was certain that they were coming alive around him, waking up. That they would look upon him with dead, yellowing eyes and reach out for him with blood-encrusted hands. And then everything in him went loose and he almost fell down, then tightened up stiff as a plank. A scream came out of his mouth, but it was dry and scratchy and barely more than a hissing sound.

The dead were just dead.

But the idea of three of them coincidentally moving, falling over or sliding out of their seats, was just too much and Louis could not accept it. His heart hammering and his breath coming very fast, he forced himself to move. To step over the body of the fallen man. He expected them to move again, to reach out or whisper his name, but they were just dead. And to prove this to himself, he went right over to the state cop— avoiding the reflection of his grinning, staring face in the mirror— and pulled the gun from his holster. It was a 9mm. And soon as Louis pulled it out, the cop's corpse fell over like a tree.

Louis stepped around him, the gun in his hand.

Outside, he heard something that made him go white: the high, joyous peals of laughing children. Just for a moment, but it had been there. Something passed before the window of the café and Louis turned, bringing up the gun and pulling the trigger. But nothing happened. His hands shaking so badly that he almost dropped the gun, he found the safety and clicked it off.

He heard running feet.

He ran to the window, the gun out before him. Out there, the streets were empty. Completely empty. His entire body shook and his bladder felt very full. His heart was pounding so hard he thought it would blow out of his chest. He could see his Dodge from where he was, see it very well.

And the doors were wide open.

Behind him, something moved...

50

They had the girl now.

They dragged her into the shadows while the man was in the café. He never even saw them or suspected they were near. That's how the clan knew that he was not a hunter, that he was soft and weak, his senses still deadened by who and what he was. Nothing but prey. They could have charged in and taken him but the Huntress did not want that. She would call them to the hunt. She would select the prey. She would find the meat and show them how to bring it down.

She was strange.

She was careful.

But she was also very cunning, very dangerous, and she killed without warning. The others let out a cry of anger when they struck, but not the Huntress. She smiled, exuded a scent of calm, then slashed your eyes, your throat.

The hunters stared down at the girl in the grass.

The men sniffed her. The women pulled at her hair.

She was theirs now...

51

Louis turned, his heart pounding mercilessly.

He turned and found himself staring down the barrel of a double-ought shotgun. The woman clutching it had crazy eyes, messy blond hair. She was dirty, bruised, her shirt was ripped open in the front and he could see most of her left breast quite plainly. But it was those eyes that held him: they were blank, almost unfocused like the eyes of a sleeper.

In a voice that was too calm, too easy, she said, "You just set that pistol on the countertop, mister, and I won't blow your fucking head off."

She spoke clearly. Her speech was not garbled or filled with snarling glottals like the regressed ones. He thought she was still human. Yet...her eyes were scary. They made him feel weak, vulnerable, everything inside him running like tepid water.

"Easy," he said, setting the 9mm down carefully. "I'm not like *them*. I'm not an animal. I'm still human."

"No shit? Well, excuse me, fuckhead, if I don't exactly believe that."

Louis realized then that she wasn't crazy, just scared, confused, and more than a little desperate. She would kill if she had to. But he saw that she did not really want to.

He kept his hands in the air. "I'm human and you know it. If you doubted it, you would have shot me. Have you ever seen one of them with a gun?"

She sighed. "I guess not."

"It's the regression," he told her. "A return to the jungle, to the original man, the original woman. They are like our ancestors. They hunt. They kill in packs. They reject anything of our world. I think it might almost be a phobia with them."

"Listen," she said, lowering the shotgun, "I don't have any idea what you're talking about. But I'm glad I found you. We might be the only two left. I'm Doris Bleer. You?"

"Louis Shears." He crossed over to the window. Practically dark. "We don't have time for this. There was a girl with me. In that car out there. I think she wandered off. I have to find her. She's in shock."

Doris shook her head. "She didn't wander off, Louis. They took her. The crazy ones. I saw 'em from the window in the back room where I was hiding."

"Then I have to go after them," he said, grabbing up the 9mm.

"Louis," the woman said, looking very compassionate for the first time. "I'm sorry about your girl. But you'll never see her again. Next time you do, she'll either be dead or she'll be one of them."

"You're fucking crazy," he said, filled with emotional turmoil that turned within him like a steel screw.

"Wish I was. But I'm not. Neither are you." She looked at him with those lost eyes. "They rushed in our house. They killed my husband. They...they cut him in two. They took my daughter. I escaped."

"I'm sorry," he said.

She shrugged, almost bulky beneath her defensive armor. Nothing could touch her. Not now. Not with what she'd seen. "An hour ago...before I hid out here...a pack of them chased me. My daughter was running with them. My own fucking daughter, Louis. She had a knife in each hand. *She was hunting me. Do you understand? She was hunting her own mother!*"

Louis bled for her, but there was only so much blood in him. Right now his blood was reserved for Macy and Michelle. "I'm going out. I'm going to get her back."

Louis scrambled over to the door and something let out a sharp, piercing ring. His cellphone. He fumbled it from his pocket.

"Hello?" he said, his voice tinny and weak. "H-hello?"

There was breathing on the other end, deep and drawn-out.

"Who is this?" he said. "*Who the fuck is this?*"

There was a muted giggling on the other end and then a voice. "Hello, hello, hello."

An echo.

Michelle.

But *not* Michelle.

This was an imitation of Michelle's voice. Flat where it should have been bright; hollow where it should have been full; scraping where it should have been smooth and silky. Like a recording slowed down or sped up. A synthetic voice, a deranged voice. Some insane woman had borrowed Michelle's voice and this was the blasphemy she was doing with it.

"Michelle?" he said. "Baby? Baby? Is that you?"

More breathing. The sound of a tongue licking lips. "Hello."

"Michelle, please—"

The line went dead.

And Louis went dead with it...

52

They had her now and Macy knew it just as she knew that whatever came next, whatever unimaginable horror that might be, it would be the end of her. She was still gagged. She imagined she would always be. They had dragged her into a sporting goods store and threw her on the floor. Some of them left, but others stayed to guard her. A boy and girl who were probably grade school age, their eyes shining in the semi-darkness, and a woman who wore a red-checked hunting shirt, unbuttoned, naked beyond that.

They all had the same eyes...red-rimmed, almost translucent like those of wolves, just staring with a fixed blackness at their world.

The new world they would inherit.

A man came in, carrying a club with a nail driven in the end of it. He set it aside and helped the kids drag Macy into the back room, some kind of storeroom behind the counter. She fought against them and they kicked her, hit her. She punched the girl in the face and the girl went berserk. She made a hissing sound like a mad dog and proceeded to slap the hell out of Macy, her arms windmilling, the slaps landing hard and hurting one after the other on Macy's face until she stopped moving. The boy grabbed an arm and bit it. The girl did the same with her leg. Not just a nip like the boy, but biting down hard until Macy screamed behind her gag.

She could feel the blood running down her bare thigh.

The woman came in now. By the light of a nightlight—which they all seemed just absolutely fascinated by—she looked up into the woman's face. It was shrunken like the face of a corpse, deep-cut by wrinkles that looked almost like scars. Gray hair hung in her face like moss. She bent down, sniffed Macy's throat, then licked her cheek.

Her breath was like tombs.

Grunting in her throat, she rallied the two children who began to strip Macy under the watchful gaze of the man.

Good God, more than just savages, animals, but a family of them: mother, father, two children.

They tore off Macy's shorts, her shirt, ripping them right off her. And when they wouldn't come, they used their knives to cut them free, slicing her in the process. Naked now save for bra and panties, they rolled her face-down and tied her hands behind her back. She was trussed like a swine ready for the roasting pit.

She cried out, fighting against her bonds. The girl grabbed her hair and rolled her over. Macy tried to shout behind the gag. The girl slapped her again. Then something hot and wet, almost burning sprayed in her face: *urine.* The boy was standing there, pissing on her. The stink was rank, gagging. Not normal human urine at all...this was wild with a sharp-smelling musk to it.

Then, as the woman watched over her, the children joined the man.

She heard them wrestling with something, something heavy. They were grunting and puffing, making snarling sounds in their throats from time to time. She could hear the man straining. A pounding noise. *Rap, rap, rap-rap-rap.* Macy did not want to know what they were doing...but she craned her head and looked. Needing to see.

That scream again, held in check by the awful-tasting gag in her mouth.

By the glow of the nightlight and the fading illumination coming in from the street, she saw...oh dear God...she saw—

She saw a corpse hung by its feet.

She did not know who it was and it was really too dim by that point to see, but it was the corpse of a woman. Oh, how meticulous and wicked were they. They had nailed the feet right to a beam overhead. That was the pounding she heard. As the man hoisted the woman up, the children nailed her feet by standing on crates. Her arms were still swinging back and forth from it. It was the corpse of a middle-aged woman, heavy in the breast, bunched with fat at the belly and hips. There was a glistening scar across her abdomen probably from an old C-section. Her flesh was impossibly white, almost luminous in the nightlight that buzzed on and on. The crown of her head and hair were clotted with blood that looked black.

There was a shattering noise out in the store like a case had been broken into and the man came back. He threw something on the floor: knives. He'd been in a knife case. Dozens of hunting knifes, blades sliver and razor-sharp gleaming on the floor.

They were going to slaughter her like a steer.

Like autumn's first kill—

Taking a handful of the dead woman's hair, he yanked her head up and stabbed a hunting knife with a seven-inch blade right into her throat, sawing and sawing as blood splashed down his arms and over his chest. It sounded like the noise of sawing the lid off a Halloween pumpkin: meaty, muscled. He sawed, then jerked her head to the side with cracking motion, then pulled it right off and tossed it.

He went down on his knees and drank from the flow. The children fought their way in, drinking, slurping, sucking at the stump. The woman knocked them aside and lapped at the stream of blood, smacking her lips appreciatively.

The boy untied the gag and pulled it from Macy's mouth. She dared not scream. He studied her face. He snapped at her with his teeth and giggled when she jerked in fear.

Then the girl cupped her hands, filling them with blood.

She crouched by Macy, careful not to spill the nectar.

"Here," she said in a grating voice. "Here, here, here..."

She opened her hands and let the blood splatter over Macy's mouth, rubbing her bloody hands all over her face and lips so that she got a good taste of it. "Good," the girl said. "Good."

Macy screamed, her face red and glistening. She thrashed and screamed, turned her head and vomited.

The man used his knife, cutting shanks of meat free from the dead woman's thighs and belly. The family fed upon them, chewing and snapping and tearing, eating it raw and bloody like tigers in the jungle. Cutting free a slab of meat from between the woman's legs, probably her vagina, he handed it to the woman. She sniffed it, licked it, then she stuffed it into her mouth whole, chewing it slowly. She kept taking it out, working it with her fingers, then stuffing it back in and chewing it some more.

And in Macy's mind a voice was screaming: *she's not eating it! She's not eating it at all...she's tenderizing it, chewing it to a soft fleshy mush.*

And that's exactly what she was doing.

She went down on her hands and knees, breathing hard, her face glossy with blood, the thin juice of what she had been chewing upon smeared on her lips. She spit it into her hand along with a snotty tangle of saliva. She held it out, shaking it at Macy, grunting deep in her throat with an almost bleating sort of sound. The others went down on all fours with her.

Then together, like beasts of the field lowing in the grass, they crept in closer, blood-drenched ghouls with huge black eyes, their teeth white and shining, drool falling from their mouths.

They moved in closer...and closer.

Macy screamed because she *knew.*

While the children and the man took hold of her, the woman forced her jaws open. She stuck the handle of a knife in her mouth and pried them open. Then she brought the thing she had been chewing on closer, forcing it into Macy's shrieking mouth...

53

When Louis stepped out of Shelly's Café, the streets were empty.

Oh, *they* were out there, somewhere, but he could not see them. He could feel them, though, gathered thickly in the spreading shadows like locusts in a farmer's field. Just as destructive, just as lethal, just as patient. He thought he could even smell them—their sweaty bodies and sour breath and bloody hands, the ripe stink of death hovering over them.

As he stepped out into the fading sunlight, the precarious uneven illumination of twilight, he could certainly feel their eyes on him. It was very unsettling. Like being some beast of the field ringed in by the hungry eyes of predators. They were watching him, gauging him, seeing what kind of defense he could put up and how easy they could take him down. He felt like a suckling pig in a pen surrounded by ravenous wolves. He actually thought he could smell their hot breath and drool.

Doris was behind him and she felt it, too. She kept the shotgun in both fists. She would kill anything that moved. There was no doubt of it. "We better find somewhere safe. And fast. I don't think we have much time."

Louis was terrified.

There was no way around that.

He was utterly terrified and instinct told him to run, to get the hell out, but he wasn't going to do that. He knew he was in terrible danger. But what worried him most was Macy. So he would not run. As he stepped out onto the sidewalk, the cop's 9mm in his hand, he did everything he could to look calm and in charge, even if he was lights years beyond these things. He was a man and he was going to act like one. Maybe they'd kill him, but he wouldn't make it easy. He wouldn't give them the pleasure of his fear.

Confidence.

Just a word any other time, but suddenly Louis seemed to understand what it meant. How it was a tool you used. If you panicked and bolted, those *people* out there would come running and howling, smelling his fear like wild dogs and sensing an easy kill. But if he was confident, they'd be cautious. They were playing mind games on him and now he would play them, too.

But it isn't just mindless, murderous strangers out there, he reminded himself. *Michelle is out there. Michelle is with them. If she attacks...can you kill her? Can you point the gun at her and put a bullet in her if it means saving Macy?*

Louis couldn't think about that.

He loved Michelle completely. He would have done anything for her. But now things were different. Yesterday, he would have rather put a bullet into his own head than harm her...but now? If she was some savage, blood-maddened beast? He did not know. He did not want to know.

He stepped off the curb, wanting to give himself some distance from the buildings, the alleys, the cellar stairways cut down into the sidewalk. Too many places to spring an ambush from. And although he had never actually used a 9mm automatic before, he knew enough about the weapon to know that its magazine carried enough rounds to do some serious killing.

Okay.

"You're not going to find your girl," Doris said. "Be sensible. You'll get us both killed."

Louis ignored her.

He moved down the street. He was very aware of how long his shadow was growing. Darkness was coming fast and he had a pretty good idea that they wanted it to come, that reduced to what they were now, they would probably be much better in it than he. He could see the Dodge parked up the street from the police station, the shadowy hulks of bodies scattered around it. The driver's and passenger's side doors were wide open. The windows were shattered. He preyed it was still drivable.

He wondered if Michelle was out there. Maybe she had taken Macy.

Oh, not her, not Michelle, not my wife.

Louis walked on very slowly for ten or fifteen feet, then paused.

Doris nearly bumped into him.

He thought he heard that childish giggling again. His flesh crawled anew. Wasn't it amazing that one of the sweetest sounds in the world, the delightful laughter of a child, was also one of the most foul and obscene? And particularly in a ghost town. He breathed in and out, readying himself for it, whatever it was, because it was coming. It was building around him and he could feel it. Like a frightened animal, he could sense the waiting teeth out there, the claws and hunger. Tensed like a spring ready to explode, sweat running down his face, he remembered driving up Main with Macy, how dead the town was, how he'd speculated earlier that maybe everyone was dead. But it had all been a ruse, of course. Macy and he had been watched from the moment they pulled down the street. These people were organized, then. They had laid a trap and waited for him to step into it. And, boy, he'd bested their greatest expectations, hadn't he? Leaving Macy alone in the car even when, deep inside, he'd known it was a mistake.

Sacrifice.

He'd offered her up for sacrifice.

"No," he said under his breath.

"What?" Doris asked him.

"Nothing."

He went across the street, stepped up onto the sidewalk. They could have had her anywhere. Or blocks away for that matter. It was hopeless, but he couldn't give in, couldn't crumble. He walked over to Indiana Video. He pushed his way through the glass doors. It was silent in there. There was a light on behind the counter, another near the back of the store. Enough light to see by.

"Macy?" he said.

There was a moaning sound.

His heart leaping with possibility, Louis charged over by the children's movies. A young girl, maybe eight or ten, was squatted on the floor, entirely naked. Arms wrapped around herself, she rocked back and forth.

She was a redhead.

Not Macy at all.

"Honey?" Louis said, still fearful. "Are you all right?"

The girl looked up at him. Her face was dark with ground-in dirt, her hair greasy and stuck with leaves. There were bruises and contusions all over her. Louis held a hand out to her, afraid she might bite it, but the humanity in him demanding that he try.

Doris kept the shotgun on the kid. "Jesus Christ, Louis...are you fucking blind as well as stupid? Look at her. That's not a girl. It's one of *them*. Can't you see that?"

But he couldn't be convinced of that. The girl was sobbing, shaking. One of them wouldn't do that...would they? After a moment the girl took his hand and stood up, breaking into a wail of tears. She pressed herself against him, shuddering. She smelled bad. Like blood and decay and dirt. Her flesh was hot, moist. He could feel her heart thudding.

"They dragged me through the streets," the girl said. "They...they...they..."

But she couldn't go on; she shook, whimpered.

"All right," Louis said. "You're going to be safe now. My car is outside. We're driving away from here."

Doris didn't move. "I'm not going anywhere with you. Not with that *thing*."

"Stop it!' Louis told her.

"You're an idiot. You'll get us both killed."

He turned towards the door, the shadows thicker and more tangled out there than nesting cobras now. Death waited out there. In every shadow, in every doorway, and behind every tree. Death. The girl shook in his arms. And then she tightened against him. He could feel the flex of her muscles, the heat of her skin. It was nearly feverish. He tried to pry her away so he could walk, but she circled her arms around him, jumped up and swung her legs around his hip.

"Honey," he said, "listen now..."

She looked up at him from beneath strands of filthy copper-colored hair.

She was grinning.

Her eyes were filled with a stark malevolence that was beyond mere insanity. The tips of her teeth were filed into points.

Louis felt something sink inside him, he felt her repellent flesh against his own. Darting her head, she buried her teeth into his shoulder, breaking through his shirt and puncturing skin.

He screamed with pain.

He heard Doris cry out as the other savages rushed in.

A trap, it had all been a fucking trap...

54

Painted for battle, the hunters came out of the back of the store. Another rushed right through the front door. And the most amazing thing was, he held a spear in his hands. And from the barbed point to nearly a foot down the shaft it was stained red.

The girl dug her teeth into the man.

This was the one. The one the Huntress wanted. She must not let go of him, she must hold him tight until the hunters could take him down. But he was wild, enraged. He did not shrink with fear as she'd hoped. He tore at her back, digging welts into her skin. He beat at her. He pounded her. Then, gun in hand, he banged the butt off the back of her skull until she pulled her teeth away and cried out. He hit her with the gun again and something went in her skull with a sickly popping noise. Inside the girl's head, things went dark, then sank into mist and she...she could...not...*hold on...*

The man whirled around in a circle, yanking her free with a handful of bloody hair and throwing her as he did so. His locomotion propelled her through the air. She crashed into a case of movie collectibles, her face shattering the plate glass window. A shard of glass went right into her throat and she died kicking in a pool of her own blood.

The hunters saw it as they charged.

But they were too late to stop it, nor would they have considered it worth their time: not all members of the clan survived the hunt, the few must perish so the many could survive.

A spear barely missed Louis as he turned and fired at the three coming out of the back. His first shot was wild his hand shook so badly. But his second and third were right on target. He put a round through a guy whose entire body was blackened with what looked like ash or charcoal. The bullet caught him right in the sternum and threw him backwards in a drunken semi-circle. Blood fountained from his wound and he pitched over face-first, gyrating on the floor, screeching with a high, piercing noise that scarcely sounded human. The second round caught another hunter in the throat, in the Adam's Apple, and the effect was instantaneous: his throat was blown apart in a spray of bloody mucilage and his head slumped forward. His legs went to rubber, but forward momentum carried him right past Louis. He stumbled right into a wall of DVDs and took them down with him in a clatter of plastic clamshells.

The third hunter did not hesitate, did not slow.

He didn't even throw his spear. When he got close enough, he brought it up over his head and leaped with it, going airborne and bringing it to bear on Louis. Louis pulled the trigger as the man jumped. The bullet was wild, but it caught him in the ribs, glancing off them, spiraling into his body cavity and chewing its way through his stomach like a drillbit.

But again, forward motion carried him, and he hit Louis. The spear gouged Louis' right shoulder, but it was off-balance, undirected. They went down in a heap. And gutshot or not, the naked man was not ready to die. He kicked, he scratched, he clawed. He got his hands around Louis' throat and squeezed with unbelievable strength, making black dots pop before Louis' eyes as his air was completely shut off by those gnarled, blood-crusted hands.

He forced Louis down, never breaking his grip and pounded his head off the floor which, thankfully, was carpeted.

Louis knew he was done.

He could not fight the maniacal strength of his attacker.

Blood spilling all over him from the guy's wound, Louis took the last of his strength and pounded the guy in the face, then he jabbed his thumbs into his eyes. The grip was broken immediately. The man made a squealing sound like a stepped upon dog. Rubbing his eyes, blinded, he launched himself at Louis who was still gasping for air. The guy hit him with his bleeding, loose bulk and they went over together. The guy somehow got his hands on Louis' head and smashed his face into the floor again and again...but not with as much power as before as his blood spilled out in a steady gushing flow.

Louis let out an enraged battle cry and brought his elbow back, catching the wild man in the ribs. Once, twice, three times. The man weakened, grunting and squealing. Then Louis reached his hand back between the naked loins of his attacker and grabbed his balls in his fist, savagely twisting them and then squeezing them with a ferocity he did not know he possessed. The man doubled-over, howling with agony.

Louis wrenched and crushed what was in his fist until it went to a moist pulp.

Doris' battle was no easier.

About the time Louis's third attacker leaped, the painted man who came through the door threw his spear with a fine, powerful agility and grace. Doris fired, but her aim was off. Buckshot peppered her attacker's thighs, but by then his spear was already in flight: it sank into the meat just beneath her collarbone. It punctured through fat and muscle, buried in her a good three inches. A couple more and it would have went out her back.

She screamed with fear, with pain, with everything inside her that had boiled black by that point.

Then the man hit her.

She felt the shotgun slide from her hands.

He hit her, forcing the spear in deeper and she cried out, clawing at him with rage. The buckshot that hit him was basically scattershot. The real blast took out a cardboard standee of Brad Pitt and Angela Jolie. The scatter that hit him peppered his thighs and belly, but did not penetrate deep enough to do any real damage. Regardless, by the time he hit her, he was wet with blood. Her fingers could get no real purchase on him, they scraped over his bloody belly and his chest and face that were painted up with earthen reds and browns in a thick grease. He grabbed the spear shaft and yanked it to pull it free, but it was wedged along the inside of her scapula, the barbed tip caught on a slat of bone. When he yanked it, she came with it. He threw her to the floor, then pulled her back up again by the spear and bounced her off display cases, the wound below her collarbone ripped wide open and spouting blood by this point.

With a growling animal cry, he put all his weight behind the shaft and slammed her up against the counter, the spear point scraping over bone and puncturing out her back. He withdrew it and Doris went down in a shuddering heap, barely conscious.

She looked up through blood-glazed eyes, seeing him above her with the spear raised to strike.

Standing over her, he brought it down again and again, sinking it into her belly and thighs, hip and breasts. Then he brought it down into the original wound. He put his bare foot on her throat and yanked with everything he had. There was a wet snapping and the barbed point came free, snapping out a shattered section of collarbone in the process that broke through the skin in a bloody shard. Then the spear came down again—right into her open screaming mouth. It sheered her tongue in two and went through the back of her throat, punching into her cervical vertebrae—

She was dying and nothing could help her.

The hunter brought up the spear and let out a wild yelping cry of victory.

Then there was a thundering sound and his left eye blew out of its socket in a spray of tissue with most of the socket itself. He fell over straight as a board, his upper jaw catching the sharp edge of the counter with a violent thudding, teeth scattered over its surface. He folded up, already dead.

Doris, through a mask of blood and a haze of pain, saw Louis standing over the thrashing body of one of the savages. He had the 9mm in his hands. His eyes were wild, his mouth hooked into a manic sneer...

55

Somehow, Doris' mind cleared and she felt the agony that threaded through her body. Her heart leaped, then leaped again. Her mind swam in and out of the darkness, trying to focus, trying to maintain. She had lost so much blood by that point and suffered so much trauma that she hovered on the edge of shock. She heard more gunfire, heard screams, heard running feet.

And when her eyes did focus, Louis was gone.

They must have gotten him.

The air stank of blood, smoke, and voided bowels. She saw two men standing there with a woman between them. All were naked, all painted-up and covered in something viscous and shining like grease. Their eyes blazed with a flat animal hunger. Light reflected off the filed points of their teeth. They looked like Mesolithic hunters.

Realizing she was indeed alive, they crept forward, soundlessly.

Oh God in heaven, no more, no more, just let me die...

But she did not die. Blinking away the dreams that pushed into her skull, her body felt like it was on fire. Every inch of her flesh was laid bare, it seemed, everything inside ripped and gouged. She tried to swallow the blood that filled her mouth, but her damaged tongue was like a flap of rubber. She was in so much pain that she was literally *beyond* pain...notched up a level into a place of floating emptiness where she could feel her pain, yet did not seem attached to it. Such is the magic chemical bath of endorphins.

A grunting, a snarling, a fetid animal stink...

When Doris again opened her eyes, the three savages were crouching down by her. The woman had a knife, a damn big knife, and, grinning, she jabbed it into Doris' belly just below the navel, putting her weight on it until it cut deep and sure. As they stared down, the beast-woman sawed the knife clear up to Doris' sternum.

They looked pleased.

With filthy fingers, they pulled the cleaved flesh apart.

Doris could see what they did, feel the pressure and pulling, yet not the pain. It was divorced from her. They pulled the wound wide, tearing at yellow fat and pink strands of connective tissue. She could see the glistening bulge of her stomach, the coiled ropes of her entrails. She was aware of only the pressure and the pulling as the grunting, drooling creatures yanked things out of her, rooting around in her abdomen, searching, digging, probing.

They found something.

They bristled with excitement, chattering their teeth, making low moaning sounds that were nearly orgasmic. All three had their hands in her now, ripping, jerking at something, cutting at it with the knife, finally working it free as they cried out with a strident communal baying. Doris saw it. Saw that great fleshy mass they yanked from inside her...a heavy, pinkish-brown slab of blood-dripping meat that could only be her liver.

They held it up like a prize.

Growling and grunting, they brought it to their mouths and bit into it.

This was the very last thing that Doris saw before the darkness took her...

56

Night came then to the Greenlawn.

It came over the rooftops and from cellars, from dark corners and alleys, crawlspaces and attics and graveyards...all the places it had been tucked away and coveted during the hours of daylight. It came with teeth and intent and degeneracy. The darkness concealed a thousand sins, a thousand terrible deeds, wreckage and corpses and packs of men and women and children that were no longer human, just creeping night things running wild and insane and loathsome through the narrow streets and weedy backlots, the dusky arteries of the town. These were the ones that welcomed the night, that understood it and worshipped it and called it their own. With fixed eyes, primal appetites, and a yawning malignancy where their souls had once been before a certain dormant gene was activated, they returned to the dawn times. Repressed demons and parasitical desires that had long clung to the undersides of their psyches were released with gruesome abandon. In Greenlawn atavistic evil was brought to term and was allowed to bear its pestilent fruit. And the growing season was rich.

Heeding the primordial call of the wild, filled with an archaic killing instinct born in the pre-Cambrian slime, overjoyed to return to the jungle at last, they took to the streets in wolfpacks, hunting and maiming and devouring.

And the night went on forever...

57

Although she was sore from being raped repeatedly, Leslie Towers was nothing if not completely connected to her surroundings. Though bound as she was, tossed into the grass, she was alert as any animal, sensing the night around her and the things that hunted it. So while Mr. Kenning and Mike Hack slept off their meal of dog—both greased slick with yellow dog fat, Setter hairs and leaves stuck to them—Leslie heard the hunters circling beyond the light of the fire. They had been out there in the darkness for some time.

Now they were coming.

Leslie was tense, ready. Her wrists were tied behind her back so there was no chance to gnaw her way free. Trussed-up as she was, she could only lay there, an unwilling victim. She longed to run free and wild through the grim, silent night. She also longed for a knife to protect herself with.

The hunters crept in closer.

Mr. Kenning slept on as did Mike Hack.

Silence.

Heavy, pregnant with foreboding and dread.

Soon now.

They were closer.

She could smell the stink of them: gamey, rich, hot. There were males as well as females.

Now she could see them...hulking shapes, but small and lithe. Children. Children led by a large man who was shaggy and stealthy. Their faces were darkened with tiger-striped bands, bodies slashed with browns and blues. With a shrieking battle cry, they rushed in. Mr. Kenning leaped to his feet and two spears sank into him, one in the belly and the other in the back. A knife slashed his eyes into bleeding holes. A hammer crashed down on his skull with a sickening popping noise. He went to his knees, more spears jabbing into him. Blood poured from him and an insane doglike howl roared from his contorted mouth. Mike tried to help and was put down under a rain of fists and clubs.

The hunters ravaged the camp, looking for weapons, for food. They kicked over the spit that the dog had been roasted on. They scattered the coals of the fire into a heap of dry kindling that immediately began to blaze.

Leslie thought they might not notice her there in the grass, away from the fire. But the rekindled blaze made the yard glow orange and yellow, flickering. Then a form jumped down by her, a girl with long hair knotted with wildflowers and sticks. Her painted face was like that of a wild boar...fat, puffy, greasy, her eyes glistening black. She stank like shit and blood.

She dragged Leslie by the ankles over towards the fire.

The other girls snarled and snapped at her, kicked her and spit on her. The boys rushed in, gripping her breasts and the globes of her ass. One of them bit into her shoulder. They fought over her, yanking her in all directions, their dirty nails scratching into her back. They were all hard and she could smell the brine of their balls.

She screamed.

She hissed.

Fingers groped her face and she bit one of them to the bone.

Then the huge shaggy figure waded in, tossing the boys aside, screeching at all of them until they drew back and away. Leslie looked up at him. He was a huge man, shining with sweat. His hair was white and bristly, his face set with deep-hewn wrinkles and ruts. He wore a shaggy fur coat with the arms torn off, his chest on display. He had many tattoos. There was a hatchet and a knife in his belt. A necklace of blackening ears was strung around his throat.

Leslie recognized him for what he was: the baron of the pack.

He pulled her to her feet, sniffed her face, then licked it. His breath was foul like he'd been chewing on rotten meat. "Did they take you, child?" he asked.

She nodded.

"Did they force you here?"

She nodded.

"Would you hunt with us? Kill for us? Be with us?"

"Yes," she said in a dry, cracking voice.

The man spun her around, pulled his knife and cut her the binds from her wrists and ankles. He shoved her away towards the other girls. They touched her hair and face. They sniffed her breasts, between her legs, and especially her ass. This was how they would know if she could be one of them. They were sniffing for the telltale trace of adrenalin, which would indicate fear. They smelled none.

A spear was thrust into her hands.

She liked the feel of it. She would use it. She would bring down prey and her simple little animal mind wanted nothing more.

Mike Hack, forgotten in the grass, leaped to his feet and tried to escape. Three of the girls jumped on him, took him down. He fought madly, but they bit and scratched and hit him, beating him into submission. They tore at his eyes and worried his testicles until there was no fight left. He was pulled to his feet. The pack did not like runners. It respected those who stood and fought; it despised cowards. While five or six of the pack held him, another cut the tendons behind his knees, the others behind his ankles. He flopped uselessly in the grass, blood rushing out of his wounds.

Mr. Kenning was lifted up, hoisted by the half dozen or so spears sunk into him. He could barely stand. He was wet with his own blood, gagging and grunting, a spray of vomit at his chin. He was pushed over to the tree where he had earlier hung the carcass of his Irish Setter, Libby. The noose was still there. It was looped around his throat, drawn taut. The spears were pulled from him, blood gushing out of the holes. Six of the children took the rope and pulled on it, yanking him up off the ground by the noose around his throat.

The pack baron pulled out his knife and began to slash Mr. Kenning, hacking and slicing with wild abandon until he was flayed open, slabs of flesh dangling by threads of red gristle, his intestines hanging in slimy loops. Laid raw, Mr. Kenning was still alive.

Leslie, excited by what he had done, rubbed herself against the girl next to her whose flesh was hot and slippery.

All were watching, all were breathless, all excited sexually.

With a few deft movements of the big knife, the Baron slit off Mr. Kenning's balls, then his penis. He threw them into the grass and the girls went after them, fighting over the scraps, biting and clawing each other. The boys went after the viscera, yanking it out in coils that they chewed on.

The Baron turned towards Mike Hack. He put away his knife and took out his hatchet. Bleeding, broken, Mike squirmed in the grass as the Baron towered over him, his eyes filled with a primordial malignance.

"Mr. Chalmers," Mike moaned. "Please, Mr. Chalmers..."

The Baron let out a piercing cry and brought the hatchet down. Again and again and again. Such was the punishment for disobeying the rules of the pack...

58

He ran because there were too many of them. He shot and killed two, wounded a third, and as the others set on them to feast and three more went after Doris, Louis ran into the back of the store and out the rear entrance. He cut down the alley, moving through the shadows. He waited for shapes shaggy, meat-smelling and vaguely human to jump out at him...but none did.

He made it onto the street.

There were bodies everywhere.

Had there been that many before? Two or three were lying by the car. He couldn't remember if they'd been there before. Carefully, he stepped forward and then he knew. Maybe one or two them had been, but not these others. If they had, he would have run right over them. These bodies were dirty and ragged, but they were alive. Crazies playing dead and setting up an ambush.

Very clever.

Louis scanned the darkened buildings, the rooftops, the shadowy storefronts. Even with the streetlights on, the main force could have been just about anywhere. So many places to hide. He moved forward, pretending not to notice the ones on the pavement...a man, a woman, a teenage boy. But he gave them a wide berth. He heard one of them stir behind him and swung back with the gun.

"You can get up now," he said, "nap time is over."

The boy made it to his feet first, bringing out a carving knife. Louis pulled the trigger and the kid took a round in the chest that knocked him flat. He twisted and thumped on the pavement, hissing and gagging and that was it. The man ran off, but the woman came right at him. Louis fired point-blank at her. The slug caught her in the belly and she went down, a river of blood running from her hands which were clenched over her stomach. She had no weapon. Just fingers and teeth. Her face was smudged with dirt, her eyes huge and glistening, staring black holes. She was gutshot and she wouldn't make it. She squirmed around on the ground leaving a blood trail, coughing and wheezing.

Louis was sickened by the killing he had done, yet exhilarated. There was power in holding a gun, using it. He could feel the darkness welling inside him then, something huge and organic and clutching, the beast within clawing up, scrambling for hold, wanting to own him. It *liked* the killing. It fed on it like an engorged leech at an artery.

He fought it back down.

He would kill to survive. Not for pleasure. That was the difference, that was the difference between civilization and the primal call of the jungle.

Louis stared at the bodies. They had thought him easy prey and now he had shown them different. There was a satisfaction in that.

"All right!" he called out, his voice echoing off the buildings. "You wanted me and here I am! Come and get me! You hear me? Come and get me!"

He heard sounds from between the stores, from alleys and shadowy tangles of shrubs. Rustling sounds. They were there, but they did not want to show themselves.

Sure, not much more than animals, but certainly not stupid animals.

"DID YOU FUCKING HEAR ME?" he shouted now. "SHOW YOURSELVES! WHERE'S THE GIRL? WHAT HAVE YOU DONE TO HER? YOU LET HER GO AND WE'LL DRIVE OUT! YOU CAN HAVE THIS PISSING TOWN!"

More rustling, some subdued voices, nothing more.

The woman on the ground was still squirming. Louis was suddenly filled with a hatred he had never known before. The blood, the carnage, none of it could touch him. *Macy, dear God, poor sweet Macy.* He walked right over to the woman and *kicked* her. She grunted and rolled to the side. When she tried to get up to crawl, he kicked her in the ass. When she turned to bare her bloody teeth at him, he kicked her in the face. Her eyes rolled back white and she flopped to the ground.

That got them.

He was abusing one of the pack and they simply could not allow such a thing. Whatever had rotted their minds and swept 7,000 years of recorded civilization into the dustbin, it had not taken away such very human traits as devotion and loyalty. Maybe they were animals and madmen, but they were a clan and they lived and died for the clan.

They came running out. First five or six, then twice that number and twice it again. They emerged in twos and threes, joining together in a mob. They carried axes and pipes, knives and shards of broken glass. But most simply came empty-handed. Men, women, children. Even a woman nursing a child. They were a filthy and ragged lot, looking little like modern humans and very much like a Neolithic tribe. Hunters and gatherers. And wasn't that the most amazing thing of all? That they had degenerated so quickly in just a matter of hours? Maybe that said something about the human race and maybe it said something else about the contagion that had afflicted them. The only thing that betrayed their primitiveness were the Nike shoes and cargo shorts and Wet Seal t-shirts some of the women wore. Though many were shirtless and barefoot, many others were stark naked and painted for battle.

Like New Guinea headhunters.

They assembled on the other side of the Dodge and stopped. Louis could hear them breathing, smelling the body odor and blood on them, a stench of urine and feces and something like vomit.

Behind him, he heard the pattering of feet and some red-haired kid, maybe seventeen or eighteen, came bounding out with a broomstick in his hands. He was naked, his genitals swinging from side to side. He had painted up his body with blue and gray streaks of makeup like a Celtic warrior, bands set under his eyes, his lips painted white.

Louis fired and missed.

Fired again and caught him in the arm. He could plainly hear the kid's humerus snap like a green stick. The kid skidded to his knees, screaming and spitting, a pink slime of foam on his lips.

Louis put the gun back on the others. "I want the girl," he said. "I want the girl now and if I don't get her, I start killing you sonsofbitches."

They just stood there, holding their weapons, clenching and unclenching their fists. Drool ran from their mouths. Contorted faces were twisted into sneers. Eyes were wide and staring and glassy. There didn't seem to be any intelligence in them. Hunger and need and hatred, surely, but nothing more. Louis could not believe that any of them were smart enough to orchestrate this little trap.

"Hello," a voice said.

Michelle stepped from behind the clan. She was still wearing her skirted business suit, though her nylons were torn and her usually carefully coifed long dark hair was matted and there were leaves stuck in it, what looked like flowers and sticks braided into it. There was blood all over her shirt from the killing she'd done. Even with the suit, she was unbearably tribal, vicious. This was her clan, her pack, Louis knew then with a yawning emptiness opening inside him. She was their warrior queen. They were all ritualistically painted with snaking bands, symbols, and tiger-stripes. But their faces...*yes*...they all bore the individual insignia of the tribe, the ceremonial sacraments of the wild hunt: the likenesses of skulls. Every face was painted the same. A flat marble-white base that covered face, ears, and throat, black upturned crescents around the eyes, a black oval around the mouth, and an elongated black triangle down the bridge of the nose.

The effect was chilling.

Michelle was painted the same, the dark glittering jewels of her eyes staring out from that grim death mask. She was no longer human; she was an animal now.

"Michelle...baby, come over here with me," Louis said to her, everything breaking loose inside him, tears welling in his eyes. Her glare was fierce, hungry, lethal...yet, he wasn't afraid, not really. Just the sight of her, painted up and bloody or not, crushed him, made him want to weep at her feet. He pitied her, he pitied himself. That their love should be shattered like this, torn asunder by some primordial horror from the dawn of the race. It was an obscenity. *"Please, Michelle, please..."*

She just looked at him. There was no recognition in her eyes...and yet, there was...*something*. She seemed almost hypnotized as she stared at him, unblinking. Inside, deep inside, she knew him and the knowledge made her blood run and her heart beat and her chemistry long to be joined with his.

"They're...they're all crazy, Michelle. Come with me. I don't know what the hell got a hold of you and the rest of them, but we can figure it out. Come on, baby. I love you and you know I love you. Don't do this." He felt the tears well up in his eyes and overflow onto his cheeks, felt his throat constrict until his voice sounded like that of a whiny little boy. But the emotions he was feeling were almost too much. They paraded through his head with the memories and each one laid him open. He held out a shaking hand. "Come over here, Michelle. I'm your husband. I love you. I won't let them hurt you."

She just stared. Maybe her mind was a little more intact than the others, but something essential in her was burned away. There was no love in those eyes. There was manipulation, madness, a means to an end, but certainly not warmth. They were the eyes of a spider as it hunts down its prey, prepares to suck the blood from a fly in its web...a favored fly the spider is drawn to, but a fly nonetheless.

She grinned then and for the first time he saw her teeth...Michelle always had very long teeth, perfectly straight and perfectly white...and now he saw that they had been filed to deadly points, those beautiful teeth. So when she grinned at him, it was the lewd grin of a snarling wolf, a grin of fangs...fangs that were stained pink from what she had been feeding on.

He almost went out cold at that.

She was gone. Not only had she killed, but she had torn and rent her prey with her teeth, filling herself with bloody meat.

Oh, Michelle, oh baby...oh dear God...

The primal fall.

He could hear the guy on the radio and he fully understood it as he hadn't before. You had to see someone you love regress into a beast to appreciate those words:

Bonfires and stone knives by this time next week, animals hunting in the streets...most of them of the two-legged variety. Now comes the time of the primal fall...

He made a gagging, whimpering sound in his throat that was partly repulsion and partly deep-hewn pain.

It stopped Michelle for a moment. She seemed to understand inarticulate noises better than words. Inside she felt them and understood. She cocked her head to the side, softened, but it didn't last. She closed her mouth, pursed her lips, then shook her head frantically like a dog trying to throw off bothersome flies. "Come with...us," she managed. "Walk with...us...the night, the night...*the night*..." she said to him, her words breaking off into a coarse barking sound.

Oh, it would have been easy, but he did not want to be one of them. "No," he said very loudly.

Bands of shadow fell over her face, making her already skullish appearance unpleasantly cadaverous. Her eyes were seething with a fathomless darkness. She brought up her hand and pointed one long, bloodstained finger at him. And then she said it. Said it without remorse: *"Kill him!"*

She was their queen and they were just mindless drones and soldiers. The stupor that had consumed the mob broke like the snapping of fingers and they vaulted forward. Some coming around the car, but most scrambling right over the top of it.

Louis fired three shots into the mass and then ran, pausing and shooting, pausing and shooting, dropping half a dozen of them. Then his gun clicked on empty and the others poured forth like hungry insects looking for something to tear and feed upon. Behind them, near the car, Michelle just stood there, supreme and malefic and insane, grinning and grinning at the idea of her husband's grisly death.

Louis ran...

59

They had failed...all of them, failed! And the task was so simple!

The man bolted away and with surprising speed. So quickly, in fact, that it was several moments before anyone thought of pursuing him. The Huntress fumed. She bared her teeth. She screeched into the night.

"AFTER HIM!" she cried with every ounce of volume she had, so loudly that her voice seemed to bounce off the face of the moon itself. *"BRING HIM DOWN!"*

They already knew what she was capable of. They already knew what she would do to them. She did not like failure. She did not understand it. For those who failed there was the knife, there was the cutting, the rite of the blooding. Already in those precious few hours they had been together she'd already flayed two hunters.

She watched them scatter into the streets, threading into shadow like worms into meat, all anxious to be the one who

228

brought back the pelt of the man. There would be benefits bestowed: the first choice of mates, the best food, the best weapons.

The Huntress raised her knife to the moon and howled like a wolf.

It was simple, was it not? The girl used as bait to trap the man, then the others hunters taking him, bringing him bound and broken to dump at the feet of the Huntress. Yet...the man had proven himself clever, deadly, treacherous.

As she faded into the darkness herself, she knew they would bring him down.

There were only so many places to hide in the hunting grounds and already the clan had his scent. They would cast for it, locate it, force him out of hiding and then run him, the way wild dogs would run deer to their deaths.

You can run but you can't hide.

That gave her pause...the words seemed familiar for some reason. She liked them. She would use them again. When the man was found, she would make a spectacle of him...

60

It did no good to cry, it did no good to plead, it did no good to beg: this is what Macy learned very quickly about her captors. They were not human, not anymore. Only human minds, *civilized minds,* understood the high concept of compassion and these things were not human, they were animals. Dirty, smelling, vile animals.

So she did not fight.

She did not beg.

She allowed herself to be dragged naked through the streets, through secret channels of night. Her hands were bound. She was naked and smeared with gore, stinking of urine and sweat. They had thrown a noose around her throat and now she was their pet, their slave. Why they didn't just kill her, she didn't know. But she prayed for it.

She prayed for death.

In those rare moments when she wasn't overwhelmed by horror and repugnance, Macy was amazed at how her world, a world that had been perfectly ordinary twenty-four hours ago, now resembled something out of prehistory. When she was lucid enough to examine things objectively, the absurdity of it floored her. It couldn't be. It just could not be. But it was and, try as she might, this was one nightmare she could not awake from. Her world, once somewhat dull with repetition yet bright with possibility, had become this: a narrow, nameless void where she was now the victim/plaything/pet and prey of a family of predatory savages. Cannibals. Killers. Animals. Absolute fucking monsters.

And Louis? Where was Louis?

It hurt to think about him because a few days ago he was just the husband of the lady next door, that being Michelle Shears. But today, with all they'd been through, he had become something more: guardian, friend, mentor...God, too many things. Her heart pounded at the memory of him.

It was funny, but before all this she'd never said much more than hello to him when she saw him out washing his car or raking the leaves, that sort of thing. Oh, Michelle and he had those backyard parties every summer, but Mom made such a fool of herself that Macy slipped away soon as possible. So before today, she had not known him. Not really. But they had been through a lot together and she felt herself missing him terribly like some strong emotional bond had been cemented between them. She ached for him in her heart, not because she was hot for him or anything, but because he was the only thing stable she'd found on this awful day. He had been there for her. He risked his neck for her. He'd done it all without a second thought or with any ulterior motives. She held the image of his face in her mind and it calmed her. She knew that if he was alive, he would do anything he could to rescue her.

If he was alive.

Thinking this way, she began to realize that she liked him in a way that was not strictly platonic. It was stupid and she knew it. Really, really stupid. She was sixteen for godsake and he was like forty or something. He was married to Michelle and she was gorgeous, tall and leggy with long dark hair sweeping down her back. Carried herself with that stature, that poise that was simply beyond Macy. Louis would never even consider for a moment, he would never think—

But what if he did, Macy? she asked herself. *What if he did? What if they were still together and he put an arm around her...what then?*

And she knew. She could feel the heat inside her that she'd only felt once or twice before and never for boys in school, always for older men. The boys at school were gangly and silly and immature. They were not men. Not like Louis was. Sure, if he tried something, she would melt in his arms. She would let him lay her down. She would let him inside her. She knew that now. Maybe she'd tried to pretend otherwise ever since this afternoon when they'd hooked up, but she didn't doubt it anymore. She felt it building in her, that blaze, ever since they'd sat on his porch and he had looked at her with that...that *hunger.*

She'd thought it then. There had been precious few boys at school that interested her, but often older men intrigued her. And Louis intrigued her like no other. She wanted her first time to be with him. Not a sweaty, groping, inexperienced boy...but a man. An older man.

Get a grip!

Yes, yes, she had to. Where was all this nonsense coming from? It had to be the stress and weirdness and fear. That had to be it. Because this wasn't the way she thought. This was how Chelsea or Shannon or one of the slutty cheerleaders thought. They fantasized about things like this, about having sex with older men and spreading their legs and feeling someone pushing into them with a slow and deliberate rhythm that would speed up and speed up until you couldn't take it anymore. The feel of flesh against flesh, tongues mating with tongues—

Macy was breathing hard now, her flesh hot to the touch. If Louis had been there, she would have blushed.

Or maybe you'd just go down on your knees...

Oh, good God, it was happening again.

It was taking control of her again. She'd been worried all day since she'd attacked Chelsea that it would return, that it would come back and claim her...that boiling darkness. That whatever iniquitous flower that bloomed in her head and closed back up, would bloom anew and take her back to that awful place. That primal and destructive place where you acted on any and all urges with sinister delight. She could remember it now. How it had felt, how it had

(excited)

offended her. How all the dirty and dark desires in the pit of her mind had jumped to the fore and she had no control, had not honestly wanted control or even understood what control was. Was it happening again? Was it taking her over again? If it was, she was only glad that Louis was not here, because if he was, she would want him. She would put her mouth on his and her hands on him and demand that he put his on her, do things to her, use her and use her again.

Still breathing hard and trembling now, too, Macy realized that it was *not* happening to her. At least, not how it had happened before. Though she would never have admitted it, she'd felt *free* when the madness had taken her. She was feeling that way now. But not in a dangerous way. She was just feeling the stirrings of who and what she was. She was feeling desire and lust and she was not honestly uncomfortable with it. The woman in her was making herself known and although it scared her to a certain extent, she felt liberated by it. Because she had been expecting it for a long time and now it was here.

But she had to be realistic here.

But if Louis is not dead and we find each other, then...then...

She only hoped that if he was dead it had been quick, relatively painless. Something that would take him fast. She had been dehumanized to the point now that she was becoming almost desensitized to everything. She didn't care what they did to her, she just hoped that Louis Shears died quickly.

The girl who was leading her stopped.

Macy realized she had been stumbling along for a long time now, totally disconnected from reality. She knew

Greenlawn well. But in the darkness, she could not say exactly where they were. The man did not seem to be sure either. He was standing there, looking around. He said something to the woman and she went down on her hands and knees, crawling through the grass of somebody's yard and *sniffing*. Sniffing like a dog. She jumped up excitedly, started making grunting sounds and gesticulating madly. The man seemed to understand what she was saying. Macy couldn't. That grunting and snorting...like the guttural language of wild hogs.

The man walked to a tree and pissed on it, scenting his trail. The boy hopped over there and started to do the same, but the man hit him, clopped him upside the head, knocking him down. The boy did not seem angry. Better to be hit than put on the spit.

They moved on.

The girl gave the noose a jerk and Macy stumbled forward. The boy kept watching her. He couldn't have been more than ten or eleven, but every time he looked at her with those dead amethyst eyes, a leering depravity came over his face that was elfin, carnal, unspeakable. And when it did, he groped himself.

Whenever the woman saw him do it, she kicked him.

The man trudged along. He had a black plastic Hefty bag tossed over one shoulder that was bulging from what it carried. Now and again what was in there shifted with a moist, slopping noise.

The remains of the woman they'd butchered.

Macy had tasted her blood, her meat. There hadn't been a choice. She could still feel its texture on her tongue, its flavor that was rich and sweet and nauseating. Yet...yet, part of her almost *liked* it. That dark part that kept trying to insinuate itself. Macy did not want it, but she really didn't have the strength to fight it and why fight it anyway? Inch by inch, it was taking her over. Something had shut down in her and something else was waking up.

But she wouldn't be like *them*.

Never.

Ever.

She refused.

But part of her, maybe instinct, was much sharper than before. For she was hearing everything, feeling everything. Never had a night been like this, never did the breeze seem to be overloaded with the scents of night blooms and dark earth and green grass. The odors were so pungent, each almost seemed to have a flavor. And despite the shadows shrouding the streets, she was seeing exceptionally well...everything vibrant, vivid. Like a cat.

It all scared her...and intrigued her.

The girl yanked her lead and Macy moved forward. They were taking her to their lair and she could not even conceive of what sort of place that might be. Down alleys, through vacant lots thick with hay-smelling weeds. She thought they were down by the city park. They moved along until they reached a high, whitewashed building with a steeple above brushing the stars. Macy knew where they were now. Yes, by the park, 8th Street and Holly Avenue: the Salem Evangelical Lutheran Church.

This place? This was where they were taking her?

She was led up the stairs, pushed through the doors. It was a narrow edifice, the walls pressing in from either side, rough-hewn beams overhead. A crowded aisle, pews to either side. Like some goddamn frontier church in Dodge City or one of those places, she thought.

Claustrophobic.

Cave-like.

Yes, the den of animals, the warren of beasts.

She smelled the stench of death right away. There were shadows clustering amongst the pews, many of them. The shadows came out to greet them, becoming people or something like people. They rushed in towards her. Dirty, oily hands fondled her. Moonstruck faces. Grinning sawtoothed mouths. All those people were taking hold of her and the smell that came off of them...sweat and body odor, blood and meat and filth.

She was pushed up towards the altar.

It smelled like urine and bloody viscera.

Bodies were dumped there, three or four of them, all slit open like salmon, what was inside carefully cleaned out and dumped into buckets. And high above, where Christ had spent so many years nailed to the cross, there was another effigy now. Christ was gone.

There was a corpse nailed up there.

The corpse of an obese woman that was dark with dried blood. Her breasts were immense and flabby, her stomach swollen, her thighs pale and meaty. She was open in places and Macy could plainly see the crude black stitchwork that held her together. But the suturing had burst in places and it was evident that she had been stuffed with dry leaves, hay, cane straw.

Yes, gutted...then stuffed.

A totemic effigy.

A straw hag.

Macy stared up at the abomination speechlessly. It was profane, grotesque. Candles had been thrust into the corpse-woman's mouth and the hollows of her eyes. They were lit, burning, guttering, casting eldritch shadows over the blood-drenched obscenity the altar had become.

The girl yanked Macy's lead and tossed her to the altar, into the dirty straw and bloody carpet, there amongst the slaughterhouse of human husks, limbs, and snaking entrails. Macy squirmed in the bile and slime, staring up horrified and awestruck at the plucked, stuffed, and slit goddess of the new church...

61

Louis was running.

Maybe from the town and maybe from himself, but mostly from the clan coming after him. He was running and running, trying not to think of what had just happened back there. Trying not to think of anything else but the clan hunting him down. Trying not to see Michelle and that look in her eyes or to remember that it was her, really, that had put the clan on him.

He couldn't think about that.

Because the only reason he'd stayed in this goddamn town was because of her and now she was a stranger, a sadistic queen wasp with her very own hive. If he hadn't stayed, then he would not be a player in this nightmare and Macy would be with him. Not out there. Not dead or raped or worse...just like *them*.

Not now, though, not now.

He couldn't worry about any of that now.

Already his lungs were aching and his feet were getting sore, his clothes drenched with sweat. Jesus, he was too old for this shit. Just way too old. He needed a hiding place, but everything he saw—house, alley, or hedgerow—just looked alive with threat. Dark places where gnarled hands could find him, bring him down and do the most awful things.

He rounded a turn on Main Street and paused. He could keep going and maybe run right out of town...if he could keep this up for another mile or so. Or he could find a car or a building, some place to hide. There simply wasn't the time to check every single parked car for a set of keys. If he started that, they'd be all over him.

He looked down Main, looked down the side streets and interconnecting avenues. He stood there, hands on his knees, panting and panting. Jesus, he just couldn't go on like this. If he didn't find a safe place or a car to get out of town with, then this would go on until dawn, maybe even longer than that. The clan would run him right to death like dogs running a stag.

Main Street twisted and turned like the back of a snake, lots of sharp corners and tall buildings and leafy trees to obscure things, little rolling hills. There were so many places to hide. He imagined that most of the stores and buildings on Main would be locked. One or two might be open, but again, he just did not have the time to be checking doors. His instinct was telling him just to go home. But if Michelle wanted him dead, then she would no doubt direct the clan there.

If she remembered where home was.

Louis looked behind him and, yes, they were coming. He saw them crest a hill behind him, maybe a dozen of them washed down by the moonlight. He could hear their pattering feet and their shouting voices. Why the hell didn't they just give up? Why didn't they go after someone else?

Maybe there isn't anyone else, Louis. Maybe you're the last one.

Christ, that was unthinkable. If it were true, if there were thousands of them out there...he'd never make it. He just couldn't make it.

He took off running, getting a second wind now. His body was aching and he was just glad that he had not smoked in like seven or eight years. He'd picked up jogging about three years back, but that hadn't lasted. He wished now that he'd kept up with it.

More of them now.

The fast ones had come over the hill first. The young and fit ones, the middle-aged people lagging behind. But now they were all coming down the hill.

Louis put forth a burst of speed, coming around one of those sharp corners and sprinting through shadows thrown by a row of buildings. He darted down an alley, came out the other side and jogged down an avenue, cutting through yards and the parking lot of a gas station. He paused, trying to catch his breath. He could still hear them.

He ran down a narrow side street until he linked up with Providence, which itself ran south to north right through the middle of town. He crossed the Providence Street Bridge which spanned the Green River and the sounds of his pursuers faded into the distance. He kept going, trying to put as much distance between himself and them as possible. If he followed Providence Street for about six or seven blocks, 7th Avenue would cut across it and then it was just a short hop to Rush Street. If he wanted to do that, of course. And he was thinking he did. Because he knew that neighborhood and though people were crazy there, too, he knew where quite a few of them kept the keys to their cars.

Providence was one of those streets that was partially commercial and partially residential. You'd pass two blocks of private homes, hit a couple bars, maybe a furniture outlet or a truck depot, pass some more houses and there was a beer distributor and a little hole in the wall hamburger stand or a fried chicken joint. Lots of little shops and taverns, their storefronts changing all the time as an archery supplier went out and an upholstery place came in. Lots of the storekeepers lived right above their businesses as their parents and grandparents had.

Louis had grown up just off Providence on Middleton Street. Though his parents were long gone as were most of his relatives, the house he grew up in still stood, though the second story had been taken off following a fire fifteen years before. But he had grown up on south Providence Street and he knew every nook and cranny, every courtyard and cul-de-sac. Every old empty shed and tucked away warehouse. When he was a kid there'd been a big red barn on the corner of 5th Avenue and Providence with a large fenced in yard where they used to play. Years ago it had been a livery stable, but that was long before his time as were the old street cars that used to run up and down Providence. The tracks were still there, he was told, under the present street, along with the remains of the brick road that had housed them.

He came to 4th Avenue and collapsed under a row of spreading oak trees, just panting and gasping. He knew these trees. As a kid he'd climbed them. You could shimmy out onto the branches that overhung Providence and watch cars and trucks pass beneath you. He knew his initials and those of his friends were still carved up there on the tree above him. Just down the block was the Sloden Mortuary, a looming gray concrete edifice flanking the town cemetery, and across the street from that there was a creamery on the corner—Fretzen Brothers—and lots of old houses pressed in tightly together.

Sure, it hadn't really changed much.

Except they weren't really houses anymore, just block upon block of cages. Each one filled with one or more slavering things that used to be human. In fact—

They were coming.

It didn't seem possible, but they were. He started to wonder if they were not only a pack in appearance, but in reality. If maybe, somehow, they had his scent or were going to run him to ground. He'd taken a pretty circuitous route and still they'd found him, casting around for his scent like true dogs.

Louis didn't think he could run anymore.

They were still a long way off. He looked up at the moonlight dappled tree above him. It rose a good thirty feet above Providence, if not forty. Looking around, he checked the trunk which was so wide that two men could not have put their arms around it. Some of the old footholds had been broken off by storms or children. But there was enough there. He reached up and grabbed a limb above his head, getting his foot on one of the old knobs. He started up, straining and cursing under his breath. Definitely feeling his age. His foot slipped once and he dangled there by the limb, but finally he pulled himself up, breaking spiderwebs with his face. Stout limbs came out from the trunk like spokes. He ducked under some and climbed up others until he was a good fifteen feet up. He sat on a branch and hugged the trunk and just waited, sweat dripping off the end of his nose.

He could hear them.

When he caught his breath, he climbed higher like a frightened monkey.

They were getting closer...

62

When Macy came to, maybe an hour or two later, she was suspended in midair about three feet off the blackened carpet of the altar. Her wrists were noosed with hemp ropes that were tied off above. She was hanging there, the ropes cutting into her flesh like hot wires, seeming to wind tighter and tighter, cutting off her circulation. Her arms felt numb, but her shoulders—which were bearing the brunt of her weight—were burning with a dull, constant throbbing.

But the pain seemed distant.

She was in a den of them.

They were everywhere, huddled in the smoky darkness, moving about like primordial shadows in the tenebrous haze. The only lights burning were from candles that threw a flickering, uneven illumination that reflected off clouds of slow-moving smoke in the air. They had built a fire using sticks and pews shattered to kindling. About a dozen of them were huddled around it, men, women, a couple dirty naked children. An old woman, also naked, with terrible pendulous breasts pocked with sores was tossing leaves or herbs into the fire, chanting something beneath her breath.

Macy could not hear what it was.

But the others answered her with harsh, throaty groans that did not sound human at all, more like the low rumbling growl of wolves or dogs. Now and again, one of the children would make a yipping sound that reminded her of hyenas fighting over a carcass.

The smoke burned her eyes, a greasy film lay over her bare flesh. She could just make out things scattered over the floor that looked like bones and hides, maybe a few jawless skulls lying about. She could not see them clearly, but she could smell them. Smell the death on them, smell the tallow and blood of the skins.

Her first instinct was to shout, to twist and fight against the ropes, to scream for help. But she'd already done that and knew very well the futility of such things. Sometimes, sometimes when you were laid out as meat in the cave of a bear it was better not to draw attention to yourself.

She saw that three other women and one man were roped together at the foot of the altar. One of the women was looking up at her with shocked, fearful eyes. And that meant she was not like them, not an animal. *Normal.* Macy felt pity for her, but there was nothing to be done.

This was no longer a church, Macy saw. It was no sanctified place but the rotting, filthy den of depraved things like troglodytes, cave-dwellers and man-eaters, walking pestilence from a forgotten age.

And realizing this, realizing that these people were not just crazy, not just a bunch of lunatics out on a binge, but primeval and animalistic things, a flesh and blood regression of the species, she was terrified. For a darkness had taken the world and those that hunted it did not seek the light, they were content to scratch in the shadows of reason. The church was a cave, a warren, a lair now. Those things out there were not men and women any longer, they were just...animals. God was not here. This was not his house. This was a place of pagan evils now. The corpse-woman on the cross was evidence of that. And Macy did not doubt that with regression, with the reaffirmation of race memory, that this place was thick with primordial spirits, with long forgotten dark gods of fertility and sacrifice. And maybe, just maybe, if she shut her mind down and let it hum along at its lowest level she might see them: creeping, shaggy things from the misty past that demanded burnt offerings, demanded the flesh and blood of the faithful, expiation in its purest form: *Give unto me your firstborn for I would find their flesh pleasing.*

She looked around, squinting. The main doors were open, the night breeze sucking out the smoke. She could see them, the savages, coming in out of the night, dragging things behind them (one man had a naked girl on a rope). A couple were screwing atop a heap of bloody hides. An old woman picked things from the scalps of children, often eating what she found. A man sharpened a bone into an awl. A teenage girl cut designs into her skin with a razor blade while another girl painted her face with the blood from a carcass of a dog while a boy sawed the pelt free with a knife. Others crawled over the floor, picking at bones and refuse, scratching symbols into the stones, gnawing on meat and offal, licking their fingers and groping themselves and snorting in the shadows.

Jesus.

Is this what human kind had evolved from?

Is this why the species fought so hard for civilization, for order, why they adopted a church that was brutal in its dealings with paganism and adapted strict laws to punish any who acted...*uncivilized?* She thought so. This was why people were so offended by cannibalism, by headhunting, by ritual murder—yes, it was a cultural thing, of course, a *taboo* and it was taboo because this was the sort of thing that was skulking in man's past, the very thing man had finally risen up from, stamped out, was horrified at his core *of.* For every sadistic murder, every cannibalistic act, was a reminder of our past, what we had evolved from and what we were afraid to backslide *into*.

But how had it happened?

How had the darkness of the past returned? How had grim racial memory swallowed the civilized world and plunged it back to this degeneracy?

Maybe this regression into primitivism is natural. Maybe like the Dark Ages of Europe that followed the collapse of the Roman Empire and thrust things like culture and learning into the pit until the Renaissance, this was pre-ordained somehow. Maybe the beast within was always more active than anyone ever guessed, much closer to the surface, teeth bared and claws out, ready to pounce. For there was a simplicity to it, wasn't there? The beast with his rudimentary wants and needs, feeding and fucking, hunting and breeding, living only from one day to the next to satisfy the simple drives of aggression, procreation, and instinctual craving. The world had gone native, it had gone savage and tribal. A new Dark Ages had been heralded in. Like maybe the race was fed up with the burden of civilization, with progress and culture and law, greed and envy, religious intolerance and political corruption, it wanted to return to a time when all men were truly considered equal, when you were only as successful as your last hunt, your innate cunning, the children you bore, the weapons you fashioned with your own two hands. Yes, the call of the wild, an atavistic longing in every man, woman, and child to return to an age of basal simplicity wherein the fire that roasted your meat and warmed your cave also lit your world.

The law of the jungle.

Survival of the fittest.

Darwinism rendered to its simplest form.

These were the things Macy was thinking. She had always had an intellectual bent and prided herself upon it. Any thick-headed idiot could score on the field and any bimbo could jump up and down and cheer, but thinking, *real* thinking, that was a gift, that took mental power, discipline, and drive. And realizing this, realizing that she was still an intellectual, she knew she was absolutely fucked.

There would be no place for thinkers in this new world of darkness.

She stared out, watching them. There wasn't much else to do. Some of the smoke had cleared and she now wished it hadn't. Things were revealed now that she did not want to look upon. For suspended over the fire from a tripod of what looked like aluminum tent poles secured at their apex with electrical tape, was the body of a boy. He was being smoked and from the smell—that sickening odor of blackened meat—he had been cooking for some time.

Macy squirmed now.

She had seen things, witnessed things, been humiliated, beaten, and abused, but this she could not look upon...a child cooked over a fire.

But what came next was infinitely worse.

A man and woman came to the fire. The man had a knife and the woman had a metal pail. He prodded the boy's corpse with his knife, making it swing back and forth with a slow grisly motion. The boy's flesh was blackened in places, his belly was bloated pink-yellow and shiny like that of a roasted pig. The man jabbed the knife into him and hot juice ran into the fire, sizzling. Using the knife, the man began slicing slabs of meat, sawing them free. He tossed these to the crowd. He hacked off the boy's genitals and dropped them in the pail. Then he peeled the flesh from his belly and chest, carefully carving it until it came off in a single sheet he yanked free.

The savages around him, their faces oily and flickering with impure light, could barely contain themselves.

With a forceful plunge, he buried the knife just below the navel and slit the boy gut to throat. He cut free the stomach, liver, kidneys and intestines. It took some time. As he did so, the others were eating, chewing on the flesh, their faces smeared with blood and fat. The internals went into the pail. Using the haft of the knife, he broke through the boy's ribs, pounding and pounding until the bones gave. Using his hands, his snapped the ribs free and tossed them aside. He cut through the lungs, peeled them back, and sliced the muscled mass of the heart free. It, too, went into the bucket.

The crowd of savages were roaring and squealing with delight.

Macy did not want to look, but she could not help herself. She looked over at the roped-up man and the three women. The one woman looked up at her as before. She was gagged like the others so she did not scream. But judging from her wide, tear-filled eyes, she wanted to.

The boy's corpse was cut free.

The man dumped it on the floor. Using a hatchet, he chopped off both legs, then the arms. The crowd took charge of these, fighting over them, biting and scratching. The head he did not share. He chopped at it until the cranium was smashed and then he peeled the scalp and shards of bone free, snapping them like crab's legs. He slit the membrane and exposed the brain. Several women had gathered around him now and he happily shared with them. They sat in a crude circle, dipping their scabby fingers into the skull and scooping out hunks of brain that they chewed almost delicately, sucking them between their lips and pulping them with their teeth.

Meanwhile, the woman with the pail divided up the intestines which were quickly spitted on sticks and roasted in the flames. Blood and fat dropped from them, sputtering on the coals.

Macy saw the heart get pierced with a stick and looked away.

She needed to throw up and not so much from the sight but from the smell. Out of the corner of her eye, she saw one of the women licking the inside of the boy's skull clean while the bloody man with the knife violently fucked one of her friends.

Oh God, that stink.

Then Macy realized someone was behind her. Her bra was cut free, then her panties. Callused fingers gripped the globes of her ass, slapped them, poked them with stubby fat fingers. A man. It was a man. He was pressed up against her and she could feel his hardness spearing between her legs. He licked her neck and breathed into her ear. His breath stank like a gangrenous wound.

He reached up and cut the ropes holding her wrists. She hit the altar and prepared to fight him. She had no doubt she was going to be raped. But she would not make it easy. He grinned down at her, his eyes like open infected sores.

He reached for her with crusty, bleeding hands...

63

Getting down out of the tree was not quite as simple as getting up it, Louis found. After the clan had gone and he had a chance to breathe, he waited a time and then began his descent. He went slowly because he was no kid anymore and a drop out of a tree might mean a broken limb. And something like that tonight in Greenlawn was deadly. So he climbed down slowly. Then about eight feet from the ground his foot slipped off a limb and he nearly fell right onto the pavement. A lucky grab saved his bacon. His hand hooked around a limb and he lowered himself to safety.

And then he ran.

Like a hunted animal he ran home.

When he finally made it to his house on Rush Street, he was panting and sore and drenched with sweat. He collapsed in his front yard and just breathed. He looked up at the stars through the tree branches and was amazed that they were still the same. Shouldn't they have changed, too?

Finally, he sat up.

It wasn't safe to be lounging around like this and he knew it.

His brain kept telling him he needed a plan, a mode of survival...but there was nothing. What could he do? Where could he hide? The world had fallen to barbarism and the wild things were everywhere.

He looked down Rush Street.

The streetlights were still on, moths and insects circling them. All the houses were dark as tombs. The Merchant's next door. The Maub's, the Soderberg's, the Loveman's. Even the Gould's. There was only a dead silence coming from the Starling's and Kenning's across the street. Nothing but shadows, the breeze stirring tree limbs. Usually at night like this you could hear a few cars in the distance, the distant rumble of trucks out on the highway. But tonight...nothing.

He heard a dog howl in the distance.

A shouting voice from several streets away.

He smelled smoke on the breeze from burning neighborhoods and firepits.

Nothing else.

Just the steady sighing respiration of the night world. Probably, he imagined, exactly how summer nights had sounded during the Pleistocene after the retreat of the glaciers.

He got to his feet and walked across the yard and there, stopped dead. Two of his windows had been shattered. The front door was standing wide open. Within was the blackness of plundered crypts. There. Now what? Did he run off or did he dare go in there and face what had done this, what might still be waiting inside?

A weapon.

He would need a weapon. He still had his lockblade knife in his pocket, but he wanted something bigger that he could strike from a distance with.

His mind frantically searched for something. There were plenty of things in the garage. But his keys were still in the Dodge on Main. He remembered there was a rake in the backyard. Better than nothing. Carefully, staying in the shadows, he scouted his way back there, expecting long-armed, hollow-eyed slavering things to leap out at him at any moment.

There was the rake right where he'd left it two weeks before after cleaning up the weeds in the garden. He could hear Michelle's voice bitching at him to put it in the garage before it rusted.

Michelle, Michelle, Michelle...Good God.

But he couldn't think about that, he couldn't—

The door to the garage was wide open.

Dick Starling had escaped.

Now the night seemed more dangerous than ever. But he knew he had to look, to find out. He crept over there. It looked like the door had been kicked in. Dick Starling had been rescued by one of them. It was quiet inside. Raising the rake with one hand, Louis groped in the darkness, found the switch, clicked it on. The light would be like a beacon to them, but he had to take the chance.

Dick Starling was gone, of course.

Louis had a crazy, demented hope that one of them slipped in here and killed him...but no. He was just gone. The duct tape had been cut free of his wrists. It was all over the floor like shed snakeskin. The chain and Masterlock were nowhere to be seen.

Get moving.

He set aside the rake and grabbed a hammer. Then he shut off the light and tip-toed across the yard. He went in the back. Creeping up the back stairs into the kitchen. Silence. He waited, waited some more. He moved down the hallway, sweat running down his face. His heart was pounding so hard he was certain someone would hear if they were there.

He smelled blood.

In the living room, he clicked on the light. There was a body sprawled on the carpet. A woman. Naked, pale. Blood was splattered up the walls, soaking into the carpet. She had been gutted like a steer, her entrails stretched across the room like dead snakes.

He turned away.

Bonnie Maub. It was Bonnie Maub from a few houses away. She had come here, maybe looking for help and...well, *they* had gotten her. Maybe Dick Starling. Maybe the ones that had set him free. His stomach in his throat, Louis looked at her a little closer. Other than her abdomen being ripped open, there didn't appear to be any other damage. He was no anatomist. He couldn't be sure, but it looked like whoever had killed her had taken some of her guts with them. She looked awfully... *hollow.*

Enough.

He was going to the Soderberg's. Mike Soderberg had guns. Back outside then, hammer gripped tightly, waiting for death to come for him. He slipped past the Merchant house, moving quietly down the sidewalk to the Soderberg's. It was dark. He crouched by the rose bushes, his head rioting with their perfume. He could see no outward damage. Maybe the savages had overlooked it.

Cautiously, his heart in his throat, he crept up to the house...

64

Macy, the rope still binding her wrists, was dragged over to the foot of the altar where the other captives were herded. Here was the man, the other three women she had seen. All roped-up like swine ready for the spit. There were others in the shadows, she knew. She could hear them sobbing and crying out, but could not see them.

The man who had brought her over had left her.

She had thought for sure he would rape her, but the old woman at the fire called out to him in some coarse tongue and he went over to her. Macy was forgotten. At least for the time being. The stench in the church was indescribable. Just filthy and low. Blood and meat and carrion. A high, hot stink of absolute dark corruption like the den of buzzards or vultures must smell. And these things that held her captive were no more human than that. Just beasts. Crawling, flesh-eating beasts. Many of them were still at the fire, feeding on the corpse of the roasted boy. He had been sheared down to bone in many places. His ribs were standing out, shining and well-plucked. She could see the vertebrae at his throat.

How long?

How long before it's me they cook like that?

The stink of the burning flesh and meat was probably the most offensive thing she'd ever smelled. It revolted her and...intrigued her at the same time. She did not know exactly why. Only that somehow, some way, it was almost...*familiar.* Like she had smelled it long ago in a dream. And realizing this, she wondered if it was not some warped race memory kicking to life in her, remembering the smell of roasted boy from some dim, bone-heaped cave of prehistory.

God.

The old woman with the pendulous breasts came over with two boys. They were naked, their bodies blackened with ash. The old woman wore nothing but a sort of shawl made of canvas or maybe skin. She pointed at the captives with dirty fingers, mumbling something under her breath that was absolutely unintelligible. The boys seemed excited. Down on their knees, they crawled past the captives, poking them with their fingers. The tied man was oblivious to it. The woman who'd looked up at Macy with shocked eyes just sobbed. The other two women gasped.

The old woman stomped her feet twice.

The boys untied one of the women who'd gasped. Macy recognized her from somewhere. She was maybe thirty with long red hair. Rough-looking like the sort that might have chummed around with her mother out at the Hair of the Dog on the highway. When they untied her, careful not to free her wrists, she came to life fighting and kicking at them. A man came over with a length of iron pipe and hit her three or four times until the fight drained from her.

"Please," she moaned, spitting out blood. "Please...please just let me go..."

She might as well have tried to talk a snake out of biting her, it had as much effect on them. They dragged her away by the ankles, pulling her up onto the altar and depositing her at the feet of that gruesome straw hag nailed to the cross. The burning candles stuffed in the hag's eyes and mouth guttered and dripped wax. Macy saw something she had not seen before: the hag was like a pincushion. There were things stuck into the flesh. Knives, needles, screwdrivers. It only made that gutted, stuffed corpse look that much more perverse, that much more pagan.

The old woman barked something.

One of the boys gripped a steak knife thrust in the hag's thigh and pulled it free. He studied the blade with the rapt fascination all boys seemed to have for weapons, save this was infinitely worse. Not curiosity, really, but an almost religious awe. He pressed the blade to his lips, then went down on his knees, yanked the woman's head up and quickly slit her throat.

The woman flopped and gagged, drowning in her own blood. It did not take too long. That's all the ceremony there was to it...though Macy knew they had not slit her throat at the hag's feet for no reason.

It was ritualistic.

It was an offering.

They had sacrificed her to the hag.

The boy slid the knife back in the thigh and then he and the others began painting their bodies with the pooling blood. And when their faces and chests were gleaming red, they both painted a weird little symbol on the stitched belly of the hag.

Macy was offended, of course, but not shocked, not really. She had seen so much by this point that trifling things like ordinary shock were beyond her. That intellectual part of her brain that was finding it harder and harder to swim upstream against the currents of atavism that were trying to drown her, knew that it had just witnessed some primeval tribal rite that had not been practiced for eons.

And maybe Macy was fascinated in some way by this, but the woman next to her was not.

She was screaming.

Her gag had come off and she was screaming manically. Macy kept telling her under her breath to shut the hell up, but it was too late. The man and woman who'd first butchered the boy came over. Covered in drying blood, they were savage and insane things. They were whispering under their breath with a chilling sort of hiss. They untied the screaming woman and dragged her off maybe five feet. The man held her arms and forced her down on the stone floor. The woman grabbed her legs, forcing them apart, gripping her thighs and opening them like she was about to deliver a baby.

She brought her head between the woman's legs.

Is she going down on her? some crazed, near-hysterical voice in Macy's head wondered. But Macy knew that whatever was going to happen would have absolutely nothing to do with passion, forced or otherwise. She saw the savage woman grin. Her teeth had been filed to blood-stained points.

Macy gasped.

The bound woman screamed again.

And Macy saw it, though she knew she should have looked away. The savage woman opened her mouth and bit down on what was between the legs, bit down on it with a snapping of her jaws. As her victim screamed with a high, mad treble, she tore and ripped at what she had bitten into, worrying it like a dog trying to shred a piece of tasty meat from a bone.

The screaming women went silent, fell limp. Maybe it was trauma and maybe it was shock. Macy never knew. She saw the savage woman. Her face glistening red, a flap of meat in her jaws.

Macy went out cold...

65

Louis entered the Soderberg house. He stepped in there, sensing immediately that he had just made a very bad mistake. The house smelled like shit and blood and God only knew what else. A steaming odor of waste and offal. He moved through it, fighting against his own fears. He had to find that gun cabinet. He had to have a weapon that could drop those animals from a distance.

Perfectly good plan.

It took a moment or two for Louis to get his bearings. He'd only been in the Soderberg's house once or twice. He entered the living room, trying to remember where Mike Soderberg's den was. Because that's where his gun cabinet was. He seemed to think it was on the other side of the house, somewhere near the kitchen.

Louis, his heart galloping wildly in his chest, moved through the dining room, barking his shin on a chair and cussing under his breath. So much for stealth. As he came into the kitchen, he thought he heard something out in the backyard. A thumping sound. He cocked his head, listening, sweating and trembling.

Nothing.

Nerves, probably just nerves, he told himself.

He moved on, the moonlight coming through the windows thick as curdled milk.

He became aware then of a particularly vile smell that was sharp and revolting that he could only acquaint with something like rotting onions...or *hides*. Because when he'd been a boy his class had gone on a school trip to a mink farm. The heaped mink hides had smelled something like this, pungent and unbearably musky. They were told that the stink came from the mink's scent glands. He was smelling that now. Or something like it.

It was far too strong to mean nothing.

And that's when a man stepped around the side of the refrigerator. He had something in his hand that might have been an axe. The stench was coming from him. He let out a little shrilling cry and swung what he had at Louis, missing him cleanly. Louis did not hesitate. He swung his hammer with everything he had and felt it connect with the guy's skull with a sickening hollow thud.

The guy folded up.

The backyard suddenly exploded with light, flooding the kitchen. Louis crouched down. He thought at first it was an explosion of some sort, but from the quality of the light he could see it was a fire. A big fire. He raised himself up and peered out the windows above the sink. Yes, there was a bonfire burning in the backyard. He saw five or six naked forms dancing around it. They looked like kids. Somebody was tied to a tree and kindling had been banked up around them.

They were burning.

The kids were hopping around happily, burning someone. And from the way the bound figure was squirming there was no doubt that they were alive. Tied and gagged, but alive. Something snapped in Louis. He couldn't watch this. He charged out the back door with a fierce cry, a rebel yell that came from deep within him. He charged with the hammer in one hand and his knife in the other. One of the kids, a teenage girl, launched herself at him and he staved her skull in with the hammer and stabbed a boy in the belly. The girl fell limp at his feet and the boy hobbled away.

The others ran off, taking the girl with them.

Panting, slicked with sweat, his hand holding the knife bloody up to the wrist and the hammer clotted with gore, he looked very much like a savage himself. He whirled around, expecting attack from every quarter. But none came. The tree was engulfed in flames as was the person tied to it. They were beyond help. The flames were so high he could barely see them. But the stink of roasting flesh was thick and nauseating.

Louis fell to his knees, needing to cry, to vent himself somehow.

And from the shadows a voice said, "Over here, Louis. I'm over here..."

66

For some time, the thing that had once been Angie Preen and her tribe of hunters had been shadowing the teenage boy and his females. They had watched in rapt fascination as the boy led them on one conquest after another, running down strays and dogs and attacking smaller packs for food and weapons. They took no slaves. They killed and feasted on all. But mostly, they just killed for the sport of it.

Angie had killed for the sport, too.

But that was just to get the scent of blood into the tribe's nostrils. To get them a taste of meat. It was necessary to get them enraged, to get them hungry and aggressive. None of this was truly a conscious decision on Angie's part. She was going purely on instinct and race memory now. She knew these things without thinking them. For in the politics of survival only two things really mattered: territory and dominance. The boy and his females were poaching what Angie considered to be her territory and as she exerted her dominance over the tribe, so must the tribe exert their dominance against intruders to protect their hunting grounds.

The boy and his females were resting now.

In a vacant lot they had stopped and built a fire. Their blood-slicked bodies were lying in the grass. Several of the females were licking each other's wounds. Two of them lay with the boy, their heads resting against his naked loins. One female was on watch, casting a wary eye into the darkness. She was alert and ready.

Streaked with blood and paint, Angie rose up from the cover of the hedges and stretched her bowstring with an arrow. She sighted in on the female who was watching. As her eyes swept across the field, Angie sucked in a breath of air and then slowly let it out between clenched teeth, releasing the arrow at the same time.

There was a barely audible whooshing noise.

The arrow pierced the female right in the center of her back, puncturing through, the tip exploding between her breasts with a gout of bone and blood. She made a gasping sound, then fell face-first into the fire.

By then, Angie's tribe—bodies painted with scarlet and green bands for war—was charging from cover, howling and brandishing their weapons.

Kathleen Soames was the first into the fight. She jabbed the sharpened end of broomstick into a female's neck and then turned on the boy. Before he could pull his knife she swung her axe with both hands and split his skull wide open.

Then it became a war of spears and knives and hatchets. Deadly close-in fighting. Angie's tribe was numerically superior and had the advantage of surprise. They cut down half a dozen of the enemy before they could even mount a counterattack.

One of the females, blonde and fierce, well-muscled, gutted two of Angie's best hunters with agile slashing motions that disemboweled them. Then she herself went down with three spears in her.

Angie was in the battle by then, shrieking her war cry as one of the females jumped out to meet her with a carving knife in each hand. There was no fear on her. Nothing but bloodlust. She slashed admirably, almost taking Angie's head off, but then a hatchet caught her in the neck and Angie seized the moment. She leaped, bringing her foot down on the girl's kneecap. There was a pleasing snap and a pleasing cry from the female who was instantly hobbled. Angie sliced her across the breasts with her butcher knife, then sank it between her legs, pulling upwards at the same time, opening the female wide. Her blood splashed against Angie and it was invigorating.

Another female with dark lustrous hair had gored two of Angie's hunters.

As Angie approached her, she had just eviscerated one of them—a man—and he crouched there on his knees, his hands filled with the white coils of his own intestines. The female slashed him across the eyes, turned, and began stabbing the other hunter—a woman—in the face, throat, and chest.

Then Angie jumped her, knocking her down and stabbing her through the throat. The female fought and screamed, but Angie yanked her head back, felt the female's teeth bite into her hand with an explosion of pain. Angie shrieked and slit her throat, sawing through the windpipe and carotid artery, hacking through meat and muscle until the blade bit into the cervical vertebrae. And even then, filled with pain and anger and a wild animal dementia for the kill, she cracked the vertebrae and sliced the head free. She held it up to the sky and the mother moon above in glory, blood splashing from the stump of neck down her face and making her feel more alive than she ever had before.

It went on for maybe ten minutes, probably not even that long. Knives cutting and axes chopping. Blades grinding against bone and clubs shattering ribs and spears punching through soft white underbellies.

And then...silence.

Nothing but corpses and parts there of.

Hacked victims still squirming on the ground.

And the victors, blood-drenched and meat-smelling, rising up from their kills and howling to the sacrificial moon high above. Angie, spitting out blood, surveyed the scene of carnage. Three of the boy's pack had run off to regroup, but the others had been slaughtered. Angie noted that six of her own were dead, five others mortally wounded.

Kathleen Soames had already eaten the boy's genitals as was her way. Then she had disemboweled him and was now rolling in his blood and entrails, scenting herself with the kill. Others of the tribe were imitating her.

They did not touch the heart.

Angie carved open the chest with her knife, shearing through muscle, snapping ribs in her bare hands. She slit the arteries away, sliced the heart free of its protective membrane. As the others watched with almost religious awe, she bit down deep into it, feeling the strength of its owner becoming *her* strength.

The boy's cunning was her own now.

As a hunter devours the flesh of a wolf to absorb its ferocity, so she ate the boy's bloody heart, tearing strips of it away with her sharpened teeth, enjoying every taste and texture. She fed upon it with a mystical rapture, feeling his spirit entering her with each bite.

When she was done, she went around to the mortally wounded and slit their throats one after the other. It was the way a warrior must die. Not slowly like a pig in the straw, but with blood in their mouths and a glaring steel memory of killing.

As she stood over her tribe, watching for other packs that might try and poach their kills, her hunters took trophies of bones and ears and body parts. One woman was fashioning a necklace of vaginas that she had slit free then threaded onto a necklace of beads around her throat. More heads were taken and speared on broomsticks.

Kathleen Soames, her red and green banded body now entirely red, stood by Angie's side, appraising the night. Killing to her was not only ritual and necessary, but almost sexual in nature. She drew her strength from the taking of lives, from her victim's blood washing her down, from the select remains she then fed upon. She was a fearsome sight standing there, blood still dripping from her. The moonlight gleamed off the sticks and rodent bones braided into her hair, the bone inserted through her nose.

Her lips long since sliced free, she grinned with gums and teeth.

"Enough," Angie told the tribe and they rose up from the field of blood, bones, limbs, and torsos.

The men urinated on the remains so all would know the penalty of poaching the tribe's territory. The women squatted near where the men pissed and wetted the ground themselves.

Then, Kathleen Soames leading the way with a decaying head on a broomstick, they faded into the night, glutted and pleased at the offerings of the mother high above...

67

Don't you touch me. Don't you dare touch me.

One of them had taken notice of Macy now. He was a hulking creature, stinking of excrement, his oblong face and body thick with a crust of something that must have been mud, dried blood, and congealed fat. In the flickering firelight she could only really see the gleam of his bared teeth, his eyes like two bloody holes.

He was standing there, watching her, his feet placed right in the pool of blood that was pretty much all that was left of the screaming woman after they'd dragged her remains away. Macy knew it couldn't go on. They simply wouldn't ignore her forever. She tried to be quiet, not to draw attention to herself, but now that just wasn't enough. At best, she would be raped. At worst, they would make her suffer unimaginable agonies before putting her on the spit.

He went down on one knee, arms outstretched, fingers splayed in the pool of blood. He looked like a runner waiting for the start of a race. He was grinning. He knew she was frightened, probably could smell the fear on her as she could smell the filth on him. And the really awful part was that he was enjoying it. She could see that. He was actually enjoying her discomfort, getting off on it, copping a sadistic thrill.

He laughed beneath his breath with a hoarse, grating sound.

Macy was getting angry.

That this inbred, barbaric piece of shit would enjoy her suffering was just too much. Yes, she wanted to run as fast and far away from him as she could. But part of her wanted to stand and fight. To smash his head open with something, wipe that mocking, vicious grin off his face.

He inched forward; she recoiled.

He pulled back, laughing.

A game. That's all this was. She did not doubt that it would end in something terrible for her, but for now it was just a game. Macy's wrists were still tied behind her back, but the knots were sloppy and loose. If she only had a few seconds unobserved, she knew she could squirm free.

He was creeping closer, smelling like he'd been eating dead things and garbage.

Macy waited. She would not flinch.

He reached out to grab her ankle and she moved quickly, instinctively. She lashed out with her right foot and cracked him in the face with her heel. He let out a barking sound and fell away.

Macy moved.

She'd spent the past three years in gymnastics and it paid off now. She rolled onto her back and brought her roped wrists down to her ass, wriggling, squirming until she got them around the mounds of her buttocks. Straining every muscle and ligament, she got her wrists to the back of her knees and slipped her legs out.

The man was staring at her. Not quite recovered from the kick in the face, but very much ready to pay Macy back in kind.

Do it now or just forget it.

Macy leaped to her feet and as that caveman sonofabitch tried to grab her ankle, she jumped away and kicked him in the ribs. He grunted and fell. Then she ran, knowing the chances of escape were futile. A boy stood in her way and she knocked him aside, knocked aside another woman and darted around a man with an axe in his hands. And then something hit her from behind, bowling her over to the stone floor and scraping the skin from her knees. It was *him*. The filth-covered man. He held onto her and she kicked him, hit him, felt her raw knees bounce off his chin. She was almost free—

Then a fist collided with the back of her head.

She saw stars and was thrown into the grip of her adversary once again. This time it was not games. He smashed her in the face, clouted her upside the head. Punched her in the belly and grabbed her hair and kneed her in the ribs. She went down and he reached for her.

Those scabby, filth-covered hands groped her.

Macy came up fighting and even she didn't know where the strength came from. He was huge, savage, bristling with muscle and fat. He easily outweighed her by a hundred pounds. She clawed his face, gouged his eyes, tried to get her knee into his groin and he hit her again, this time her lower lips split open and a tooth came loose. She went down, spitting it out along with a tangle of blood and saliva.

Breathless, dazed, she waited for retribution.

A ring of savages closed them in, waiting for it, too. Like hyenas surrounding the fresh kill of a lion, they were excited, yammering and snarling and squealing. They wanted a taste, but they wouldn't touch Macy, not until the apex predator had had his fun first and the apex predator in this case was a tall, heavy man covered in mud, blood, and animal fat that had dried, cracked open in jagged crevices, making him look hideously mummified, something feral and embalmed come to life here in the gutted bowls of a desecrated church.

Macy looked up at him in the flickering light of the fire, a thing of shadows and primal appetites. He was breathing very hard, grinding his teeth, flexing his muscles so that the crust covering him continued to crack and flake away. His eyes were shiny, wild.

She hated him. She lived only to see him suffer. If a knife were placed in her hand, she would have slit his throat.

Standing there, he seemed to know it, and it excited him.

Staring down at Macy, he gripped his penis. He squeezed it. He was already hard. With a bloody hand, grunting like a pig, he masturbated with firm, sure strokes. He looked into her eyes the entire time, his gaze black, bestial, and deranged. He made sure she watched.

He let out a cry and came, his semen striking Macy's cheek in a hot gush than ran down her face.

A day ago, a week ago, she would have screamed.

She would have gotten sick.

But now she did not even flinch. Debased, humiliated, there was nothing left now to flinch *with*. She did not feel exactly human anymore. Because it was happening now and she knew it and she wanted it to happen: *the regression.* A civilized, reasonable, intelligent person could not hope to survive with them or against them. You could not reason with them. They did not understand logic. They were territorial. They were animals. They were shaggy, psychotic, shit-smelling, crawling horrors straight out of the Pleistocene. They knew only the politics of the tribe, the mechanics of the hunt, the anatomy of murder and survival and blood sport. It was their liver and lights and soul. Regression was taking Macy with a hot surge of genetic impulse, sinking her slowly, steadily into the black pit of prehistory, down into the primal earth cheek by jowl where she could feel the cool moist soil of atavism and smell the secret animal musk of the race and taste the sweet blood of the primordial void.

She was one with it now.

And as the savage with the flaccid penis glared down at her with an appetite barely slaked, she felt herself falling into a shattering metallic silence.

But sometimes it took a snake to kill another snake...

68

She watched the man by the fire.

He was tall, well-muscled, lean. In the moonlight, a bloodied hammer in one hand and gore-dripping knife in the other, he looked every inch the dawn man that could be at once feared, understood, and desired.

Kylie Sinclair trembled.

In the darkness of the bushes, she was just touched by moonlight. She was wearing a crown of sticks and leaves that was not decorative, but meant to break up her silhouette in the night. It was an ancient technique of the hunt. Her sister and mother waited nearby.

The man just stood there.

She was smelling the pig roasted on the fire, the bubbling seams of fat and well-marbled slabs of meat that dripped a tantalizing hot juice into the flames. She was waiting for the man to pluck the carcass free and begin eating. Perhaps he would render it to bone and pack the meat off with him.

No.

He did neither.

He went down on his knees in the grass, shaking. Kylie was confused. For surely this was his kill, slit and spitted, he had drawn first blood and would be the first to taste the sweet bounty of the hunt. But he did not seize it and claim it as his own.

Kylie waited.

She could smell the pungent odors wafting up from her body...leaves and loam and black earth, a telltale stink of musk and animal oils that just barely masked her own ripe body odor. Good earthy smells. Smells that did not confuse, but invigorated and gave confidence. She ran fingers over the ceremonial welts and upraised scars of citricization that mottled her flesh. Like the paint made of blood and marrow fat that she decorated her body with, these were the symbols of who she was, what she was, her tribal affiliation.

She sniffed her fingers, tasted them, intrigued by her own odors and flavors.

She touched fingers to her armpits, her vagina, her rectum. Each smell and flavor was more heady and organic, each one making her giddy.

The man moved.

He had heard something. Kylie was certain of it for the smell coming from him across the yard had changed. This was sharper: *fear.* Yes, he heard something. A voice. Weapons in hand, he was going to investigate.

Kylie, peering through the bushes with eyes like glittering black stones, tensed in the dappled moonlight. Her muscles were drawn tight. She could smell violence coming from the man. It made her loins tremble.

Deep inside the dark chest of her mind, biochemical signals had been activated and Kylie knew instinctively that the zenith of the cycle was fast approaching. She could smell it on herself. Taste it on her skin. Tomorrow, perhaps, she would be in estrus—heat—and already she was aching for the filling and the release. She hoped the dam would give her the man. She would bait him with the scent of her womanhood, draw him in, let him spill his milk into her. Then the cycle would be complete.

A voice had spoken to the man.

Kylie did not like the voice. She could tell by its tone that its speaker was not like she, not a hunter but prey. Something to harvest with the rest. The breeze brought her his smell and it was perfume and soap and synthetic fibers, only a ghost of sweat and animal purity.

It was time.

Kylie went back to join her sister and the dam. They had found a bucket filled with white fireplace ashes. They had dumped water into it, mixed it into a smooth white paint. She watched them cover themselves in it. She did the same. The three of them looked like marble-white ghosts. When it was dry, the dam took red lipstick and painted her daughters. She colored both ears red and then drew a wide red band from ear to ear and filled it in so that their eyes were looking out from a belt of bright scarlet. She painted similar bands over their mouths stretching to both jawlines.

When they were done, it was time.

Clutching her spear, Kylie led them on the hunt...

69

"Nice job, Louis," the voice said to him. "Very nice, scaring off those little savages. Commendable. One might think you were a savage yourself."

Earl Gould.

Louis went over to him in the grass. "What the hell are you doing here, Earl?"

"I was kidnapped by the little horrors."

He was tied-up in the grass. Louis cut him loose, wondering if it was such a good idea or not. "I'm telling you right now, Earl. I've been through the shit, okay? You try and attack me and I swear to God I'll kick your fucking ass."

Rubbing his wrists, Earl managed a laugh. "I'm okay, Louis. How about you?"

Louis didn't bother answering that. What could he say? He had a bloody hammer and a bloody knife in his hands.

"Thanks for getting me out of this...jam," Earl said. "I was next on the barbi. Nice show of aggression, by the way. You scared the hell out of them."

"I thought they'd stand and fight."

Earl shook his head. "Most animals rarely do. When faced with a life-threatening show of aggression even a grizzly bear will think twice."

"We're in a hell of a situation here, Earl."

"Yes, we are, Louis. We are in the jungle," Earl said. "This is where seventy million years of primate development has led us: right back to the beginning."

Louis led him into the house and made him sit in a recliner in the living room. He did not turn on any lights. He went into the bathroom and washed his face, drank a few handfuls of water. When he came out, he grabbed a poker from the fireplace and sat on the couch. He could see Earl just fine in the moonlight filtering in through the picture window. He was grinning, but it was an awful sort of grin. A mad grin, but hardly dangerous. Just the grin of a man who had parted the black velour curtains of reality and peered deep into the fires of Hell, maybe saw something looking *back* at him. Something he recognized.

An ex college prof, Earl dressed very neatly, was always well-groomed and on the ball. But today, all that was gone. His white hair was mussed, his clothes dirty and unkempt. There were bruises on his face and a smear of blood at one cheek. He kept taking off his glasses, cleaning them on his shirt. Putting then back on and repeating the process.

"Okay, Earl," Louis said, his voice very weary. "Tell me about it. Tell me what you did."

Earl just kept grinning. His eyes were wet in the darkness. "I...I killed, Louis. I killed Maureen."

There should have been some shock, but there was nothing. Had he told Louis that he bought a new Weed-Eater, the reaction would have been about the same. "Are you sure?"

"I hit her."

"I saw that."

"But you ran off, Louis! You ran off!"

"I had to, Earl."

Although Louis could not see his eyes, he could just about gauge the pain in them. But he figured there was more than pain. Probably recrimination.

"But you let me hit her, Louis."

"No, Earl, I didn't let you do anything. I didn't have time to stop you. Somebody was attacking Macy. I couldn't help you." Louis sat there, looking at him. "*You* hit her, Earl. *You* hurt her. Not me. *You.* You're the one that let that fucking madness take you over."

Earl sat right up and walked over to Louis like he was going to attack him. "*I didn't have a choice!*" He grabbed Louis by the shirt, shook him. "*I couldn't fight against it! You can't fight against it! It just takes you and you belong to it and there's not a fucking thing you can do about it! Do you see? That's why I hit her and that's why I kept hitting her!*"

Louis slapped him across the face. Slapped him hard enough to snap his head back and he wanted to keep slapping him. He was just sick of it all. Sick of the shit his neighbors had been doing to each other, to themselves, to the whole goddamn town. He didn't know why the madness had not gotten to him, but he was starting to think that everyone who was infected was weak. *Goddamn fucking weak.* So he slapped the old man and he wanted to keep slapping until his hand was red and numb and Earl was on the floor, bleeding and sobbing and pissing himself. To Louis, the old man was the embodiment of all of them. Their weakness. Their inhumanity.

Earl was down on one knee, still grinning, though his eyes were filled with tears.

"Tell me what you did, Earl. Tell me what the fuck you did to your wife and how it felt when you were doing it," Louis said, needing to rub the old man's face in the stink he had created. "C'mon, tell me all about it."

Earl was blubbering now. Just beside himself with guilt and anguish and Louis actually found satisfaction in that because he wanted to see them *all* like that, down on their knees feeling the pain of their actions. And particularly Michelle. The woman he loved. The woman who had betrayed him now in ways Louis himself could not even begin to catalog.

Jesus Christ, you idiot! She's sick! They're all sick! You can't blame them for it any more than you can blame an alcoholic for hitting the bottle or a junkie for sticking a needle in his arm! Sick! Sick! Sick!

Louis knew it. He knew it was true, but it wasn't buying beans with him now. Not after what he'd seen. Not after what he'd experienced. Not after what his own goddamn wife had done to him. Finally he sighed. "I'm sorry, Earl. Really I am. Tell me what happened. Take your time."

It took some time, all right, but Earl did. He opened the flue and all the heat and smoke and suffering blew out of his soul. It had been itching in the back of his skull for hours, the insanity, the need to run free like an animal, the dire compulsion to act out his most debased fantasies and urges. He refused to tell Louis what these were, but Louis could just imagine. There's nothing more sordid and filled with crawly things as the human subconscious mind, that pit of fears and desires, wants and needs, repressed feelings and anxieties that the rational, conscious mind will simply not allow to be expressed. Louis understood what Earl was saying, because it was much the same thing Macy had told him. Earl said it was caused by a gene. Regardless, it first infected the subconscious, releasing images and ideas and primal wants, flooding the mind with them, and by that point, such things as inhibition and restraint no longer existed. The infected became, essentially, an animal with a human brain, though highly degraded, primitive. It had taken complete charge of Earl as he talked to Louis over the hedges. Maureen's shouting had acted like some sort of trigger and there was no turning back. He hit Maureen, put her down. Kicked her and kept kicking. She was old, she was frail. She should have been dead, but she wasn't.

"So I kept hitting her," Earl said, his eyes wide in the moonlight coming through the window. Like mirrors reflecting the awfulness inside his head. "But she wouldn't die, Louis. She just wouldn't."

"Take it easy, Earl."

He uttered a cold and sterile laugh. "Oh yes, take it easy. How can I take it easy, Louis? How can I possibly take it easy? She wouldn't die! She wouldn't die so I went into the garage and got a hammer. You know what? I remember doing it, I remember *wanting* to do it. Can you understand that? No, you can't. You can't understand or know what it was like, Louis! I went and got that fucking hammer and I was whistling the whole time! *Whistling!* Like I was going to fix the back door! When I got back there, when I got back to her—"

"You don't have to do this, Earl."

"Oh yes, I do! I got back there and...and she was gone! She had dragged herself around the side of the house! I followed the blood trail and when I found her, found her curled up and bleeding, I bashed her goddamn brains in! I kept swinging and swinging and I never wanted to stop! I liked it! I *loved* it!"

Louis was feeling sick to his stomach now. Yes, he'd seen his share, but this was so much worse. So intimate. A peak into the mind of a lunatic. He thought if he looked deep enough, he might see something in Earl's eyes that would validate what was in his head. Something looking back at him and grinning.

Earl was kneeling on the floor, rocking back and forth, just devastated by what he had done. "But you don't know the rest, Louis, you don't know what it was like."

"Please, Earl. Stop this."

But Earl shook his head. "It got her too, Louis. It got in her head and she was just as loony as I was. When I found her there, around the side of the house, she laughed at me! She fucking *laughed* at me! Started saying all the terrible things she'd always wanted to say to me! And then, and then she..."

Earl broke down into tears and Louis went to him, tried to put a hand on his shoulder, but the old man just batted it away.

"I killed her because I had to! And because she *wanted* it!"

Louis sat back down. "What do you mean?"

Earl uttered that awful, bitter laugh again that maybe wasn't insane, but was living right next door. "I mean she *wanted* me to! After she said those things, something snapped in her, Louis! Just snapped! It was a violation of everything that dear woman was! She couldn't live with it! So...I killed her! I killed her because she *begged* me to do it! Begged me to smash her head in!"

Louis could say nothing to that.

He was speechless and simply worn out by all of this. Earl sobbed and shook and eventually the tears just went away and he was silent, just silent. Not even moving. Not doing anything but dying inside.

"When did you come out of it?" Louis finally asked.

"Before...earlier...I don't know. It just fades away a little at a time. And now I'm sane, I'm perfectly fine, aren't I?"

"It wasn't your fault, Earl. Not really."

"Don't bullshit me, Louis. Please don't do that." He pulled himself up and sat back on the recliner. "Anything but that. I'm like the others now. A killer. I'm nothing but a killer..."

70

The pack waited patently on the hillside.

In the moonlight, their bodies reticulated with bands of mud-brown, blood-red, and midnight blue like jungle serpents, they were nearly invisible. Only their teeth gleamed in the moonlight, their staring eyes. A slight breeze was carrying the smell of prey, the delicious odor of live meat, and a ripple of excitement ran through the pack.

Down below, in a tree-lined hollow at the edge of what had once been known as Lower Fifth Street, a group of prey had hidden themselves away. They thought they were safe from the things that stalked the night. They were wrong.

The Baron examined the gleaming edges of his weapons— the K-Bar knife, his hatchet, his spear, and his machete which was really just the razor-sharp blade from a paper cutter with a handle at one end. They pleased him. Their edges caught the moonlight, held it. Touching the necklace of ears at his throat, he made a grunting sound under his breath.

The pack rose from the grass.

They were his children. They surrounded him, pressing up against him, smelling the raw blood-stench of brutality that he wielded like a weapon. It made them feel strong.

Without a word, the Baron slipped down the hillside with the others following him. He avoided the sparsely placed streetlights, haunting the shadows, *becoming* the shadows, sliding through their ebony depths like a snake skimming a pond.

There were three houses and he broke his pack into three hunting bands, each led by his fiercest warriors.

It was time.

Letting out the wild cry of a wolf, he charged through the first yard. He came to a locked door, but it was flimsy and he kicked it open, his band rushing in. Inside, there were lights and screams. His hunters had found a woman and two children cowering. They impaled them with their spears, hacking them with hatchets until patterns of blood were sprayed up the walls and spattering the ceiling.

A man lay dying on the carpeted floor in a pool of his own blood.

There was a hatched imbedded in his skull.

He had fought, fought hard for what was his, shattering the skull of one hunter with a baseball bat and beating another to a faceless wreck. But that was all he did. The hunters were fighting over the scraps of the woman and children, others slitting trophies from the dying man with their knives.

The Baron heard gunshots.

Shattering glass.

More screams.

He ran outside and to the house next door. One of his hunters lay on the porch, a bullet hole in his temple. A window was smashed. Inside another hunter was dead. Then the Baron saw that three of his own were busy gutting a woman and another was feeding the body of an old woman into the fireplace. She screamed as the flames engulfed her. Another hunter was gut-shot on the stairs, a trail of blood marking his progress.

Two more gunshots from above.

Then the howling of hunters. Thrashing noises and a screech of pain. The Baron smiled. Whoever had been doing the shooting had been overwhelmed now. He could hear them shrieking just above the noise of blades hacking into flesh and splintering bone.

Outside again.

The next house. A back door opened as the Baron came around the side. A woman was trying to escape. She got one look at the Baron and tried to slam the door shut. He shouldered it open. She screamed and slashed at him with a steak knife. He beat her down, kicked her until she was nothing but a sobbing heap, and then yanked up her head and slit her throat.

He came across three more of his hunters who had cornered a boy. They were jabbing him with their spears. And in the living room, a sight which even gave the Baron a moment's hesitation as some shred of humanity kicked in his head.

His hunters had a pregnant woman on the floor. She was dead, slit open from throat to crotch. One of the boys was urinating on her. A group of girls had torn her unborn child from the womb.

They were eating it, the umbilical still attached to its mother.

The Baron slit the woman's ears off and threaded them onto his necklace as his children devoured, their eyes black and staring, their faces smeared with gore.

He went out onto the porch. There was a man out there, bleeding from spear wounds, hobbled by axe cuts, but not dead just yet. Letting out a cry of victory, the Baron scalped him...

71

The girl was refusing so the Huntress knew she had to be broken much as a young colt must be broken by whatever means necessary. What must come now must not be crude or low in nature, but ceremonial, for it was a rite. And it would be carried out as such.

The Huntress looked down on the girl. "Hunt with us, as us."

The girl looked up at her. There were tears in her eyes. "Michelle, please—"

The Huntress was taken aback by that name. It was what the man had called her. She feared that name for it was a name of power that made her feel helpless, uncertain. She could not have the clan seeing this. That name. *Michelle*. It was a magic name, a spell of power. The others must never learn of it or they would break her with it.

The girl opened her mouth again and the Huntress slapped her.

She reached out and took the girl by the throat, squeezing her while she trembled and gasped and fought weakly in her grip. The Huntress slammed her up against the wall again and again until there was no fight left.

"Now," she said, "ready her."

Macy was suddenly gripped by hands, so many white reaching hands they were like the ensnaring tentacles of a squid, grabbing her, fondling her, pinching her and scratching her leaving deep welts. There was no fight left. Everything had drained out of her and she was limp there on the cool flagstone floor, naked, exposed, vulnerable. They pressed in, savage faces, primordial things from a nightmare, sharpened teeth gleaming and fat-greased faces grinning. The Huntress stood over her, dark and cruel, her eyes cold glistening jewels. Macy looked up at her, but there was no pity. The woman she had known as Michelle was a savage warrior queen now, her face painted white and black like a skull, things knotted in her hair, a necklace of tiny bones at her throat. There was no sympathy, no pity, for Michelle was now from a time of long ago. A dark, misty time where men were little better than the beasts of the forest.

The clan pressed in, stealing her light and her air.

There was nothing but the greasy feel of them, the stink of the pelts they wore and the marrow-grease they coated themselves with, rancid, revolting, meaty-smelling stuff. They were all touching her, feeling her. Nails scratched blood and teeth tore her skin even as tongues licked the sweat from her breasts and moist blubbery lips suckled her wounds and were pressed to her own lips. Clammy hands forced her legs apart and there was no air to scream with, not a single muscle would obey as more hands pushed in, rubbing her down with fats and oils until she glistened as they glistened and then, and then—

Then she did scream with a raw, shrieking sound that echoed through the church as her head thrashed from side to side with the horror of what was happening. The scream was silenced by many mouths and many tongues covering her face.

So Macy did not see.

Did not see the painted, grease-shining man who wore the bloody, ragged pelts of men and animals, the leering snarling-mouthed headpiece of a slaughtered dog. She did not see him or the hands that pressed him down on her, but she felt his penis as it slid along her inner thigh like an engorged snake, pushing higher and higher, sliding into her as she shuddered and kicked and called out the name of the only man she thought would protect her.

Please, please, please, Louis, please don't let them, don't let them, don't let them do this to me, don't let them destroy me like this—

But there was only the clan, clutching and feeling and holding her, gripping her with dirty fingers until her flesh bruised, kissing her and sucking on her and nibbling her with the serrated edges of their teeth. She was buried alive in their bodies which stank of blood, excrement, and peeled hides as the man on top of her, the one chosen by the Huntress, pushed in and out of her, bringing pain, riding her, grunting like a hog, drool hanging from his mouth in fetid ribbons.

When his seed flowed into her, his body stiff and jerking, she let out a final rending scream that tore her open inside, ripped her soul wide open in a vicious, bleeding chasm that swallowed everything she had been, ever was, or could be into the black seething nothingness of prehistory...

72

Louis watched the darkness outside the window. He knew he should have run as far away as he could before they came back. But he just didn't seem to care. Everything was collapsing, both within and without, and he had lost focus. In his mind he could see Earl that afternoon, out by the hedges:

We are the instruments of our own destruction! Inside each and every one of us there is a loaded gun and radical population explosion has pulled the trigger! God help us, Louis, but we will exterminate ourselves! Beasts of the jungle! Killing, slaughtering, raping, pillaging! An unconscious genetic urge will unmake all we have made, gut civilization, and harvest the race like cattle as we are overwhelmed by primitive urges and race memory run wild!

It sounded crazy then; now it simply sounded practical.

"You still sticking to the gene theory?"

Earl buried his face in his hands. "Yes, absolutely. Let me indulge in some Darwinism here, Louis. For if the survival of the fittest is a true thing, then what we have locked up inside each and everyone of us is a genetic propensity towards hunting and killing, taking down prey and destroying our human rivals. I'm talking about the beast inside. The beast that is the very core of who and what we are. That's what's causing all this: *the beast.* The primal, ravenous other inside us all, the dawn-child, the shadow-hunter, the savagery and cruelty that forms the framework of the human animal."

"The beast," Louis said. "I've seen it. I've looked in its eyes."

Earl nodded. "Yes, and what a disturbing sight it is, eh? At our roots, animals, nothing but animals. Beasts. We crawled from the immortal slime of creation with the will to kill and that will is still upon us. Upright animals with savage instincts and an inheritance of acquired, barbaric characteristics. We can write poetry and make music, build cities and microcomputers and send probes to Mars, but in our hearts, our black beating little hearts, still Miocene apes and pithecanthropoid hunters. Love, hate, greed, want, violence, war. Love is a romanticized adaptation of the breeding/brooding impulse. Materialism is simply an expression of the animal instinct to covet. Nationalism, our flag-waving patriotism, nothing more than the ancient animal drive to maintain and defend a territory and war...yes, even *war*, nothing but an overblown, exaggeration of the territorial impulse to raid, to kill, to take what belongs to another and make it our own."

What Louis wanted to know was: what activated this monstrous gene? What set this regression, this primordial memory—or whatever you wanted to call it—into action? "What was the mechanism, Earl? What was the machine or influence that set it all free and on such a massive scale? Just overpopulation? Stress?"

"We'll never really know, Louis. Anymore than any other herd animal will know. It's inside us, though, my friend. These impulses, this sadism, it's inborn and inbred. We're the product of our ancestors. No more, no less. Why do people murder each other? Why do they kill their own children? Their neighbors? Their wives? Why do they allow genocide to happen? Why do they lynch people of a different skin color? Why do they hate those with more or with less than them or with different religious affiliations? The beast, Louis, the beast inside. The imperatives to descend into our prehistory, into our savage past, are locked up in all of us.

"How many times have you read that somebody killed another and they really weren't sure why? The Devil made me do it...except, we all carry the devil inside of us. Our animal past is why. We all have terrible buried impulses, but most of us don't act upon them. But now and again, a select few or even a mob does. It's a combination of our brutal heredity acting in accordance with deep-seated, repressed wants and desires. That's what you're seeing here: all the awful, dirty, hateful, and twisted things growing in the underbelly of this world, this town, in its *collective* mind, have been unleashed. All the terrible things festering inside these people have been released. It was genetically preordained, I suppose. The conditions were right and it just happened. That's no answer. Not really. But the potential was there and has been in every human population since we evolved from a lesser primate. God help us, but the world is now a great living laboratory of the human condition and the mechanics of violence, primal instinct, purge and atavism. The evil is here, Louis, and the evil is *us*. We made the Devil in our own image."

"But what about the animals, Earl?"

"Animals?"

Louis swallowed thickly as he told Earl about the police station. The dogs there. How they had died fighting men or fighting *with* them.

"Hmm, interesting." Earl considered it. "Well, there's only one logical explanation. Hormones."

"Hormones?"

Earl nodded. "Yes, hormones, pheromones. It was long thought that pheromones were the province of insects. Not so. Recent biochemical studies tell a different story. All species have them. Most are species-specific, but certain kinds can be read by other species. There are aggregation pheromones which function to herd species in defense against predators or for mating purposes. Primer pheromones which trigger behavioral changes in reaction to environment. Releaser or attractant pheromones which attract mates for miles. Territorial pheromones which are carried in the urine to mark territorial boundaries or lairs or to warn off intruders. Sex pheromones which indicate the female is ready for breeding. All sorts of chemical signatures. And then there are alarm pheromones which alert a species when one of their own is under attack. Studies have shown that these pheromones, in mammals, trigger the fight or flee instinct. They make animals quite aggressive. A harmless tomcat becomes a beast. Prey animals will tend to flee, predators will generally fight. Those primitives out there—that's a *kind* word for them— must be letting off alarm pheromones of absolute aggression and the dogs are responding in kind. It's a chemical thing. The dogs cannot help themselves. They fight. If directed against a common enemy, they fight with our primitives. Lacking the same, they fight *against* them."

Louis hated Earl at that moment. He was reducing man to a laboratory rat. Maybe that's all any species was, a victim of their own chemistry, but he still hated it. It was so...dehumanizing.

"The regression, Earl. Can it be stopped?"

Earl didn't even attempt to answer that one. "Have you ever heard of a man named Raymond Dart?"

Louis told him he hadn't.

"Raymond Dart was an Australian anthropologist and comparative anatomist. A true giant in the field. In 1924 he discovered the fossil remains of *Australopithecus* in a South African limestone quarry. In time, he also discovered more fossils of this extinct hominid, along with great heaps of fossilized bones that were the prey of the *Australopithecine*. He also discovered crude weapons such as clubs made from antelope bones and knives fashioned from jawbones, as well as heaps of animal bones and baboon skulls which bore the marks of death blows from these very weapons. As did the skulls of other *Australopithecines*. Evidence that was supported by forensic experts who examined the remains. The dawn of organized murder, Louis! A quarter of a million years before man! From this Dart theorized that we evolved not from a gentle vegetarian ape as established paleoanthropology would have it, but from a savage, predatory ape with a lust for killing. It was called the "Killer Ape" theory. He perpetuated it in his paper, 'The Predatory Transition from Man to Ape.' In the paper he said and I quote verbatim: 'The blood-bespattered, slaughter-gutted archives of human history from the earliest Egyptian and Sumerian records to the most recent atrocities of the Second World War accord with early universal cannibalism, with animal and human sacrificial practices or their substitutes in formalized religions and with world-wide scalping, head-hunting, body-mutilating and necrophiliac practices of mankind in proclaiming this common bloodlust differentiator—this predacious habit, this mark of Cain—that separates man dietetically from his anthropoidal relatives and allies him rather with the deadliest of Carnivora.' Well, don't you see, Louis? Don't you grasp it?"

Louis was way too tired for thinking, for anything this heavy. "We evolved from a killer ape, I guess. Not that I'm really surprised."

"Yes, basically," Earl said, very excited to be lecturing once again. "The innate depravity of our species comes directly from the killer ape. Civilization is only an attractive cloak, for beneath we are murderous beasts. We are territorial, aggressive, and murderous—to our species and every other. This is why we wage war, this is the foundation of mass murder, serial killings, genocide, and our instinctive cruelty. We are killers. Listen to me, Louis. Dart further suggested that we did not evolve intelligence and then turn to killing, we evolved intelligence *because* we turned to killing. At some point, our ancestors branched off from their non-aggressive cousins. These early hominids became predatory probably because of the scarcity of food and probably by imitating other predators as primitives will do. We learned to stand erect to hunt, to give chase to our prey. Hands free to grip and tear, but lacking teeth or claws, we developed weapons. Crude imitations from bone, rock, wood. Ah, now the use of weapons entails great coordination, thus our nervous systems were challenged and our brains enlarged. The development of hunting tactics enlarged our brains still further. We are men today, Louis, because our ancestors were killers. As Robert Ardrey said in African Genesis, *man had not fathered the weapon, the weapon fathered man.*"

Earl said the "Killer Ape" theory was controversial as hell. Many anthropologists dismissed it and probably because it pretty much swept their conservative, bloodless little theories into the wastebasket where they belonged. But there was no need to doubt it now. Because out there, in the streets, the killer apes were running wild.

"The devil, as it were, has risen up from our chromosomes, Louis. Like certain diseases, cancers that are hereditary in nature, the genetic impulse to regress is irresistible.

Fighting against it will be like fighting against the color of your eyes. It's preset, preprogrammed, and absolutely immutable."

Louis sighed. "But why did Macy regress and come out of it again? Why did you? Why haven't I gone native yet?"

"Who can say, Louis? The gene may have been bred out of your family line at some point. There may be thousands like you or only a handful. As to me and the girl...I fear that the reassertion of reason is only temporary. A remission of sorts, if you will."

There was nothing Louis could say to that. It was wild and impossible, but it was probably also true. And that was the most disturbing thing of all. For man was a beast at heart and civilization, at best, was an illusion. As Earl said, a fancy cloak you could drape over the ugly monster within...and you could hide those claws and those teeth and that bloodthirsty appetite in its folds, but it was still there. Waiting to get out. As Earl also said, it got out pretty commonly on an individual basis and now and again on a communal level. But this, what was happening here, was probably one of the first times it had reached such a proportion, had infected and degenerated so many in such a short span of time, gone global. But it had always been coming, right from the beginning. Now and then the gene was activated— accidentally, no doubt—and you had a serious body count. But the big one, the Big Bang, the Doomsday Effect, of the human race had not come until now.

To think that all man had strived for and accomplished was now being destroyed by a primitive gene, by biochemical reactions deep in microscopic cells. That was scary.

"I'm frightened for the race, Louis. Terribly, deeply frightened. For what if this regression continues?" Earl pondered. "What will a year bring? Will we continue to devolve? Those people out there, they still have language skills and reasoning powers. But I'd say they're rapidly devolving from *Homo sapiens* to *Homo erectus*. That's just a guess, of course. But what will we be like in five or ten years? Will our culture completely have been forgotten? Will we have degraded into *Australopithecine* hunting groups, forging tools from animal bones, roaming the veldt, forest, and grassland with our ancestral bloodlust intact while our cities slowly turn to rubble and memory?"

"I don't know, Earl. I can't think anymore."

Earl shook his head. "This is what the Greeks call *hubris*, Louis."

"Hubris?"

"Yes, *hubris*. If man lifts his head too high or raises his achievements and ambitions to a godlike level, the gods will be threatened. And threatened, will react in kind by destroying him. And we've—all of us—have certainly acted like gods, haven't we? Killing one another, waging wars, raping the planet, exterminating other species, crushing any that stand in our way...yes, certainly the province of gods not *men*. And now nature or God or what have you is putting us in our place. If that's not karma, I don't know what is."

Louis felt like crying as he waited here on the threshold of doomsday. He wanted to weep at the sullen marble grave of civilization and mankind. Jesus, the absolute horror of it all.

Earl sighed. "My head hurts. Dear Christ, but my head hurts. I need to use your bathroom, Louis. I have to wash my face. And piss. Yes, piss in a toilet like a man and not against a tree to mark my trail." He got up, started walking out of the living room and then turned back. "You've been a good neighbor, Louis. The very best. I always thought you were special and now I know that you are."

But Louis shook his head. "I'm not. I'm nothing special."

"Oh, but you are," the old man said. 'You haven't lost it like the rest of us. Not even for a moment. It hasn't been able to get its claws in you and that makes you special, Louis. Very special. You may be the last of the reasonable men. A species nearing extinction. The last man to study other men rather than simply killing them. What a waste. The nature of man is to study the nature of man, I always thought. But I was wrong. The nature of man is to *kill*. The territorial imperative, Louis."

"I don't know what you mean, Earl. I don't understand."

"Learned response, cultural instinct, my friend. These things make up the basis of any creature's behavior. You have to be taught how to make a paper airplane, but no one has to teach you how to make a weapon. You know. It's instinctive. Just like the desire to kill."

"They *are* making weapons, Earl...spears, clubs, you name it. And you know what? They work. I would think making a spear that could be thrown and actually hit its target might be an art form of sorts. There's engineering involved. You wouldn't think those savages could figure it out so quickly."

"They didn't have to, Louis. They knew instinctively."

Earl gave him a quick example. In France, in the Rhone valley, beavers made their dams and lodges for centuries, right back to—and before—antiquity same as beavers did everywhere. But then with the coming of the European fur trade, the beavers were hunted to near-extinction. Only a few remained. For several hundred years, no dams, no lodges. Then the French government extended protection to the small beaver population in the Rhone valley. Their numbers swelled over a period of decades. Then, for the first time in several hundred years, the beavers began building dams and lodges in the tributaries of the Rhone River. Building dams and lodges is a very complex, communal effort...yet, no one had to teach the beavers how to do it, they *knew*. And those dams in the Rhone were perfectly identical to those built by American and Canadian beavers. Cultural instinct at work.

"And our friends out there, Louis. Nobody has to teach them what their ancestors knew. It's race memory. They know how to survive. How to kill, how to make weapons, how to dress a carcass and peel a hide. Cultural instinct."

While Earl was gone, Louis found Mike Soderberg's gun cabinet. He broke the glass with his hammer and sorted around in the moonlight. He wasn't much of a shooter himself, so he grabbed a weapon that he was familiar with: A bolt-action Winchester Featherweight .30-06. His father had had one. He'd shot it plenty of times as a boy. He loaded the magazine with Springfield cartridges, stuffed more in his pockets.

"We better get the hell out of here, Earl," he said when the older man came back.

"Where to?"

"Just out of here for now."

They stepped out on the porch together. The streets were quiet. But right away Louis got a bad feeling in his stomach and it did not answer to such trifling things as reason or logic. This was an ancient sense. A sense of impending doom.

"I don't think we're alone out here," Earl said.

Something moved in the hedges and Louis did not even hesitate: he brought up the rifle, worked the bolt, and fired. There was nothing but the echo of his shot. No movement.

"Let's get out of here," he said.

Holding the rifle high, he led Earl away out to the sidewalk. He knew it wasn't safe to stay in the house and it was no more safe out here. *They* were near and he could smell them: the stink of oily hides and wet dogs. Something moved across the street. Louis hesitated. Something moved behind a parked car. He fired, taking out the windshield. Earl turned to him, mouth opened to say something...but then he grunted and stumbled forward. There was a sharpened spear shaft jutting from his lower back. Blood filled his mouth and he made a gurgling sound and went to his knees.

Louis fired a shot.

He heard a whooshing sound.

He turned, made ready to fire again and his head exploded with stars. The rifle fell from his hands. When he opened his eyes he was flat on his back on the sidewalk. He could hear Earl gasping. But he paid no attention to that. Because somebody was standing over him. They smelled of urine, meat, and shit.

At first he thought it was a monster. Some horrible, walking cadaver that had forced its way out of a muddy grave. But it wasn't that. It was a woman...or something like one with huge breasts and an axe in her hands. Her flesh was clotted, lumpy, white as bone, glistening. That's when he knew that she had covered herself in slimy white clay or maybe ash. She had coated herself with it and slicked back her hair, giving her the appearance of a bloodless wraith. Bright red diagonal bands at the mouth and eyes contrasted this. He could see the yellow of her teeth which had been filed sharp, the shining orbs of her eyes. She wore a necklace of fur which he soon realized were maybe a dozen human scalps sewn into a garment.

The stench of her.

The absolute obscenity.

He tried to move, but his head was spinning. Two other women—younger, thinner, breasts like small cones—stepped out of the gloom. They were smeared with ghostly white ash, too. One carried a sling which had propelled the rock into Louis' head. The other stepped over to Earl, planted her foot in the center of his back and yanked out the spear. Earl screamed and she stabbed him three times in the throat.

I'm next...they're gonna kill me next.

This is what Louis thought as he hovered at the edge of unconsciousness. They gathered around him for the killing. The older woman crouched down by him, running her hands over him. When one of the younger girls groped at his crotch, she slapped her hand away and hissed at her like a snake.

"Mine," she said. *"Mine..."*

73

The Baron was scalping his prey.

The body of a man was facedown in the grass. The Baron—or Mr. Chalmers as he had once been known—was kneeling on his shoulders. He pressed the lethal, razored edge of his K-Bar knife just behind the man's left ear and slit along the back of his skull, above the right ear and along the forehead/scalp line and back to his original incision. Then he peeled the scalp free from the skull with no little exertion, holding it up for all to see.

The pack howled like animals.

They screeched.

They bayed at the moon high above.

The Baron wiped his bloody fingers on his sleeveless fox coat, then he tossed the scalp to the pack. They fought wildly over it. And as they did so, the Baron cut off the man's ears and then, punching holes in the cartilage with the tip of his knife, threaded them onto his necklace.

He had six sets on there thus far.

He told them he would fill the necklace by morning and the greatest hunter among them would be awarded the necklace of ears as a symbol of their stealth and ferocity. For amongst the pack, these were the things admired the most.

A pair of young boys came running back into the yard. The Baron had sent them scouting for new prey. They were breathless, filthy things who wore only pants and both carried long-bladed hunting knifes on makeshift slings around their necks. The Baron heard them out, his black-striped face grim, impassive. It would be his decision.

"Lead us," he told them.

The pack howled in honor of the blood sport to come. Then, maintaining the pack discipline that the Baron had told them was so very important, they quieted down and there was only the sound of a summer night. Crickets. A light breeze in the high boughs of the oaks. And in the distance, the screams and war cries of other packs as they raided from neighborhood to neighborhood.

The Baron's pack moved out in single file with flank guards to either side and the two boys taking point far ahead. Soon there would be scalps for all...

74

The girl was broken.

The ritual began.

The Huntress watched the clan seize the girl, take hold of her and drag her from the shadows where she cowered. She did not fight at first. She was becoming of the clan, but she still acted stupid and helpless like prey. Her brain was not yet the brain of a hunter.

But soon.

Soon she would hunt with them.

The Huntress was certain of it. Because just as she could smell fear or the telltale scent trail of other hunters, she could smell what was going on inside the girl. The more like them the girl became, the more her blood ran hot and bright.

At my side. When you have proven yourself, you will hunt at my side.

Then she could wear the paint of the skull, but not before. Only the ones the Huntress selected were given this privilege. Her inner circle.

The men wanted to have the girl, of course. Many of them. They could smell her ripeness and hers was a fruit they wished to pluck so very sweet and juicy was it. But she had been broken by the one the Huntress chose. That was enough. For now. The others would not have her nor the women who wished her for sport. This one was special and she belonged to the Huntress and none dared violate that taboo. The Huntress had other reasons for wanting the girl. She was somehow connected to the man and the Huntress desired to have the man.

But he was sly.

He was cunning.

She would use the girl as bait.

Even now, the Huntress could hear his strange, mystical words:

Come over here, Michelle. I'm your husband. I love you. I won't let them hurt you.

The Huntress did not understand what he said exactly, but she knew there was a special meaning to those words. The pain and depth of emotion in the man had been all too apparent. And his voice, what he said and *how* he said it...it had touched something in her, made her feel warm, weak, and soft. And so she had set the clan upon him before they smelled her uncertainty.

The girl cried out in pain.

The clanswomen had thrown a rope over the naked beams above and, tying the girl's wrists, were hoisting her up by them. The girl was crying out. Her wrists were raw from the other ropes she had been tied with, the skin scraped red. A trickle of blood ran down her left forearm.

"Let it begin," the Huntress told them.

This was the ritual. The Huntress remembered it from another time and that time seemed to be long ago. When she tried to recall it, everything was dim and misty and what faces she could see were not faces she recognized, *yet* she was certain that she knew them. And well. No matter. The ritual was ancient and correct. It was a test for a true warrior maiden. If the girl did not cry and whimper like an infant, if she withstood the ordeal, then she would hunt with them.

If not, there were the men.

Then the women and their skinning knives.

It started with sticks from the fire. Once the ends were blazing hot, the women withdrew them and, chanting archaic words under their tongues, they spun the girl so that she twisted on the rope and as she rotated, they jabbed her with the hot sticks. The blazing ends hissed as they sank into her pale white skin. She would forever be marked and forever remembered for this. None that looked upon her would doubt her courage or importance.

The Huntress knew that some died during the ritual.

It was unfortunate, but necessary. If this one died, her ghost would be released from the shell of her body and would be angry. It would seek vengeance as ghosts often did. Young ghosts were always angry.

The girl did not beg for mercy or even whimper during the burning. She just twisted on her rope from bloody wrists, her eyes glazed over and staring. The women were angered by their inability to break her. They took up branches and whipped her mercilessly, drawing blood, tearing open the burned pink flesh until red creeks ran down the girl's belly and legs.

The Huntress raised her hand and she was cut free.

The women now knotted her hair and tied it tight with the rope. Again, the girl was hoisted above. The men had sticks in their hands. As they passed, they swatted her with them. And when they were finished, they urinated on her.

She was left to hang like that.

Maybe for hours...

75

The tribe moved through the shadows, the dappled moonlight from intertwined tree branches overhead enhancing the red and green serpentine stripes covering their naked bodies.

Angie, with Kathleen at her side, two hunters cast ahead, led them.

Dawn was hours away yet, but until then they would hunt. For the tribe lived, breathed, and was of the hunt. Without it they were nothing. It was their blood and soul and purpose. Without it they would be no better than any other pack of animals rooting in the dirt for grubs and worms. The hunt gave them focus, it gave them reason, it was the blood in their veins. Angie knew instinctively that her kind rose above the beast of the field *because* of the hunt.

When dawn came, they would slink back to their lair and sleep away the daylight hours like the rest, waiting for darkness.

But for now, they hunted. Being that they were more than predators, but creatures of opportunity, scavengers even, they were following another hunting clique. The one led by the old man in the animal skins. He had an army of children following him. They were raiding from neighborhood to neighborhood, killing and slaughtering and laying waste. The tribe followed along because the pickings were so good *and* out of sheer curiosity.

There was another reason, of course.

And that reason was Angie's and hers alone.

The old man. He was an excellent hunter, a great leader, savage, bloodthirsty, and exceptionally cunning. Angie learned many things just watching how the old man led his raids. His hunters were very well disciplined.

She respected and feared him.

She emulated him.

She wanted to kill him.

Yes, that's what she really wanted because that's how it was done. When you killed another, drank their blood and feasted on their meat, you *absorbed* what they were. Their strength, their wisdom, their spirit became part of you. Angie knew as her ancestors had known that the center of it all, the nucleus of the being, was the heart itself.

She would kill the old man with one well placed arrow. Then she would bathe in his blood. And lastly, while the others fought over the tidbits, bones, and sweet meats, she would carve out the old man's heart and eat it raw, filling herself with his spirit and vitality. For the heart was the center of the all, the hub of deeper mystery, the pulsing artery to the beyond. And when she had eaten it and filled her veins with his cruel potency and thrumming life force, then she would skin him and wear his flesh as a garment...

76

While the dam saw to the gut sack that smoked over the fire, jabbing it from time to time with a stick, and seeing to what roasted in the coals, Kylie played with the man.

He did not like to be played with.

After binding him with clothesline, they dragged him back to their lair and deposited him in the corner. He had slept for some time—or pretended to—but now he was awake. His eyes were open, wide and bright.

Still covered in ghostly white ash, Kylie grinned at him.

He did not smile back.

Kylie crept over to him on all fours. He tensed. His muscles were good. She straddled him, her long flaxen hair hanging in his face. She studied his eyes, his scent, his facial expression...all the things that would tell her what she wanted to know.

She pressed her crotch down on his own, rubbed it again the coarse material of his jeans. The texture, the pressure excited her. She could feel him getting excited, too, only from what she saw in his eyes he did not like that.

She brought her mouth to his own.

He trembled.

She pressed her lips to his own.

He did not move. She pushed her smallish breasts into his face, daring him to suckle them or nip at them. He did neither.

He just looked up at her with eyes that were shocked and glassy. They looked very wet. He was frightened and she could smell it on him.

Frightened. Yes, Louis was frightened. This girl...Jesus, painted white like something dead, completely naked, red bands of paint on her face, red slashes across her breasts and belly and arms. And her skin...it was beaded with welts like she had been burning herself, only the welts were formed into symbols of some sort, concentric patterns and diamonds and half-moons. Like those tribes on TV with the beads under their skin. She hovered over him. Teasing him, rubbing herself against him...he guessed she was no more than thirteen. Younger than the other girl who sharpened stakes in the corner. The older woman at the fire must have been their mother.

And this...this house of horrors...their den.

Their warren.

Louis saw human remains scattered over the dirt floor, bones and scraps of meat. There was a head in the corner. Severed limbs were dangling from the beams overhead on ropes of gut. There was garbage and filth everywhere. The air stank of putrescence, burnt meat, smoke, and excrement. The girl toying with him smelled like urine.

Grinning, she licked his face.

Elissa came over now. She turned to make sure the dam was still occupied; she was.

Kylie gripped the man's throat with her hands. Spreading her legs wide, she rubbed herself on him faster and faster until she began to tremble. The man's face was a contorted mask of dread. This excited Kylie more as she rubbed herself against him harder and harder, making communion, feeling her heart pounding, her skin hot and moist.

Still, he resisted.

"Get the fuck off me," he suddenly said.

Kylie brought her face to his own and he flinched. She buried her face at his throat and licked him, tasted his skin. As wave of ecstasy rolled through her, she bit down on the bare flesh of his shoulder and kept biting until she drew blood, until it filled her mouth. He screamed and she bit down harder, harder, filling her mouth with the taste of his blood, his flesh.

"No!" the dam cried.

She grabbed Kylie by the hair and tossed her aside. She kicked Elissa and then kicked her again when she dared snarl at her. She dragged the man over to the fire and pressed her mouth to his bleeding shoulder. She sucked the blood away and then pressed a rag to the wound. He was shaking, squirming.

The dam poked the gut sack. Hot juice sizzled into the fire.

She drew a rib bone from the coals. It burned her fingers. She gnawed at the meat and pressed it to the man's mouth. But he would not eat of it. She hissed at him and struck him in the face with her palm. When he refused the meat again, she struck him harder. He was defiant. But she was confident that she could break him. And if not, she would slit him open and yank out his intestines. While he still moved she would roast them and eat them.

It was an ancient punishment.

Kylie and Elissa crawled over. The dam bared her teeth at them. She crouched over the man and scented him with her urine. Then she clawed out at the girls.

"Mine," she said. "Mine, mine, *mine...*"

77

The Baron's pack now numbered upward of a hundred. As they moved through the night, raiding from one neighborhood to the next, driving prey from hides, holes, and coverts, none dared stand against them. They raced up streets and down avenues, scattering other hunters and hunting them down if they did not flee. The Baron's strategy was simple: seize anything worth taking, slaughter the stragglers, burn the houses, and generally lay siege to anything in their path with a horrendous scorched earth policy.

They ran afoul of other hunting packs, of course, and put them down or enslaved their numbers, always moving, always taking more territory and leaving a trail of butchered corpses, dead animals, and flaming neighborhoods in their wake. Soon, the Baron's ranks included not just children but adults, dozens of them. They wielded axes and pikes, spears and knives, hammers and baseball bats with spikes driven into their ends.

Women were raped and men skinned. The elderly used for sport. And tiny children of no use to the pack were given to the flames, for all knew that a sacrifice must be offered to ensure a successful campaign.

And on it went.

They were an irresistible, relentless force.

Then, on the south end of Providence Street, they were met by another pack. Just as determined. Just as ferocious. Just as territorial. The only difference was this group came with dogs. What seemed to be hundreds of barking, yapping, howling dogs. Things driven mad by the scent of aggression and the rich, tantalizing odor of blood in the air.

Battle was joined.

Energized by bloodlust, hysterical fury, and animal ferocity, the two opposing armies of savages—all painted for war, some naked, others dressed in rags or fresh hides, many brandishing death totems of human scalps, heads, and assorted body parts—charged at each other in howling groups. To a casual observer, it was a deranged display of psychotic frenzy unmatched since the barbarian invasions of Europe. But to those involved it was strictly territorial, the sort of manic blood-rite that the tribes lived for.

The Baron led the first charge, hacking and cutting his way through the intruders. Bodies were cut down by spears and hatchets and machetes. Bones splintered and heads were smashed in, limbs were sliced free and bodies fell disemboweled in the streets. The first five minutes was nothing but wholesale murder, the packs beating one another down, slitting throats and chopping on the fallen.

Then the dogs charged in.

The Baron, pulling back with dozens of wounded, watched them tear through the ranks, biting and clawing and feeding on the injured. A huge shepherd gripped the head of a boy and shook it in his jaws while three others fed on his writhing body. The dogs ravaged both sides and even themselves.

When an axe dropped a Doberman, its head nearly cleaved in two, a group of beagles tore it apart, fighting over the bloodiest chunks of meat. Men killed men and children killed children and both killed dogs and were killed *by* them.

As the Baron watched the atrocities, there was a vague memory in the back of his mind: driver ants. South American driver ants cutting a killing swath through the jungle. Trees and bushes stripped, animals eaten down to bones. Nothing escaped them, not even men who were stupid enough to get in their way. It flashed through his mind and vanished as quickly.

The dogs were like that.

The main force was an army of teeth and claws and hunger. A huge and voracious machine of destruction. The smell of blood, meat, and death drove them wild.

They attacked people. They attacked parked cars. They charged through screen doors and dove through windows. They tore sidings loose and chewed at woodwork. They ran roughshod through gardens and tore small trees up by the roots. If they couldn't kill it or maim it, they pissed on it.

The Baron saw dogs fucking. Dogs eating people. Dogs eating each other. A fearful feeding frenzy. A group of armed women had been caught in their masses and the dogs went insane tearing and ripping and biting. Pretty soon so many dogs had pressed into the melee, you couldn't see the women. Just dogs biting each other. Biting themselves. Blood was flowing, was gathering in a heaving, stinking mist over the streets. And still the killing continued.

Both packs were under siege now by the animals and fought side by side.

Tribal affiliation was forgotten.

A raging group of men with machetes, most homemade, tried to slash through their numbers. But the dogs were like ants sacrificing themselves madly for their queen. They literally piled up their own crushed bodies until their attackers had to withdraw...into an onslaught of dogs and crazy solitary hunters who claimed no true affiliation and slaughtered anything that moved.

Providence Street that night was a cacophonous hive of noise...barking, howling, screeching, wailing. Some was from the animals that walked on four legs and some from those that walked on two. Just absolute, thundering chaos.

Slowly, though, the dogs were dropping, being overwhelmed by cutting blades and devoured by their fellows.

The Baron, with so many of his pack littering the street, charged in again and again, dealing death and fighting tooth and nail. Swinging his machete like a sword, he gutted cockapoos and boxers and spaniels while to all sides the wounded were drowning in the living, biting sea.

The Baron was bitten, gouged, bloodied, and torn.

But he never stopped killing.

He saw a poodle hanging from a hunter's face by its teeth. He decapitated it, but the head still hung, jaws locked in a death grip.

Dozens of hunters took his lead and frantically waded in, chopping at the animals, chopping at blood-covered savages, and in the end, chopping at one another. The leader of the other pack, whom the Baron had sighted as his kill and his kill alone, was overwhelmed. He'd once been known as Dick Starling and he'd once been knocked cold by Macy Merchant, but by then he was just a savage wearing the bloody pelt and peeled headpiece of a Great Dane. A Rotweiler—split neatly in half—was hanging from his belly by its fangs, still biting, still clawing. The Baron, dragging an Irish Setter with him whose teeth were in his leg, moved in and decapitated him.

Finally, even the Baron withdrew from the killing fields.

He slashed the Setter until it released its bite and stood there, bloodied but unbowed, viewing the carnage around him. The decimation of both packs.

Then a final group of dogs came at him.

A hodgepodge of shepherd, collie, and Great Dane mixes, they advanced. He stood his ground. They moved with a slow, economical shambling, fur bristling, jaws open.

The first one made its move and the Baron slashed the business end of the machete across its eyes. He pivoted and split open another's skull. Still another hit him and he tossed it aside, eviscerating it. The teeth of yet another sank into his leg and he chopped its foreleg clean.

Then he ran as a howling, barking pack thundered across the killing fields at him.

He made a nearby porch and turned, swinging the machete with blind wrath, splitting the maw of a beagle and then throwing himself through the open door. They ripped the screen door right off its hinges, seven or eight of them, and began to fight over it like a tasty bitch.

The Baron pressed his back against the inside door as they battered and rammed it. Way they were going, he knew, it wouldn't last long. The door was hardwood and he could hear them smashing themselves against it, their bones popping and crunching. There was a thin pane of glass that ran the length of the door and the Baron forgot about it until the head of a huge, filthy Rotweiler crashed through it, its muzzle catching him in the back and sending him sprawling. But the pane of glass was not safety glass that spiderwebbed with cracks and fell into itself. It was plate glass. It shattered, but a six-inch triangular shard from the base lodged easily into the dog's throat. The more it wrenched and flopped its massive, heavily-muscled body, the deeper the shard sank until it was impaled there, whimpering.

But it wasn't dying fast enough for the Baron.

There was a pile of lumber near the stairs, a wall that had been stripped to lathing. Home improvement. The Baron saw a gun-shaped apparatus sitting on the lumber. He went for it, palming it. A cordless drill with a half-inch bit threaded into the chuck. Part of him seemed to recognize it, but there was no conscious memory.

But he knew a weapon when he held it in his fist.

He pressed the trigger. The drill bit whirred around.

Grinning, he ran the bit right through the dog's thrashing skull. Its eyes glazed over as he scrambled its brains. It slumped over dead, its sheer bulk keeping the others away from the opening it had shattered in the glass.

The Baron pulled the drill back, studied the bit that was slimed with gray matter, bone chips, and strands of coarse hair.

Some time later, he wandered outside.

The street was filled with gutted corpses, human and dog, parts of them, blood and hair and entrails. A few savages devoured raw joints of meat or fought over juicy shoulder portions. What dogs were left scavenged the dead. There was nothing but the moaning of the wounded, the whine of dying dogs.

What remained of the Baron's pack were beaten, bloodied, exhausted. They stepped amongst the bodies, slipping on blood and corkscrews of intestines.

They gathered at the Baron's side.

Although he was bitten, blood-streaked, and in considerable pain, he had never felt so joyously *alive* before...

78

They're in the dark, Louis. All around you, slithering hideous things that feed on children, that sharpen their teeth on bones and decorate their lairs with human hides. Wake up! Wake up, you fucking idiot, you're in the cannibal's kitchen, you're in the ogre's cave, you're in the musty rot-smelling cellar of the wicked witch and her wicked offspring...

Louis opened his eyes, fighting on the edge of sleep. Inside, he had given up. He had been beaten, cut, dragged through the streets, dry-humped by a cave girl and then pissed on by her mother. It didn't really seem to him that there was much to live for because the world had shit its own pants and here he was a prisoner of these fucking *things*.

But he opened his eyes.

Something plopped in his face. Cool, moist. It plopped again. He looked up and there was the corpse of a man hanging from the rafters...part of a man really. His legs were nowhere to be seen. He was hanging upside down, chained and gutted, ghastly white in color. And what had plopped onto Louis' face was something dripping from one of his hollowed eye sockets.

Louis recoiled, squirmed away from it best he could with his ankles and wrists tied.

He looked around.

The mother—he now suspected it was Maddie Sinclair, though she had degenerated so much it had been hard to tell at first—was nowhere in sight. Either were here daughters, whom Louis could not remember the names of.

The air smelled rank, heavy, and musky: the raw animal stench of the women themselves. The sort of smell you might acquaint with the shit-stained, blood-spattered, bone-strewn den of a wolf pack.

He lay still for ten minutes that became twenty, refusing to entertain any hope that they had abandoned him. He could not be that lucky. He waited. Breathed. Tried to get his mind working, trying to pretend he couldn't smell the woman's piss on him.

Something bit his ankle.

He jerked and a rodent went scampering away. A rat? Must have been. Too big to be anything else. He looked around the cellar. Had he been an anthropologist he might have appreciated the primordial squalor of prehumanity. But he certainly did not appreciate it. Bones and hides, human remains, bodies and parts of them hanging from the rafters. A sack— which must have been a human stomach stuffed with something and stitched closed—was hanging over the fire from a tripod.

Vile, was the only word for it.

But honestly, with all the boxes and bags and crap piled everywhere, Maddie Sinclair's basement had been a pigsty to begin with.

Imagine that. Uppity, snobby, Little Miss Perfect Maddie Sinclair's basement was a rat's nest. Ah, the secrets we hide from our neighbors.

He heard a sound and started. He was expecting them to come back, those white-painted wraiths with their necklaces of human scalps and fingers. He expected them to return to their kills...and their captive. And maybe this time, it would be no simple dry-hump from an overeager teenage savage.

Maybe it would be the real thing.

He thought that if Macy was truly dead and he was the last civilized person in Greenlawn then maybe it would be better off if he just cashed in his chips here and now.

But to die like that, to be peeled and quartered...

His senses were very alert these past hours. So he listened. Processed it all. Outside he could screams of terror or perhaps pure unbridled joy in the distance. Crickets chirping. Nothing else. A calm night. Warm, pleasant.

You better find a way out of this.

You don't have much time left.

He could feel the numerous gashes and bruises on his body, each one a separate catalog of pain. It would have been unlivable a few days before, but now it only served to reinforce his waning will to live. He was alive. He was a man. Men like him would be needed to straighten this out if such a thing ever became possible.

He had to live.

He squirmed across the floor, smelling the piss in the dirt, the shit that Maddie and her daughters buried in the sand. Jesus.

Footsteps.

Shit.

The three of them came padding down the stairs—and *padding* seemed appropriate here, because they no longer walked like women, like human beings, they shuffled along like apes or cantered like hunting wolves—and crowded the doorway.

Maddie came over and squatted about four feet from him. She had a bone in her hand that looked roughly about the size and shape of a human femur. It was stained brown and one end was sharpened for stabbing. She said something, a series of guttural barking sounds that he could not begin to decipher. She grunted and then stared at him for response.

When he didn't respond, she pounded the floor with her bone.

He just shook his head.

She pounded her bone with authority now.

As dangerous as the situation was, it reminded Louis of that scene in 2001: *A Space Odyssey*. He could have laughed at the absurdity of it had he not been so close to tears at that point.

There was something she wanted him to understand. She kept pounding the bone, offering him the toothy grin of a baboon.

Maddie Sinclair had been an attractive woman before this happened to her. Yes, elitist and pompous, but also the sort of woman men watched, the penis having no true shame. She was not thin and willowy like some TV spokesmodel, but shorter, hips and ass well-rounded, breasts quite large, long hair just this side of bronze and large liquid black eyes. Sexy. That was the word for it. She had it and she carried it well and that's all there was to it.

But now...good God.

Naked and painted white, that brilliant red war paint at her face and breasts and loins, the streaks of dried blood and filth mottling her. Her hair hung in her face like strands of wet straw, her mouth hooked into a contorted, evil funhouse sort of leer. And those eyes—could you really call them eyes?—wicked crevices peering into a pestilent sewer blackness.

She edged in closer, slapped the ball joint of the bone in her palm.

The way she smiled was not the way human beings smiled. It was the lurid, carven grin of a crocodile. A smile of teeth and bone-crushing appetite. She glided forward on hands and knees, the stench of her enough to put Louis' stomach in his throat. Her breath was sharp smelling like rat poison.

She had him and there was no way out.

Despite the crawling beast she was, the craven leer in her eyes was unmistakable. She did not want to make love, hell no, she wanted to screw, to fuck. And even that was far too dignified for a rodent like her. She wanted to rut like hogs in the mud and breed like wolves in the brush and apes in the trees. Rutting season. She was in heat and she wanted what he had.

And if he didn't give it?

He knew the answer to that. The ones that had refused were hanging from the rafters, salted, boiled, tanned, or bubbling away in pots.

Maddie's mouth was open and he could see her tongue worming in there like a maggot considering blackened meat. She crept closer, her breasts swinging from side to side like the teats of a cow. Louis could feel the heat coming off her. It was feverish, diseased, sickening. Not the sort of heat you associated with a human body, but maybe a cooling engine block.

He tried to squirm away from her and she did not like that.

She dove on top of him, grabbed him by the ears like a school bully and smacked his head off the hardpack of the floor five or six times. She was an absolute horror close like that...the greasy feel of her, the loose boneless gyrations of her body, the molten heat rising from her pores, and worse, oh God yes, the smell of her which was like dirty straw in a monkey cage. A unique and revolting effluvium of urine, scabby hides, and simian drainage.

Don't throw up, Louis. Jesus Christ, don't you dare do that.

She grinned down at him with that obscene drooling blow-hole of a mouth and he almost lost it right there. Some things were not meant to smile and she was one of them.

She ran her hands all over him, letting her fingers do the walking while he trembled at her touch and his stomach contents bubbled up the back of his throat. There was no escape, that was the most horrifying and demeaning part of it all. She groped his balls and squeezed his legs. She slapped his chest and gripped his shoulders while she slapped her thighs against him until he felt that his full bladder would burst. She pressed her fetid smelling corpse-face into his own, nibbled his throat and covered him with sloppy kisses, licked him and *tasted* him with a tongue that was coarse and gritty like that of cat. And when she pulled away, she left a rope of spit that broke wetly against his cheek.

The entire thing was not so much violation or suggested rape, but more like being a piece of meat: seasoned and tenderized, made ready for the stewpot.

Or maybe the marriage bed in this case.

She crawled away and he saw just how filthy her ass was. She turned, saw him looking at her, grinned almost childishly and spread her legs apart. She jabbed a thumb up inside herself and pushed it in and out and there was no mistaking what she had in mind.

Louis pissed right down his leg.

He had never felt so unclean in his life, contaminated by her touch, her smell, his own helplessness.

She went over to the fire.

She had a bowl in her hand.

She slit a few stitches of the gut bag and pried it open. The hot stink that came out was meaty and blood-smelling. She scooped something out of there with her fingers and brought the bowl to him. She wanted to feed him. Steam rose off the bowl, the juice inside congealed and fatty, the meat itself flabby and pale. He could not say what it was...a bit of lung? A strip of heart meat? A slice of kidney?

He drew away from it.

She opened her mouth with a sawtoothed grin and snapped her jaws shut. It was all so simple in her mind: meat was meat. No inhibitions against cannibalism, against feeding on your own kind, absolutely no cultural taboos because they had not yet been *invented* at her level of psychological evolution.

She shoved the bowl in his face and some of the juice spattered him, running down his cheek. It smelled like hot vomit.

He recoiled.

She stuck the bowl in his face again and he butted it out of her hands with his head. It flopped to the floor, right into the dirt. She made an enraged growling sound, snapping up a piece of meat and shoving it in his face.

I won't.

I will not eat that, you foul fucking cunt, and I don't care what you do to me but I will not eat human meat. So just...piss...right...off.

She saw the defiance in his eyes and jumped on him, scratched ruts in his face with her nails. If he didn't want the offered meat, then he must want something else. She grabbed his pants and fought with the zipper while he fought against her. It was no use. Hands tied, legs tied, he was about as offensive as a wriggling worm. She yanked his pants down and he could feel himself shrivel to nothing. She brought her face down there, sniffing his balls. She jabbed her fingers into them, making him jerk with pain, but she kept right on doing it like some confused bratty child who did not comprehend why her Jack-in-the-Box just wasn't working.

Then she straddled him again.

Rubbing herself against him while her daughters watched in breathless fascination. She stuck her breasts in his face, leaving white streaks on his cheeks. She kissed him, licked him, melted her rancid body into him. And when she slid her cankerous tongue into his mouth, he did the only thing he could.

He bit down on it until he drew blood...

79

When Macy pulled herself off the floor, she was aware of the pain thrumming through her body, but it was ancillary, removed, like the beat of her heart and the pulsing of her muscles it was simply part of her identity now. She was grimy from dirty hands, lustrous with grease-fat. A trickle of blood ran down the inside of one leg, it was crusted over her breasts and belly, reddening her lips and smeared over her chin. Her hair hung in filthy strands over her face.

They had ringed her in, the clan.

Facing her was another girl, older than she. Like Macy she was naked though carefully painted with black and white stripes. Her hair was dirty, though a lustrous gold.

The girl hissed through clenched teeth.

Macy steeled herself.

Her eyes, go for eyes, then her throat.

The girl backed away, seemed almost submissive and when Macy let her guard down for that one instant, she charged. She leaped three feet and hit Macy square in the face, then hit her in the head and gave her another jab to the chin. Macy was overwhelmed, seeing stars and funny lights in her head. She folded up and the girl pounded on the back of her skull.

The girl made to kick her and Macy rolled away, more out of dizziness than anything else.

The girl jumped on her back, locking an arm around her throat and yanking her head back until it felt like her spine would snap. The girl grabbed her own wrist and tightened the hold, applying more pressure until Macy thought she would pass out. She clawed at the girl's scabby arms, tugged at her hair.

The girl only squeezed that much tighter.

The clan was excited, cheering and howling. This was a blood rite, an ancient test of strength and cunning and also one of the few true entertainments that existed in the prehistoric world.

Macy's vision began to blur.

She couldn't draw a breath.

She's killing you! Killing you! Killing you!

A strangled growl started in Macy's throat. She bared her teeth, drool foaming from her mouth. She reached back and grabbed the girl between the legs, filled her hand with her womanhood, and twisted it with every ounce of strength she had left.

The girl screamed and loosened her grip.

Macy went wild, writhing and squirming with reptilian gyrations. She got her chin under the girl's arm and bit down on her forearm until she felt her teeth break through the skin and blood filled her mouth.

The girl, screeching madly, released her and hopped away, tripping over her own feet. When she turned from babying her wound, Macy was on her. Letting loose a snarling, wolflike sound, Macy snatched up a handful of the girl's hair and twisted her head on her neck. The girl raged, scratching and hissing. Macy stuck her thumb in the girl's left eye and she cried out again, going nearly limp. Then Macy had both her hands in the girl's hair. She yanked her head down and started kicking her. In the belly, the groin, the legs.

The girl fell back.

Her left eye was swollen purple, nearly closed, but her right was huge and staring, filled with murder.

The girl came at her.

Macy tried to sidestep her, but the girl rammed right into her, throwing her off balance. She jabbed her elbow back and felt the impact, heard the girl's nose break with a sickening popping sound. She brought hands to her face. Blood ran between her fingers.

Macy went at her.

And to Macy, at that moment, the girl epitomized the suffering, the degradation, the violation that she had endured and been put through. She punched her in the face again and again and then kicked her in the ribs. The girl screamed and tried to fight back, but it was no easy bit with being half-blind. Macy came from every direction, battering her with fists and feet.

The girl fell to one knee, bleeding and dazed.

She tried to rise up and Macy kneed her in the side of the head and kicked her repeatedly when she fell back.

Then she jumped her, clawing her face and then sinking her splintered nails into the girl's hurt eye. Tearing right through the lid and scratching her eyeball, laying it raw. The girl screamed with an agony that was shattering and bone-deep. She fought and bit, but Macy would not quit digging at her eyeball. She had it now, her nails speared into it, her fingertips worked into the socket. With a primal yell, she ripped it free. It came out with a bundle of pink muscle and an oozing length of optic nerve.

Throwing her weight behind it, Macy yanked it right out until it came away in her hand, still pulsing with life.

The girl was a blubbering, shuddering mass of flesh by that time, overwhelmed by agony and barely conscious. Macy hit her a few more times. Then something was shoved into her fist.

A knife.

There was no conscious thought on the matter. Macy gripped the knife and what she did with it was done out of reflex, entirely instinctual. She pulled the girl's hair back by the roots and slashed the knife against her throat, blood spraying in her face and over her breasts. She slashed the girl again and again until it looked like both she and her victim had been dipped in red ink.

The girl struggled a bit, then flopped over into Macy's lap.

The clan was wild from the violence, from the stink of raw blood in the air. You could see it in their eyes. They wanted to cover themselves with it, swim in it, paint the walls of the lair with it.

This was nectar.

This was the juice of life.

This was the fluid of the great mystery.

They were screaming and jumping around, beating on each other, rolling on the floor, fucking, spitting, scratching themselves bloody. It passed from one to the next and the next and the next like some kind of hideous circuit was completed.

Macy was not immune to it.

Her heart was pounding, her flesh wet with blood and sweet-smelling sweat. She felt the heat between her legs, in her belly, and especially in her mind like some all-consuming firestorm.

The grotesque faces of the clan staring out at her in rapt anticipation, Macy buried her face to the girl's throat, wrapping her lips around the knife wound that had split her carotid open. The blood still gushed. It was hot and salty as it filled her mouth and flowed down her throat, as she sucked and gulped, more content than a baby suckling mother's milk from an offered breast.

At last, she pushed the corpse away, blood running from her mouth. She raised her hands into the air, cocked back her head, and screamed her rabid lust to all creation. For she was blooded now. She was of the clan. She was a hunter...

80

The pack needed to be careful now, they needed to rest and lick their wounds, recover from the physical injuries of the open warfare on Providence Street and soothe the psychological ones. Both kinds were still wide open and hurting.

But the Baron would not have it.

The more lives he took, the more blood and guts he spilled, the more pain he took, the more *alive* he felt. He could not and would not roll into the straw like some beaten dog, not when there was hunting and the night called to him. He was energized, mainlining the very honeyed ambrosia of life itself.

The pack lay in a grassy field, licking their wounds and calming one another, a few of the more daring ones clutching weapons, ready for the hunt. The Baron stood up and walked towards the street. A few of his hunters went with him. The others perked up their ears, concerned, alarmed, but not following.

There was an odor on the breeze.

The baron had caught its scent and it enlivened him. It was tantalizing, pleasing. He followed its trail, curious and excited. It awoke cravings in him he had not felt in some years. It made his heart flutter, his blood run hot. His penis stood hard. One of his hunters, a teenage girl was down on all fours, sniffing the trail. The Baron went up behind her, grasped her hips, pushed her open and penetrated her. She shrieked and snapped at him, but she had offered herself and the chemical signature of that was unmistakable. He took her as she wanted to be taken with fierce thrusts, his thighs slapping against her ass cheeks.

When he was done, the odor was stronger.

He followed it, the other hunters coming now, too, sneaking through the grass, weapons in hand, eyes glittering with moonlight. The odor was of dead things, meat rotting and fly-specked. It left a trail of rank, green stink, exciting canine impulses in the entire pack. They all wanted to roll in it and scent themselves.

The Baron led them forward, through yards, across vacant lots.

The smell was getting stronger, carried by the breeze.

They followed it to a yard of night-blooming flowers and sweet grass, the smell of running plant sap invigorating. Down on all fours, the Baron could smell the scent trail of another. The stink of urine and musk was unmistakable. This yard had been marked as another's territory. The other hunters smelled it and quivered. They did not like it. There was something wrong here.

But the Baron was too intrigued by the other odor: that delicious stench of rot.

He pissed on the trail to obliterate the smell of the other. Several other hunters, male and female, did the same.

Still, the Baron could smell the other's urine. He did not like this. It was an affront to him. It raised his hackles, challenged him, usurped his authority. It made him angry. It made him want to seize another by the throat—

Still, that other smell... he needed to find it, to cover himself with it.

He was getting furious. The urine smell was female. There was no mistaking it. There were a series of scent trails laid out in the vicinity of this yard, all leading up to the darkened house before him. It was confusing. The Baron knew that it was necessary to proceed with caution, but his blood was up. The scent trail. The other delicious odor of rot. It made him feel very aggressive. He let out a low growling sound and several other males imitated him even while many of the females pulled back, suddenly concerned about the nature of this place.

They had been led here. There was no doubt of it.

But the Baron didn't care. He was challenged. It was now a matter of territory and dominance. He would find the females who had sprayed these conflicting scents—there were several, he knew that now—and make them bow down to him.

The pack was tense.

The Baron cast several of his males forward. They peered in bushes, around the garage, pawed through flower beds. One of them made a sharp yelping sound of surprise and pleasure; he was calling to the pack. The others followed him around the garage, past the potting shed...there was a sudden cry of surprise, a crackling sound, and then a drawn-out whine of agony.

The Baron rushed forward.

His male was down in a pit about ten feet, the walls of black earth carefully squared off. The male cried out a few times, shook, and went still. The entire pack smelled his death, his terror, the blood trace he left in the air. Whoever had dug the pit, had lined its bottom with four-foot stakes that were sharpened to lethal perfection. The young male was impaled upon them. They were thrust through his groin, belly, and throat. One pierced his arm and another thrust from his wide open mouth.

The Baron let forth a bloodcurdling cry that echoed throughout the neighborhood. The other males, again, imitated him. This was an insult to the pack, a blood crime that would have to be avenged.

Much more cautious now, the Baron crept towards the house on all fours...

81

Maddie tasted the blood in her mouth and savored the pain.

She had marked this man as her own. She would mate with him and perhaps produce offspring...but he was defiant, he was willful and arrogant. She would not have that. If she brought him in for a breeder and spared him the knife, then there were things expected. She would not be rejected.

Not here in her own lair.

Not by this pig who spurned her offered meat.

In the hazy corridors of her mind she could remember other men, shadowy figures without faces, and never had they rejected her like this. She always had her fill when the season was upon her.

Grinding her teeth, she watched the man by the fire. He was well-muscled, firm, he would have made a very good breeder. Too wiry for the eating, but that did not mean he wouldn't know the knife. As she sharpened a carving blade against a dull stone she knew there were ways to break pigs like him.

The heat inside her was almost unbearable...pulsing, wet, hungry. It would need to be fed and if he would not feed her then another would be found. Maybe if she punished him, cut a few things off, let her daughters toy with him a bit.

Then he would beg for what she offered.

Because it was his and she had already selected. He would fill her needs or she would flay him alive...

82

Wearing the shadows, Angie's tribe remained hidden.

For some time they had been trailing the Baron's pack. It was not too difficult. At first, Angie had been impressed by the Baron...his strength, his cruelty, his knowledge of hunting and stalking. But the more he killed, the more drunk with power he became and the more careless was his leadership.

Angie's tribe had watched with amusement as the Baron's pack waged war with the other pack on Providence Street. He had lost the majority of his hunters. His bravado was stronger than his wisdom. Such was the way with males.

Now they had been drawn to the house.

Angie knew it was a trap for she had been past the place several times that night and each time did not linger. But the Baron had been drawn in effortlessly. Just by a hanging bag of rotting meat and dead fish outside the back door. It drew males from blocks around. This combined with the crisscrossing female urine scents was enough to drive any male wild.

And so it had.

As Angie watched, she saw the females of the pack hang back. They knew instinctively that the yard was not a good place to be. But the Baron would not submit to their fears just as he would not submit to his own.

The tribe waited to see what would happen next.

That there was death in the house, Angie knew without question. Her only concern was that the females who lived there would get the Baron before she did. And she needed to bring him down.

Even now, she could taste the juice of his heart in her mouth...

83

Louis heard screams and instantly jerked out of his fugue.

One of the woman's daughters—Elissa—stumbled down the stairs with a spear punched clean through her. She clutched it and clawed at it, her own blood that was very dark in the firelight gushing from the wound, dripping off the shaft. There was more than just pain on her contorted face, but *surprise*. Absolute surprise.

A group of savages rushed down the stairs.

They were children.

Louis saw them and was amazed, though he shouldn't have been by that point. Just kids. Most of them were grade school age, a few teenagers amongst them. All naked and painted up with blue, brown, and red stripes, brandishing spears and hatchets, their eyes flat black and predatory.

They converged on Elissa and brought her down with their hatchets, chopping on her until she was a writhing, red-splashed thing, her head split open, her face hanging by a thread, one arm on the floor.

The children went wild.

They screamed and shrieked their primal delight, hacking on the girl and splashing themselves with her blood. The oldest amongst them, a boy, shoved the others aside and peeled the girl's scalp.

Louis knew they would see him by the fire.

He was next.

Where was the woman and the other girl?

Good question and one soon answered. For now they charged out of the shadows with axes. Four children had split skulls before the others could organize themselves. Maddie and Kylie, still painted ash-white, were soon spattered with blood and meat. The other children were terrified as these ghosts attacked them. They could see the scalps at their throats. The meat and limbs hanging from the rafters, the human remains and refuse scattered over the floor, smell the gut sack that smoked over the fire.

While Kylie swung her axe from side to side, Maddie hobbled about, circling the invaders who bunched together. She sang a high, shrill song that clearly frightened the children as she lumbered about them, her axe held high for the taking of lives. Even though Louis knew she was no ghost, he wondered if the children were frightened of her for that very reason.

By the looks of them, they weren't exactly the passive, non-violent types.

But the woman had struck dread into them.

She circled them, singing her song louder and louder and something about it even chilled Louis. He did not know what any of it meant—it did not even sound like English or any other language that he had ever heard—but the threat behind the words was without question.

He fought at the ropes that held him.

If somehow he could convince the children to attack.

But they were submissive now, terrified. Several had even urinated. Who or what did they think the woman was? Granted, smeared with white ash, red bands enclosing her eyes and mouth, her teeth yellow and sharp, and her eyes like two windows looking into a madhouse...she *was* a real horror.

"You kids!" he called out. "She's not a ghost! She's not a spook! Kill her! Do you fucking hear me? Kill the bitch!"

Kylie hissed at him and Maddie broke off her song, snarling in his direction and there was absolutely no doubt in Louis' mind that he was no longer the favored, coveted plaything, but a shank of meat to be slit and deboned, salted and cured. She would slit his throat, disembowel him and bathe in his blood, wear his skin and gather his bones in a red-stained heap.

He was definitely a dead man.

But then...he hadn't been brought down to this awful place to be treated as a favored guest, now had he? And murder, violent and brutal as it would be, was far preferable to being used for the amusement of the witch and her daughters.

"Kill her!" Louis cried.

It was a terrible chance to take, but if he could goad the children into fighting back then maybe, just maybe, he had a chance. Regardless, his shouts disrupted the spell that Maddie was putting on them.

"Kill her! Goddammit, kill her!"

Maybe it was an authoritative adult voice, but one of them jabbed his spear at Kylie. She deflected it with her axe. But the others took the cue. A spear sank into Maddie's leg and her axe nearly cleaved a girl in half. Now it became a nightmare of blood. Spears thrusting, hatchets slicing, axes chopping. Louis watched it momentarily with insane glee, wanting the blood like somebody watching a football game secretly wanted violence. But unlike sports, he truly got it as the children clashed with Maddie and her mother who fought with insane, raging hysteria.

That's it, kids, Kill the witch. Slice her right fucking up.

Louis rolled closer to the fire, ever aware of that grotesque sack of human entrails smoking on the tripod. There was a carving knife on the other side of the pit and he planned on having it. Maybe he was going to die, but he was going to die with a knife in his hand, he was going to go down fighting.

A window shattered and something exploded on the floor, spraying flames over the wall and up a stack of cardboard boxes that started to burn right away.

Louis inched around the pit like a caterpillar until he saw the knife and brought his hands around until he grasped it. He immediately started sawing at the ropes on his wrist. It was expertly sharpened and right away the fibers began loosening one by one.

In the flames and the smoke, the blood sport near the stairs went on unheeded. It was like some twisted, blood-drenched nightmare. The children fighting in a pack, glistening red, Maddie and Kylie both slashed and bleeding but refusing to go down. Knives bisected skins and hatchets laid flesh open, spears sinking into bellies and axes shearing heads from necks.

It ended on the floor with the three remaining children chopping on Maddie while Kylie, split wide open and clutching her intestines in one hand, lurched in Louis' direction. She had a knife in the other hand. Her hair was plastered to her face with blood. She limped forward, dragging a bad leg behind her that was nearly severed at the knee.

She made a low growling noise that was wet and gurgling as she choked on her own blood.

Louis' hands were free, but not his ankles.

He had a knife but he didn't know if he was any match for Kylie who was by that point beyond anything as simple as a savage. She was a gruesome, hobbling zombie, a monster who understood nothing but killing.

"Don't do it," Louis told her.

She spit out a glob of blood and came closer. She would have had him, too, and her last act in this world would have been to make him suffer unbelievably. But a spear plunged through her belly and then another through her chest. More children were rushing around. They sliced limbs and meats from the rafters overhead, kicked over the tripod which spilled to the floor, the gut bag bursting with a sickening hot smell as organs and entrails steamed over the dirt.

They were destroying everything.

Throwing bottles of gasoline at the walls and roaring with delight as the flames spread, consumed, and the air became as hazy as fog.

Louis slit his ankles free.

His legs were numb but he made them obey. He knocked a couple kids out of the way, dodging and darting towards the doorway. A spear just missed him. A girl swung something at him that he realized was a severed arm. And then he was jogging up the steps, coughing on the smoke.

More savage children.

They were pissing on the walls and pulling the stuffing out of sofa cushions, tipping over furniture and tossing their scat at one another. Several of them saw Louis, hesitated, maybe unsure if he was one of their own or not. They decided and bared their teeth.

Then a huge, bristling man stepped forward.

His face was tiger-striped with black slashes of paint, old and seamed, the eyes glittering with dementia. He wore a vest made of fur, his bare chest and arms filthy with blood and dirt. There was a necklace of what must have been human ears around his throat.

Louis hesitated.

Good God...was this Chalmers? Frank Chalmers from a few streets over?

He knew it was and then Chalmers dove on him. They rolled to the floor, knives forgotten, fighting tooth and nail. Chalmers was old, but in incredible shape from so many years in the Army humping it through jungles and leaping out of airplanes. Louis hit him three times and Chalmers barely flinched. His hand like a claw, he took hold of Louis' windpipe and squeezed it close. Louis fought and tried to throw him off, but it was useless. The world went dark and he went limp.

When he opened his eyes again, he was lying in the grass.

The house was burning.

Two girls squatted by him and both had knives. They were no more than eight or ten years old and seeing them there—painted for war, splattered with flesh and blood, their eyes just gone wild—it was ludicrous. For a few days before they might have been selling Girl Scout cookies door-to-door. Now they were hunting people, slaughtering anyone or anything they could catch.

Louis licked the blood off his lips.

The girls moved in closer, crawling on hands and knees towards him like Preying Mantises stalking their prey. They had been waiting for him to come to. It would have been no fun for them to gut a sleeping man. One of the girls raised her knife for the kill...there was a human scalp on a thong around her wrist, the hair red and lustrous.

Then Louis heard a whooshing sound and a hatchet came flying end-over-end with a perfect throw, imbedding itself in the skull of the girl with the scalp.

Other savages charged in and it was war to the knife...

84

Macy was outside the lair, the church, and sucking in the not-so clean air of Greenlawn. She had status now. She was one of the Huntress' clan. By blood-rite she had secured the right to stand with them, to hunt with them and butcher, and to die with them.

She heard a noise behind her.

She turned quick with sharp animal reflexes.

A man was standing there.

He was tall and filthy, hair hanging to his shoulders in greasy curls. His face was painted like a skull as all those of the inner circle. His body was likewise painted with white and blacks streaks, though smeared with ground-in blood, dirt, and animal fat.

He held a scalp in his hands, still bleeding from its owner.

The hair was lustrous gold, beautiful, like something spun on a spinning wheel. The moonlight caught it, held it, made the golden mane glow.

Macy recognized it.

The scalp of the girl she'd killed in the blood-rite.

Yes, she remembered it as she remembered the man who held it out to her. It was an offering. The scalp belonged to Macy. Golden, beautiful, any warrior would be pleased to have it hanging upon their scalp pole. He made sure it was brought to her.

Laid it at her feet.

Like burnt offerings.

Macy just stared at him with something leagues beyond hate. A mania that was all-consuming and burned bright.

She remembered him, too.

The wet dog stink of him as the others held her down and he mounted her. She remembered the pain between her legs and the oily feel of his skin against her own.

Having set the scalp at her feet, believing them to be conjoined now like fetal twins because of the rite, he looked up at her and smiled.

Macy slashed her knife against his throat.

He stumbled away, gagging on his own blood, shocked, mortified, beyond himself by what had just transpired. How could she do this, how, how, how, how—

Macy stepped over to him with her knife and smiled with a blood-stained mouth at the huge slaughter moon high above...

85

As the hatchet was embedded in the girl's skull with a wet thudding noise and she pitched over on top of him, eyes glazed in death, Louis saw the barbarian hordes rushing in from all directions.

People screamed.

Howled.

Bayed like animals.

Spears were thrown. Axes cleaved off limbs and shattered bone and arrows punched through chests and bellies.

And there he was, barely conscious, his mind reeling in every imaginable direction as the warfare broke out in every quarter. He was confused...but *happy*. For just as the children brought hell and death down upon Maddie Sinclair and her slinking, animal daughters, now hell and death was coming down upon the children and their leader which had once been a fellow named Frank Chalmers, though only God knew what he was now.

Children dropped all around him, screaming with spears stuck in them. A boy with an arrow in one eye stumbled about, his face red and shining, then fell over. Louis looked for Chalmers because he knew he was out there somewhere delighting in this. A sixty-year old man who could fight better than any two twenty-year olds.

The other girl Louis had seen when he first opened his eyes was leaping around, trying to avoid the blades of older women who were cutting and hacking their way through Chalmers' perverse pack of hunters and killers. She made a good show of it and then a woman with a sharpened stake in her hand—like something you went to slay a vampire with—took her by the hair, broke her over one knee and pierced her in the throat with it. Then she proceeded to decapitate her.

And look at how much she loves it! Chopping the head off a little kid! Have you ever, ever in your life, Louis, seen such genuine unadulterated pleasure on someone's face? Such concentration, such conviction in the rightness of what they were doing?

And honestly he had not. And if there was anything left that could frighten him and maybe even unhinge him it was this: they were not human anymore, these people, not even remotely. Men, women, and, yes, children were just game.

Game for sport.

And game for meat.

On the slaughter went and he had a front row seat and never, not since the dawn of what men referred to as civilization, had there been a contest this bloody, this savage, this unrelentingly grisly.

The children, he soon saw, were really no match for this new army of butchers who seemed to come sliding out of every shadow like snakes, leaping from every bush and even dropping from the trees. Primeval, obscene, anti-human—that was *exactly* the word that flashed through Louis' crowded mind—and somehow reptilian, they prowled in for the kill, meat-hungry pythons and slinking human pit vipers and deadly rattlesnakes and fang-toothed mambas. The fact that they were covered in not just old blood and dirt, but a crazy warpaint/camouflage of red-and-green bands only heightened the effect.

They were human reptiles.

Many of them had bows and arrows and Louis had not seen that up to this point. They had axes and pikes, homemade spears and knives and you name it. And they were very good at what they were doing. The children went down beneath the slashing of blades and when they went down, they were instantly harvested. Trophies were slit free: ears, fingers, scalps, even genitals.

Louis had not been noticed yet, so he decided now was a good time to slip away.

Two women held a boy down, slit his mouth open into a bleeding, clownish grin and proceeded to cut his tongue out.

Louis almost fell right over them, but they paid him little attention.

He yanked a butcher's knife out of a girl's back and slashed a woman across the breasts who tried to take hold of him. The air was filled with smoke from the burning house, it lay across the yard like a thick and pungent fog. There was a mist of blood, bodies sprawled dismembered and still kicking at every turn. A scalped boy crawled in his direction. A woman dragging her own viscera grabbed at his legs as another strode out of the haze carrying a bloody dismembered head in each hand, swinging them by the hair.

Louis hopped over corpses, dodging savages with axes and body parts, slipping on the blood-covered grass, and finally tripping over a torso.

When he came back up he was no longer anonymous.

Recognized.

Frank Chalmers stood there, huge and shaggy with the blood-matted fur vest on, like something from a Pliocene cave. He had a hatchet in one hand and a sickle in the other. Louis did not doubt for one moment that he had come to kill him. His body swayed back and forth as if to some unheard melody, his muscles bunching beneath his skin, his knotted hands gripping his weapons and anxious to put them to use.

Louis got up and faced him.

He knew Frank very well, but Frank was dead. This was not Frank.

He felt very useless with his butcher knife facing down this grinning, war-painted bear of a man who at sixty still bristled with corded muscle, his flesh like alligator hide, slit and cut and scarred but still holding together.

Chalmers let out a cry and came right at Louis.

Louis tried to get away from him, but there were too many bodies, too many savages crowding in. The sickle nearly took off the end of his nose and the hatchet came down at what seemed the same time, striking the blade of the butcher knife and knocking it out of his hand, leaving his arm numb right up to the shoulder joint.

That's how easy it was for Frank Chalmers, the pack Baron.

Louis was his and he knew it. That after all he had been through that it would end with this crazy sonofabitch just wasn't acceptable. When Chalmers moved again, Louis jumped away, tripped over someone, found a broomstick that had been sharpened into a spear and came right at the bigger man.

It was sheer suicide.

But it worked.

The counter-attack threw Chalmers off his guard and bought Louis enough time to make a valiant jab at him or to run like crazy. It was at that moment that arrows thudded into Chalmers' left arm and ribs. He cried out and fell back and Louis vaulted in and gave him the spear right in his exposed belly, sinking it deep with all his strength until he felt it hit something in there, maybe bone, and become firmly lodged.

Chalmers screamed and swung his sickle.

Had the blade hit Louis it would have probably split his face open, but Chalmers swung it backhand and hit him with the unsharpened edge. Still, it was quite a blow. Louis was hit in the face and knocked backwards. Just in time to catch an arrow right above the kneecap.

He went down.

He hit the ground, rolling in the bloody grass, and when he opened his eyes Chalmers was gone and there was that arrow sunk into the meat of his leg, a patch of blood soaking through his jeans.

Then the pain hit him.

Things hadn't exactly been easy for him that night. His body had taken its fair share of abuse...but this was beyond all that. At first, when he went down, there was just the sting of impact...but now, the *real* pain arrived. It hit him blindly and with full force. There was nothing remotely subtle about it. It exploded in his leg and made him cry out, made something inside him roll over as wave after wave of agony moved through him tearing up everything in its path.

And when he again was able to take in his surroundings, his face covered with a warm, sour-smelling sweat, he saw a woman advancing on him. She carried a human head on the end of a spear...

86

Macy had him on the ground and no one interfered.

Most of the clan had followed the Huntress off on a hunt and those that remained did not interfere. Macy stood over him, the man that had raped her, with a bloody knife in one hand.

There had been a time, perhaps ages ago, when Macy Merchant had been a very shy, bookish girl who cringed at the idea of swatting a fly or stepping on a spider, but that Macy was as extinct as the tribes the people of the world had regressed into.

She watched him bleed to death but it was hardly enough.

She raised her knife over her head and jabbed him in the belly, the spray of hot blood in her face invigorating as she put both hands on the hilt and forced the blade upwards, gutting him like a trout.

He died squirming in his own blood and entrails and Macy watched death take him with a cold, almost clinical eye. She rose up from his carcass, studying the blood on her knife, her hands, her arms.

Unafraid, raging with primal memory, she licked it off her fingers...

87

Louis watched the woman approach him and he was not entirely sure it *was* a woman. She was wearing a freshly peeled human hide and a looping scarf of bowels around her throat. As she glided towards him, she was muttering something under her breath in a hoarse, gargly sort of voice, brandishing the head of a teenage boy on a sharpened pole in one hand and an axe in the other.

What the hell is this now?

It was a woman, naked, washed down with blood and ceremonial paint. Her hair was a tangled, snarled mess plaited with what looked to be bones and sticks and shining beads. Her face was an absolute atrocity, like some gruesome tribal mask: flesh peeled away from her mouth in a lopsided oval so that her red-stained teeth were on full display, a slat of bone shoved through her nose, eyes like bleeding holes.

Frank Chalmers had been bad enough...but this...*God.*

She saw him there, singled him out from the masses in the streaming moonlight, and gestured at him with her axe, her teeth parting and a high, keening howl of rage and savagery cutting through the night.

Louis got to his feet and it was no easy thing with the pain throbbing in his leg. But he did get up and he faced her uneasily with the butcher knife in his hand.

The warrior woman charged, tossing the head pole aside. She came swinging her axe, absolutely deranged and filled with primitive wrath. She looked like some kind of living voodoo fetish doll, a surreal version of a cannibal witch-doctor.

Louis ducked under the axe and slashed out with his knife.

But he was far too slow or maybe she was just too fast.

He missed her entirely and as he regained his balance and brought his knife-hand around, she lashed out with a foot and kicked him in the side. His leg gave out immediately in a baptismal of pain and he went face-first into the grass, his head spinning and the breath gasping from his lungs.

She jumped on his back, a hot, greasy hand grabbed his hair and yanked his head back for throat-slitting. At least that's what he expected, but the blade never came, but her teeth did. She seized his ear and bit right through it. They were filed sharp as daggers and sliced right through the cartilage. The pain made Louis forget about his leg. He thrashed beneath her as she held on, his bloody ear clenched in her jaws. He threw himself this way and that. When he got her off balance, he brought his elbow back and felt it mash into her face.

That did it.

She came up right away, grinning cadaverously in the moonlight, her teeth glistening with fresh blood. She looked at him with those dreadful vulpine eyes and uttered a growling guttural sound that raised the hairs on the back of his neck.

"Bitch!" he cried at her. "*Stinking rotten fucking bitch!*"

It meant nothing to her, of course, but it did wonders for his adrenaline and hatred. She dove at him and he met her and they fought tooth and claw in the grass, rolling through the blood and spilled viscera. No weapons, just the rage of the primitive and the absolute loathing of the civilized man for such racial backsliding. It was like fighting a serpent. She writhed and squirmed with a fluid muscular grace, her teeth biting into him and her nails tearing him open.

Finally, he again threw her.

On all fours she faced him, a primordial thing of bloodlust, eyes wide and almost luminous like new moons. The stench of hot urine wafted from her. That and a sharp, gagging musk that was revolting.

She could have easily grabbed a weapon, but she did not. She was going to take him down like an animal with claws and teeth and nothing less would be acceptable to her.

Louis never had time to get his knife because she came again and he met her, raining down a series of blows on her that had no effect. He managed to get behind her, to lock an arm around her throat. He rode her like that while she thrashed and growled and snapped, coming alive beneath him, but he held fast, forcing her head back with a strength he didn't know he possessed.

She lost balance and collapsed under his weight.

He yanked her head back, fingers digging into her eyes until she screamed and still he kept yanking and straining until she began to make wheezing, gagging sounds in her throat. Things began to pop and snap in there. He kept stretching it back until his face was buried in her oily warm throat. Until he could smell her filthy reek and taste her foul dog-smell.

He felt something pulsing in her throat.

Something throbbing and pumping and straining.

Without thought, wired mainly on instinct, he sank his teeth into her throat, biting and gnashing and tearing until that pulsing thing sheared open and sprayed hot, salty blood down his throat and into his face.

But he did not let go.

He kept chewing and ripping as the woman went slack beneath him.

He held onto her until she was limp beneath him. He limped maybe three or four feet and went down in the grass, vomiting, cleansing himself of the unclean, polluted taste of her.

When he gained his feet, there was nothing but corpses scattered in the moonlight. The hunters had moved on...

88

Angie closed in on the Baron.

It was not difficult. After the warfare broke between her tribe and the Baron's pack, he had few followers. His pack was mostly killed, wounded, or driven off into the night. It was only a matter then of following his blood trail.

That he had come this far was testament to his strength.

His vitality.

Angie had tracked his blood spoor for nearly three blocks until it ended here, at the athletic field behind the high school where the Greenlawn High Wildcats strutted their stuff on the gridiron come September.

Angie was ignorant of all that, of course.

She followed his blood trail to the fence, circling it quietly, looking for some means of egress. But even the gate was locked. She lost the Baron's spoor for a moment, but then caught his scent where he'd urinated on a tree. Angie sniffed this for telltale signs of his condition. The urine had a weak smell. She could scent the blood in it and the waning trace odors of the hormones usually associated with a healthy, fighting animal.

The Baron was dying.

She found where he'd gone over the fence. Shouldering her bow, she climbed up and over, dropping silently on all fours into the grass.

The spoor was simple to track now on the freshly-shorn grass. He was bleeding badly and it was splashed in copious amounts everywhere. Yes, she could see him now. He was staggering, moving for a few feet, falling, then rising, pushing himself on through willpower and little else. There were woods beyond the field and this is where he was going: he wanted to die in the forest where his kind had always been born.

His darkened shape was simple to pick out on the flat field in the moonlight.

Angie put an arrow in her bow, stretched it, sighted in on the feeble shape in the distance. Clenching her teeth with a slow exhalation of air, she let it fly. He let out a garbled cry as it struck him in the back.

He pitched forward, limbs jerking.

Now! Take your kill! Make it yours!

Angie rushed out and he heard her coming, tried to crawl away from her. But it did no good. She stood above him, a painted and bloody tribal warrior maiden, breathing deeply, smelling the death of her pray and reveling in it as only the hunter can.

Menstrual blood ran down the inside of one leg.

She leaped on him, landing hard, his breath coming out in a whooshing gasp. She grabbed the arrow in his back and yanked it out. He moaned and tried to crawl away. She let him. When he made it a few feet, she blocked his path and stabbed him lightly with the arrow until he turned. And when he crawled in a different direction, she stabbed him again. She toyed with him a bit as she liked to with her kills. It amused her. To toy with prey was the world's oldest form of foreplay.

He stopped crawling, looking up at her with fixed hatred.

He made a grunting, puffing noise. He coughed out ribbons of blood. His fur pelt was shiny and wet with it. Still, even weakened, he was huge and vicious. His tongue lolled from his bloody mouth, his nose sniffing.

Angie dropped to her knees to watch his death throes.

He closed his eyes...then, with a final burst of strength and a terrible muffled roar deep in the chimney of his throat, he leaped at her.

She was caught by surprise, knocked into the grass.

He pinned her down, his eyes filled with a deadly intensity

Angie slid her knife from its sheath.

She did not fight.

This stopped the Baron momentarily. He cocked his head sideways.

She slashed him in the face, slicing a strip of meat from his temple to jawbone. He tightened his grip on her throat and she buried the knife in his eyesocket.

He made a drawn-out growling sound...and attacked again, filled with a hideous, primal rage. Streamers of vile-smelling saliva oozed from his jaws. Blood and tissue dripped from his ruined eye. Then as his jaws came at her, she buried the blade of the butcher's knife into his belly right to the hilt.

The Baron released her with a squealing, miserable sound like a run-down puppy...then he went crazy, snapping and biting and clawing.

Angie was howling herself: an atavistic war cry pulled up from the forgotten, shuttered basement of human history.

And as she did so, as the Baron's fangs nipped at her face, tearing a hurting channel into her cheek, she drew the knife up from his belly to his sternum. His viscera, hot and steaming and slimy, spilled over her and its reek was raw, horrible...and delicious, ultimately invigorating.

Angie threw him to the ground and began to slash and hack his corpse. The knife rose and fell and blood splashed and flesh was bisected and she kept going until she'd thoroughly mutilated his hide, his head nearly severed from its neck.

Hurting, but alive because of it, her veins surging with electricity, Angie let out a deafening shriek and buried the knife in her kill. Then she broke open his ribs and carved his heart free. It was hot and pulsing in her hands. She brought it to her mouth, licking it, tasting it, coveting the muscled, marbled mass. Then bit into it with a shuddering carnal moan.

She tore it apart with a violent feeding frenzy until her face was covered in blood, tissue, and hot juices.

She fell back into the grass, sated, fulfilled, feeling the Baron's strength and cunning becoming her own. Beneath the waning eye of the moon, the night was made complete...

89

The Huntress returned to the place she remembered.

It was a lair.

A lair she had once shared with the man, but long ago for she could not scent herself there. She immediately set about marking the place with her urine, her blood, her scat until her smell was everywhere and those that dared come here would know, would sense the warning and the danger and flee.

She brought in meat and stuffed it in nooks and crannies where it would season and age properly. She salted several hides, brought in leaves and sticks and brush for the nest. Then she brought in the carcass of a freshly-killed man. She set out her collection of knives that she had scavenged. Knives for scraping and boning, skinning and slitting.

When the man returned he would see these things.

He would smell her upon them.

He would know this was his lair.

When things were ready, the Huntress went back out into the night. Already the horizon was stained with indigo. The sun would be up soon and she knew the man would come here to lair. He had to. He would be drawn here as she was.

The Huntress moved off into the night.

For one last kill, one last feast of blood to give thanks to the moon goddess above with an offering of meat and death...

90

At last.

Louis found a car with keys in it. A little Ford Escort that smelled of perfume and cigarette smoke. He had checked dozens of cars since he left the fields of the dead with the taste of the warrior woman's blood still gamey and fetid in his mouth. This was the first one with keys. This was his salvation. This was his deliverance. He did not know where he was going and common sense told him there really wasn't anywhere *to* go, but he was going nonetheless. He had to escape the primeval jungle of Greenlawn and his mind did not want to think about what came after that.

He turned the car over.

It started easily enough.

He shifted, released the clutch, and drove through the battle-ravaged streets of his home town. There was wreckage everywhere. Entire neighborhoods were still burning. Bodies were sprawled in the streets. Some were hanging in the trees.

He would not think about it.

He would not let himself understand what it meant, that Greenlawn was just another piece in a huge puzzle that had, in the course of less that twenty-four hours, completely gutted civilization from one end to another. He turned on the radio but there was nothing but dead air. All the power was out in Greenlawn now.

Yes, finally, a world lit only by fire.

An unconscious genetic urge will unmake all we have made, gut civilization, and harvest the race like cattle as we are overwhelmed by primitive urges and race memory run wild...

Earl Gould.

Jesus, Earl Gould.

Somehow he had forgotten about him as he was beginning to realize that he was forgetting about a lot of things. He would not think about it. He followed Providence Street until it crossed the river, then turned onto Main. He followed it right out of town, knowing that it hooked up with the county road and eventually led to highway 421. But where then? He did not know and he did not want to ask himself.

The sun would be up soon...and what would it see? What would it light? A world thrown back in time to the Pleistocene and all because of a gene. A microscopic chemical transmission of heredity.

Louis could not make sense of it. Not any longer.

He touched the bloody scab at his leg where the arrow had been. It would need attention soon or it would become infected.

Faces passed through his mind—Michelle, Macy, Dick Starling—too many to make sense of and each of them bringing pain to him.

Just outside town there was a sign the Kiwanis had put up: WELCOME TO GREENLAWN. His headlights splashed over it. Somebody had speared a human head atop of it. How fitting.

Ahead, there were silhouettes in the road.

Many of them.

Naked people standing in the road as the car sped down on them. They had regressed to the point that they did not understand what the car symbolized. That it was a moving machine that would crush them. Like deer, they stood there, transfixed by the headlights. Louis slowed down, knowing that he would have to drive right through them. The idea was not as offensive as it once might have been for he wanted to kill then. They represented everything he hated now.

He sounded the horn a few times and they only moved forward.

They were going to attack the car.

They were charging it with axes and spears, hammers and pikes and God knows what, all with that crazy animal gleam in their eyes. They were prehistoric hunters who had discovered a monster in their midst and they were going to kill it. They were going to slay the beast, bring the mastodon down.

Louis stopped the car, just amazed by what he was seeing.

Now he shifted into gear and slammed down on the accelerator. Fucking idiots. *Fucking primitive idiots.* Bear skins and tribes and stone fucking knives. It was incomprehensible. They charged the car and he plowed right into them, knocking three aside and rolling over the body of a fourth. But one of them swung something at the car and it had shattered the passenger side window. The Escort rocked with the impact but kept rolling.

Thank God, thank God.

Dammit.

More of them.

The same scene all over again. They were attacking the car. He hit a few of them and one of those was knocked up from the impact, crashing into the windshield. The glass went white with spidewebbing, the body still wedged there, blood running down the cracks. By then Louis could not see where he was going. He let out a mad scream as he saw that they were everywhere, naked people crowding the shoulders and standing in the road. He hit two or three more.

The wheel spun in his hands.

He screamed again as the car was pelted with rocks and the body of the person on the windshield fell into the car as the blood-streaked safety glass let loose. The body slid across the dashboard and fell right into his lap. He jammed the brakes as he tried to fight the bleeding husk off him. The car skidded through gravel, bumped and rolled, and then found a ditch and flipped right onto its side.

Louis could hear them howling in the distance.

He wasn't injured.

The corpse—a man—had fallen into the backseat when the car went over. There was no time. Louis crawled through the missing glass of the passenger side window, pulling himself out. He slipped and fell into the ditch, right into about three feet of stagnant water. He splashed free, up the grassy bank. In the light of the rising sun he could see a farmer's field spread out, sheep grazing.

He limped forward, his lungs aching, his breath hot in his throat.

The world was still shadowy and he stumbled right out into a pack of the savages. They had come here into this field after the sheep. The sheep were all dead. Skinned. What he had seen was not sheep grazing, but savages wearing their blood-spattered white hides.

Dozens of them rose up around him and he tripped over his own feet, going down in the grass.

He heard birds singing. The rooting, grunting sounds of the savages as they moved in on him. This was it. They had him and there was no more running, no more hiding, no more anything. But maybe better, he thought, to get it done with. For how long can you run when you're the last man on earth and the monsters are closing in from every side?

Better to die than become like them.

He watched them come on and they offended him on every level. Throwbacks to a time when humans were nothing but filthy, shaggy predators covered in hides and ritualistic tattoos and piercings. Things that picked through bone heaps and fashioned crude weapons, coveting the skulls of their ancestors and the scalps of their enemies, chanting to long-forgotten pagan gods of the hunt, rearing their foul young in shadowy, meat-smelling caves where flesh was smoked—animal *and* human—over the ritual fires which lit their tenebrous, malevolent little world.

No, he refused to become something like that.

As they pressed in around him, pulling at him and scratching him, he lost consciousness and what a delicious fall it was headlong into the darkness, into the oblivion of nothingness. Even they could not get him here.

He was safe...

91

He awoke later and the sun was up.

He was whole.

He had not been sliced up or spitted.

His leg did not hurt so bad and he saw it had been packed with a crude poultice of mud, leaves, and herbs. Whatever that stuff was it was working.

But he was not alone.

He was in the grass, the stinking pelt of a sheep thrown over him. There was a woman with him, her naked back pressed to his chest and her ass pressed to his groin. They had always slept like that, curled into one another—

Michelle.

He was with Michelle as crazy as that sounded. And he dared not move because it would shatter the fantasy, destroy the dream...but then he realized it wasn't a dream at all. He was with her. *Really with her.* She was alive and breathing and warm. She smelled like blood and dark earth and raw meat, but it was still Michelle, her body painted or not.

Swallowing down his fear, he pressed into her, let his hands glide over her smooth tanned flesh. She felt the same. She responded immediately, grinding her ass into him. And he grew hard, despite the violent smell coming off her—or maybe because of it—he grew hard, engorged, and he thought at that moment that he'd never, ever been that hard before, that aroused, that hungry for the act. He trembled for it. His blood burned in his veins. He reached out. Michelle moaned. Still behind her, he grasped her ass in his hands, reaching down and pulling one of her long legs up so that he could enter her.

She was wet for it.

He pushed into her violently, his thighs slapping against her ass cheeks and she made grunting, groaning sounds of pleasure that he barely heard above his own. He pounded into her until he could stand it no more than he buried himself in her, gripping her legs and trembling as he came.

Then he fell away, barely able to breathe.

It was like he had just emptied himself of something more than just semen. She turned around and grinned at him with bloody teeth, still a beast of the night, still a regressed animalistic hunter. Her dark hair was slicked with grease, braided with bones and beads. Her face was still painted white, eyes set in blackened hollows, nose and lips darkened. She was savage, primordial, but still beautiful, maybe even more so reduced to her simplest form. A sleek and hungry cat...but submissive now, not deadly, his wife as she'd always been his wife.

She dug a piece of raw meat from somewhere.

She offered it to him.

No, he would not eat his meat raw. If he did that then he was no better than they were and he had to hang onto his humanity. He had to. But the hunger. It opened in his belly, it chewed at his stomach. He could smell the salty blood, the meat marbled with veins of fat. He began to drool.

Don't do it. Please Louis, don't do it. You're right on the edge now. The gene is active in you. You're standing on the edge of a huge black pit and beneath is the crawling blackness of prehistory.

Do not eat the meat.

Do not even taste it.

One taste and you will not be a man.

You will be shoved into the darkness.

The primal fall...

He snatched the meat from her and bit into it, moaning with pleasure. Oh, how good it was. How wonderful. How delightful and sensuous it felt upon his tongue as its juices filled his mouth and made him feel a simple joy he had never known before, one long denied him, but one that somehow owned him and made him part of what it was and what he would never be again.

Michelle watched him eat.

She smiled.

When he was done, he curled up against her again and was instantly aroused. His wife. His female. The meat had excited him and now he needed to have her, to dominate her. He took her again. He was crude, physical, forcing pain upon her and delighting in the fact. When again he was spent, there was blood in his mouth and he realized he had bitten into her shoulder.

He closed his eyes, content now.

His dreams were simple and fulfilling.

When he opened his eyes he was alone. He started awake, peeled the sheep's hide from him. The sun was high in the sky. There were abandoned sheep hides everywhere but no people to go with them. Naked, but unashamed of the fact, he stood up and, listening, sensed for danger. They were gone and he was alone. Where had the clan gone?

He looked around for a weapon. Something he could grip in his hand and kill with. For in his mind he dreamed the dream of the first man, the primal man, the original man. And that dream was the dream of a weapon.

The sun hot on his bare skin, he looked for something to hit or stab with. Because only then, only with a weapon in hand, was he above the beasts...not a grubbing root-eater, but a man...*a man...*

Epilogue

I

Louis shambled through the streets carrying a bone.

He slapped the ball knob of it in his other palm, knowing it could cause damage, knowing it could bring down enemies and also prey. And a man, he knew, was judged by the weapons he carried and the game he killed.

I need to find the girl. It is the season for the girl.

He had covered himself in river mud so that his enemies could not spot him so easily. The stench of the river bottoms also made his scent harder to pinpoint. He knew these things without thinking them. They were part and parcel of who he was. Imprinted onto the blueprint of his being.

He had found the rest of the clan.

Something had happened. They had all rushed off and left him. He found hundreds of corpses in the river. So many that he could have walked across them without ever getting his feet wet. He understood only that they were dead. It meant little more to him than that. He did not know that the gene that had been activated within them had reached fruition with a mindless mass migration wherein everyone—or nearly all—the town's former residents heralded the call of the wild and left in a mad rush, trampling and killing one another, each seized by the inexplicable desire to run and run and run, to seek new feeding grounds and nesting habitat. The old, the wounded, the weak and diseased were purged in the process, their bodies lying everywhere. The others kept running through the fields and forests until what was inside them, what was activating them, finally ceased.

And by then, only a third of them were still alive.

In the coming days, they would regroup and form tribal units for the hunt.

Louis was unaware of this. Such things did not concern him. He was only interested in finding food, shelter, water, and possibly a mate. When he had the previous he would have the latter for the females always came when a male had built himself a handsome lair.

He walked through the town, pissing his scent so others would smell it and remember him.

He stepped over mutilated cadavers, snarled at dogs that were feeding upon them. A few people were digging through overturned garbage cans. He paid them no mind. Nor the few others that walked on past with distinctively simian strides. Brushing flies from his face, he saw only Greenlawn which lay before him like a ravaged and violated corpse.

By instinct and memory, he found the house.

The walls were painted with shit and blood. There was a carcass in the corner and a collection of fine cutting knives. Someone had made a comfortable nest of leaves and sticks and boughs. He would sleep in it. This would be his lair. He could smell something very familiar here. A trace odor of the woman he had laid with under the sheep hide. She did not concern him.

She was called something once and her feel was velvet, her skin like satin, her taste that of honey and secret sweetness—

He studied the symbols written in shit and blood on the walls. He picked at a scab on his foot, examining the numerous injuries, touching them, picking at them until fresh blood ran. He sniffed his armpits, his crotch, licking his fingertips and remembering the field of sheep. He could remember little else.

The girl.

Yes, he could remember the girl.

She was young and ripe and firm.

She would come, yes, he knew she would come. Even now she was probably looking for him as he had looked for her in the streets. He had marked scent posts with his urine throughout the city. His scent would lead her here.

Scratching his ass, he hummed a song and picked at his teeth, finding tasty bits wedged in them. Each one reminded him of things. Many made no sense. He found a piece of meat under a chair. It was old and its smell was intriguing. Sometimes, the worse something smelled, the more a man wanted to roll himself in it or taste it.

He ate the meat and curled up in the nest.

He slept...

2

He came awake later to a smell of blood that was rich and gamey. It came from the girl who stood over him, watching him. Yes, *the* girl. She had found her way to him. He looked up into her big chocolate brown eyes, studied the curve of her smallish breasts, the roundness of her hips, her tangled hair the color of wheat chaff. Her skin was scabbed with dried blood.

He grunted at her.

She licked her plump lips, gathered saliva with her tongue, then spit on him so he would know her smell. He rubbed her saliva on his fingers, smelling it, tasting it. It was pleasing and good.

This is the girl who lived in my heart. She has come here. It is her season.

He got to his feet and took hold of her roughly. She fought and clawed and he threw her down in the nest. He urinated on her to mark her with his scent. Once he did so, she accepted things and did not fight so.

He jumped on top of her and pressed a hand to her mouth and she bit it. He struck her and she scratched him. She seemed to find the play amusing. She watched him as he spread her legs and made ready to take her. He penetrated her and she gasped, grinding her teeth and hissing at him. This and only this is what she had been dreaming of, even before in those times she could no longer remember, she knew she dreamed of this and wanted it and felt it in her blood until it became part of her, the heat that had simmered before but now made her burn.

As he rammed into her, grunting and growling, a light passed through her eyes and in that momentary burst of light there was absolute horror because this was not how it was supposed to be at all, *oh dear God, not like this, like this, like this...oh please, Louis it was not supposed to be like this...*

But then it was gone and he pumped into her and she squirmed with the feel of it, knowing this was who and what she was and who and what he was, that they were joined in the ancient dance of the heat, his hands wrapped around her neck and her nails dug deep into his flesh and the blood ran and the world swam with tiny black dots and a voice in her head screamed until it became a howling, an atavistic baying, as every cell in her body electrified with primal starving estrus, *yes, yes, yes, just like this, just like this, do it faster and faster, kill me kill me kill me—*

—The End—

Breinigsville, PA USA
20 September 2010
245741BV00001B/27/P